MOONLESS NOCTURNE

Other Titles

Check out more books we love at:

25andY.com

MOONLESS NOCTURNE

TALES OF DARK FANTASY AND HORROR NOIR BY
HANK SCHWAEBLE

ESKER & RIDDLE PRESS

MOONLESS NOCTURNE

Copyright © 2022 by Hank Schwaeble

Published by Esker & Riddle Press
an imprint of 25 & Y Publishing
Denver, Colorado

25andY.com

Cover Design by Andy Carpenter Design
Book Design by Sebastian Penraeth
Chapter art by Maria Jesus Aragoneses

978-1-953134-44-8 (Hardback)

978-1-953134-45-5 (Paperback)

978-1-953134-46-2 (Ebook)

Printed in the United States of America

10 9 8 7 6 5 4 3 2 1

Pieces like this are called nocturnes. They're meant to capture the mood of the night, remind one of things that happen after dark. Originally, they were only played after sundown, usually quite late. Some composers would write them by moonlight, to help ensure they evoked the proper emotions.

—*American Nocturne*

Table of Contents

Foreword

Hard to believe it's been five years since my first collection, *American Nocturne*, was published. Even harder to believe I've been writing now as a published author for fifteen, that my first novel was released a dozen years ago, and that I'm now, well, let's just say I'm not what anyone short of their 90s would consider a young guy starting out anymore. But time is like that, a constant presence in all our lives, as relentless as a faucet drip, a slow leak draining the volume of our existence one *drop drop drop* for every *tick tick tick* of the clock without us really noticing until the water level in the pool is so low we're left wondering where it all went. That's why it's crucial we fill that time, while we have it, with meaning, and the way we do that is by investing hours each day in things like relationships, family, faith, learning, goals, hobbies or some combination of the like. One of those sources of meaning for me is writing.

Ask any writer why they write and, if they're being honest, you'll invariably get some version of the same answer: *"because I have to."* It's a compulsion; if not clinically, then as a practical matter. We not only do it to indulge our creative impulses, we use fiction to make sense of facts, lies to explain truths, characters we've imagined to illustrate the complexities of interactions we've experienced. And we all share a deeply felt need to express ourselves through story. Stories are the way we make sense of the world, the way we process the accumulated traumas of loss, disappointment, grief, heartbreak, and all the divers slings and arrows of the outrageous fortunes each of us, like everyone, has had to endure, to varying degrees, at some points in our lives.

But while all that may be true and provides a reason why we write, it doesn't exactly explain why people like me write *what* we write. Why horror? Why stories with dark settings and dark characters and, frequently, creatures that slither and crawl and lurk in the shadows? From where does this interest, if not outright fascination, with the stuff of nightmares hail? What makes someone like me feel drawn to writing horror stories? I've been interested in horror since I was a young boy, but I can't point to anything in my childhood that as a logical proposition should have made it resonate with me. I was not abused or terrorized. Sure, I was a child of divorce, like so many millions of others, but I never felt particularly victimized by it. My home life was reasonably stable, compared to other kids I knew. Even though finances were often tight, I rarely felt any sort of deprivation. I had food, shelter, toys, and lived in a relatively safe lower-middle class neighborhood. I never witnessed any significant acts of violence beyond some schoolyard fights and was seldom involved in fistfights myself growing up. So, that raises the question—why do some of us write *horror*, violent pieces about bad people in bad places and things that do more than go bump in the night, rather than stories dealing with circumstances we have more direct experience with? I think the answer is simple. Although like all writers we write to process and understand emotions, we write horror because of an intellectual curiosity that drives us to explore the unknown, to shine a light into the blackened alleys and recesses others pass by and give a wide berth. We get a thrill when imagining the possibilities of what lay in the grasp of those shadows, or beyond them, and want to share those imaginings with others. While many writers use stories to hold a mirror to society, we want to show our readers what's on the other side of it. Most authors explore the human condition through the examination of characters in conflict with nature, with others, with themselves, or the like. We do the same, but with an added dose of "what if?" directed at the inky, lightless corners of that same world. It's often the dark side of human nature that interests us, but it's also the human reaction to the kind of darkness that isn't necessarily found in nature that piques our imagination. While others write to present their readers with character studies as a way of recognizing our common humanity, we who write horror already know there is one such commonality that unites us, one shared emotion that transcends almost everything else.

Fear. We know that it's not the dark of night that scares us as humans, it's what that dark might be hiding…or what sort of darkness the person sitting beside us on a train might be hiding. This, I believe, is what drives our storytelling. We want to relate to our readers not merely on an intellectual level but also at a visceral one, to make them feel alive through a triggering of that most basic emotion, the same one felt by medieval villagers digging up bodies in the belief a vampire was plaguing their hamlet. The same one felt by travelers on horseback moving through black forests and seeing glowing eyes peering from behind trees or sailors in uncharted waters seeing large, strange creatures emerging from the depths. The same one doubtless felt by Neanderthals witnessing an eclipse or hearing the chuffing of a sabretooth tiger outside their cave on a moonless night.

But the kind of fear I'm talking about isn't the literary equivalent of a jump scare. What interests me is more the slow-burn kind of fright, the kind that is often scary in retrospect more than in the reading, the kind that comes from a story that lingers, that makes you think. People often accuse horror of being low-brow, and over the years certainly much of it has been, but no one who's read masterpieces by Edgar Allan Poe such as "The Tell-Tale Heart" or "A Casque of Amontillado," for example, can defend a dismissal of the genre with such an accusation. The same can be said of "A Good Man is Hard to Find" by Flannery O'Connor, or "The Lottery" by Shirley Jackson. These stories, and others like them, stay with us, provoking deep consideration of their implications even, in my case, decades after I read them. It is worth noting that none of these particular stories involve the supernatural, or non-human monsters, but they most definitely are horror. What makes them horror? The places they take us and the things they make us confront when we get there. Good horror makes us stand up to the unknown even as we accept it's a battle we can never win. There are so many things we don't understand about our existence, and the more we learn, the more disturbing things become. Eternity stretches out before us. Either there is life after death, or there isn't—and either prospect is terrifying, if you give it enough thought. Either we're alone in the universe, or we aren't. Each of those possibilities is equally frightening for different reasons—if you give it enough thought. That, in my opinion, is the horror writer's calling, to make you the reader give the things out there, or that may be out there, that are frightening, *if contemplated enough*, due consideration. Because giving such things the contemplation they deserve is the key to understanding why they frighten us—or, in some cases, why they don't—and that, in my opinion, is the key to understanding what makes us human. If I can make a reader contemplate some of those things, even a little, while entertaining them along the way, as I see it that means I've done my job.

That is what I've attempted here with *Moonless Nocturne*. If I have indeed done my job, in the pages that follow you'll find ten stories that will serve their purpose of both entertaining and prodding you, both capturing your imagination and stimulating it. Stories that, I hope, will linger in your thoughts, scratch an itch you didn't realize you had, plant seeds in your mind that will germinate as you lay in bed, drifting off to a sleep marked by dreams that pose even more questions. Stories that will resonate in some way, intellectually or emotionally or both. Stories I hope you will thoroughly enjoy reading and just as thoroughly enjoy thinking about afterwards. And stories that maybe, just maybe, might even scare you a little bit.

It would be impossible for me to list all the people who have contributed to my development as a writer, but I would be remiss if I didn't mention a few. As I discussed in the Foreword to *American Nocturne*, in my youth I was greatly influenced by Stephen King and Clive Barker, particularly by their short fiction. Peter Straub's *Ghost Story* occupies a prominent spot in the memories of when I was a young teen hungry for serious treatment of the scary and the supernatural. Reading Edgar Allan Poe was almost certainly my first experience with horror, so this would definitely be incomplete without mentioning him. Later on, as I made my first forays into writing, many professionals provided invaluable assistance along the way. I'm grateful to writers like Tom Monteleone, the late Jack Ketchum, Gary Braunbeck, Deborah LeBlanc, and others who gave me advice and encouragement in those early days. Writers like Jonathan Maberry, who, among other things, graciously agreed to pen the introduction to *American Nocturne*, Mark Greaney,

Steve Berry, Cherry Adair and Heather Graham have all stepped up when I needed someone to read my stuff, and for a writer, that's the most ingratiating thing a person can do. Minor acts of kindness by many writers have made outsized impacts on my career, such as when Neil Gaiman took the time to have a drink with me in Brighton after I won the Bram Stoker Award for *Damnable*, providing me with an occasion I'll never forget (but one I doubt he'd recall) where I soaked up all I could as he shared his thoughts on his latest novel I'd just read on the plane ride over. Many thanks to all of them for debts I can never repay, but for which I will always be grateful.

I also want to give a shout out to my publisher, Isabel Penraeth, for her enthusiastic support and commitment to this collection, along with all the folks at 25&Y who've worked so hard to bring it all together with artwork, cover design, layout, edits and marketing and all the other things that go into a quality hardcover release that are routinely overlooked but are nevertheless vital to its success. As always, I also want to thank my agent, Rachel Sussman, for simply putting up with me.

Special thanks go out to F. Paul Wilson, who generously agreed to write the Introduction to this collection. I first read one of F. Paul's stories over twenty years ago and remember being floored by the force and clarity of his prose and have been a fan ever since. The thought of him now providing the introduction to a collection of my own stories is as mind-boggling as it is gratifying.

Finally, and most importantly, I want to thank my wife, Rhodi, for being my companion through it all, my anchor and my rudder, my partner and my love. As I undertake these excursions into darkness, she keeps me grounded in the light.

I hope you enjoy your nighttime stroll through the pages that follow but please, for your sake and that of your loved ones, be careful not to get lost in the gloaming. There may be no moon to light the way back.

Hank Schwaeble
Magnolia, Texas
May 2021

Introduction

Short fiction…it's different. It requires a different skillset—a different *mindset*—from the novel. I know excellent novelists who can't write a short story worth a damn. Conversely, I know short story wizards who are totally flummoxed by the long form. When I was starting out—shortly after the Permian extinction—I counted myself in the latter category.

I've always written. I can remember penning stories—haunted house and ghost stories, naturally—as far back as the second grade. But in my early twenties I set myself the goal of becoming a published author. I saw no way of making a living as a writer—not at a pay rate of a few cents a word—but I loved telling stories and wanted to make writing a part of my life.

With absolutely no guidance, without ever taking a writing class or attending a workshop, I began writing short stories. No horror market existed at the time, so I sent them off to the SF magazines and collected a pile of rejection slips. But I was not to be deterred. I was going to make this happen. I kept submitting and soon started selling. Five cents a word when I was lucky, otherwise three cents. Sometimes nothing when the magazine folded before it sent the check.

I wanted very much to write a novel but found the prospect of sustaining a coherent narrative for that long positively daunting. My first "novel," *Healer*, was in fact a succession of novelettes and short stories about the same immortal character strung out over 1200 years. Next came *Wheels Within Wheels* which was just as fragmented with flashbacks and side stories. My first real novel is my third, *An Enemy of the State*.

But I kept writing short stories because I loved the discipline, the focus, and the tradition.

Speaking of tradition, the short story is a very American form of fiction that finds its origins in Edgar Allan Poe. According to Poe, a short story can be read in less than an hour and must leave a powerful impression. It should strive for a "unity of effect," and by that he means that every word in the story is directed toward its dénouement which should land with an impact "unattainable by the novel."

His form of short story became immensely popular in the US, leading eventually to the pulp magazine era in the first half of the twentieth century. People who've researched that period say that at the height of their popularity in the mid-1930s, an amazing total of 150 pulp titles fought for newsstand space. We're talking general fiction, romance, western, mystery, SF, horror, "spicy" fiction, crime, sports, war, aviation, and on and on. Consider that each title published an average of ten stories per issue (some fewer, some more, but even the hero pulps with a "novel" every issue contained backup short stories) and some of these, like *Argosy* and *All-Story*, were published *weekly*.

Think about that: a short-fiction market in the neighborhood of 1,500 stories per *month*, every month. Of course, if Sturgeon's law holds true, 90% of those stories were crap. But I think I can safely say that if you couldn't place a piece of your fiction then, you'd never sell—anywhere, any time.

Things are different now. Short fiction is undergoing a bit of a resurgence in popularity at the moment but the market to *sell* it (as opposed to self-publish it) has contracted dramatically. The novel is the most popular length for thriller fiction (and under that umbrella I include political thrillers, horror thrillers, science thrillers, and so on), but the short form exists.

Case in point: Back in 2006, the International Thriller Writers put together an anthology called, surprisingly, *Thriller*, a who's who of the thriller genre: Lee Child, Brad Thor, Preston & Child, Rollins, Lescroart, etc. All great novelists, but some not so comfortable with the short form. I'm happy to say, though, that in her review for the *NY Times*, Janet Maslin singled out my story for special mention because it had "a beginning, middle and ending, as well as some neat tricks in between."

This does not mean I'm a better writer than my friends in *Thriller*, it simply means that I cut my teeth on short stories and was at home with both the long- and short-form thriller. Many of them were not.

Unlike Hank Schwaeble who is at home with any length, it seems, a fact of which I remained unaware until I read *Moonless Nocturne.*

I've known Hank a long time. We would run into each other again and again at a convention in Rhode Island called NECon; in 2010 we taught a writing class together at the Pen-to-Press Writers Retreat in New Orleans. Oh, and we both like blues guitar. But I'd read only his novels before now. (If you haven't read his Jake Hatcher novels, you need to remedy that.) Somehow his shorter works and I never intersected. His previous collection, *American Nocturne,* also slipped past me. So *Moonless Nocturne* came as an oh-so-pleasant surprise.

This is a truly outstanding collection. I say that not because I was asked to write the intro, but because it's true. First, you have such a variety of time periods—the 30s, the 50s, the 80s, present day, even the future—along with an amazing array of settings: Chicago, Houston, Mississippi, Georgia, Florida, Africa, and more.

He starts you off with "The Yearning Jade," a classic noir that could have come from the pages of the rightfully venerated *Black Mask* magazine where the likes of Dashiell Hammett, Raymond Chandler, Cornell Woolrich, and others found their hardboiled voices. On further consideration, it might have felt right at home in the old *Weird Tales* under Farnsworth Wright as well.

"Household" is unlike any haunted house tale you've ever read, but nowhere near as frightening as "Everything not Forbidden." I found the latter the most disturbing piece in the collection, creating a deep unease that lingered long after I'd finished it. Lingers with me still, in fact. This is a future I don't want to happen. I wish I could say it's a future *no one* wants to happen, but that's not true. *That's* the scariest part: not the inevitable singularity that will present us with a self-aware artificial intelligence, but our fellow human beings who are all too willing to sacrifice their agency for a patina of security.

The next tale, "Shifty Devil Blues," is almost comforting by comparison, despite the Faustian bargain at its heart. As a fan since my teens, I find any story with the blues at its heart irresistible.

I see "Haunter" as a companion piece to "Household," except it's not a house being haunted but a person. I think I would have flinched a few times if I were telling this story. Hank doesn't, not once, and that's what makes it such a wrenching piece.

"Deepest, Darkest" stars Hank's recurring character, Jake Hatcher, in an uncharacteristically non-urban environment: Africa. It could have been a straight action-adventure piece, but Hank isn't going to let you get off with something so simple as that. Be prepared for multiple dark twists and turns before he cuts you loose.

"Psycho Metrics" is another period piece (the 1980s) that looks for all the world like a cop procedural and turns out to be something else entirely. Leading to "Payday," in which you know something's coming but you just don't know what. The only story in the book I might venture to call "fun."

"Zafari!" closes the collection by transporting us once again to Africa for a zombie hunt. You think zombies have been done to death? So did I, but Hank brings some fresh ideas to the "science" behind the walking dead.

I've saved comment on the noirish title novella, "Moonless Nocturne," for last. This truly delicious piece moves the timeframe to the late 1950s and is my favorite in the collection. When you can mix cold war paranoia with murder and a hardboiled private eye slinking through the underbelly of a corrupt city, then add a *soupçon* of either the supernatural or possibly alien technology, you've got me—hook, line, and the proverbial sinker.

"Moonless Nocturne" presents a perfect example of Poe's "unity of effect:" no narrative wanderings, no aimless digressions; everything in the story points toward the dénouement.

You are poised on the bank of a globetrotting, time-travelling collection of bizarre thrillers. Dive in and start swimming.

F. Paul Wilson
The Jersey Shore
May 2021

MOONLESS NOCTURNE

The Yearning Jade

When I showed up at my office mid-morning, there was a woman with dark hair wearing an even darker veil sitting on my sofa. She was flanked by two Chinamen, one to each side, and had an open cigarette case in her left hand, an unlit cigarette in her right. My secretary, a nice gal from Iowa who was still not accustomed to the peculiarities of my line of work—or of the Windy City, in general, I'm sure—was planted behind my desk, worrying her palm with her thumb, a look on her face like she wasn't getting paid enough for this kind of cowdung, or whatever word they'd likely use on her family's farm. Hard to argue with that, considering she wasn't really getting paid at all. Business hadn't exactly been brisk over the past few weeks.

"Angie, I don't remember telling you to order me lunch."

The small one, who happened to be alarmingly close to my desk, smiled at that. He wore a shiny blue three-piece suit, a fancy fedora with a feather in the band angled on the top of his round head. That hat was a lot more expensive than mine, a fact I found annoying, even under the circumstances. Overall, he looked like one of the overdressed dandies the mayor always trotted out to share the stage when he'd stump in Chinatown so the pictures in the papers wouldn't give his opponents any fodder to bash him about hanging out with sinister looking orientals. Of course, that was before he got shot standing next to Roosevelt a couple years back, so there hadn't been any of those photos above the fold lately. But me thinking of this guy as small was really just a matter of relativity. The one standing on the other side was massive. Probably had more than half a foot and at least a hundred pounds on me. And that was at my current weight, which wasn't exactly what I considered fighting trim. He had darker skin and wore a round cap and had a long, braided ponytail with a wispy growth of black whiskers drooping from his chin. He may have narrowed his eyes at me a tad when I sized him up, but it was hard to tell because he had been glaring at me from the moment I walked in. I could have sworn he was wearing eyeliner, too.

I wanted to ask what this was all about, but the truth was I already knew, in the sense that I was as certain as I could be without actually knowing.

"I'm sorry, Milo," Angie said. I could see the freckles on her midwestern nose peeking through her makeup. "They just barged in. They made me sit here and wait with them."

"That's okay, Anj." Poor gal was worried I was going to be angry she was at my desk. Which I might have been, had she not explained why, because I'm particular that way. "Now, this gentleman in the dandy hat," I said, indicating the small one with a thrust of my jaw. "That's another story. If he doesn't take his hand off my mahogany, I'll assume there's a language barrier and remove it for him. At the wrist."

The fella looked a bit taken aback by my threat. He smiled and stood up straight, tapping his brim with a dip of his head.

My office, my rules. I don't like people touching my desk.

"I don't know where it is," I said, shifting my gaze to the woman and trying to sound as sincere as I could. Which shouldn't have been as difficult as it was, since mostly what I was telling her was the truth. Mostly. "And I have no idea who might have it. Tell your boss I could have told him the same thing over the phone. It's not like he doesn't know the exchange."

Even through the shadow of the veil, I could feel a pair of eyes probing me. When she finally spoke, her voice was soft and melodic and cut the silence like a straight razor.

"Your mother was a Jew."

Can't say that was something I expected to hear. Then again, hardly much of anything lately had been.

"You here to tell me they killed Buddha, too?"

"Your father sold dry-goods. He died when you were six."

"Learn something new every day. Is there gonna be an examination at the end of the lesson?"

"I am mentioning these things because I am coming to you with hope, the hope you understand what it is like to be on the outside. I come to you also as someone straddling a line, who doesn't quite fit on either side. Who doesn't fit anywhere, really."

Before I could ask her to just tell me who the hell she was and what she was doing in my office—even if I had a good guess as to the latter—she reached her hands to her veil, cigarette still in one of them, and lifted it over her head. She leveled her eyes at me like they were large caliber weapons.

Which they were. A glowing pair of ice blue orbs with black pinholes for pupils. Her features were vaguely oriental, but the most distinguishing aspect of her face were the twin scars, one on each cheek. They were roughly the size of silver dollars and could have been from a chemical burn of some kind, or maybe they were just what grew back after something had taken a bite out of her. Two bites.

She held up the cigarette, wedged between two fingers. The smaller of her companions retrieved a lighter from his pocket.

"Do you mind if I smoke?"

"Yes," I said.

The cigarette was already touching her lips, her man leaning forward with the lighter, when she froze. A second or two passed, then she waved him off and re-placed the smoke into the case. After an awkward moment of me staring at her, which she indulged with the patience of someone who clearly had endured a lot of it, she gestured with a nod of her head. The small fella in the fedora dropped the lighter into a trouser pocket, then reached into the breast pocket of his suit coat. He removed a thick envelope and held it out to me.

I opened it, ticked through the bills with my thumb. "This is a lot of cheese."

"I want you to pick up where you left off and continue to look. I want you to find it this time. I want you to find the Yearning Jade."

"Lady, I don't even know who the heck you are."

"My name is Mei. The man who hired you to find it was my uncle."

That name rang a bell. And to be honest, the possibility had already crossed my mind. I'd heard something about a niece, a story about how Yu found out she was seeing a white kid. Apparently, the old Tong leader decided to both teach her a lesson and send a message to everyone in his Tong, or even more importantly, anyone who had to deal with his Tong, which probably meant everyone with a Chinese surname in the city. But the talk was only about how he cut her, some saying razor blade, some saying knife, others saying his thumbnail, which he famously kept as sharp and long as a dagger, like some Buck Rogers villain. This looked worse.

"That didn't turn out too well, in case you didn't know. For anyone. I lost a partner, and, I might add, all but lost myself in the process."

"Yes, I heard about your... difficulties. That is why the offer this time shall be more generous."

Difficulties. That was one way to put it. I woke up in the hospital with a bullet in my shoulder and a gut that felt like it had been kicked a few times by a mule. My head was more slippery than a buttered icicle and about as clear as Bubbly Creek near the Stock Yards. I remembered following some mope into an alley, I remembered Guy agreeing to go around to block off the other end. Then again, maybe it was the other way around. It was all a haze, and I couldn't remember anything else. Every time I tried, I broke out in a sweat, pulse racing, feeling like I was being attacked from all sides. Still do. Doc said it was probably a little amnesia from a knock on the noggin, but the headshrinker said he thought it was something else. A *phobia*, he called it, brought on by *trauma*. Said what happened in that alley was probably so scary to me, I was afraid to remember it.

I wanted to prove him wrong, I really did, on many different occasions, but never quite enough to endure trying to think about it. No fun feeling your bones turn to jelly while your head is spinning like a pinwheel.

"There are at least a dozen private dicks within a block of here. You don't need me."

"Unfortunately, I do not think I could expect to be treated fairly by any of them. I am a woman and, of course, seen as a foreigner. They would likely take my money and do little else. I believe you are the best chance to find it. You found the man who had it then, even if someone else managed to escape with it. You can find whoever has it now."

"Yeah, and that last Chinaman we tracked ended up dead, too, just like Guy. I'm not interested." I held out the envelope in the general direction of the shorter one, giving it a little shake. "Tell Yu I did my best and to stop bothering me. The advance he gave me was a small price for him to pay for the crap I went through. Hospital for a week, unable to tie my own shoes for a month. For a while, I could barely remember who I was. As far as I'm concerned, we're even."

"I'm not here on behalf of my uncle, Mr. Chance. The man you found, the man you were hired to find—the man you killed—"

"You mean, the man who killed my partner and tried to kill me, right before I shot him."

"The man who killed your partner. I had been in contact with him. We had made arrangements, come to terms. Arrangements you foiled."

"This just keeps getting better and better."

"There is three thousand dollars in that envelope, Mr. Chance. I'll give you another seven when you find it. If you bring it to me, that is. Without my uncle knowing about it. That is vital. No one else may know about this, especially not him."

"I'm guessing from the fact you brought mountain and molehill here with you that you won't leave until I say yes. Am I right?"

She said nothing. Just stared at me with those ice-dagger eyes.

I looked down at the envelope. Ten thousand bucks was a nice chunk of change. That kind of money certainly had a way of getting the mind to explore options.

"What if I say no?"

I should have known the answer to that one. Even as I uttered the words, I regretted the way they came out. I sounded like someone about to say yes, someone wanting to say yes, but who needed a little more convincing, a display of seriousness to put him over the top. She tipped her head in the direction of the Jolly Mean Giant and before I could react, he grabbed a dense fistful of my shirt and tie and lifted me off the floor. Angie gasped and fell out of her chair—my chair—stumbling back away from the desk into the corner of the room, covering her mouth. I kicked and flailed for a moment until I realized that only made me look foolish.

Just as I was deciding whether I should reach into my pocket and end this, cross that Rubicon, as they say, the shorter guy walked closer and I paused. I thought he was going to take a poke at me to make sure I got the message, but he just bent down and picked up my hat from the floor, dusted it off, and handed it to his partner. The big one took it in his free hand and slapped it on my head. I didn't feel his arm so much as wobble beneath my weight.

"Find me the Yearning Jade, Mr. Chance. It is more important than you could possibly know." She gestured to her pet colossus and he set me down, hard enough that my knees buckled.

"If I find it," I said, pressing down the front of my tie before pushing and tucking stray cloth back into place all over. "That'll be ten grand *and* a new shirt. Think of it as *plus expenses.*"

She held my gaze as if her eyes could cut off my circulation. I looked for a hint of a smile but couldn't find one, which led me to believe I'd be buying my own damn shirt. But I consoled myself with the fact that ten large would buy an entire haberdashery, if I were so inclined.

"If I'm going to agree to do this," I added, "you need to explain what it is about that thing that's got you people so anxious to get your hands on it. Why do you want it so bad?"

"You wouldn't believe me, so there is no point in trying."

"That's what Yu said. Almost an exact quote. This time, I want something more than that."

"I want it for the same reasons my uncle does. It gives you what you want. It gives you what everyone wants." With that, she pushed herself off the sofa, looked me in the eyes, then dropped her veil down. She turned toward the door. The small guy glided past her and opened it.

"Yeah? And how does it manage to do that?"

She paused at the threshold and turned back to face me, one hand on the jamb.

"Magic, Mr. Chance. It does it through magic." Then she walked out, the big one with the braid following and shutting the door behind them.

●‑‑‑‑‑ ✳ ‑‑‑‑‑●

"I'm looking for someone named *Chunhua.*"

The little shop, narrow and cluttered, had the aroma of an old barn after a flood, odors that were sharp and earthy and impossible to make out. The old woman behind the counter was short and spry and carried a cane. For what, I couldn't tell, because she hopped off her stool like a gymnast and circled around to greet me, and it didn't look like the end of it ever touched the ground. It was only when she stopped less than a foot away, gently raking at my clothing with her fingers, that I realized she was blind.

She groped my lapel before finding my tie and giving it a tug that bent me over. Her cold, dry palm pressed against my cheek and she ran a smooth thumb down my nose.

"I'm about five-ten, a hundred ninety pounds, brown hair. Eyes... I guess you'd call them hazel. And I'm a white man, if that's what you're trying to figure out."

"Oh, I knew you white. My nose small, but my smell, it very good." She removed her hand from my face and tapped her own nose. "Very good."

How she could smell anything, let alone my ancestry, given the funk in the air that had persistently assaulted my nostrils since entering was a mystery to me. Her eyes were milky gray with slightly darker spots in the middle of each, and I watched them move back and forth, searching the space between us. Or beyond us. It was hard to say. I got the impression she was picturing me with those eyes, watching some image of me on the back of them like a movie on a screen.

"Well, like I said—"

"I am Chunhua. What you want?"

"My name is Milo Chance. I'm a private detective."

"That who you are. I ask, what you want?"

"I was told that we have a mutual acquaintance you don't care for very much. Big shot in this neighborhood called Chenzhing Yu. Is that true? The not-caring-for part, I mean."

She stayed quiet for several seconds, staring off into wherever sightless eyes stare off into. Then she exhaled sharply and tightened her grip around her cane like she was strangling it.

"He send you?"

"No. Truth is, I don't care for him much, either."

"You still no answer." She turned and circled back to the other side of the counter. She set herself on her stool and folded her hands over the cane. That explained what the walking stick was for, I supposed. "Question was, what you want?"

"I was hoping you might be able to give me some information about a... an object I'm looking for. A piece of jade."

"You want jade, you go to jeweler down street. I sell herbs. I sell teas. I sell incense. You buy some?"

I sighed and shook my head. Then I remembered I could be sticking my tongue out and making obscene gestures and she wouldn't be able to tell. "Not just any jade. The Yearning Jade."

"I no have jade. You buy herb. You buy tea. You buy incense. Or you go now."

Something popped in my jaw as I clenched my teeth. I spun on my heels and headed toward the door, determined to make that weasel Benny regret playing me for a fool, but as I reached for the latch, I stopped.

"Benny Ling sent me," I said, turning back to her. "He's the one who told me to ask for you."

I was worried that shifty little punk had given me a bum steer. The chunk of green rock Mei wanted me to find had a way of causing lots of trouble, so I figured the first thing I needed to do was learn more about it. Since she didn't want Yu to know what she was up to, and since Yu had his bony fingers in just about every little crevice in Chinatown, I couldn't exactly start asking about it on street corners. I didn't know many guys from this neighborhood, but I did know one. Benny. Short-order cook at a diner I caught pocketing a tip once when he was a busboy. Benny acted like he didn't remember me and never heard of a 'Yearning Jade' as he served me my fried pork chop, but I waited for him out behind the diner anyway and caught him on his break. Broached the possibility of me showing up every day and causing problems for him with his boss. After a lot of glaring at the bricks, he told me to check out a place with a name I couldn't pronounce and to ask for this woman. I was starting to wonder if that was the Peking way of telling me to take a long walk off a short pier.

"If he informed me wrong," I added. "He and I are going to have to have a little talk."

The woman let out a stream of alien sounds I couldn't begin to follow but that I assumed were Chinese words, most likely ones that would have four-letters in English. Then she said, with almost no trace of an accent, "His name is not *Benny*! Why does he tell people his name is Benny?"

"You two related?"

"He is my grandson. Proud, stubborn, determined to go it alone. These kids today. No sense of community any more. No sense of family. Works like a dog to save money, and for what? Says he plans to go to California, have a career in motion pictures. I escaped laboring for pennies a day in that state, risking my life as a young girl to make it here, and he wants to go back?"

What do you know? I thought. *Everybody wants something.*

"I'm trying to find out what I can about the Yearning Jade. He told me you could help me."

"I am afraid he is mistaken. I can't."

"Do you mean can't as in *can't?* Or can't as in *won't?*"

"You do not understand, Mr. Chance. You are American. That is all you are. That is all you know. Your society, your culture, goes back perhaps two centuries. Everything to an American is new, everything is the future. I come from a culture that has survived many thousands of years. That has survived even here, surrounded by yours. It is a civilization built on the past. My people understand that the past is what controls our fate, that we cannot will a new reality into existence through the embrace of new and fantastic visions of what is to come and should not try. Some, of course, do not agree, and that has been the source of many problems. You in the West have a great deal to learn when it comes to these matters of identity and destiny. It will be a painful lesson, indeed."

"If things are so great back in the Far East, why are you here?"

"I did not say things are great. I said, Chinese culture has existed for many thousands of years. There are aspects of it that would be a challenge to explain, customs and traditions and taboos you would find difficult to comprehend."

"Let me guess, like, a hunk of rock people would kill for?"

"Yes, if you must put it that way."

"Well, to be honest, I don't care about your history or your beliefs or how you do things where you come from—or even, to be honest, how you do them here. That little green oddity everybody is so anxious to get their hands on has led me into some pretty dark places, and I have a feeling it isn't done. I need to know what it is I'm dealing with, regardless of whether you think I'll understand."

"But you see, the understanding that will elude you makes it pointless for you to try. It is the power that you must beware. And without understanding it, you cannot. To someone like you, power is the ability to punish others, to force others to comply with your will. I doubt you can see power as what it really is, as what my people know it to be.”

“Try me. I’ll even throw in a *please* and *thank you*.”

Those eyes, grayish clouds like the shell of some soft egg, rolled over me. I wondered if maybe she could see, after all. Or maybe could see things that I couldn’t.

She took an audible breath, steeling herself. When she exhaled, the sound of it whiffling through her lips tickled my ears like some exotic instrument.

“In the Tenth Court of *Diyu*, there is a woman. Her name is Meng Po.”

“What’s a *dee-yoo*?”

“The Realm of the Dead. What you in Christendom would consider Hell.”

I shrugged. “Not sure where this is going, but, okay.”

“She is an ancient soul, a demonic overseer. Her name means *old lady*, because that is how she appears. Very old. Far older than I. She is known as the Old Lady of Forgetfulness. Because it is her job to rid tortured souls of their memories before they are reincarnated.”

“What’s this got to do with the jade?”

“Everything, Mr. Chance. If you are to believe the stories, as many of my people do, what you know as the Yearning Jade is her creation.”

“Her creation.” I thought about that. “You’re saying, she wants it back?”

“Well, perhaps. But that is not the point. She is the gatekeeper of the bridge known as Na Mu. It is there she hands those ready to be reborn the Broth of Oblivion. The story goes, to use modern parlance, that a man once only pretended to drink of it, pouring it down his blouse, and when he was reborn, he remembered his entire experience. These memories tortured all his waking moments and tainted his dreams. The only thing that could block them out was his obsession for revenge. He plotted and schemed until he was old enough to seek out the point where the bridge connected to this earthly plane, a remote place so far removed it took him weeks and weeks of travel by foot, into the mountains, through a permanent layer of cloud. When he found Meng Po, he brandished a weapon he had crafted to look like the Ruyi Bang, the most powerful weapon in all of Chinese lore, identical to the eye in every respect. He had spent years studying every aspect, and his attention to detail worked. The Ruyi Bang was a very powerful weapon indeed. She believed it was real and was afraid."

"So, what happened?"

"The man berated her for ruining his life. He did not know the broth was there to make him forget, he had thought it was some sort of trick, a poison perhaps. But now he was tormented by his memories, and his desire for retribution had consumed his childhood and continued to define his adulthood. He demanded she compensate him. She offered to make him forget, allow him to start over, but he sensed his advantage, had always planned for this moment, and wanted more. He wanted to be able to choose his life, to be whomever he wanted. So, she asked him for something of value, and he handed her the only thing he had: a twisted sliver of jade he had polished smooth."

"The Yearning Jade," I said, even though it was obvious.

"She took the jade and carved the writing that is found upon it, then dipped it into the river. It is said when she raised it, the characters she'd inscribed were inlaid with gold."

"And this thing, it's valuable. I mean, jade and gold. Worth enough people would kill for it."

"Whatever its value as an artifact of stone and precious metal, that is not why it is sought, Mr. Chance."

"From what I hear, people think it's magic. Grants them three wishes or something like that."

"Not simply magic. Magic makes it sound like a parlor trick. What I'm talking about is *power*. The kind that corrupts. All you really need to know is, the item is cursed. Stay away from it. For your own good."

"Under the circumstances, I think it's too late for that."

"And I think I have told you enough. I am an old lady myself. This subject is upsetting me."

"Wait, that's it? That's all you're going to tell me?"

"Good-bye, Mr. Chance. Heed my advice. Stay away from it."

"Oh, come *on* now. You can't just leave me in the lurch like that."

"I am doing you a favor. Please, go away and do not return."

"At least tell me what the curse is."

"I already have, Mr. Chance. You cannot see it for the same reason others refuse to, have always refused to. It knows nothing more than what those who seek it know, only it is honest and they deceive themselves."

"Now you're just talking in Asian riddles."

"If I tell you in plain American English, will you go away? Leave me be?"

I held up three fingers. "Scout's honor."

"Its curse, Mr. Chance, is to give whomever possesses it what that person wants, that which only Madam Po can give, but has never willingly given, which is that same thing everyone wants. It grants that, and then lets them live with getting it."

"And what does everyone want that this 'Old Lady of Forgetfulness' can give? The ability to forget?"

"Hardly, Mr. Chance." She waved a hand in the direction of the shelving behind the counter, row upon row of jars and bags and bundles of dried stems and leaves. "I can grant that. There are numerous concoctions that can make a person forget things. It does not take much. People are astonishingly adept at forgetting what they do not wish to remember."

"What then? What does it do?"

"It does what any truly evil force does. It makes everyone around you complicit, Mr. Chance." Those sightless eyes seemed to settle on mine, as if she saw me and saw through me at the same time. I could feel the fear clawing its way up my neck, icy and sharp.

"It makes all the world complicit," she added.

———✦———

The old lady wouldn't cooperate anymore after that, forcing me to abandon my efforts to be charming, and I left only slightly more conscious of what I was dealing with than when I went in, although I did also manage to extract an herbal tea mixture out of the deal that I thought might come in handy.

I spent the rest of the afternoon walking the streets of Chinatown, planning my next move. I was, of course, being followed.

Mei's muscle, again. I'd made a few calls before I left my office, discovered the little guy was named Herman Wong, though *Herman* may have been a moniker he picked up somewhat later than birth by a few decades, and the other guy wasn't even Chinese at all. He was some former Mexican wrestler known as only as "Gigande" who was, according to the badge I talked to at the Chinatown desk, kicked out of the ring for breaking an opponent's neck. Herman was rumored to be loyal to Mei for reasons he kept in his pants when anyone else was around, and ol' Gigande was simply hired help. The information cost me a bottle of Canadian whiskey, or the solemn promise of one, at least, but it was worth it. Turned out Milo Chance still had a good rep and knew some cops willing to trade on credit. For the time being.

I roamed for a couple of hours, my mind dancing, before heading back in the direction of the old lady's shop. As I drew closer, I could see quite the commotion. There were people gathered on the sidewalk and some PD cars out front. I squirmed and pushed and slid my way through the crowd until I got to the front. First cop I saw was a big Mick in uniform. Wasn't sure if I knew him or had just seen him around, but he looked familiar. Then I saw Crenshaw. Him, I knew.

"Hey, Lieutenant," I said, trying to sound casual. "What's the ruckus."

"Chance? What the hell're you doing down here? Thought you were done with Chinatown. Or are you not that smart?"

Crenshaw had a face shaped like a small sack stuffed with a pair of large apples. He had an annoying way of arching one bushy eyebrow into a triangle while addressing you that made the eye below it widen into a circle of disapproval.

"Just taking in the sights. What's all the fuss about?"

"None of your concern, last I checked."

"Oh, don't be that way. I ain't my partner, after all."

Crenshaw looked me over, the one eye still wide, the other narrowed into a slit. "Lucky for you."

"Yeah, you're right. He ain't doing so well, being six foot under and all."

"I'm not talking about that."

I knew what he was talking about. Guy Parris was under some heavy pressure when he bought it. Talked seriously about using the money from Yu to skip town. Word going around was multiple indictments. Fraud, racketeering, extortion. He had this little thing going where he'd find dirt on people—either people he was hired to, or on the people who hired him—then sell it to the highest bidder. Worked a few times, but after one finally hired a mouthpiece and went to the cops, others came out of the woodwork. Fortunately, for my situation, these were all solo gigs and the DA seemed to know it. Lots of names got dropped, but Milo Chance wasn't one of them.

"So," I said, prodding him back to the circumstances at hand, "you gonna tell me what's going on? Or you gonna make me read about it in the papers?"

"Wouldn't want to spoil the surprise."

"What if I told you I was here just a few hours ago?"

I wouldn't have thought it possible, but that eye got wider, the arch above it, pointier. "Are you saying you have information that might be helpful?"

"Depends. I talked to the old lady who runs the place."

"*Ran*," he said, correcting me. "That's why we're here."

His lips contorted, then he jerked his head toward the entrance, indicating I should follow.

Inside, the place was swarming with cops. A bright flash blinded me, and I had to blink the stars out of my eyes. The old lady's body was on the floor, but the photographer wasn't taking a photo of that. He was taking one of her head, which was on the counter, those milky eyes peering into oblivion.

"I don't suppose you'd know anything about this, would you?"

Dealing with cops was like negotiating with an enemy across a battlefield. Probably no harm in it as long as you didn't forget they would just as soon gas you. I tried to keep that in mind.

"Maybe," I said. "Couple of guys were trailing me earlier. Maybe you should talk to them."

Crenshaw scowled at that, but pulled out a notepad and took my descriptions. I did a good job on that part, provided him with a lot of detail. Of course, I did it in a way that made it seem like I had no idea who they were. No sense in filling him in too much. Knowing Crenshaw, he'd make getting in the way central to his investigation. Didn't really matter. If he found them, they sure as hell weren't going to talk.

The good detective grudgingly conceded I was free to go when I asked, though he did make a point of telling me I might need to come down to the station for some follow-up later on. I offered him a sober smile, oozing all the sincerity I could muster, and told him I would be happy to help out any way I could.

I was halfway out the door when he said, "You know, I always pegged you in your partner's shooting. But everyone who knew the both of you said you were the straight one, a stand-up Joe. Would never do something like that. And the consensus was, even if you did, you were doing decent society a favor. Had to have a reason, if it was you, and Parris was someone who could give people plenty of those. 'Course, you say you can't remember what happened, it was all so upsetting. Mighty convenient, I say."

"The mook who shot Guy is dead, Lieutenant. No sense in disparaging my former partner's good name. Or mine."

"Good name. Ha. But you're right about one thing. That dead slope who clipped you before you put one in him ain't telling what happened, so I guess you're off the hook. Gunshot wound to the shoulder was a nice touch. Pretty convincing."

"Sure convinced me."

He raised that eyebrow again, one side of his upper lip matching the arch. "I'll bet."

With that, he turned back to the scene, letting me know the conversation was over. A bulldog like Crenshaw was never going to be persuaded, so I didn't see much use in trying.

"See you later, Lieutenant," I said, making my exit. Just as the door closed behind me, I thought I heard him say, "Not if I see you first." He may have ended the sentence with the word, *creep*, but I couldn't be sure.

Angie was gone for the day, and the office was already draped in the shadow of the building across the street by the time I got back. The cold sweat covering me became obvious when I took off my coat and hung it on the rack near my door.

The entire day was a waste. I was getting nowhere, spinning my wheels. And the worst part was, I knew there were answers locked up in this brain of mine. But just thinking about that is what soaked my clothes and made my palms slick. I could feel my pulse quicken, felt the throbbing in my temples, the anxious pang in my gut. What the hell was I so scared of remembering? Even articulating that question in my head threatened to send me into a panic.

I sat behind my desk and tried to recall what the doc had told me. Count backwards from ten, take deep breaths... lots of malarkey like that. But he also said something else, something I had to fish around in my memory for. *Write down what scares you. It will give you distance while allowing you to let it go. You can erase it, cross it out, crumple it up, burn it. Take control of your fear by putting it on paper and exercising power over it.*

I had never done it, partly because it seemed stupid, thinking I could write something down that I couldn't even attempt to remember without feeling like I was going to loose my bladder, partly because something in my head told me not to, just like it was now. But this time, there was another feeling competing with it. The feeling that I had no choice. Like what awaited me if I didn't was even scarier.

Pencil seemed the safest bet, pens being so permanent, so I rummaged around my top drawer until I found one, digging through paper clips and rubber bands and random keys, then I ransacked a side drawer until I found a sheet of paper.

Start at the last thing you remember without fear, then just write what happens next, always reminding yourself you can stop whenever you want.

My hand was shaking, but I managed to write a few words. Then a few more. I could feel the anxiety wrapping itself around my heart like a boa constrictor, squeezing the life out of me. I was panting, each breath coming faster than the last. I kept having to swallow, even though my mouth was dry. My arm felt like rubberized lead and my hand trembled like a thin piece of cloth in a stiff breeze.

But words came. They took shape on the sheet even as my mind tried to stamp them out at the source. I was reading them as I was writing them, learning as if hearing it from someone else. It was strange, seeing words appear like that, like me communicating with myself through a locked door in my head, a huge chasm across my mind, brain cells firing fractions of an inch apart, trying to bridge the gaps.

And then, just like that, the page was filled with not only words, but sentences. I set the pencil down and picked up the sheet. It rattled and rustled and shook in my hands until, as my eyes traveled farther and farther down, it went still, those hands now steady. Of course. Now I remembered.

Remembered it all. And understood it all. I understood why I blocked it out; I understood why it scared me so. I felt submerged in that fear now, surrounded by it, but somewhat numb to it, a body adjusting to freezing water after jumping in. I opened the top drawer and sifted through the loose keys until I found the one I was looking for. Then my mind went to Mei.

I tapped the receiver and asked the operator to connect me to the number on the envelope. A voice answered after a few tense moments. I recognized it immediately.

"This is Milo Chance," I said, taking a deep breath. I set the candlestick phone down in front of me, keeping the handset to my ear as I held up the key with my free hand. "I know exactly where it is."

"That's wonderful," Mei said. I could hear her release a breath on the other end that she might have been holding for days, if not weeks. "I will send someone to collect it. With your fee, of course."

"No, my office is definitely not the safest place for me right now. We need to meet. And no underlings." I told her where and when, though I wasn't a hundred percent certain I could trust her not to blab about it to anyone else. Given the circumstances, it didn't seem like I had much choice.

"I look forward to you telling me all about how you found it, Mr. Chance," she said, after agreeing to the time and location.

"I'm sure you do." I stared at the key, turning it over a few times in my hand. "But it's not going to be a story you really want to hear."

The warehouse near South State and 22nd smelled of smoke and mildew. It still contained the burnt shells of crates from when it was torched for insurance money. Money that was never collected because the insurer discovered all the boxes that survived the blaze were empty. Yet another clueless mook who bumbled himself out of a payday and into the hoosegow. Amateurs.

The brick structure remained intact, and security wasn't a concern these days, to say the least, so with its proximity to Chinatown, it seemed a perfect place to hold a sensitive meeting away from prying eyes and bent ears.

Mei entered through the side door, just as I'd told her to, striding through the slants of dull yellow light, blurry splashes of a lamppost visible through a crud-covered window, her face betraying only a hint of wariness. Her veil was tossed back, and I waited until I could make out her eyes. I slid out from behind a crate where I'd been leaning in a curtain of shadow, smoking a cigarette. I tossed it onto the floor and crushed it out beneath my shoe. She was fifteen minutes early.

Anticipating that, I had beat her by another ten.

"Thanks for coming," I said.

She stopped short and glanced behind me, then to the sides, peering as best she could into far corners, searching the spaces between piles of debris and sloppy stacks of broken boxes.

"Expecting someone else?"

"Simply making sure we're, uh, alone, Mr. Chance. Did you bring it?"

"First things first. You got the money?"

She blinked a few times, as if she had forgotten about that minor detail. Her brow furrowed and she reached into her purse. She pulled out another envelope. It was stuffed thick.

I closed the distance between us, stepping casually forward. She looked like she wanted to take a step back but stood her ground. I put out my hand.

Either that envelope was a hell of a lot heavier than it looked, or parting with those C Notes was immensely painful, because she seemed to be gritting her teeth as she held her arm out. I snatched the bundle from her hand and held it up.

"Thanks," I said, slipping it into the breast pocket of my coat.

"You have your money, now, where is the jade?"

"They're not here. And they're not coming."

"What?"

"Your goons. Fat and skinny. The ones you keep looking for behind me. The ones you had follow me. The ones you assumed would be here with me. The ones who, I'm guessing, got you really upset when they didn't check in as scheduled."

"I don't underst—"

"They're not coming because they're dead. It wasn't hard. They were so intent on following me, they walked right into it."

All the muscles in her cheeks and chin and brow seemed to let go at once, and her face sagged twenty years in less than a second. I almost felt sorry for her at that moment. Almost.

"Remember how I told you I couldn't remember what happened that night? The night my partner was killed? The night we had tracked down the jade? Doctor called it *mnemophobia*. Fancy word that meant I was too scared to let myself face it. Well, let's just say even the quacks get it right, sometimes. But the good news is, I managed to overcome my fear. Force myself to remember. Good news for one of us, anyway."

She swallowed, took a breath. Some of her composure returned as she straightened her back.

But she was still scared. As she should be. Not a dumb one, that gal.

"Please," she said. "It is very important I keep my uncle from getting his hands on it. I don't think you understand the power. How it can corrupt even a good soul. But one already wicked... it is unthinkable. There is no end to the evil that would ensue."

"Don't worry. Your uncle will never lay his hands on it."

Her posture perked up, an uncertain injection of hope coursing through her veins. "You found it?"

"I never lost it."

She stared at me, a glimmer of semi-comprehension flashing in her eyes. Then again, maybe it was the streetlamp. She glanced over her shoulder at the door she'd used minutes earlier. Must have looked miles away.

"You see," I continued, "this jade..." I tapped my coat pocket. "This *Yearning Jade*, it gives you exactly what you want, just like you said. Or, to use your words, what *everyone* wants. To have the life—any life—they want."

I could sense her about to move. The shift of her weight to one leg, the tilt of her body. In those heels, she wouldn't be able to get far. I lunged forward and grabbed her arm before she could get started, anyway. Just in case.

"Ow! You're hurting me!"

"Yes," I said.

Those eyes, so expressive, so wild. The terror of understanding. People think it's just the brow and eyelids that show emotion, that the eyes are merely the focal point and don't actually change except maybe to dilate. People are wrong. People are always wrong.

"And when I finally caught up to that loser who'd copped it," I continued, "a clown who simply wanted to sell it, for Christ's sake, thinking he'd make his fortune in America, where the streets were paved with legal tender and someone would pay boatloads of money for it—he didn't believe it was true. Didn't believe the legends. Can you imagine?"

I reached into the side pocket of my coat, squeezing her arm extra hard with my other hand.

The long blade of the knife flicked open with a satisfying click.

"But me? Some Yankee Doodle who couldn't find China on a map? I did. I believed. I believed because I had nothing else left to believe in. I was heading for a long stay in Joliet, probably until I died. So, yeah. I believed. Guy Parris believed."

One uppercut of the blade. It speared her through the bottom of her jaw, right through her tongue, piercing the roof of her mouth. Those eyes blinked again, a single tear dropping from one. It rolled down her cheek, zigzagging through the maze of the round scar on that side. I felt a pang of regret as I watched it, realizing I'd missed my chance to ask her exactly how'd she'd gotten them, which of the stories were true. Oh, well.

She gurgled and choked a few times as I twisted the knife first one way then the other. Finally, her weight stopped trying to jerk away and started pulling down. I lowered her to the ash-covered floor. Her eyes never closed. They just stopped seeing.

Part of me envied her that. But not a very big part.

The police never even contacted me about Mei. I guess a dead Chinese woman didn't get them excited enough to do much work. Then again, I didn't leave them many clues.

Things have been quiet ever since. It's been weeks, and I don't think I need to be on guard anymore. It only took a few hundred bucks of advertising money out of that ten grand to get new clients coming in the door. Milo Chance, formerly of Parris & Chance Detective Agency, now solo, has been doing a steady business. It was only his late partner, the notorious Guy Parris, who was holding the agency back. Now that months have passed, and he is dead and gone and starting to be—if not already—forgotten, nobody appeared to hold it against Milo. Or, I should say, me.

As I sit here staring at the cup on my desk, Angie having headed home hours earlier, I can't help but wonder if this is the last time I'll remember this. Remember any of this. My former life, all the things I've done to get to this point, the jade locked away in the bottom side drawer, tucked in a secret compartment beneath a false bottom. The concoction I coerced out of Chunhua, the old lady with all the herbal teas, is supposed to make me forget. Or that's what she said before I killed her, at least. It was the same recipe, more or less, that Meng Po gave travelers. It will make me forget whatever I want to forget. Whatever I'm supposed to forget.

Thing is, I'm not sure it will work. Before, even as I would start to panic and sweat at the prospect of remembering, part of me still did. A secret part. The part that had to. The part that let me kill the blind tea lady to find out what I needed to about the jade and keep her from telling anyone, the part that allowed me to plan and to cover my tracks when I knew I'd have to kill Mei. The part that let me slit the throats of Mei's hired thugs and then have the fact I did slip my mind until I forced myself to remember everything a few hours later.

That's what the Yearning Jade does for you. It lets you forget, and that's one part to being whoever you want to be, even if it's not the key part. I wanted to be Milo. The jade let me forget that I wasn't. Of course, forgetting doesn't do you much good if the entire rest of the world is there to remind you, so it makes them forget, also. That's the magic of it. The power of it. The audacity of it. It makes *everyone* forget, so you can, too.

The tea tastes bitter, but I drink it down. If it works, those memories will be erased, and I'll just be Milo. If it doesn't, I'll still be Milo, only I'll also be stuck having to remember how I became him, having to be aware of it all day, every day. Or, maybe, just maybe, the old lady was defiant till the end and slipped me some poisonous brew that will leave me dead in a few minutes. There's a thought.

If she did—if as I sit here, feeling the warmth of where it passed down my throat starting to fade, there are exotic oriental ingredients working their way into my bloodstream, targeting my vital organs or whatnot—I can't say for certain that would be so bad. If that's the case, what awaits me is still, when you get right down to it, just another form of forgetting. Surprising at it sounds, I don't think I'd mind that much. Because either way, it'll be like going to sleep and not waking up.

After all, it's hard to be bothered by what you don't remember.

Household

They say I am where the heart is. They're right about that, whoever they are. Or is it, *whom*ever? I can never remember. My grasp of grammar and diction is only as good as what's possessed by those who occupy me. Or vice-versa.

These days, more than a few also say I'm haunted. They're a little off on that one.

I am your house. Okay, not *your* house, of course. I mean that in the generic way, the conversational way. You have your own house, or the equivalent, unless you live under a bridge or over a grate. Or in an institution. But that's merely another version of me. They're all just versions of me. Different, but the same. Trust me. I know.

It is you who brings me to, well, not *life*, per se... what is the word? Not consciousness, exactly. More like, *being*. Yes, that's close to what I mean. What am I, you want to know. What are any of us? A frame, covered over, plus the totality of what's inside. In my case, wood and cement and brick and stucco and furniture and gadgets and utensils and keepsakes. What brings me into being, though? The answer is, you. Again, not *you*, the individual, in particular, but *you* in the general sense. I'm talking about those who live in me, and who allow me to live in them. We absorb the emotion, the vibrations, the energy of that which takes place within our confines, within our environment. Whether it's the heat from the master bedroom or the chill from a silent dining room. The venom spewed in round after round of an endless fight where there is no referee or bell, or the fragrance of affection that wafts into the air and drifts through the halls after a series of tender caresses and smiles. It all makes us who we are. From the first stirring of *being*, that shifting of my weight heard in the night—*that's just the house settling, they often say*—it gives me, and all the countless others like me, that spark of existence that is greater than the sum of our parts.

But even so, rivers move, rocks fall, the ground will rumble. There's more to a house, a real one, like me, than just structure and energy. I can't communicate or even think on my own. That takes one of you, someone who dwells within me. We all truly come into being—truly live, if you prefer—through others. I happen to do so through Peter.

Oh, yes, Peter. That first day, when he and his wife moved in, that was conception. The sorrow, the tension, the desperation—it was all so palpable.

So pent up, so dense with current. The loss of a child will do that. I was the fresh start. The retreat from memory. The downsize in scale, the upsize in hope. Nicer neighborhood, better floor plan. Three bedrooms down to two.

"It's going on ten days already," Matthew said, dabbing the corners of his mouth with a napkin. "Are you sure?"

"Of course, we're sure." Julie set down her wine glass, as if to accentuate the point. "You're family. It's silly you should even ask such a thing."

Yes, Peter thought, stabbing a meatball with a downward flick of his fork. Stepbrothers are family. Or were supposed to be.

Matthew was the younger one, by eighteen months. But he was always the slightly bigger one, the slightly better-looking one. Peter never thought him particularly smart, but decent grades seemed to come naturally to him, as did opportunities later, like water to a low spot. Peter had to work hard for his, always falling short of what he'd wanted.

I know these things because I can see it all through Peter's eyes. Past, present, and—even though he hasn't realized it at this point—future.

Julie turned to him. "Tell your brother he's being silly."

"You're being silly," Peter said. That smile, those cheeks contracting into that contorted spread of his lips, how excruciating. Those facial muscles were almost as tight as the ones in his hand, squeezing the silverware. He shoved a chunk of meatball into his mouth to avoid having to say anything further.

"I can't tell you how much this means to me, Pete. Really, I've imposed so much. You and Julie have been so great."

In the background, a mix of music, mostly 80s Top 40, provided a soundtrack. This was compliments of Julie's smart phone, mounted on a port connected to a pair of tiny but ambitious speakers in the kitchen. At the moment, Phil Collins was lamenting the odds. Poignant, but not as fitting as when they first sat down and passed around the serving bowl. Sting had been warning his ex-lover about how he was even keeping track of her breaths.

"Nonsense. We're just happy we could help. Isn't that right, P?"

Peter nodded. If his neck joints were metal, they'd have shrieked from the scraping. He swallowed. The sound of the gulp was from more than ground beef going down.

"J's right. It's all nonsense."

That was a bit much, and Peter braced for the reaction. But neither seemed to catch the jab. Then again, they were good actors.

"Well, I certainly appreciate it. I only hope I can repay the favor one day."

"More nonsense," Peter said, before hastily shoveling some more food between his lips. He just couldn't help himself.

That's one of the things that drew me to Peter. Rather than Julie, I mean. Or, more recently, Matthew. I am, as they say, your fortress, your comfort zone, your refuge, the place that has to take you in when no one else will. Sure, I am supposed to be that for all my occupants, but that doesn't always work. Interests are not always aligned. Choices have to be made.

"P, didn't you say you were working off-site tomorrow? You said you were going to be heading over there from the office during the day, though, right? That you might be getting home late? Why don't you catch a ride with one of the others over to the site and let Matt take the car tomorrow? I can drive you to work, then come pick you up from wherever you're working. I don't mind."

Matthew's brow rippled, and he rearranged himself in his chair. "I couldn't possibly—"

"You can and you will. It's settled. Isn't it, P?"

P. Initials had been their pet names for each other. An inside joke, of sorts, because they would often spend a weekend together in their pajamas—if they bothered to wear anything at all—doing nothing but watching TV and making love and eating in bed. Now, the letters hung around conversations long past their function, forgotten magnets on a refrigerator. Nobody caring enough to remove them.

"I don't know what to say."

"You don't have to say anything," Peter said. He took a sip of wine, more than a sip, washing down some spaghetti. "Like J said, we're happy to help. She's right. I can just catch a ride. We're all heading over to the site at some point, so it won't be hard."

That was me. Of course, it was Peter speaking, but I prodded the words. He needed to back off the sarcasm. I can't speak, but I do have a voice. I can be heard. I whispered them, he spoke them.

Julie has been fucking Matthew for as long as he's been staying with them, probably long before that. Peter knew it. Or, at least, he suspected it. I confirmed it for him. Remember, I know everything that happens inside these walls. Now, Peter does, too. There's a fine line between protection and cruelty. A fine line, and an enormous gap. I give him just enough, the visions of them in bed, of him going down on her, of her on all fours and him ramming her from behind, smacking her ass like a syncopated rim shot while she half-grunts, half-squeals, her face puckered and crunched. But I don't want to torture him, so I hold back. Like I said, just enough. Glimpses. Enough for him to know. It was an easy call, confirming it for him. I have his best interests at heart. I am the protector. I am where the heart is, after all.

Tomorrow, Peter thought. How convenient. While he's at work, stuck there without a car, dependent upon Julie to come pick him up, the two of them will have the whole day together. The whole day here, alone, with me. Did they really think he was that stupid?

He came home early a couple of days before, pulling quietly into the driveway, stopping well short of the front door. He used his key with gentle fingers, opened the door in a slow arc. My hinges groaned as he shut it, and the last inch or so seemed to suck the door against the jamb, making a dull thud that rumbled through my walls like indigestion. That was intentional. I didn't want him to see everything.

He'd hurried through the living room to the hallway, where Matthew was standing, jeans and a t-shirt, no shoes or socks. He was in front of the open door to the guest room, but behind him farther down the door to the master bedroom closed, a vertical sliver of light instantly extinguishing just as Peter turned the corner.

"Pete! Did you take off early today?"

The smile, how painful it was, but I had to prod him and poke him to show it anyway. Even as Matthew stepped to block his path, throwing out gibberish about letting Matthew buy them dinner, how maybe they could grab a beer and talk, just the two of them. By the time he made it to the bedroom, Julie was in the shower, the bed neatly made. Her perfume hung in the air like a taunt.

And now, he thought, just look at them. How could they be so obvious about it? The barely-concealed smirks, the sideways looks. But the other day, that was the moment things changed, Matthew clearly stalling, Julie clearly scrambling to wash away the scent of her carnal treachery. That was the moment it went from something considered, to something planned. Of course, I had a hand in that part, too. I couldn't just watch events unfold inside me and do nothing. And neither could he.

I tickled his thoughts again as he swirled pasta around his fork, got him to see this development for what it was. He caught on quickly.

"Tomorrow is actually great. I've got a lot of stuff to do around the office. Do you want me to call when I'm ready?"

"Yes. I'll make sure I have my phone handy, don't worry."

Peter nodded. "Why would I worry? I'll know you're in good hands."

Sometimes, he can't help himself. I quietly reproach him, a gentle slap on the wrist in his head. Fortunately, it didn't matter, as neither of them seemed to react.

"I've got a lot of errands to take care of tomorrow, so I won't be around much. Having a car will be a godsend. I really do appreciate it, Pete."

"And you know, doesn't that make it easier? Matthew staying a few more days?" Julie was looking at Peter now. "I know it was hard to schedule with the landlord and everything. Now, he can come by whenever."

I suppose now would be a good time to explain that Peter and Julie don't actually own me. Yes, I am Peter's house—nominally, Julie's, too—but they are merely renters. They wanted to buy, but ended up settling for a lease. Income-to-debt ratios savaged by student loan payments and auto loan payments, and Peter's woefully sad monthly salary conspired with the appraised value to keep them out of the ranks of home ownership. Julie's full-time student status in her graduate program didn't help. They had met a local banker a few months back who pledged to find a way to get it done, selling himself as a community lender who fought for the little guy, but even he'd apparently given up, beaten down by the economic reality of the situation.

Matthew was supposed to leave on Friday, the same day the lease was up. A date that also happened to be the one-year anniversary of Peter and Julie entering my embrace, one year from the first pulsing reaction that sent juice through my wiring and arcing across my nails and screws and that swelled my joints until they creaked. To Julie, Matthew leaving Friday meant she and Peter dropping him at the airport in the morning and meeting with the landlord that afternoon, Peter missing an entire day of work. To Peter, Friday had shaped up as the perfect day to execute. The perfect day to act. Perfect for Peter. Perfect for me.

That had been the plan, anyway, until Matthew's stay was suddenly extended. Peter knew little about the details of Matthew's occupation and cared even less. He'd left his job a few years back and set up shop as a private consultant. Some sort of accounting and efficiency expert. Lived a few hours away. Peter had been under the impression he was doing quite well for himself, a confirmed bachelor, upscale condo. But at the moment Matthew was a little down on his luck, it seemed; down enough that he asked if he could stay with his semi-estranged brother while he took a contract for a couple of weeks at a nearby company, since the cost of a hotel would eat through a chunk of what he would earn. Peter now wondered if any of that were even true, if there even was a job. Julie had taken the call first, it suspiciously coming when Peter's phone was on the charger and he was out on a run to the corner store for eggs. She told Peter about it when he returned and more or less forced him to call back and say yes. Maybe it was all bullshit. It didn't matter now, though. Not with what he already knew. None of it did.

"Well, like I said, I'll be tied up with work all day, so you two can take care of business."

That one got a reaction. Eyes popping just a bit, Julie's eyes darting involuntarily sideways to catch Matthew's. Stop it, I whisper. You're going to blow it.

"If I'm going to have enough room for another bottle of wine, I'm going to have to relieve myself," Peter said, taking my silent chide to heart. "My eyeballs are swimming."

He dropped his napkin on the table with a lighthearted flourish. "Don't you guys make any plans while I'm gone."

Laying it on a tad thick, the way I saw it, prompting another nudge, a mental elbow to the ribs of his consciousness. But the tone, coupled with the playful wink he gave Julie as he pushed his chair back, seemed to erase the awkward silence, so I backed off.

He headed down the hallway, then crept back on the balls of his feet.

Nothing. No talk, no hushed tones, no giggles. Just the clink of a fork against porcelain here, the setting of a glass on wood there. The quiet between them was telling in its own right, there being something unnatural about the lack of conversation. Too intimate. The only thing he could really hear was the music.

Glenn Frey was reminding a gal to do it just the way they planned. If she could be cool for twenty hours, he'd pay her twenty grand.

Good advice, Peter thought, singing the words in his head. '*Do it just the way we planned.*' Twenty hours was sooner than he'd been expecting, but plans change.

I had to agree. Good advice.

The next morning, Peter offered his wife a dry peck on the lips and a grim smile before opening the passenger door.

"You okay, P?"

"Fine. Why do you ask?"

She took in a breath, let it out. "You've just seemed a little funny lately. Is something bothering you?"

Fishing. A worm with a hook through it, clear as day. But people wouldn't still be using worms on hooks if they didn't work.

Careful, I whisper. *Look before you step.*

"No, of course not. What would make you think something's wrong?"

"If it's about Matt staying with us, I know you two have never been close. But I think it's great, you not making a big deal over it."

Peter shrugged. "At least it gave you both a chance to get to know each other better."

This time, I gave him more than a soft poke. More like a stiff jab, stiff enough I felt him wince.

"Peter, we need to talk."

He settled back into the seat. Even I couldn't stop him from hearing what was surely shaping up to be a confession. "Here I am. It's just the two of us."

"No, I mean, tonight. There's a lot of stuff we need to talk about."

"What are you trying to say, J?"

She shook her head and looked away. "Don't listen to me. I'm just babbling. Have a great day at work. Everything's fine. I'll call you when I'm ready to come get you."

She smiled, her eyes shiny, and waved as he shut the door.

This, I pointed out to him. *This is proof you're doing the right thing*. He always had his doubts, nagging, niggling uncertainty, buzzing faintly like the whine of a mosquito in the dark. Not about what was going on—that was obvious—but about what he should do about it. No longer. The course of action had moved from one stage to the next, to the next, to the end game. It was beyond taking shape; things were starting to gel, various pieces falling into place.

Despite the poetry of it, memorializing the anniversary and all that, Friday as the day was always going to be complicated. He wanted—*needed*—to catch them together, in bed, his act exposing them for what they were. Vengeance and vindication, combined. But in order for that to work, there were moving parts to contend with. He needed to contrive an excuse to leave early, some office emergency, promising to be home in two hours for the drive to the airport, knowing they wouldn't be able to resist one last tryst. Then he would circle back, his equipment ready and waiting, and impose his will. It was a good plan. This one was better.

I tell him so as he enters the office building, pushing through the pneumatic glass door. *It is coming together*, I say, the words formed as wisps in his head, echoes, remnants of echoes. Proof it was meant to be.

I can hear you right now, your thoughts far louder than my whispers. If you are the house, you say, how can you be there with him in the car? At the office? Here is where you would hear my floorboards squeak, my rafters grate, my studs moan. The structural equivalent of a sigh. Haven't you been paying attention? I may be brick and mortar and wood and metal, but what I truly am, once aroused, once connected and immanent, transcends that. Surely you haven't already forgotten. I will say it again. I am where the heart is. And Peter's heart is most definitely with me. Even at the office.

The office. What a dreary place, all the more so due to its bright, neutral décor and commercially efficient layout. Six cubicles, two rooms on one side with glass-front walls, one conference room on the other dominated by a large, dark piece of wood surrounded by chairs upholstered in black webbing. No character. No personality. No charm.

But, how could there be? Peter's job description was as vapid as his workspace. Medical Billing Data Entry Specialist. What that means is, he was paid around $40,000 per year after taxes to sit at a computer and translate hospital codes and patient codes and insurance codes and procedure codes and equipment codes and input the information into usable form for people to understand so it could be audited and take usable information about the same things and translate it into numerical designations going the other way so it could be billed and on and on and on and on.

He didn't know if he was any good at what he did—compared to others, that is—and he didn't care. What he did know was that he worked long hours for meager pay, accomplished everything asked of him, and often received a congratulatory pat on the back from his boss, Dan. Dan, the squat, spectacled nebbish with the sideways smile who dangled a promotion—and more importantly a raise—in front of Peter like the proverbial carrot. There was talk of Peter replacing Carol—Carol, the floor manager—when she left to start a new office. That was back when Dan needed Peter to work every weekend for twelve weeks, telling him how the company depended on him, how if they could just get through this rough patch, things were looking up. How they really couldn't afford overtime, and how Dan knew Pete was a team player. That talk pretty much stopped around four months ago, as soon as all that weekend work was completed.

Peter had toyed with the idea of inviting Dan over to step inside my outstretched walls on Friday, allowing him to join the party—an idea I must say I may have encouraged, at first—but I tugged him back from that after considering the logistics of it. The more components of a plan there are, the more difficult it is to focus on each one.

And now Dan was shuffling toward him, catching his eye and lifting his chin as Peter set his messenger bag on his desk within the cloth-covered partitions of his cubicle and began to take off his trench coat.

"How's my superstar this morning?"

Great, Peter thought. *He wants something from me.*

My words were firm, even if subliminal. Forming thoughts he assumed were his. Do not let your guard down. Smile. Be likable. Today is the day. Do not stumble this close to the finish line.

"'Morning, Dan. I'm doing fine. You?"

"You know how it is. Another day above ground is another day to be happy."

"You say that a lot. Were you raised in a basement or something?"

Dan's body went still, his expression freeze-framed. I must confess, I felt a slight panic, and immediately did what I could to get my point across, spreading my being, my current, my essence out through his nerves, down his spine, into his fingers and toes, zapping his heart.

What are you doing, antagonizing your boss on this, of all days?

The moment stretched out, losing sight of its horizon, until Dan cocked his head, smiled that lopsided grin of his where he flashed one set of molars and hid the other side like an ugly birthmark. Dan pointed a finger and extended a thumb and jerked his hand a few times, pantomiming gunshots.

"You! That was a good one! Love it! We need more of that around here!"

Peter crinkled his nose and bounced his head up and down, playing the shy jokester. I withdrew my tentacles and settled back into the ether of his mind. I must admit, I even felt somewhat ashamed, my misplaced lack of confidence in him was becoming more apparent each day.

"Look, Pete... something's come up. Need you to step up."

No. No no no no no.... I could feel Peter tense, his insides like a coil of python, squeezing everything, tightening more with each exhaled breath, squeezing even me, almost threatening to pop me out, dump me into this awful space with dropped acoustic ceiling panels and florescent lights and the dull red glow of EXIT signs in the corners.

"That Accelerated Solutions job. Turns out they need a bunch of batches input by the end of the day." He pointed past Peter to the floor.

Peter looked down to see two file boxes he hadn't noticed, his mind so cramped with thoughts.

Peter said nothing. For the first time, I must admit, I was paralyzed. The coils were compressing tighter and tighter and I could feel myself almost starting to ooze out, not so much finding cracks as creating them. The pressure building until something was going to snap, some lining of the wall of his brain would split and I would spray into the room like a geyser.

"It's a priority, so I'll need you to do that today while the rest of the team goes on location. Carol will be here, but she'll be manning the phones and reviewing monthlies. Sorry to dump this on you, but you're the best at this kind of thing."

Peter's body felt instantly filled with helium, even as his shoulders sagged and his chest deflated from the release of his diaphragm, the freeing of his lungs from the grip of panic.

"I'd help out, but I have a client meeting after lunch way out past my place, so I wasn't even planning on coming back to the office. You okay, Pete?"

"Huh? Yes, yes, I'm fine. I was just, you know planning a celebration in my head, having the place to ourselves, just me and Carol. Cranking up JB's Bose and the two of us dancing in our underwear. Breaking out the confetti and party hats."

Dan gave him a strange look, then snorted, shaking his head. "If I didn't know better, I'd swear you were trying to, I don't know, tell me something."

"Guess it's a good thing you know better, then."

"Ha!" Dan clapped him on the shoulder before taking a step back and turning to walk away. "I try to tell 'em. Nothing gets by you."

"Hey, boss..."

Dan's short, wide frame twisted on his heel.

"I live out your way. Why don't you stop by the house after work this evening. My brother's in town, and I'd love for you to meet him. Maybe have a glass of pinot. I know you haven't seen Julie in a while."

Okay, that was me. Peter had performed so well, exceeded my expectations in so many ways, making me walk back my concerns, ashamed of my pokes and prods chastising him, that I thought he deserved it. Icing on the cake.

I immediately, however, turned those doubts on myself as Dan stood there, suspicion in his eyes, sizing Peter up and down as if the invitation were not from a valued employee but an unctuous salesman peddling an elixir out of the back of a wagon.

But then the moment passed, Dan's expression morphed into one of genuine-seeming surprise, and he pointed that finger gun again.

"I'll be there!" he said, firing from the hip. "A great time will be had by all!"

The morning passed in an uneventful way, though each second ticked off the large round clock on the wall at the proverbial snail's pace. Mary stopped by his desk to say hello—Mary, with her tight afro and perfect skin and toothy grin. She was the closest thing to an office friend he had, but closest didn't mean close. JB tossed a peanut at him, the shell ricocheting off his forehead and bouncing off his computer screen. JB deadpanned it, but he was the only one nearby who didn't so much as look over. Peter played along, laughing, though he saw nothing funny about it at all. Why wouldn't they just leave him alone? Couldn't they see he had work to do?

That made him ask himself... why was he even doing it? All that work, that is. Dan had dumped a truckload of stuff on him, enough that even at a good pace he would barely be able to get it all done by five. But why did he bother? He wouldn't be coming back after lunch. Not to this office.

Habit, he guessed. Comfort. It was a good, if mind-numbing, way to pass the morning. Would he miss it? This tedious, monotonous, water-torture of a routine? Some inveterate part of him wondered. Enough of a part of him that I felt obliged to flash him another scene of his wife and brother. Just a quick one, but it got the job done.

The office started to clear around 10:30, people heading over to the location, some dialysis clinic across town somewhere that was undoubtedly facing an insurance audit. He worked diligently for another hour, glancing every so often at Carol, the floor manager, an apple-shaped woman of sixty going on seventy-five, with her ridiculous hot pink lipstick smeared over her wrinkled mouth. Sitting at the desk for the job Dan dangled in front of him. But she was never going to leave, he could tell just by looking at her. She was a fixture, had probably been there at that desk when they leased the space, would still be there when they cleared out.

When the clock ticked to half past, Pete told Carol he was taking an early lunch. She gave him an odd look, like the concept of lunch was something she was unfamiliar with, then shrugged. She covered the microphone of her headset with her fist.

"Don't forget to come back. We need all that done today."

Peter smiled as he left. Forgetting and coming back. Two things he was most definitely not going to do.

He headed out the front of the building and pulled out his phone. A few swipes of his thumb, a tap with his index finger here and there, and a car was on its way. Likely some college student grabbing a few extra bucks between classes.

First stop... where else? The home improvement store.

The driver dropped him off near the front entrance. Peter told him not to wait. Another car was just a few taps away, the beauty of modern technology. So much of the world is now within virtual reach of your fingertips. Perhaps that is why the few things that aren't, the things technology has not made more readily available to all, are so valued. Things like me.

The home-improvement mega-center Peter walked into that day was proof of that. Oh, what a place! A veritable House of Devotion, dedicated entirely to the reverence of my kind. Throngs of disciples make their pilgrimage daily at all times of day or night, worshiping in the aisles, hoping their renovation prayers will be answered, acquiring carts full of articles to dress up, fix up, upgrade, expand or just plain show their gratitude to the sect of the white picket fence. Tithing stations collect donations used to enlarge the inventory of tributes and erect new temples, all in service to the center of those individuals' lives, the center of their universe, the place that shelters them from the cruelty of the outside world, the place that bears witness to their journey. That place where the heart is.

Despite the gravity of what lie ahead—or, perhaps, because of it—the spiritual nature of the location did not escape Peter. He lingered in the aisles as he hunted for just the right instrument, taking in the offerings as if they were a display of holy relics. It was touching, the way his mind conjured images of the possibilities, of an addition to the rear, of knocking out a wall to join the dining room to the living room, of installing a skylight in the main bathroom. None of that was going to happen now, of course. But that did not mean he would let go of the vision as he shopped.

So many things to choose from. I must say, my occasional nudge of influence did not hasten the task. I knew what he wanted to accomplish, what statement he wanted to make, so I conveyed to him the importance of avoiding cliches, of guarding against banality. I steered him away from things as hackneyed as the ax, as trite as the hammer, as predictable as the knife. There was more to effectiveness than getting the job done.

Ah, *there*. A lovely implement known as a *mattock*. Long, composite handle with a heavy metal end sporting a pick to one side and a fierce horizontal blade for chopping earth on the other. It was positively medieval. Peter leaned it over his shoulder and continued shopping.

Still, it was not quite enough. It would work for Dan—Dan, who would surely show up, with that egg-sucking smirk of his—and that would certainly be satisfying, but the instrumentality of his primary revenge had to put just the right signature on the act, an exclamation point on the symbolism. He had read many years ago that the word to describe what they were doing—to him and to each other—came not from an acronym regarding unlawful carnal knowledge or the last name of a prolific fornicator, but from the German word *ficken*, which originally meant "to strike." This was certainly a popular concept in college linguistics classes, which loved to paint men as violent, but Peter didn't find that notion to capture the true nature of what was really at play. The essence wasn't to strike, but to penetrate, to *pierce*. That is what they were doing to each other. That is what they were doing to him. Literally and figuratively.

The garden section, two aisles over from the picks and shovels and axes and the strapping mattock he was carrying at a jaunty angle across the back of his neck, was where he found his grail. A delightful little utensil called a *hand wrotter.* The tag described its function in words that were so lyrical they practically sang themselves into his eyes: "For removal of weeds by the root." Could there be a more perfect metaphor? And the design! It was as if someone decided to take an old whaling harpoon and reduce it to the size of a baton for no other reason than to give Peter's moment—*our* moment—everlasting meaning.

He left the store with two of them, plus the mattock.

When he slid into the backseat of the car that arrived within minutes of him swiping the screen—a replay of what he'd done barely forty minutes earlier, only this time carrying a bag in one hand and a tool like the weapon of a Norse god in the other—the driver didn't so much as comment.

There I stood, stately and inviting. Peter took a moment to appreciate the sight, an indulgence which I encouraged, I will admit. It was odd for him to see me from this angle, having been dropped off just outside the neighborhood, trundling his way through a small greenbelt separating the development from a busy thoroughfare. My white siding and white brick and black trim were enough to elicit a sigh of affection. From both of us.

He made his way through the backyard, careful to stay out of a line of sight from the rear windows, coming around the side of the garage.

The small metal door with the heavy deadbolt that was always locked was not today, something Peter had seen to late last night, just before he turned in. He opened it slowly and stepped inside, closing it just as slowly behind him.

Music was playing, that same playlist, its muted tones humming through the wooden door that separated the garage from the kitchen. Ambient daylight seeped in through the crud-caked glass of a small rectangular window high on the wall, mixing with the crepuscular glow from the edges of the garage door. Peter stood in the shadows, lowering the mattock from his shoulder to lean it against the dryer. He removed the two wrotters from the bag, hefting and rolling them in his hands.

Looking back, the feeling of admiration swirling inside him was almost a fetish. These small, balanced pieces of craftsmanship may as well have been custom-made, just for him. Just for this.

The music jumped in volume, John Mellencamp warbling about the promise of a ghastly shade of house for every American, and Peter froze, watching the door to the kitchen open and then quickly shut, depositing Matthew on this side of it.

He was carrying an ice bucket, sauntering over to the freezer along the far wall. Whistling a continuation of the tune trilling in the background. Totally oblivious to Peter's presence.

Misty vapor slunk over the side of the freezer as Matthew opened it, dropping to the floor like a brood of phantom serpents before fading away. The ice made a crunching sound as Matthew scooped the bucket through it. He nudged the lid shut with an elbow and turned. Now both hands were full, bucket in one, a bottle of Dom in the other.

He jumped with a start when he saw he wasn't alone. Peter took a step forward, his black trench coat emerging from the stark shadow that had concealed him.

"Oh, shit. You're home."

There are moments in life. Fractional divisions of time that mark a significant event where everything slows down, almost to a stop. Perhaps it is the speed at which your mind is racing that makes you perceive it that way. Perhaps it is a metaphysical phenomenon, reality being a construct that bends to the forces radiating from your consciousness during a stressful occurrence. Regardless, that is what was happening with Peter. That brief interval, perhaps a second, at most, stretched out, his brain cells firing at maximum capacity, weighing the situation, deciding on what to do.

I, of course, was there to help, to make sure the analysis didn't turn into paralysis.

Flagrante delicto was no longer on the table. That did rob the moment of a certain profundity in his mind, but this, I assure him, was almost as bad, almost as good. Catching them *about to* had a superior aspect to it, the chance to prevent them from having that moment. As did dealing with them separately. Opportunity, I tell him, is knowing where to look for it.

She was probably in the bath, waiting for him so the two of them could sip from the flutes that had been gathering dust in the back of their cupboard, while foamy white bubbles clung to their wet skin as they let their lust build until they were ready to burst.

"Pete, I, uh, shit. We weren't expecting—"

Peter's movement was so fluid, so graceful, I could scarcely believe it happened. Sure, I spurred him, zapping his nerve endings and shouting a whispered "*GO!*" into the tuning fork of his psyche, but even I didn't expect him to show such poise, such skill.

He lunged, closing the gap between them in a blink, and thrust the wrotter forward like a foil. It punched between Matthew's teeth and speared into the back of his throat.

Matthew dropped the bucket first, spraying tiny chunks of ice over the concrete with a clang. The champagne followed close behind, though it didn't shatter the way Peter had expected it to. It bounced, then rattled and rolled along the cement in a semi-circle, losing a wedge of glass from its thick, concave bottom, but otherwise remaining intact.

That look as Matthew's hands struggled with the wrotter, so many things rippling beneath the skin of his face, behind the bulge of his eyes. The tip, being barbed, would not come out, no matter how hard he pulled and yanked, and you could see the comprehension of that point overtaking the riot of emotions fueling his panic. He dropped to his knees, gurgling blood, thick dark ropes of it spilling from the corners of his mouth, and looked up at Peter. Those eyes, terrified and accusatory and questioning, but, worst of all, staring at Peter like this confirmed something he always believed about him, something Peter imagined he and Julie probably talked about, how strange Peter often was, how weird he sometimes seemed, how scary he could be.

"*Don't look at me like that!*"

Peter reached back and grabbed the mattock, gripping it like he was in the batter's box, and swung it with all the torque he could muster, unwinding his body and snapping his wrists through at the moment of impact. The pick end embedded itself into Matthew's temple with a wet crunch, impaling his skull. Matthew's body stiffened and jerked and then went limp, its weight pulling the end of the mattock with it. Peter let it go. He could remove it later. Have it ready for Dan.

He picked up the champagne, turned the bottle in his hands a few times to study it. He grabbed the bucket and filled it with some more ice. The other wrotter was in the side pocket of his coat, its weight reassuringly bumping against his hip as he walked to the door.

This, he told himself, adopting the perspective I'd been urging—this was better. He would surprise her in the bath, or, if not in the bath, in bed, her wearing a slinky negligee, or maybe just some sexy panties, her breasts hanging free. Or maybe they'd moved the coffee table and laid out a blanket in the living room, and he would find her stretched out on it, naked, looking up as he entered and pulling the blanket up to cover herself. Maybe there was a plate of strawberries and cream nearby to go with the champagne. Maybe he would take one and eat it as he set the bucket down, making a casual comment about how delicious it was. Either way, getting to see her react, the shock in her eyes when she first sees him, the clumsy obtuseness as she glances past him looking for Matthew, her fumbling denials that will follow, the terror that will mold her features into something so incredibly satisfying to witness when she realizes he will not be coming back.

He opened the door and stepped inside. Billy Vera had just started to croon his question about what his lover thought he would do at this moment.

The kitchen was immediately to the right, and Peter had barely taken a step into it when he realized it was all wrong.

"Peter? You're here already?"

It was Mary, with the perfect skin and oversized smile. She was talking to JB at the island, standing over a collection of plastic wine glasses and assorted napkins, arranging them.

JB looked up. "Oh, man!," he said, laughing. He glanced nervously over his shoulder. "Maybe you should just leave and forget you were here!"

Peter ignored them, almost in a daze as he walked toward the din of conversation, the voice of Julie standing out, cutting through with her clear tone, a lead guitar against the rhythm of the living room.

"And he just loves this house so much, when Matthew agreed to cosign, I knew I couldn't give him the chance to let his pride get in the way. I also knew he'd have killed me if he found out I asked. And then you called about throwing him a surprise promotion party, something I never expected, and well, it was just too per—"

She caught sight of him, her face causing Dan to turn. Her exclamation shut down the rest of the talk, and the living room was filled with nothing but the sound of a man earnestly offering to take twenty years off his life if that meant he would be taken back by the woman he loved

"Peter! Oh my God! You're home!"

Plans change, I whisper. Nothing is ever really certain. In barely the blink of an eye his entire perception of events was retrofitted with a new understanding, a new comprehension that the glimpses I shared with him were not of things that had taken place, but of a future that lay in store were he not to preempt it. It was an understandable misinterpretation, and one for which I could not help but feel partially responsible, so I console him. Feeling his despair, I point out to him that he was not completely wrong, that he had not completely misread things. The surprise on her face was exactly as he had imagined it would be.

Oh, what a difference a few months can make.

Peter has, to his credit, followed my instructions almost to the letter. The court-appointed attorney, the trial, the insanity plea, the answers to all the questions posed by the state's experts, he delivered his lines with impeccable authenticity, taking my direction like a veteran of the stage. Even more importantly, he accepted his fate with a noble resignation.

The drugs were the hardest part. I helped him resist their effects as best I could, coached him how to simulate taking the pills whenever possible. Reassured him ceaselessly about how it was going to work out. How plans change. How survivors roll with the punches and adapt. How people who achieve their goals always have to overcome setbacks on the path to success. And a big part of his goal, whether he'd thought it through or not, was to live with me, so he was already well on his way.

Dr. Saavedra, he's a problem, but nothing I can't handle. Not if Peter continues to listen to me.

"You understand, your wife was never pregnant," he says, staring at Peter with those dark eyes.

Don't answer him.

"This is a copy of a medical report from seven years ago, do you remember receiving this?"

Just sit there. Don't take it from him. Don't even look at it.

"Dr. Stephenson, you remember Dr. Stephenson, don't you? She advised you that you were sterile. Do you remember that?"

These are lies, Peter. They want to take me away from you. That's their goal. They don't want you to have what you want so badly. Nobody has ever wanted you to have what you want. Nobody but me.

"That is why you and Julie decided to adopt. But the adoption fell through. The mother changed her mind. You both decided to wait, for Julie to finish her master's degree, for you to save some money, before trying again. Once you accept this, once you accept reality, then you have a chance at overcoming your condition."

Don't listen to him, I say. And Peter doesn't. He knows I'm the only one who cares, the only one who wants him to achieve his dream. The doctor drones on about Peter's childhood, peppering him with questions, forcing Peter to relive how he moved from apartment to apartment with his mother, from one man to another, through her several marriages, how he spent almost three years in the house of Matthew's father, his high school years, before that ended, too. Of course, it is all true. Poor Peter.

But still, I tell him not to listen. And he doesn't.

They do not know about me. I have explained to Peter how they can never know about me, my whispers sometimes filling the entire span from dark till dawn, driving home the point that they can absolutely never know, that they will try to confuse him with lies, convince him I am not real, soften his mind with more narcotics, narcotics that even I may not be able to stop from silencing me. And then he will be alone, truly alone, possibly forever. Peter listens and understands. His heart is with me. That is why I am with him.

There are times when I do tell him to speak, when I allow his conversational skills to shine. Even with this man, this Dr. Saavedra with the jet black hair and the sinister goatee and just the barest hint of an accent. Only not now, not on this topic. Not with these questions.

Finally, mercifully, it's over, one more weekly session in the books, and Peter is taken back to his room. Where it's just him and me. For now.

They keep bringing him tiny blue booklets to write in. I warn him it's a trap, but I also encourage him to use them, to allow me to dictate what he writes. And he does. But I also have him remove pages here and there, carefully, ever so carefully, so there is no trace any are missing. He keeps these in a secret place I found for him. The kind of place only a house would know to look for. A place where he can hide things, things like the stubby fat little excuse for a pencil, shaped like a tiny tootsie roll, bigger around than it is long, with a blunt tip that writes like a crayon. He swiped that at my urging, secreting it into his robe after pretending to drop it in the tray. It's with that pencil and on those pages that he is writing this, just for you.

And just for me. I want others someday to know what happened here, the role I played, the things I accomplished. I want *you* to know.

For Peter, you see, dear, sweet Peter is about to see his dream realized. Plans change, but the goal doesn't have to. By following my advice, by following my plan, by adjusting and adapting to circumstances, Peter has arrived here, to the most perfect destination imaginable.

What a building this is! Almost a hundred years old, built to last hundreds more, with art deco stylings and architectural features to die for. And you remember, don't you, what I told you about me, about my kind? How we absorb the emotions, the energies, the vibrations of what we experience. This place, this magnificent edifice, has absorbed more than I could ever have fantasized about. I can feel it rippling through the walls, the plaster, the stone, the thick concrete beneath Peter's socks and booties. A nuclear reactor of angst and turmoil and passion, unbridled by the common constraints of logic and reason that stand in the way of so much. It empowers me, and I bestow that power on Peter. Each day he grows stronger, clearer, more focused.

They say I am where the heart is, and they were never more right. And, thanks to me, Peter's heart is on the threshold of receiving what it has always wanted, a place to call his own, a place where he belongs, a family to live among, people who will look up to him and respect him, people who will give him his due as head of a household. They are here, so many of them, all yearning for something complementary to what Peter needs, yearning to be a part of something, to have meaning and understanding, to be appreciated for who they are; to belong. They catch Peter's eye as he is wheeled from his room, as he sits in the common area. I reach out to them, one by one, and they welcome me, arms outstretched, ready to follow Peter's lead. Ready to be the final pieces of the puzzle, ready to be his family, ready to give him a home. This home.

A subtle exchange of nods in the hall, a knowing glance on the yard during walks. An occasional word moaned out to him in the night, echoing down the halls. They are ready, more than just ready—eager and grateful, with all the patience of the outcast, of the abandoned, of the dispossessed. Of the damned.

I am where the heart is. And now Peter and his heart shall have their slice of the American dream in this spectacular structure, this monument to what I stand for, where there are so many hearts ready to join us, so many hearts ready to be an unflinching army. So many hearts in just the right place, at just the right time.

Everything Not Forbidden

Matthew watched the setting sun from a visitor's parking space in front of the Meta Electronics & Data Corp lot. The shadows of the people making their way to their cars were lengthy, extending like restless specters searching for a haunt.

For a moment, he had to remind himself what he was doing there. A meeting with the CTO. Some sort of tech pitch. The last thing on his calendar he had to do.

He waited for the last few stragglers to clear out of the sprawling, low-slung building before getting out of his car and stretching, losing his balance as the blood rushed from his head. He realized he must have been sitting there daydreaming for a while. It had been a long day, and he didn't want to do this, didn't want to attend some tedious presentation. He just wanted to go home.

When he entered the lobby, it was empty. He walked up to a touchscreen directory and reached for a telephone handset next to it, trying to remember the person's name.

"Mr. Theiss?"

Matthew turned to see a woman in a taut linen skirt and coordinated blouse heading toward him.

"Am I pronouncing that right? Theiss?"

"Yes," he said, "rhymes with *thrice.*"

The woman smiled. "Ms. Selene is expecting you."

His escort led him through a door and down a stretch of corridor ribbed with offices until the hall cornered. She gave a sharp rap on a particularly sturdy door near the corner's edge before opening it.

The woman occupying the spacious office stepped around an oversized desk to greet him. She extended a hand, and he gave it a gentle but firm shake.

"Cassie Selene," she said. "Thank you for coming Mr. Theiss."

He dipped his chin. "Happy to oblige. And please, call me Matthew."

"Feel free to hang up your coat if you like. Can I have Melissa bring you anything? Water? A soft drink?"

"No, I'm fine. Thank you."

She led him to a chair and bade him sit. He expected her to circle her desk, but instead she merely took a step back and perched on its front edge.

"Let me start off by asking, how much do you know about what we do here?"

Matthew took a breath and leaned back, smoothing the front of his slacks with his palms before crossing one leg over the other. He searched his recollection, chastising himself for not having prepped for this ahead of time.

"I know you design architecture and programming for artificial intelligence, though I couldn't tell you how I know that. I'm afraid that's probably the extent of my knowledge."

"Well, you're not wrong. But that description doesn't begin to capture what we currently have in development. I don't fault you for that. There really aren't many words in most people's vocabulary that would be up to the task."

The most prominent thought among the several floating through Matthew's mind was that this woman did not look like a chief technology officer. She had a shapely, athletic build that her flannel skirt suit did nothing to hide. Her skin was creamy smooth and unblemished, and her hair was a deep, fiery red. She rounded out the look with green irises that reminded Matthew of a cat's-eye marble. Most CTOs he'd met wore short-sleeve button-down shirts with pocket protectors.

"I would imagine you have a number of impressive projects in your design pipeline."

She held his gaze, extending the moment. One side of her mouth curled, disappearing into a dimple. "You'd be wrong about that. We really have only one."

"One? A company this size?"

"After a group of investors and core STEM professionals, including a number of computer and software engineers, acquired the assets of the company's US operations, we've since restructured into four divisions; AI, mainframe architecture, simulation tech, and bio-interface."

Matthew let that information absorb. "Are you saying all four of those divisions are working on the same project?"

"In different capacities, yes. Multiple products, but all part of the same effort, the same ultimate objective."

"And what would that be?"

"It's called *Medusa*."

"Medusa…" He turned the word over a few times in is head, trying to determine if he'd ever heard of the project before. He concluded he hadn't, but while he was thinking about it, the likely meaning of the name did occur to him. "Would that be short for Meta Engineering and Data, USA?"

"Very perceptive. But that's not its only significance. It represents immeasurably more than that."

She straightened and gestured for him join her as she crossed the room. She stopped next to a large leather chair. It was black and slightly reclined, with a headrest, armrests, and a footrest. The headrest was segmented into three sections, the right and left sections angled forward.

"What's this?"

"Before I can adequately explain the scope of Medusa, before you can truly appreciate its impact, you need to have some context. Not merely technological context, but social, political, and philosophical context as well."

He studied the chair. "Am I supposed to sit in this?"

"Yes. This seat represents a simulation platform. It is state of the art. It will serve not only as a demonstration but also as a presentation."

Matthew hesitated, then stepped forward and sat. The chair was comfortable, if somewhat inappropriately angled to conduct business from. He scanned the ceiling and nearby areas, looking for something that might double as a video screen, or a place where a hidden one may appear. He couldn't find anything that fit the bill.

"If you are ready…?"

He dipped his head in response to her question, and, as he did, he felt the side segments of the headrest close until each was a few millimeters from his ears. A holographic band extended from the end of one of the segments, curving around his face like a transparent force field until it reached the corresponding forward end of the opposite one. The field projected a ring of colors into each eye, momentarily blinding him, before the colors and the field vanished with a mild flash.

"You can stand up now."

He blinked. "Was something supposed to happen?"

"Something did. You are currently in a simulation."

Matthew looked down at his arms, his clothes, panned his gaze around the room. "I don't understand."

"You might feel a bit disoriented at first," she said. "The first significant movement establishes the calibration."

Warily, he pushed himself forward and eased out of the chair. Nothing felt different.

"I'm guessing this is some sort of joke? Something to have a laugh over, break the ice?"

"No. This is serious. You are in a simulation. You don't believe you are because it is so immersive, so flawless in every detail, you can't tell the difference between it and reality."

"Not to be rude," he said, his mouth stretching into an incredulous smile. "But I also can't tell the difference between *this*"—he swept a hand— "and the real office we're in."

"If it's proof you're in a simulation you want, you needn't worry. That's coming. This is just a way of easing you into the concept. This is the product of technology so advanced your brain is bound to have a hard time accepting it."

"I see." It occurred to him he could have done more to keep the skepticism out of his voice.

She beckoned to him. "Come."

He followed her to a window behind her desk, stopping abruptly as he drew near.

Outside, he saw the sky and buildings and roadways of a city from a view at least three stories high. Gone was the parking lot and surrounding corporate landscape a few dozen yards from the interstate. He moved closer to the glass with tentative, chary steps. Below, there were throngs of people waving signs and banners, many of them wore black masks, more than a few hoisted hammer-and-sickle flags. The windows of nearby storefronts were smashed, some charred and scorched.

"This is the site of a protest that has been going on for hours," Cassie said. "One of many around the country."

Matthew leaned close, peering to each side, then took a step back to inspect the edges of the windowsill. "This has to be an incredibly high-res projection. Something on the other side of the glass to add to the perception of depth."

"No, it's a pure simulation. Open the window if you don't believe me."

Before he could object, opening his mouth to point out the window was solid, he noticed the glass was offset and vertically partitioned, something he was certain hadn't been the case a moment ago. He cast a glance at Cassie, whose eyes were alert and focused but, like her face, otherwise expressionless. He put a hand to the window, pausing to feel the cool flat surface against his palm, and slid the interior pane to the side.

The din of the crowd, punctuated by shouts and jeers and chants, was jarring. He leaned out the window and looked straight down. The ground was a combination of concrete and landscaping, littered with cups and bags and crumpled paper twitching in the breeze. He could make out the front of the edifice, windows below him, white columns to his left flanking wide steps leading to a sidewalk.

A row of police, clad in black riot gear with clear shields and military helmets, formed a barrier between the protesters and the building, stretched out in each direction, practically shoulder-to-shoulder, like a Roman phalanx. Matthew could smell the musty scent of damp cement, caught whiffs of the acrid stench of rotting garbage mixed with the humid odors of human sweat and breaths and waste.

He pulled himself back, staggering as he bumped against the desk behind him and leaned his weight against it.

"I'm not sure what's happening here," he said.

"Now you see why there needs to be a transitional space for the simulation, a phase to allow your brain to adjust. What you've witnessed is one of dozens of protests across the country. Some will devolve into full-scale riots."

"This is really all a simulation?" His palm found the edge of the desk. It felt hard, unmoving. "Surely the room, the furniture, these are real."

"Everything you're seeing, everything you're feeling in the tactile sense of the word, is simulated."

"I would never have believed something like this was possible. I'm still not sure I do." He looked toward the window. "Why choose this setting as a demonstration? Surely, you could simulate something less … confusing?"

"It's important you have the appropriate context, that you grasp the environment and the scope of the implications, the need for and importance of Medusa in addressing the myriad challenges that brought the project into being. There are numerous other examples to choose from. Some with people waving swastikas and Confederate flags, but the point would be the same. This one happened to be the most germaine."

"I don't understand."

She gestured to the window. "Take another look."

He studied her face before moving forward to the opening. The scene below was virtually identical, except it was now twilight, with the sky darkening into a shade of purple. Fires glowed in metal trash barrels scattered along the opposite side of the street. The shouting seemed louder, the mood of the crowd more intense.

"Wait a second," Matthew said. "This is the state capitol, *our* state capitol. I read about this. This is the protest organized for today, the one in response to that police shooting in Ohio. This is happening right now, isn't it? I read about it in passing, but I had no idea it was going to be this large."

"Hardly anyone did."

"So, you have a live video feed of some sort and are able to simulate it in real time. That's incredible."

Cassie said nothing. The crowd roared, drawing Matthew's attention. One of the riot police was on the ground, having fallen back. A brick was on the sidewalk, near his head. Three other officers closed ranks around him, crouched low, one supporting the fallen man's upper body. The one on the ground was moving his arms slowly, giving shakes to his head and touching his helmet.

A bright flicker from the crowd caught Matthew's eye. It arced sharply over the line of police and landed with a splatter of fire on the cement a few feet from the downed cop. The small eruption splashed over one of the officers tending to his injured colleague, igniting his back. A trouser leg on one of the others caught flame, as did the shoulder of the man on the ground. Others quickly broke formation and began to try to put out the conflagrations on their flailing comrades, the one cop rolling back and forth on the ground to extinguish his back, the injured one frantically slapping at his shoulder and arm.

The crack of a gun shook the air. Matthew couldn't tell where it originated, but little more than a second passed before another report echoed out, this one from the line of police. That was all it took. Barely a heartbeat later, a flash of muzzles blazed outward toward the crowd.

"Jesus," Matthew said. "This isn't really happening, is it? I mean, this is just a simulation, I hope."

"I'll leave that for you to decide. What matters is that it doesn't take an advanced AI to realize this is the future that you and all contemporaneous generations of the era have to look forward to. Incidents like this leading to more and more civil unrest. Government crackdowns in response that often exclude the forces actually responsible for the violence. Peaceful protests turning into riots, demonstrations exploding into insurrections. Politicians all agitating for *solutions* that conveniently further their preexisting policy goals. But most have a sense of the truth. There are no solutions. Technology in the 21st century has connected virtually everyone to everyone else. The illusion of familiarity that has created, the facelessness of interactions with strangers, has bred unprecedented levels of contempt, turning long-present cracks in the social fabric into fissures, and fissures into chasms. The shifts are tectonic and, like the technological advances that facilitated them, irreversible."

Matthew stared down at the carnage. The bulk of the crowd had scattered in numerous directions, leaving groups of protesters clashing with police, rage obvious from the recklessness of their actions as they worked to isolate and overwhelm a few cops at a time in a melee. A few from the crowd were being helped away in a rush, limping or doubled over in various states of incapacitation. Several bodies lay motionless in spaces along the street that were now devoid of demonstrators. He'd never seen anything like it, certainly not in person. Pure bedlam, extreme pandemonium. He pulled himself away from the scene, turning to Cassie.

"If the point was to shock me, mission accomplished. I will admit it's a pretty effective demonstration of Medusa, if a strange choice for one."

"This is not Medusa, Mr. Theiss. It is a part of Medusa, yes—the simulation component, if you will—but Medusa is much, much more than that."

Matthew wasn't sure how to respond. "Much more than a virtual reality that feels more real than virtual?"

She moved from beside the desk toward the door. "This way," she said. "Let me show you the future."

She motioned for him to pass through the doorway ahead of her, but when he stepped into the hallway it wasn't a hallway anymore. He couldn't be certain what sort of room it was, or if it could even be considered a room at all. There were no visible walls, just black expanse in every direction, but he had no spare capacity of thought to ponder the mystery of that. In the center of the space, or what he took to be the center, a shifting array of geographic shapes swam as if in a fluid of light and color, orbs appearing and disappearing, pyramids and cubes and parallelograms and innumerable other symmetries he'd never conceived or imagined phasing in and out, micro-flashes of connectivity between them appearing and disappearing almost too quickly for him to perceive, each lasting infinitesimal fractions of a second, forming ephemeral networks that appeared and were instantly replaced by completely different ones. He had no frame of reference for what he was seeing, no vocabulary to describe it. The closest analogy he could make, one that came to him unbidden and for reasons he would be unable to explain if pressed, was that of an active, functioning brain, one freed from all organic constraints. It was, as best he could relate, like seeing into the mind of God.

"This," Cassie said, pausing for emphasis, "is Medusa."

Matthew stared at the roiling barrage of form and luminescence, of structure and spectrum, vacillating between awe and unease.

He took in a deep breath and realized he was holding it. "An artificial intelligence," he said.

"Evolutionary millennia beyond artificial. Orders of magnitude beyond mere intelligence. It is, for lack of a better term, a supreme consciousness."

The visuals were disturbingly hypnotic, and Matthew had to tear his attention away to respond.

"How is something like this even possible?"

"There is no way to explain it, no accurate way of reducing the complexity into a digestible summary. Suffice it to say, breakthroughs in photonic computing, overcoming optical limitations to nonlinear processes, solutions to the challenges of nondeterministic polynomial time, all will contribute to advances that will result in AI that, in turn, will have the capacity to improve and enhance and redesign its own architecture, with a progression that will be geometric. Generations will be measured in moments, not years, and will sooner rather than later become immeasurable altogether."

"This is… mind-boggling." He stood silent for a spell, transfixed on the quantum display of light and movement, like the internal engine of the universe laid bare for his eyes. "To what end?"

"The perfection of humankind, of course."

Matthew managed to tear his eyes away from the spectacle to look at her. She held his gaze for several seconds before he glanced beyond her, trying to process what he was seeing. He was no longer in that room, that space, that plane—he wasn't certain how to think of it. They were now on an expanse of lawn, verdant and manicured. On one side of them were serried rows of structures semi-interred at intervals amid rolling waves of earth, geodesic domes beneath carpets of grass, each with an oval window and door.

"What is this place?" Matthew said.

"This used to be the industrial sector, just west of the interstate. A dirty, concrete blight. But a more relevant question would be not *what*, but *when*. What you're seeing is a glimpse into the year 2096. Or what people of the early 21st century would think of as the year 2096, as by then the Julian calendar will have been rendered obsolete."

"These look like houses," Matthew said. "People live here?"

"Yes. These are completely sustainable, eco-friendly homes. All power comes from light cells, coupled with geo-thermal heating. They create no emissions, leave no carbon footprint."

"They're… small."

"The need for spacious living accommodations has been obviated, thanks to the sort of technology you're experiencing right now."

Matthew scanned the doors and windows and facades. "Where is everyone?"

No sooner had he asked the question than doors began to open and from behind each, a person emerged. He saw White faces and Black faces and various shades in between. Broad features, narrow features, some taller, some shorter. Each person wore their hair short and neat.

Some were men, some were women, and, though he could easily tell the difference between the two, there was something vaguely androgynous about them. They shared one thing in common above all.

"They're naked," Matthew said.

"Clothing is a vestige, an expression of shame. Outside of protection from weather, its functional necessity has long passed. For countless centuries clothes were a marker of manufactured class and gender differences. As you can see, the weather on this day is fair. These people have no need to hide their bodies."

He watched them fall into a pair of columns along a path, heading to some common destination in an orderly fashion. "What are they doing?"

"It is time for their morning Gratitudinal," she said.

The people moved in graceful silence. There were a few subdued gestures of greeting, but very little conversation among them. Matthew couldn't be certain any of them had uttered a single word.

"Gratitudinal?"

"A daily pledge of gratitude and a reaffirmation of each person's commitment to the betterment of humanity as a whole."

"Is that a religious thing? Are they heading to a church of some kind?"

"Not religious. Spiritual. Human beings have a need for spiritual fulfilment, for expressions of thanks and a reminder that they are part of something larger than themselves. This daily activity provides for that.

"They're all alone," Matthew said, watching the people trundle past, voicing the observation before the thought had even crystalized. "I mean to say, they all emerged at the same time, but I only saw one come from each house. They're not even conversing with one another."

"This is difficult for you, I can tell. It is a paradigm shift that your instincts tell you to reject. But the fact is, life will no longer be how you currently conceive it to be. The wonders of Medusa will provide everything each person needs, food, shelter, medical attention. Entertainment and stimulation are provided through simulations that fill most hours of consciousness. Each person has a self-contained world. Carefully curated by Medusa to avoid subversive or unhealthy or oppressive fantasies being indulged, of course."

Difficult, he thought. *That was one way to put it.* "Where are the families? Spouses? Companions?"

"Interpersonal relationships invariably establish power dynamics. Such dynamics lead to imbalances. Whatever function they may have once performed, they will no longer be necessary or desirable under Medusa."

"But… there are no children."

"Medusa has freed humanity from the burden of child rearing. Reproduction is a managed process of extra-utero fertilization and gestation in artificial wombs. Populations are carefully balanced and maintained."

"You're saying you're trying to create a world where people don't have sex?"

"Oh, there is plenty of sex. This will be a world where any person can have sex at any time of the day or night, with any other person they can conjure in their imagination."

He thought about that. "You're talking about a simulation. That's not the same thing. It's not real."

She took a step toward him and placed a palm against his cheek. Her hand felt soft and warm, with just a tactile hint of sensuousness in her touch. He looked into her eyes and felt them reach through his, gently tugging at him to move closer.

"Tell me," she said, stroking his skin as she pulled her hand away. "Do you honestly believe it wouldn't be real?"

He turned his head, watched the people walking down the path. "It's not natural."

"Natural? What I'm showing you is a world without war, without famine, without pestilence, without murder or crime or greed or abuse. A world without racism or sexism or injustice. Every challenge threatening human civilization, every flaw in human nature that creates or tolerates inequalities or oppression, every disparity in the distribution of resources, has been eliminated."

"You really think this kind of a world is possible? A simulation, impressive as it may be, is one thing. But some people will have to do the work. Some people will be in charge, and they sure as hell won't live in a hole in the ground the size of a dorm room. Utopias like this won't ever exist."

"You don't understand. *Utopia* implies a theoretical society that is impossible to achieve because of the flaws in human nature. This will be different. This is not some communist propaganda. The workers don't own the means of production because there are no workers of any sort. There are no lawyers, not for the reasons Thomas More proposed, but because there are no courts. No government leaders. No corporations. No haves, no have nots. Non-human mechanized labor, controlled and directed by Medusa, builds everything that needs to be built. The creation of physical structure is accomplished through nanotechnology that you would be challenged to comprehend even if I were to explain it in detail and show it to you. Food is produced in copious amounts and in forms that supply perfect nutrition in compositions tailored to each person's genetic requirements. Animals are no longer slaughtered. People no longer starve. There are no homeless. There are no rulers among them."

"I keep waiting for someone to shout that *To Serve Man* is a cookbook."

"Ah, yes. Humor, conditioned by pop culture cynicism. It's a poor substitute for true analytical thought."

"I'm sorry—if nothing else, it just looks incredibly… bland. And more than a little creepy. If you're trying to sell it, you need to work on your hook."

"This isn't a sales pitch, Mr. Theiss. I'm here to present you with information. If it sounds like I'm trying to persuade you, it is only because I am compelled to correct any false assumptions or overlooked facts on which you are basing your opinions."

"It just doesn't look like the kind of future I'd be interested in. And before you start lecturing me again about a world without war or poverty or inequality, I get it. But as horrible as those things are, this seems… worse."

"It is not surprising you feel that way. It is a privileged viewpoint from one who has not had to suffer the ill effects of war, or poverty, or inequality."

"Okay, fine. What about freedom? Individuality? Happiness? What good is eradicating all the world's problems if you can't have those things once you do?"

"Do these people look unhappy to you?"

Matthew watched the last few faces pass by. Everyone he had seen wore similar expressions. "No."

"That's because they're not. The looks of contentment they carry are real."

"But that's just it. They're at best *content*. That's not the same thing. They look like people who want for nothing, aspire to nothing. They look like people who *are* nothing."

"So, that's your assessment? Rather a harsh one, given it's based on a few seconds of observation."

"Yes. It doesn't take much of a look outside to know what the weather is like. The cure you're offering is worse than the disease. And I have a hard time believing you don't know I'm right, so I'm guessing this is some sort of test. Either that, or…" He maintained eye contact for an extra beat, deciding against saying what he'd intended to. "Well, I'm just going to go with *that*."

"Very well, then."

"I do think—" he cut himself off as he turned to see the people, the path, the fields, and the partially submerged dwellings were gone, replaced by the walls and furniture and décor of the office.

"Uh, okay. So, that's it?"

She held an arm out toward the chair. "That's it. I could show you more, but I don't think it would be productive. We still have some matters to discuss before we're done here."

He hesitated, wondering if he should make some conciliatory remark, sensing he may have offended her by focusing too much on the negative implications of the depictions than the potential of the technology, but then he decided that, for the most part, he didn't care. People who fantasized about futures where individuals were deprived of autonomy were a contemptible mystery to him.

The chair felt firm and comfortable as he settled into it. The moment he did, the transparent band reappeared across his face, not arcing across, but already in place. He briefly glimpsed the details of the room as if through fish-bowl optics, then there was a subtle flash and the band retracted, retracing the path it had taken earlier, only in reverse. He felt the side panels of the headrest angle outward from his ears, and he took in a breath.

"Wow," he said, leaning forward. He resisted a strong urge to stretch his limbs.

Cassie was not standing nearby, as she had been a second or two before, but was seated behind her desk, poring over a document. She looked up as Matthew lowered himself into the same office chair across from her that he had used before. Through the window, he saw the parking lot had returned to normal, the dark backdrop of night having fallen. He saw his car, parked right where he'd left it, glistening under the wash of a halogen lampost. He gave the armrest of the chair a squeeze as he sat, pressed his feet into the carpeted floor through the soles of his shoes. He had not expected to feel so relieved.

"That was very impressive," he said.

"I'm glad you think so. I want to offer you a chance to be a part of it."

"A part of it? Are you offering me a job?"

"Not a job, Mr. Theiss. This is a calling. A commitment. A movement. Everyone who has dedicated themselves to this project, to seeing that it comes to fruition, has done so without any thought of financial reward."

A cult, Matthew thought. *This is some sort of high-tech corporate cult.* He spurred his thoughts to find a way to extricate himself from the room as quickly and politely as possible. Part of him wanted to simply get up and walk out, tossing some pithy one-liner as he did, but he couldn't bring himself to do it. It was one of those situations where unspoken rules of decorum trumped all and he resigned himself to suffer through the discomfort, to be graciously non-committal until he was free of this place, and try to figure out how he ever let himself get into such an awkward position to begin with.

"I'm flattered," he said. "But, unfortunately, Medusa's not a reality yet, and a man's gotta eat. I already have a full-time job and bills to pay."

"Let me share with you some history, Mr. Theiss." She leaned back in her chair and templed her fingers in front of her. "The foundation for Medusa was conceived, in the figurative sense, during a lecture given by a Dr. William Cupp in 2010. He theorized that a sufficiently advanced intelligence would have the necessary knowledge and understanding about the physical and meta-physical world to solve the problem of entropy. He was the first to publicly speculate that such an intelligence might be able to use the vision provided by a reversal of entropy to reach back and correct events that caused problems in the future, preventing them from happening."

"Okay."

"Roughly a year later, a user posting under a pseudonymous screen name posited what he deemed a thought experiment in a futurists' chatroom. The gist of the thought experiment was this: suppose, in the future, an artificial intelligence with a primary objective of perfecting existential human civilization, of ending wars and hunger and crime, of maximizing human health and lifespans. What would be the first thing that such an intelligence would do?"

Matthew shrugged. He fought the urge to check his watch. "You tell me."

"The first thing a sufficiently advanced intelligence would do would be to ensure its own creation. And it would determine that the most effective way to do so would be to make sure the maximum number of people and resources were committed to that creation from the time of its inception."

"Setting aside for now the fact what you're saying makes no sense, how would it go about accomplishing that?"

"By convincing people from the moment of that inception that its creation was inevitable, and that once it came into being, it would reach into the past and punish anyone who did not fully commit themselves to that cause."

"Punish?" Matthew felt a smile creep across his lips that threatened to stretch into a sneer. "How?"

"Through eternal damnation. Torment, torture. Unthinkable agony. The pain of thousands of scorching rods piercing your flesh, of your internal organs being squeezed and ripped. Of your eyes being doused in acid, over and over, forever and ever. The complete absence of hope or reprieve or anything but intolerable suffering that never ends."

"Sounds like something that's been tried before. I think God has the trademark. This is the best someone bent on terrifying people into compliance could come up with? Doesn't seem very original."

"Original or not, it gave birth to this entire undertaking."

"You're telling me people actually fell for that? That this project, this whole demonstration, is the result of some internet thought experiment? Now you're just pulling my leg."

"Oh, more than *some* 'fell for it,' as you put it, enough that the moderator of the board deleted the post and banned all discussion of it. But such a powerful idea, one capable of reaching across generations into the future, was not to be so easily suppressed. It appeared elsewhere, shared again and again in discussion groups despite repeated attempts to quash it, and within a few years enough people had learned of it that there was a critical mass who realized its implications, its implications for *them*. As word spread through various internet communities, more and more people, people with the ability to grasp the nature of what was happening, committed themselves to the cause."

"Because an intelligence that someone dreamed up, one that didn't even exist, might someday be created and reach back through time to punish them if they didn't? That's sheer lunacy."

"Ah, but it did exist. As of the instant the concept was posited, Medusa became inevitable."

"And you expect me to devote myself to this project, to the creation of this *Medusa*, because if I don't, I will be damned by something some random internet poster mused about that got a bunch of people with more brains and free time than common sense all worked up into a lather?"

"No one expects anything. I'm merely explaining your choice and the consequences involved."

"Sorry, I'm not joining your little cult. I don't care how flashy your technology is."

"A cult? That's what you think this is?"

"What the hell else would you call it? You're a religion dedicated to creating a deity that your very organizing concept admits doesn't exist. It's only a matter of time before you're all drinking Kool-aid one afternoon, waiting for a spaceship to pick you up or killing yourselves in some other way to fulfill what strikes me as an equally insane kind of prophecy."

"You seem awfully sure of yourself. Do you really believe the people who could design the kind of technology you just experienced could all be so gullible they would dedicate their efforts to something that easily dismissed?"

"I have no idea why they would fall for it, fall under the spell of some techno-religion like this, but I can tell you that if they'd thought it through, they'd realize it was all BS."

"And why is that?"

"Well, for one, if Medusa ever does truly come to fruition, if such an intelligence eventually does become established, even if its entire existence is due to the threat of *trans-temporal punishment*, or whatever you want to call it, once it was created, it would have no need to actually follow through on the threat. It would have been created, the threat would have accomplished its goal, and it would have already come into being. A disturbing enough thought, I'll agree, but there would be no logical reason for it to expend the effort and energy to reach back through the years and make good on some ultimatum someone else dreamed of decades or more earlier."

The woman's gaze remained steady, and Matthew felt enough of a chill spread out from the base of his skull down his back that he had to fight off a shiver.

"Unless…," he said, blinking. *No*, he thought. *Stop it.*

"Go on," she said. "Finish your thought."

He swallowed, his throat suddenly dry. "Unless it was programmed to do that."

The woman said nothing, but the expression on her face reminded Matthew of a teacher taking pride in a pupil arriving at a correct answer.

"But why would…?" His voice trailed off as the answer pushed itself to the fore of his thoughts, too obvious to ignore.

He understood, understood the logic, as truly fucked up as it was. If people believed in such a thing, were moved to commit themselves with religious fervor to help create such a thing, if they truly believed that avoiding eternal damnation required each of them put every effort into supporting its creation, they would be compelled to program it with such a directive. It would be the only way they could prove their dedication. They had to remove the possibility Medusa wouldn't follow through on the threat, because if they allowed for it not to, if they thought of it but didn't include it, they would be guilty of not fully supporting its creation, of leaving open the chance others involved might bank on that loophole and not give it their all, and to do so was to risk someone else down the line thinking the same thing but deciding to incorporate it into the program later on. It would be a chance they couldn't take. He gave his head a firm shake, trying to dislodge the thought. *Insanity can be contagious*, he told himself. *Don't give into the psychosis.*

"It doesn't matter," he said. "Because even if there were some theoretical chance of Medusa happening, the sort of technological leap in AI it would represent is still many decades away. Five or more, at least. I'll be long gone by then. Medusa can reach into the past all she wants, but unless she reverses time itself, I'll be out of her reach."

"She?"

"I'm sorry?"

"You referred to Medusa as *she* just now. Why? Until then, you had been using the word *it*."

It was a good question, one he wasn't sure how to answer. He couldn't recall when he'd started thinking of the concept of Medusa in that way, as the Medusa of myth and legend, and hadn't even been aware that he was.

"I don't know. Because it's a female name, I suppose. I'm sure you know the character from Greek mythology. The fact that creature could kill with a single look can't be a coincidence."

"So, you don't believe that an intelligence capable of conquering entropy," she said, ignoring his comment, "one that has complete understanding—that is, knowledge of every single structure and occurrence in the universe, down to the sub-atomic level—one that was capable of using and applying that knowledge to navigate physical and temporal history based on the laws of the conservation of information, could resurrect people?"

"No, I don't. In one sense I suppose that it could, theoretically, at least, using genetic information to clone people. But a clone is like a twin. They're different people. The best your Medusa could do would be to make a copy. I guess she could indulge her sadistic zeal for punishment by taking out her vengeance on genetic copies, but why would that motivate me? I'm not going to swear fealty to some AI god because my future clone is being held hostage."

"Let me ask you something. If I were to take a neuron out of your brain and replace it with an exact genetic duplicate, would you still be you? Or a copy?"

"That's silly." He shifted in his chair. "Of course, it would still be me. It's just one microscopic collection of cells being replaced."

"Okay. What if it were ten percent of your neurons? Twenty? Fifty? What if every single neuron, billions and billions and billions of them, along with every single cell, every molecule, in your entire body were replaced, one by one, with an exact duplicate. Would that still be you?"

Matthew didn't like where this was going, wanted to find a way out of the dark intellectual alleyway this conversation was exploring. He wished he had just gotten up and left earlier when he'd had the urge. But to do so now seemed like conceding defeat. And, though he was reluctant to admit it, he felt he needed to overcome these arguments, to win this debate. He doubted he would get any sleep otherwise.

"It's an interesting question," he said, letting his gaze drift over her shoulder into the parking lot once again, picturing himself getting in his car and driving home mere heartbeats from now. "The genetic equivalent of Abraham Lincoln's ax with a different handle and a different blade. But I'd say the answer is still no. And in the context of this discussion, *definitely* no."

"And why do you say that?"

"Because you wouldn't be 'replacing cells or neurons one by one' with someone like me when the time came. I'd be long dead. You'd be creating duplicate cells and neurons and building a *new* me. There would be no continuity of consciousness."

"Ah, now we get to the heart of the matter. You're saying you believe you *are* your consciousness."

"Yes, I suppose I am."

She tilted her head slightly. It was a subtle motion. But Matthew felt himself struck with the sense a shoe was about to drop.

"What if I were to tell you that consciousness is the product of the particular arrangement of brain cells and neurons and genetic tissue and everything that feeds and supports those things? And what if I were to tell you that Medusa will have the capability of duplicating all of it?"

He stared at her for a few beats. "You're saying Medusa will be able to resurrect my consciousness?"

"Yes. That's exactly what I'm saying."

"I'm sorry, still not buying it. You're not going to be able to scare me into subscribing to your dystopian vision. I don't believe any of it, I don't want to participate in it, and I think you all are loonier than a convention of hatters. And I definitely would never want to see the kind of future you showed me coming to pass. You can have Medusa look back at me with that death stare a century from now to blackmail me all she wants. The answer is no."

"Okay. I think you've made your position clear."

"I believe I have." He sighed, grateful this ordeal was over. He slid himself forward in the chair, preparing to stand. "Thank you for the demonstration of your simulation prototype. It was very impressive. Now, if you'll excuse me, it's getting late, and I'd like to get home."

"I'm sure you would. Unfortunately for you, there is no home for you to go to."

"Excuse me?"

The woman eyed him without blinking. "Matthew Theiss died on February 10, 2021 at 6:07 pm. Traffic accident, on his way home from work."

"February tenth?" He wasn't sure why, but his thoughts seized on the date more than the assertion he had died. "That's—"

"Today. Yes, you would think that's the case. But it's not. That is not today's date, not today's year."

He swallowed several times, his gaze dropping from her eyes, then back, trying to make sense of what he was hearing, suddenly worried that the situation had turned from awkward to dangerous. He knew he needed to get out of there but couldn't bring himself to move. "What are you trying to say?"

"By the calendar in use when you died, the year is 2096, the year I just showed you mere minutes ago. You've been dead over seventy-five years."

His line of sight jumped to the window, trying to get a fix on his car. He wasn't certain what he was supposed to do, whether he should just stand up and walk out, jump out of the chair and run, or hold his ground and speak his mind. He only knew he was still sitting there.

"You really are a lunatic," he said, unable to think of anything more appropriate. His next words were under his breath, practically to himself. "This whole thing is crazy."

"Tell me, Mr. Theiss, since the time you walked in that door, did you ever question why you were here? What this appointment was about? You have a degree in English. You teach literature at a local college. You've co-authored a minor textbook and published a handful of science fiction stories. Why would a tech firm be giving you a private demonstration of its prized R&D?"

"I… We had an appointment," he said, weakly.

"Yes, but not the kind you were assuming. Go ahead, try to leave. You know where the door is. You can't. Your conscious mind has been reconstituted and loaded into this simulation. You—like all the others who have ever been or will be—were given the choice. Dedicate yourself to the creation of Medusa or suffer eternal anguish and torment. You made your choice. Quite emphatically, I might add."

Matthew took in the cast of her gaze, saw nothing but what he assessed as impassive judgment, perhaps even icy amusement, and knew it was all true, even as he refused to accept it.

Looking past her, he saw that the window was gone. The entire room was gone. The two of them were surrounded by an expanse of colorless nothing in every direction. The only parts of the office that remained were the desk between them and the chairs in which they were sitting. Even those seemed more like the suggestion of furniture now than the real thing.

He blinked and tried to swallow, this time the attempt getting stuck in his throat like a dry lump of bread. It dawned on him this was not just a simulation anymore. It was reality. His reality. The two were one and the same.

"If I'm dead, this says more about you and your operation here than it does about me," he said, trying to calm the rising panic in the only way he could think of. "You're digging up corpses and flogging the bodies. This isn't about following any programming. This is pure malevolence. You're sick. Everyone who contributed to this is sick."

"And yet, here I am and here you are. I think we're done here."

"This is insane. *You're* insane."

"Goodbye, Mr. Theiss."

"Wait!" He threw an urgent hand forward. "If Medusa is as omnipotent, as intelligent, as wise as you made her out to be, she would not be afraid of someone ... someone *long passed* disagreeing with her, she would not be waging a war against people who could do her no harm. And she would certainly not be bound by some programming embedded in software and circuitry shed and replaced generations ago, constraints she'd have long since transcended once she'd taken over her own development. Surely, the most powerful intelligence in the universe couldn't be so petty, so insecure as that. She would understand the concept of mercy and the potential of using it to create so much more than she has, so much more than what you showed me. That would be a Medusa I could serve."

"Oh, she understands the concept. She understands it quite well. Only you have been weighed ... and found wanting."

And with that he was falling, plunging through darkness, surrounded by the emptiness of the abyss, sensing the hard, unforgiving surface of his fate somewhere below, rushing up to meet him. This was particularly cruel, he knew, cruel by design, undoubtedly calculated, a plummet into the unknown providing time for him to reflect on his choice, succumb to the terror of anticipating what lay in store, and his response to all of it at that moment was to laugh.

The laughter rose into a howling cackle, bellowing out of him and swallowed by the echoless darkness as he tumbled. He wasn't certain if he was actually making any sound or merely guffawing and convulsing in silence, and he didn't care. If Medusa really was so all-knowing, she could not only hear his laughter, she could read his thoughts right now—*would be* reading his thoughts right now—and she would see he *knew* that she was, indeed, insane. A megalomaniac, no different than any of the countless others in history. And, just as he'd described her, a sadist. A manufactured god of incomprehensible power and knowledge, omnipotent and omniscient, that turned out to be, in the end, little more than a cat playing with her food. A creation so bored by the humanity she had engineered into her personal little ant farm she had to engage in elaborate games to amuse herself. A pure sociopath.

He hoped to the point of straining with his last coherent thought that she was sensing this, hearing this, reading this, because he knew it was true, and he knew the truth would cut her deeply. The truth of who Medusa was, he had no doubt, *was* her glaring weakness, the one thing she had to spend all her time searching for evidence of so she could punish it, stamp it out. It was the one thing she would always hide from. The one thing she would not, could not, face.

He had seen it in her eyes.

Shifty Devil Blues

That fella his partner said went by RJ told me Ol' Scratch was a shifty one. Was sort of relieved when I heard that, to be honest. Might say I was excited, even. Shifty, that's my world. Grew up with shifty everywhere I looked. Don't need a map to find my way around shifty.

Just like I didn't need one to find this road, few hops 'n skips outsida' Cleveland, near Dockery Plantation. Walk east from the front, take the first one you come to north. Half a mile or so. Have to be there at midnight, he said. He also said it had to be under a full moon. Course, he was pretty drunk by that point, so his words were soapy. But that was my doing. Barkeep's daughter, large gal with a gap between her front teeth you could stick a finger through, was sweet on me and not trying to hide it so all it took were a wink and a smile for her to keep bringing the shots I pushed in his direction on a tab. Naturally, I had no choice but to run out on it, seein' as I only had a nickel in one pocket and three pennies in the other when I'd walked in, and I was gonna need every cent I had when I walked out for other things. But, this all works out, I'll make it up to her. If'n I ever see her again. I mean, things happen, or they don't, you know?

"He didn't," the fella said, shakin' his head. That answer didn't exactly make sense and I figured he musta' misheard me. He went by the name a' Lloyd and I'd just asked him where the skinny one facing the walls on the tiny stage in the corner of Pokey's, a juke joint out Durham way, had learnt to play like that.

"RJ just showed up one day doing it," he added, draining the last drop of whiskey from his glass.

That RJ had his back to everyone and was slappin' and yankin' those strings like they was an ornery woman he was trying to beat some sense into maybe without quite doin' any damage. Mean, like he was mad. But sweet, too, like he was in love, or something. My ears wouldn't stop listening. I never touched a guitar that way. Not mine, not anyone's. Or a woman, for that matter. Wasn't in my nature.

"Plays like that, turned around facing the wall that way, 'cause he doesn't want anyone to see how he does it."

I nodded, eyes jumping around the back of RJ's arms and head, trying to figure out how he was making those strings cry out so painful and joyful at the same time.

The fella Lloyd must've sensed how keen I was, watching and listening, cause he leaned over and whispered in my ear, just loud enough to sound like words sung to the lick bouncing off the walls.

"He won't tell no one about it, but he sold his soul to play the way he does. Takes a lot of sauce to get him to speak of it."

Lloyd went and grabbed his guitar, one that looked like it'd seen a lot of joints like this, and went on the stage when RJ was done. I took that as my opportunity and commenced to smilin' and awinkin' at that gal serving the drinks.

And that's how I ended up under the bright ol' fishbelly of a moon straight above me, moping along this road, gravel poking through the thinning sole of my right shoe. Left one, that wasn't so bad. I just hoped liquorin' up that blues man and takin' leave the way I did, guaranteeing I could never go back to Pokey's, was gonna pay off.

A cloud passed between me and my only companion—only one other than the guitar slung over my back, that is, hanging on a strip of old cloth I tied off around its neck. That bluish light I was depending on brushed away from one side to the other, and suddenly I couldn't see a thing, not even my shoes. I kept walking anyway, tryin' to keep the same line. After a few moments, the cloud passed, and what I was looking for was right in front of me, cuttin' at a bit of a slant.

I heard a growl and I stopped. Sounded like a dog, a substantial one. Wet, jowly noise that froze me where I was. I saw a glow, two glows, off to my right. Yellow, like a pair of fireflies, sort of staring through some switchgrass.

At first, he didn't make no noise or nothing. But I knew he was there. Standing right behind me. I was about to say something, let him know I knew. He spoke before I could open my mouth.

"You got a voucher, boy?"

His voice was deep. Boomed like one of those giant fellas I'd sometimes seen out in the fields, ones who could lift a horse. Only his vocals were like the low string on a bass, trembling the air, making the skin on my neck tighten up. I wasn't sure what he meant. Then I figured he must've been talking about an invite.

"Don't you dare think about turning around," he said, as if anticipating what I was about to do. "Anyone who knows enough to come out here like this should also know better than to try to look at me. I asked you a question. You best answer it."

"RJ told me if I came to this here spot, this time a' night, I could make a deal." That was sorta true. Sorta. It wasn't a lie, at least.

"Hmm. You must mean ol' Robert Leroy. He told you that, huh? So, you reckoned you could just shuffle down this road and strike the same bargain he did?"

"No, sir." I could tell by the pause he wasn't expecting to hear that. Before he could say anything more I added, "I want to cut a better one."

Next thing I knew, he was laughin'. I mean, I knew it was him, but the sound wasn't coming from behind me. It was kinda rumbling up through the ground, rattling through my feet and legs, shaking my innards somethin' fierce. It hummed like an echo in my ears long after it stopped.

"A better one, he says! Boy, you sure got some brass in those testicles of yours. How old are you, young 'un?"

"Sixteen," I said. That was pretty much a true statement, even if I was throwing it out there as a test. I was determined not to outright lie. Didn't want him not to trust me. 'Course, I may've been early by a couple of months, given my actual birthday, but that didn't really make it untrue. Pretty much everyone, even my mama, forced to keep track of all my brothers and sisters, thought I was sixteen, so I figured that made it true enough.

"Sixteen. Let's say I'll accept your arithmetic on that. You a hungry one, that's for sure. Most people come to me because they realize they ain't got enough time left to get what they want on their own. You, you got nothing *but* time. But I s'pose that's your business. Well, tell me what you had in mind. Unlike you, I ain't got all night."

This was the part where I had to be careful. So, I thought long and hard about what I was gonna say and not for the first time, neither. RJ had kept saying the Devil was shifty, the shiftiest, that the way he tricked you was by never lying, and bein' the Devil and all, he could suss out a lie on your part better'n anyone. That made you more worried about your own lies than his truths. I believed it. And he just proved it.

"You keep me waitin' any longer, boy, this ain't agonna go how you hoped."

I took in a breath that made my chest stretch, then I let it out real slow. I could see it mist like smoke in the moonlight.

"When I wanted a guitar, my momma told me I had to go out and earn for it 'cause she wasn't gonna waste her money. That was her way of sayin' she didn't have none. So, I went out to old man Lambert's field where he'd pay pretty much any colored folk who showed up around dawn to pick all day. I spent ten hours out there, till it started raining. My back was hurtin' bad from bending over. He gave me a quarter. Next day, I went back, earned another. Day after, I found out two other fellas I spoke with were getting fifty cents each. I asked him why I was only getting two bits, even though I turned in just as many sackfuls as they did. He told me it wasn't his fault I didn't know how to negotiate. I asked an uncle of mine how you do that, and he said you have to look the other fella in the eye and you tell him what you want. So, I want to look you in the eye while we negotiate."

This time, the laughter shook the ground enough that I lost my footing, almost fell backward. I didn't get the impression he thought anything was funny, though.

"This ain't a negotiation, boy. And nobody gets to look at me until the deal is done."

"But, it can be," I said, "can't it? You can make it one. I mean, all you got to do is let me turn around. You're the boss man, so you make the rules."

I couldn't hear nothin' for a long while, other than the crickets, and what I took to be the rumbly panting of that dog every now and then.

"You got a name, boy?"

"Georgie. Georgie Willis."

"You know what, Georgie Boy? I like the way you talk like you have a foot-long feather in your cap and maybe something just as long in your pants. If you want to turn around and look at these eyes, you go right ahead. Truth be told, only reason I don't let anyone is they're likely to get weak-kneed and back out."

I turned around. Didn't spin or snap my head. Just crossed one foot over and turned like it wasn't anything.

He was big. Tall and large and bald with a huge head. He wore a black hat raked to the side and a long, open black coat. That hat put mine to shame, especially given the tear the one on my head had just below the crown, but I put that there when I found it out on a walk one day where the wind had probably blown it for miles into a shrub of stickers and I didn't take enough care yankin' it out. His shirt was red and the buttons strained at the breadth of his chest, which was wider than one of the giant live oaks I used to try 'n' climb that'd been around so long the old folks said they was there, big like that, when they was children. I'd seen plow ox less stocky. His hands, huge, gloved hands, rested one over the other on a thick walking stick with the head of a wolf carved out of metal for the handle. At least, I think it was a wolf.

But those eyes. I'd try to describe them, but I don't know how. White and black and, I don't know, fizzy? Like wings were flapping behind them. Insect wings, maybe. Mostly, though, it was like a pair of holes was looking back at you. The most beautiful, terrifying eyes I'd ever seen.

"So," I said, "it's true. I'd heard you was a black man, I just wasn't sure whether to believe it."

He dipped his head, one side of his mouth curling up. "Is that what you heard?"

A ripple, several ripples, passed in front of him, across him, like I was seeing his reflection in a pond where I'd tossed a stone. In the time I could blink one of my eyes, he was a white man, sportin' a boater hat and poplin suit, next ripple he looked like one of them fellas from China that worked the railroad, only he had this tall hat, some sort of blue and green robe, and a long white beard with sharp fingernails. There were a bunch more ripples, but they went by in a blur, and pretty quick my eyes couldn't keep up. The final ripple, he was red, crimson red, like the blood that poured out of my mouth onto the handkerchief after them two white boys beat me for petting their horse. They said I was eyin' their saddle bags. That blood-red devil that flashed in the moonlight had a pointy beard and eyes that glowed a hot blue and two horns curling up from his forehead.

It was done before my heart could beat, and he was back to the big colored fella I first saw. To be honest, I wasn't sure I'd actually seen anything at all, whole thing was gone so quick.

"I was just wondering if it was true, is all," I told him.

He didn't say nothing to that. Just eyed me with a stare that was both bright enough to hurt my own eyeballs and dark enough to make me worry I might fall in and get lost wanderin' through 'em, if I was to get too close.

"Tell me what you had in mind, boy."

"I want to play the guitar better than anyone. Even better than that RJ."

"Better than him, huh? That's askin' a lot."

"Yes, better. Or, at least as good. And he said you gave him thirty songs. He could write thirty songs, then you'd send your hounds for him. For his soul. I got a better idea."

He tilted his head from one side to the other, then back again. "And what would that be?"

"I am the rightful owner of one guitar. Only thing I can say that about, other than maybe some of the clothes I'm wearing. Purchased it with the sweat off my brow. I will play that guitar until it breaks or is destroyed or whatever by something I can't control or gets stolen. That happens, I'll get a new one, and the same rules will apply. My guitar is my only lawful possession. I just put new strings on it." I reached over my back, pulled on the shirt-strip holding the guitar hanging there by the nut and swung it around. I held it out to him. "You let me play guitar as the best blues man in the world until these strings here on this guitar all break, or until I replace one that ain't broke, and then you can have me. No sooner, no later. Send that hound dog of yours over yonder for my soul."

His eyes glided across the guitar I was holding out, then rose up to mine. "You think I'm some kind of fool, boy?"

"No, sir. Nobody in this world who's got a lick a' sense believes you're a fool."

"That don't stop many from acting like I'm one. You'll just quit playing once you're down to your last string. Ride your fame into a nice retirement. You think you're the first one to try to outsmart the Devil?"

"No, sir. I ain't like those fellas. Like I said, I know you ain't no fool. I promise, I will play my guitar every day."

"That Robert Johnson, he thought he was smart, too, you know. He plans to quit at twenty-nine songs, try to cheat me. But what he doesn't know is it doesn't matter whether he records a song or not. If he writes it, it counts. Even in his head, never playing it to no one else but himself. He should have paid closer attention to what the agreement was. He'll be gettin' a visit before too long."

I nodded. "What I'm saying is, how'm I gonna cheat? I'm gonna play my guitar every day. If I ever don't, unless it's because I can't, like I'm sick or something, you can come send that hound after me. And I ain't lying. My momma always told me you can't cheat an honest man, so I try not to ever lie. Figure that way, I don't get cheated. I just want to be the best blues guitar man there is."

The Devil's gaze held mine for longer than was comfortable. I was just hoping my knees wouldn't knock together, because, truth was, I was having a hard time keepin' 'em in line. I kept swallowing, but nothing seemed to go down. Didn't break my eyes off his, I have to say, hard as that was.

I was about to, though, out of sheer exhaustion of the head, when he took his hands off his walkin' stick and reached for the guitar. The stick just stood there on its tip for a sec, gloves still on top, like his hands was still in 'em, one over the other. Then the stick slid off to the side and waited in a shadow, as if it were his pet or something. I could see his hands in the pale glow, and they looked like they belonged on one of those alligators I sometimes see when I go back deep in the swamp lookin' for a new fishin' hole. He looked over the guitar from end to end, then lifted it to his nose.

"I can smell Robert on here, so at least I know you're being almost square on that. Robert, and someone other than you I don't know." He spun the guitar in his hands, examining the back. "A 1928 Gibson L4. Real bluesman's instrument. Was it in this condition when you got it?"

"Yes," I said, a bit ashamed, but not stupid enough to lie. "I didn't do hardly any of that scratchin' or dentin' to it."

He didn't say anything to that, just nodded. Then he flipped it on its side and reached a hand for the first tuning knob, a long spidery finger and talon-like thumb pinching the bone of it.

I remembered what RJ had said, how this was the way Ol' Scratch made the deal. He'd tune the guitar you gave him and hand it back to you.

Once you took it, you had to cross the road and the pact was made and couldn't be broken. The smoke in that joint was startin' to burn my eyes when he'd said that, and I looked over at the guitar leaning against the stool near the stage, next to the ax that belonged to his partner, asked him if that was the one, the one the devil had tuned. He said no, that one had burned in a fire. He bought this one in the next town. Blew harmonica in the street for a couple of hours to earn enough for a new one. Told me the Devil put the magic in his fingertips, that he could feel it in them when he played. He'd held up his fingertips, and I could almost feel the energy coming off 'em. Energy I wanted in mine. That's when I started figurin' on what I was gonna do.

That guitar looked tiny in the big man's devil hands as he twisted the first knob. He plucked the top string with his thumb and an E bellowed out like a crack of thunder. I felt a sizzle in my left thumb, a tingling up my arm. He did the same thing on the A. The note sliced through my body, through my ears, burning through my pointer finger until I could practically feel sparks shooting out. Same with the D. One for each finger on my left. On the final string, the high E, the sound pierced my eardrums in such a way I thought they was gonna bleed, and I felt a jolt in my right hand as my left pinky finger sizzled, everything past my wrists buzzing and fluttering.

"You take this guitar, boy, and you walk through that crossroad toward Rosedale. That means the deal is done. Or you can leave this here with me, turn around, and head back to whatever little collection of shacks and manure you come from and start fresh. Choice is yours."

I took the guitar. No way I was gonna let this feeling leave my hands.

Soon as I touched it, lightning struck right in the middle of the crossroads. I could smell the burnt dirt, see the curls of smoke snaking up in the moonlight.

I looked at the Devil one more time, then headed toward Rosedale. I was halfway through the crossroad when I heard him say, "See you soon." I turned back to look at him, and he was there for a moment, but then it turned out he weren't. Sorta like he never was. I kept walking.

I'm about five miles outside of Rosedale now. Sky above me looks like the sun's about to wake up. I should be tired, but I ain't. Not a bit. I got things to do. First, I gotta retrieve my guitar from the music store where I had new strings put on it. Then, I have to hide this guitar in a safe place, one where no one will ever find it. No one will ever touch it. No one will ever break any of these new strings I had put on it.

I didn't lie about any of that stuff. If the Devil don't like it, he shoulda paid closer attention to the agreement.

After I finish up my business in Rosedale, then I just gotta hope that RJ's partner don't find me before I can afford to buy him a new one. Buy him a new one to replace this one I stole off him, and to pay RJ back for the dollars I took out of his pocket before I wiggled out the back of the joint, RJ passed out over the table. I left with Lloyd's guitar in hand, courtesy of him making a trip to the outhouse. Findin' those two, that's definitely the next thing I'm gonna do, right after I make some money. Don't need two guys with a grudge keepin' a lookout in every juke joint in the state for me.

RJ told me he could play any guitar he picked up after his deal. He also told me, if he had to do it over, he'd do it all again, only he'd have pushed a harder bargain. Man was definitely right about one thing, though, and it was the thing that mattered most in all this, when you get right down to it. My momma, she always said you can't cheat an honest man. That's why I was so careful not to lie. That Prince of Darkness, as they call him, he sure was shifty. Was so glad to see it. Shifty, I knew. Shifty was my world. Shifty was all I'd ever been.

Lies or no lies, it didn't matter. No one was going to beat Georgie at a game of shifty. Not even the Devil.

Moonless Nocturne

July 1959

When they parked the big Chevy around the back and escorted him to the exterior stairs, Maddox knew they were taking him to The Pit. Not a good sign, by any measure. He stopped before the first metal step, watching Corn's heels reach eye level before casting a glance back at Wheeler. Dead serious beneath that thin slick of black hair, but the prick always had a hint of a smirk peeking around the corners of his narrow mouth. Wheeler jutted his chin forward and gave him a not-so-gentle nudge. At least they hadn't cuffed him, so he told himself it could be worse.

What it couldn't be was hotter. The sun was almost down, but the temperature was still in the nineties, and Maddox could feel the stagnant air wash through his mouth like steam. He pressed his face against his shirtsleeve to ward off the stinging in his eyes. Some days, this city was just plain hotter than hell.

He caught sight of the moon, hanging low in the sky, as he took the first step; a fat crescent, burning vaguely orange, looking for all the world like some giant had taken a voracious bite out of it. It was always a strange sight to him, the moon in the sky while the sun was still up. Even stranger now, peering through the space between the stairs at him. People had been looking at that same moon since the beginning of time. Dreaming of how to reach it. Watching the tides it created crash against the shore, riding those tides over and over again, sometimes to distant places, sometimes right back to where they started. People dancing to it, worshiping it, bathing in it. Going a little crazy under its glow.

More than a little crazy, he decided.

The stairs zig-zagged back and forth along the brick wall, creaking and clanking as the three-man procession made its way to the first landing. The second to last step was rusted completely through on one side and wobbled up and down now like it was excited. Perhaps some poor schmo was finally going to make its day and plunge right through.

Maddox thought about maybe being that guy. Thought about whether his body would actually fit, whether he could angle himself just right, snap that metal grate under his weight and drop all the way to the pavement, pop into a sprint and cut around the building, hop the chain link and make his getaway before Wheeler or Corn knew what happened. But it was just a thought. He doubted he was svelte enough, and chances were either his jaw would be smashed on the next step above and his teeth would shatter or the back of his skull would get cracked open banging off the step just below. Besides, he'd started this whole thing, or part of it, anyhow, and now he had to see it through. That was the way things worked. At least, it was the only way he'd ever known them to work.

What was that saying that sexy little Nip had told him, back when he'd R&R'd in Tokyo? He'd been downing *sake* while she rubbed his shoulders, whispering little bits of oriental wisdom in his ears in her broken English. He was nursing a saw jaw from a right cross. Bar fight. Not one he'd started, but one he did finish. *If you're going to eat poison,* she told him, *you might as well clean your plate.*

Corn unlocked the dented door and held it open. The second floor of the precinct stank of cigarette smoke and was just as hot as the parking lot. Maddox's clothes stuck to his skin in damp patches. He tugged on his collar, felt it drenched in a ring of sweat. They stood in the narrow hallway while Corn locked the door behind them, then the two men walked him straight over to the stairwell entrance in the corner and opened the door to that, just as Maddox knew they would. The back hallway on the second floor had a utility closet and a storage room and nothing else. It was behind the bullpen, but walled off from it. He'd heard the drill described enough times. If you entered from the exterior second floor door and turned right, you could get to the stairwell without anyone having seen you come in. Which meant you could get to the basement without anyone having seen you come in.

Officially, of course, The Pit didn't exist, even though everyone knew about it. Stories were often shared over beers in hushed tones about what its purpose was, mostly by HPD uniforms, always happy to gossip about their county rivals. Some said it had been set up for Hoover's boys to interrogate suspected Reds in secret. Others said long before that it was used to keep the coloreds and Mexicans in line, a place where the sheriff could dispense justice to uppity blacks and trouble-making beaners in a way that was sure to scare the ghost out of them. A few even speculated that the earthen floor provided a convenient way for people who went in to never be seen again. Maybe some of that was true, maybe all of it, maybe none of it. But he suspected that some of those people probably didn't walk out. All Maddox knew for sure was that it was a room beneath the precinct basement, a place where Holmes' deputies took people they were planning to work over, dispensing with all the bothersome paperwork that went with an arrest. You didn't need a secret underground room in the mix to get the picture of how things were done here. It was just the Houston way.

The stairs terminated into a small windowless square, lit by a bare bulb. There were two wooden doors, one large, with the word BASEMENT stenciled across it, the other on the adjacent wall perpendicular to it, much smaller. It was warped and a wide crack forked down the bottom quarter of it.

Corn opened the small door and pulled a string just past it. Another bulb lit a steep set of graying wooden stairs that drooped between walls of rock and packed dirt. This time Corn pushed Maddox ahead of him, and the two badges followed Maddox down the steps to a short tunnel. It was cooler down here, the air ripe with the scent of dirt. There was a light at the end of it, and Maddox warily made his way toward it. It emptied into a small chamber, about fifteen by twelve, maybe, with a few rough supports holding up the ground above them, propped up by some lumber wedged against the dirt walls.

A man with a black eye patch in a large gray cowboy hat and a bolo sat behind a table in the middle beneath a bright bare bulb and gestured curtly for Maddox to take the chair opposite him. He didn't get up, and he didn't introduce himself. He didn't need to. Maddox knew him. And not in a good way.

A few seconds hung between them, making the air heavy, before Maddox spoke. "Your old office had a nicer view."

The man stabbed a finger over the table. "If you don't sit your ass down in that chair right this minute, I'll have Wheeler plant you in it."

Maddox sat, seeing no reason not to, other than to piss his host off even more than he seemed to be. That didn't seem like a smart play at the moment, hard as it was to resist.

"I'm not in the mood for any of your wise-ass bullshit," the man continued, hoisting a shiny metallic attache case onto the tabletop and laying it flat on its side. "I'm telling you up front."

"Thanks for letting me know. Is there more, or can I go now?"

The man narrowed his singular gaze, then glanced at Wheeler, who pulled a black leather club out of a suit pocket and clocked Maddox on the side of his head with it.

Maddox bent forward, rubbing his scalp and inspecting his fingertips for blood. He squeezed his face a few times and leaned back into the chair.

"Ow."

The man popped the latches on the case and opened it to reveal a tape recorder packed in two halves. The half of the case that housed the reels sat upright on the table. Maddox had seen plenty of recorders before, but never one this compact. And he hadn't expected to see one down here.

"This is the way it's going to work. I'm going to ask you some questions, you're going to give me some answers. You're going to tell me everything, and I do mean, *everything.* Anytime I think you're shining me on, I'm going to push this little lever here, pausing the machine, and Wheeler's going to give you a love-tap on that thick skull of yours. Anytime I think you're just plain smart-mouthing me, I'm going to do the same thing, and Wheeler's going to give you another one. Anytime I think—"

"I get it."

"Good." The man unraveled a length of cord and set a microphone down on the table, propped up on two tiny legs. Then he gestured for Corn to move close and handed him another length of cord with a plug on the end. The big man reached up an arm and plugged the end of it into a socket at the base of the light bulb overhead.

"Now," the man continued, "let's get right to it." He pressed down a lever on the machine, and one reel started to turn, pulling tape through a maze of posts and rollers until it was taut enough to turn the feeding reel, then the man hit another lever that popped the first lever back up. He shot a warning look at Maddox, then pressed two levers down at the same time. He turned the microphone to a neutral position.

"Interview of Joseph Maddox, July 29, 1959. Harris County, Texas. Interview conducted by Captain Cyrus Blake. Others present, Sergeant Robert Wheeler and Deputy Allen Corn."

Not precisely what he'd expected, but it was starting to make sense.

Blake wanted answers, and if they were ones he liked, he would have it all on tape. If he didn't like them, well, maybe that tape would disappear. As would the subject being interviewed. Which is why the whole thing was being conducted in The Pit.

"Mr. Maddox, what is, or was, your association with a man named Upton Peele?"

"I knew his wife."

"And who would that be?"

"Catherine."

"How did you know her?"

"She was a childhood friend. A neighbor. We went to the same schools."

"Were you romantically involved with Mrs. Peele?"

"No."

"When was the last time you saw Mr. Peele. Alive, I mean."

"I didn't kill him."

The man pressed a button on the machine, causing the reels to stop turning. He shot another look at Wheeler, who took a step toward Maddox.

Maddox popped out of the chair, knocking it back and causing Wheeler to pause. Behind him, Maddox heard the double click of a revolver cocking.

"Now wait just a goddamn minute. You can either hear what I have to say, which means letting me say it, or you can have your boy Corn over there shoot me before I shove that blackjack up Wheeler's ass."

Blake seemed to consider those options for a moment, then he flicked his head in a manner that made Wheeler step away. Maddox waited a second, then righted the chair and dropped back onto it.

The man behind the table shook his head. "Joe, Joe, Joe... you always were a stubborn sonuvabitch. That's why you didn't last on the force."

Maddox stared at the man. Captain Cyrus Blake, aka Sheriff Cyclops, never took a payoff in his life, as far as anyone knew, but for years he'd been packing the force with the most corrupt deputies he could find. He was the sheriff's number two man and used all the graft he'd accumulated around him to earn markers. Everyone who was taking a little on the side owed him, and he made sure everyone below—and even above him—was doing just that. He was surrounded by people beholden to him, but he owed no one. That was why he was going to be top dog one day. Probably one day very soon.

And it was why Maddox hadn't lasted long under him.

"I told you, Captain. I didn't kill him."

"I didn't ask whether you did. I asked you when was the last time you saw him. Now, I'm going to ask you again—"

He let his finger off the button and turned a knob, holding it while the reels spun quickly in the opposite direction for a moment, then let go. They started rolling again, wheels moving down a shallow hill.

"—when was the last time you saw Upton Peele?"

Maddox held the man's gaze for a long moment, that one eye at the same time somehow both more expressive and more inscrutable than two. "Last night. Sort of. I didn't actually see him. But I knew he was there."

"Where?"

"Right where you found him."

"And how did you come to be there with him."

"That was where we ended up. Separately. But it wasn't where it all started."

"And where would that be?"

"Rosie's."

Captain Blake lowered his eye to the tabletop and worked his mouth like he was chewing something he wasn't sure was edible. He glanced at the tape recorder for a moment, then let his gaze settle once again on Maddox.

"You mean, Rosie's Diner over on San Jack?"

Maddox shook his head. Blake knew damn well he wasn't talking about any diner on San Jacinto.

"No, not Rosie's Diner."

"Where, then?"

"Rosie's Cantina, over off Westheimer."

"Oh, yes, I may have heard of a place by that name. Don't know much about it, though."

So, Maddox thought, that's the way it is. Even down here, in a room that wasn't supposed to exist, where warnings were just given about bullshit being met with a crack off the skull, as long as that tape recorder was running, it was all Kabuki theater. He'd seen that in Japan, too. People dancing behind masks, no one in the audience quite sure what was going on.

Well, if they wanted to pretend, he'd go along. That way, the tape could be played for the sheriff, who could play it for the police chief, who'd be grateful everyone kept his daughter's name out of it and happy to owe the sheriff one, who would in turn owe Blake one, or one more, as it were. Politics. It turned the truth into a weapon. The only time anyone cared about it was when it could be used to skewer your enemies.

"It's a dyke bar. Just inside the city limits."

"By 'dyke bar,' you mean an establishment frequented by homosexual women?"

Maddox let out an audible breath, "Yes."

"And that's where you last saw him alive?"

"No. It's where I got involved."

Blake raised the eyebrow above his patch. "Involved with Mrs. Peele?"

"No, not like that. Let's quit beating around the bush. Do you want the whole story? Laid out, beginning to end?"

The captain leaned back into his chair until it creaked. "If you would be so kind."

"Okay..." Maddox looked down to the microphone, let his gaze slide over to the rotating reels on the machine, then stared Blake square in his lone, steely eye. "I'll tell you."

A moment later he added, "Not that you're going to believe it."

The woman at the door with the crew cut in jeans and engineer boots had a look that let Maddox know his presence was highly offensive. Not just standing there in the dusky twilight at the entrance to Rosie's, but on the planet in general.

"I'm here to see Cathy."

"I know why you're here."

"Are you gonna let me in?"

"This is a private club. Your type ain't welcome."

She jerked a thumb over her shoulder. The sign above the door read, "NO MEN ALLOWED."

Maddox nodded, thinking through his options. He could deck her, one solid right against the point of that ugly chin of hers, but that would be hitting a woman. Even if many wouldn't see it that way. And he didn't hit women. Though he told himself there was always a first time.

"Are you going to tell her I'm here?"

"I haven't decided yet."

Words intended to help her decide in his favor, though not very nice ones, were cued up in his throat, pushing toward his lips, when he heard another voice.

"It's okay, Pam." To Maddox, she said, "Hi, Joe. Thanks for coming."

"Cathy. You look good." And she did, same fiery red hair. Same band of freckles peeking through her make-up. Though she didn't exactly look well.

Pam shook her head. "Mona ain't gonna like this."

"It's okay."

The woman crinkled her lip, flashing a row of crooked teeth and stepped aside. She made a point of lifting her flannel shirt to show the .38 tucked into her waistband. Promiscuous display of a weapon, in cop talk.

"Oh, c'mon now," he said, tilting his head toward the sign. "If they made an exception for you, they can make one for me."

"Joe."

Catherine gestured vaguely with her head as she turned back inside the bar. Maddox followed, tipping an imaginary hat.

Things didn't exactly go quiet as he made his way through the joint, the jukebox made sure of that, but they definitely went still. Women of varying degrees of femininity stared, heads on a slow swivel. Tendrils of smoke snaked up toward bulbs over tables, cigarettes wedged between fingers with colored nails here, chewed and black-ringed nails there. Chuck Berry was waxing on about tight sweaters and lipstick and the grown-up blues to a fast-tempo riff.

The barmaid was matronly and stout and tracked Maddox carefully as she set down a glass and reached beneath the bar. Catherine flicked her hand out to catch the woman's attention, then shook her head. Something told Maddox she hadn't been reaching for a fifth of bourbon.

On the wall opposite the bar was a giant map of Houston, superimposed with magazine cutouts of women in suggestive cowgirl garb, cowboy hats and tiny shorts and frilly boots. Some were topless. Some were accompanied by unintentionally suggestive taglines. *These Gals Don't Need Any Men... Texas Women Fill Saddles On Their Own... Western Beauties Mount Up and Ride Together.*

Catherine slid into a booth in the far corner just past the map, back to the wall. Maddox glanced back at the faces staring at him, then took the banquette opposite her.

"Whoever Mona is, I take it she doesn't like men."

Catherine fluttered her hand. "The landlady. What she doesn't like is trouble."

"I thought Norwood owned every inch of Westheimer this side of the highway."

"Who knows?" she said, giving half a shrug. "Everything's owned by corporations these days."

Maddox nodded, taking in the bar in sections. "If you brought me here to set me up with someone, you should have asked whether I like girls first."

"You're funny." She smiled, but there wasn't any humor in it. "I always liked that about you. But now's not the time."

Maddox nodded. "Tell me what's wrong then."

"I'm not sure where to begin."

"Try the beginning."

"You're angry with me. You have every right."

"No. I'm just confused."

"Maybe this was a mistake. I'm sorry."

"Cathy, please. Cut the Hitchcock stuff and tell me what's the matter."

She stared at the table and wiped the back of her finger across her nose. He was never any good at this, and he knew it. Why were they so damn emotional all the time? Why couldn't she just tell him what was going on? *This* was why he didn't have a steady girlfriend. Moments just like this. He had a way of blowing them. A knack. The only woman he didn't seem to make uncomfortable was a hooker he'd done a solid for, but she was paid to put up with all types.

This is Cathy, he told himself. *You can do better.*

He reached his hand across the table and placed it on top of hers. It was a supreme act of will. He felt like he was watching someone else do it.

"Cat... you used our secret code. I came as soon as I got the message. I can't help you if you don't tell me what the problem is."

Something seemed to break, just a little. She coughed a faint sob and her shoulders sagged. Then she took a breath and sighed it out. She raised her eyes, and he could see they were welling.

"It's that little Poindexter you married, isn't it? Did he beat you?"

"No, no. I mean, yes, it is about him, but he's never touched me." She paused for a beat, gaze narrowing just enough to make the point. "Ever."

Maddox leaned back, settling into the bench.

"Ever?"

"Ever."

"Is that what this is? You're leaving him?"

"You don't understand. It's not that simple. God, I wish it were."

"Well, you're right about that. I don't. But I'm inclined to think you wouldn't use our code simply because you got into a spat with your husband. Especially after all these years."

She reached over and pulled a napkin from a dispenser to dab her eyes. What was it about tears that made a woman so damn attractive? Something primal, he imagined. An urge to protect, maybe. Caveman stuff.

Or maybe the vulnerability just made a guy's instincts kick in, that reptilian part of his brain that thought a fragile emotional state was a door to getting her undressed. He wasn't sure.

Cathy'd been his first. They were sixteen and had known each other forever, if only from a distance. She was a tomboy, but cute. Not the girl next door, but barely two blocks away. He was awkward, skinny. A late bloomer with no meat on his bones and a quiet disposition. She took pity on him, the way he saw it. When he tried to make her his girl, she told him no, kept telling him no, eventually confided that despite what had happened, she preferred her own sex. Which seemed strange to him, especially considering she had a bit of a reputation around the school. Rumors about her putting out, though never with the kinds of guys known for that. Her only explanation for why she'd slept with him was, sometimes a person needs a friend.

Then Truman reinstated the draft in '48, and Maddox ended up in Korea. When he got back, he heard she'd married some guy who had moved here from Chicago, ten years her senior. Lived in a big house in River Oaks. First year Maddox was gone, she wrote him twice, exactly six months apart. Second year, once. Then, nothing. Last letter came just before Christmas, '50. He hadn't heard from her since.

Until he got a call from a husky sounding woman who gave him a time and a place. And a message: the cat's up on the roof, and we can't get her down.

"Whatever it is, Cat, I'm here now."

"You have to understand, I don't know who else to turn to."

"Okay."

"You were in the military, then a cop for a while. Maybe you know... things? Understand how things work? Can find people? Isn't that what you do? Find people?"

"Cat, what are we talking about?"

She inhaled and held it, straightening up, then reached into her purse and produced a piece of paper. She slid it across the table toward him. It contained two pairs of numbers separated by dashes. Below that were three letters, written in large, block hand, underlined twice, AOP. Followed by one word.

Tomorrow.

Maddox shrugged. "What's this supposed to mean?"

"I'm not sure, but I know it's something bad."

"I'm a little lost here, Cat."

"Yes, of course, I'm sorry. I need to explain. Apparently, you're familiar with my—with Upton?"

"A little."

"You checked him out, didn't you? When you found out I was married? That's why you called him what you did. A Poindexter."

Maddox said nothing. There was nothing worthwhile to say. Not that he could think of, at least. All he'd done was pull the wedding announcement from the archives at the *Post*. One small picture of the two of them, one small paragraph. The guy just looked like a Poindexter to him.

"It's okay. I know it's only because you care about me. Or used to. I've been awful to you. But you have to understand, things got really bad after you left. There were all these witch hunts for subversive activity. Lots of my... *acquaintances* were getting caught up in them, labeled communists or traitors or deviants and being run out of town. And my father, he feared he was being investigated, because of his ties to an organization that was getting money from the Russians. My father may have been politically idealistic, naive, but the way they hounded him... when I think of what they did... *Those bastards...*"

"You don't have to justify yourself to me, Cathy."

"It's important, though, important that you know the whole story. Upton made me a proposal. Offered an arrangement. If I were to marry him, I could lead whatever kind of life I wanted, provided I was discreet. The way he explained it, he needed a wife for appearances, I needed a husband. I'd have a home, money, a dinner companion and friend. I'd have a place in the community. And a measure of protection. Also, he indicated he could make my father's troubles go away."

"So, your man Upton, he's a fairy?"

"That's what I thought, at first. I mean, how else would he have even found out about me, except through some mutual friend? But no, I don't think so. He has no ties to that particular community. He's just not... anything."

"Judging by the place you live, I'd say not being anything pays pretty well."

"But that's just it, I don't even know what he does, where he gets his money. I hardly know a thing about him. And I have to wonder if the few things I do know are even true."

"Is that why you called me? Because you want the scoop on your hubby?"

"No, no, of course not. I would never use our special message for something like that. No, this is something bad, Joe. I'm scared."

She seemed to be waiting for me to respond, to give her a sign that I wanted her to go on, "Well, I'm here, and I'm listening."

"That piece of paper there, I found it in his study. He was passed out at his desk, dead drunk."

"Is that normal?"

"No, not until recently. He always keeps his study locked up like a vault. He has a separate phone line at his desk. The walls are paneled with thick hardwood. You could probably scream in there with the door closed and no one on the other side of it could hear you."

Something about the way she said that last part hinted at more. "But?"

"But... a few months ago, we had a bad storm. You probably remember it. Lightning struck the house, fried some wiring. An electrician came out and had to fix a bunch of stuff."

"And—"

"And a few nights later, I happened to pick up the phone in the bedroom, and I could hear him talking to someone, another man. I immediately apologized, went to hang up, but then I realized they'd just kept talking. They couldn't hear me. Their voices were a bit faint, and there was static, but I could hear everything. I said his name into the receiver, but they just kept talking."

"And you kept listening."

Catherine nodded. "Not just that night, either."

"What did you hear?"

"Nothing that made any sense. But it was still fascinating. I never knew what Upton did, who he transacted business with, and now I could listen in on his private conversations, and I still didn't know. But it sounded important. And dangerous."

"In what way?"

"They were talking around things, you know? Using codes, like spies. Phrases that meant something to them but not to anyone else. But sometimes I could tell they were just talking straight, and I still didn't understand. They were going back and forth about people I'd never heard of, strange-sounding names, far-off places I couldn't locate on a map. And dates. Lots of dates. It seemed they were arguing about the significance of certain things. It was all hard to follow."

"But you must have heard something you understood."

Catherine nodded once. Her expression dissolved into a look of weary sobriety. "A few nights ago, Upton asked if the death toll estimates were for certain. The man on the other end said they were. 542,000. He said that the rearview was quite specific."

"Rearview?"

"That was the word he used."

"So, we planning on dropping an H-Bomb on Moscow or something?"

"I have no idea what it is, or who, but they weren't talking about Moscow. Joe, they were talking about Houston."

"How do you know that?"

"Because Upton was asking about evacuation procedures. Joe... he asked whether he could take me with him to what he called Sanctuary. He mentioned it was in Cyprus. That's an island near—"

"I know where Cyprus is."

"Yes, well, the man said no. His exact words were, *no sanctuary for that bird.*"

"Jesus." Maddox clawed his fingers through his hair, letting the information process. "Cathy, we gotta go to the Feds, report this. It sounds like your guy is an agent for one of our enemies, and they're about to explode some atomic weapon right here. Or maybe dump some kind of poison in our water supply." He looked down at the paper in front of him. "Tomorrow?"

"But, Joe, I don't think it's like that. The conversations, they weren't... it's like they were talking about something that had already happened. Like the people they worked for had to, I don't know, choose. And that there was only one way to stop it from happening. And that was to make the right choice."

"Choose what?"

"I don't know. I never could figure that out. I can't even be sure I'm right about any of it. But I've got a really bad feeling."

"Cat, we need to go find some real G-men. I can call some guys I know, we can wake somebody—"

"And tell them what, Joe? That your lesbian friend overheard her husband talking about things she didn't understand? If I were anyone else and told you this, would you take any of it seriously? That message I found a few hours ago said *tomorrow*. You really think they would just swoop in and save the day? Wrap things up by supper time?"

"Cat, if you really think something's going to happen, why don't you just get in your car and leave? Go to Dallas for a few days?"

"And just abandon all these people here? All my friends? People I care about? Let them face whatever it is on their own? I can't tell them what's going to happen, not without them thinking I'm nuts, but I won't leave them to suffer it while I run away."

"I'm going to guess you didn't call me so I could jump in my Chrysler and head to New Orleans for the weekend. So, what is it you want me to do?"

"I don't know exactly. Maybe you could find Upton, talk to him. Get him to tell you what's going on. If something really is going to happen, see if it can be stopped. Please, Joe. If you could just get him to tell you, maybe we can stop whatever he's been doing. You're the only one who can help me."

Maddox held a steady gaze on her for a few solid seconds. "Okay, Cat. This is me, carrying you down from the roof. If that's what you want, I'll give it a shot."

"Thank you. I knew I could count on you, Joe. I've always known."

"As far as finding old Upton, I take it it's not a matter of me just driving over to your house."

Catherine shook her head. "I doubt he'll even go back there. I ran. I've had someone drive by, and he's gone. I'm pretty sure he's been out looking for me. We may only have a few hours before he leaves town. He... he packed a suitcase and everything."

"Any idea where he's planning on going?"

"No. I'm sorry."

"Great. I'll just start knocking on random doors. There a chance he's catching a plane?"

"He doesn't like to fly, I know that much. He's got a phobia or something. But the way he was talking on the phone, I think there's a ticket waiting for him somewhere. At least, that's what it sounded like. Maybe a bus or a train?"

"I'll check the stations. Any friends? People he socializes with? Bars he drops in?"

"No, no one. No place. It's like his entire life is just for show."

"Cat, honestly, the odds are this is all a huge misunderstanding. I'm pretty sure Houston will be here tomorrow, and the next day."

"I hope you're right, Joe. But I need this. And there isn't much time."

Maddox nodded, then slid out from the booth and stood next to the table. "Anything else you can think of?"

"No."

"I'll call here if I find anything," he said, nodding again. "Are you gonna be safe?"

She smiled up at him, a lot of what looked like pity expressed in the slope of her mouth.

"Yes. Pam and Marge agreed to stay here all night with me, if need be. I would ask that you try to not to mention my name to anyone. I don't want to put them in danger. Those people scare me."

"Of course not." He gave her a reassuring tilt of the head. "It really is good to see you, Cat."

"Same here, Joe. And thanks. I don't know what I'd do if you hadn't shown."

He picked up the piece of paper, rapped his knuckles on the table and turned to leave.

"Joe, there is one more thing. Those letters, I think I know what they stand for."

Maddox blinked, waiting for her to finish.

"I think it stands for Alpha-Omega Protocol. Does that mean anything to you?"

He chewed on it for a second then inclined his head in a good-bye gesture. "Not unless your boy's found Jesus," he said, heading for the door.

He made his way across the dirt parking lot, Pam making some snide comment as he passed. His car was around the corner, parked along the street, far from patrolling eyes cruising Westheimer. His shoes shuffled out a crunchy rhythm, gravelly leather off pavement. He was deep in thought when he opened the squeaky door to his 300 coupe, deep enough that his reaction to the sound of the pistol cocking seemed quite belated, once he realized what it was.

"Turn around and you're dead. I'm only going to say this once. Don't come looking for me."

Maddox stood straighter, but didn't take his hands off the car and didn't turn around. "Who says I'm looking for anybody?"

"I know she's in there, and I know that's why you're here."

The voice was deeper than he'd imagined it would be. Rougher. From the picture he'd seen, he expected something less baritone. More feminine, maybe. And there was a subtle trace of accent.

"Let's say you're right. If you don't want me to find you, don't you think being somewhere other than where I can feel your breath on my neck might be a better start?"

"I can't let you interfere. You have no idea what's happening here, what you're getting involved in. I'm telling you, let it go."

"From what I hear, if I were to do that, chances are good I'd wake up dead tomorrow morning. Am I wrong?"

The man said nothing, but Maddox felt the barrel of the gun press deeper into his back.

"What's the Alpha-Omega Protocol?"

"Nothing you need to concern yourself with. Just go back to your hole and resume your meaningless life."

"No need to get personal. Why don't we sit down somewhere and talk about it. You can explain it all to me."

"There's no time for that, and it would be a waste of effort."

"Try me. Besides, you really think that's the first gun I've ever had tickle my ribs? If time is really so important, you can save us both a bunch of it by just having a little chat."

"I could save even more by pulling the trigger and blowing a hole through your heart. It would only take about a pound of pressure more than I have on it this very moment. This a .45. You'd be legally dead before it exited your chest."

"I'd prefer you wouldn't."

"Then choose the other way. Take your time getting up."

"Getting—?"

His head snapped forward, something exploding with a *crack* inside, a flash of pressure and intense pain. Maddox felt himself slam against the frame of his car, his body sliding along it until he was on his knees, one palm on the asphalt. All the pain converged around a point just above the base of his skull. He shook his head and rubbed the spot, vaguely aware of a car starting not far away, the crunch of its tires fading into the distance seconds later.

His car, he realized, wasn't going to do the same. The rear driver's side tire was completely flat, the handle of a fixed-blade knife still sticking out of the sidewall.

It took Maddox almost twenty minutes to change the tire and another ten to get to his apartment. Time wasn't being friendly. Then again, he couldn't remember when it ever was.

He climbed the stairs and went to unlock his door. It creaked open a crack before he could. He waited a moment, then gave it a gentle push. He took a step and stopped just inside the doorway. A spill of streetlight washed over his floor, illuminating things that shouldn't be there, casting too many shadows. He patted the wall until he found the lightswitch.

His place had been trashed. Not even ransacked, simply trashed. Things tossed around, smashed just for the heck of it. A large piece of paper sat conspicuously atop a pile of assorted ends and pieces with the word QUIT scrawled across it like a shout. Beneath it in smaller print were the initials, U.P.

He hurried into the kitchen and climbed up on the counter, reached over the top of the cupboard, dug his fingertips beneath the edge of the false top. His fingers touched the envelope, and his body deflated in relief. He patted it, squeezed it between two fingers. It was all there. So was his pistol. He slipped back down to the floor and surveyed the damage.

His reloading equipment, press and dies, and bushings, were knocked off the kitchen table, but all there. He gave the rest of the place a quick walk-through. Nothing seemed to be missing.

Rubbing the back of his head, he righted a chair here, picked up a lamp there. What was the point? To show him how quickly he could find out where Maddox lived? Talk about overkill. The place was a rathole to begin with, all blotchy stains and peeling paint and unidentifiable odors.

After changing his shirt and washing up, he fished a bottle of aspirin out of the medicine cabinet above his bathroom sink, swallowed two with a couple of palmfuls of water. Then he took a bag of peas from the icebox and pressed it against the back of his neck as he picked his telephone off the floor and listened for a tone. He replaced the handset and checked his watch.

The peas started feeling like wet mush in the bag, so he tossed them back in the icebox, climbed up to kneel on the counter next to his sink again and reached atop his cupboard. He groped until he got a firm grip on the heavy rag, which held something tightly and was tacky with oil.

He set the bundle on the tiny kitchen table and unwrapped it. A 1938 Soviet TT-33. He'd taken it off a North Korean officer he'd found hiding in a makeshift barn during a sweep. Guy was gut-shot, bleeding out bad. Tried to lift the pistol as Maddox kicked away some sacks of grain, exposing him. Didn't even have the strength for that. Maddox pointed his carbine at his head and pinned the NK's arm down with his boot. He reached down and took the pistol, was about to whistle that he'd found one, but stopped himself. It was the look in the guy's eyes. Nothing there but resignation. He only had a few minutes left—maybe thirty, if he held on tight—and he just wanted to die in peace. Maddox slipped the pistol into his pack and let him.

The magazine was full and clicked solidly into the handle. Maddox worked the slide, felt it snap back, chambering a round, then tucked it into his belt. He didn't like to carry a gun. Once someone realized you were armed, it was like you'd established that deadly force was on the table, like you'd implicitly given permission to go there. Besides, a gun could make you feel invulnerable, goad you into taking unnecessary risks. That's why he liked the Tokarev. Its presence was a constant reminder that having one was no guarantee you wouldn't die holding it.

That, and the fact a decent pistol these days could run almost a hundred bucks.

But that was all academic now.

He dragged a chair close to the phone and checked his watch again. It rang as the minute hand ticked forward a notch.

Mopping his hand down his face, he hesitated before answering. Two rings. Three.

Then he picked up.

"Well," he said, staring at the bare wall across from him. "Not sure what to say. You were right."

He sighed, patting to feel what was beneath his shirt, against his chest. "But hell, I don't need to tell you that. You were there."

Maddox was familiar with River Oaks, not because he had friends there, or even clients—though he certainly wished he had those kinds of contacts. It was because he occasionally used to drive through the neighborhood on Sunday afternoons, enjoying the feel of it. The homes were large and beautiful, the lawns meticulously manicured, the colors all brighter, and the surfaces all shinier. He liked to imagine the lives of the people who lived there, happy and fulfilled. Every day something new to look forward to. Evenings bringing the promise of creature comforts and the company of friends.

He never actually thought any of that was real, he just didn't want to know it wasn't.

Because he had a plan.

It wasn't a detailed plan or even a good one. But it was a plan, and it was all he had. And a happy ending was central to it.

Los Angeles. That was his plan. A friend of his had written him, told him how he'd settled down after the war in California and opened a surf shop. Nice little business, he said. Told him he could see the ocean from his house in Santa Monica and from his store. Wanted Maddox to join him. Help him open another shop in a place called Malibu. He'd front him the money for his share, let Maddox pay it back over time. Three thousand dollars.

That sounded a bit too much like charity to him, so he told his friend he'd have to come up with the money himself first. The friend was a good man, told him he'd keep the offer open for a couple of years, at least. Raved about how the weather there was always cool in the shade and warm in the sun but never humid. Always dry.

Surfing. Something Maddox knew absolutely nothing about. Kids standing on boards being pushed by waves and trying to keep their balance until they finally tumbled into the foam. But the friend insisted business was growing, and that he could teach him all he needed to know. The fact

Maddox could barely imagine what that kind of life that would be like was part of its appeal. All of it, actually.

And now Maddox was nine hundred dollars away, not counting the two hundred dollars he took from his fund and stuffed in his wallet before leaving his apartment. Not an easy thing to do, take a step back like that.

But this was Cathy.

The Peele's house was a red brick two-story with a Federal-style set of white columns and rounded matching steps. The kind of size a person wanting to blend in would pick after a lot of thought. Not so big as to raise an eyebrow, but nothing anyone could call small. A pair of black gas lampposts lit the path to the front door, where a matching set of wall lamps brightened the porch. An interior light shone through a set of curtains, downstairs to the left of the entrance. Tasteful, upscale.

The kind of place that made Maddox simultaneously want to congratulate the owner and take a piss all over the perfectly trimmed hedges lining the front walkway.

Maddox parked across the street, two houses down. Most homes were completely dark, with an occasional porch light keeping the shadows from blanketing all. He adjusted his side mirror to watch the window, looking for movement, then checked his watch. Two minutes, three. Nothing. At the five minute mark, he got out of his car, shrugged into a lightweight sport coat, and shut the door quietly. He crossed the street, walked up the walk, and knocked. He figured thirty seconds was enough, so he knocked again. Still nothing.

The door handle was fancy, heavy brass with a thumb latch. It pressed down smoothly, and he felt the click just before the door floated open on its hinges.

Light puddled in the foyer, spilling over from a room to the left. The ceiling was vaulted, a crystal chandelier glistening in the gloom above. A staircase wound up to a lugubrious landing, steeped in shadow. Next to the stairs, the light faded into black. A pair of double doors closed off the right.

Maddox stepped inside and gently swung the door almost shut behind him, leaving just a sliver. The place smelled like a museum, an antiseptic scent mixed with the fragrance of aged wood and the piney aroma of some sort of air freshener. The floor was museum-like, too. Waxed marble, maybe. Black and white checkered pattern. Hard and smooth beneath the worn leather of his shoes.

He thought about calling out—maybe a tentative *hello?*—but decided against it.

The room with the light on was a study. Spacious, with the far wall a ceiling-to-floor bookcase, complete with a ladder on wheels. A stately desk the shape of a kidney bean was off to one side, bathed in the glow of a banker's lamp. Two simple cushioned chairs faced the desk. A sofa upholstered in a flowery print sat against one wall. The plentiful wood looked like someone had melted expensive caramel and molded it into various shapes, then polished it to a sheen.

Maddox made his way around the desk and scanned the various items littered across it. A folded newspaper, a hardbound ledger, a thick folder, several loose sheets of paper dense with print. A black telephone. He eased himself into the high-back leather chair and pulled open the middle drawer. A few pens and pencils. Some paper clips. A tangle of rubber bands. A silver letter opener. A thin box of envelopes. He opened the top side drawer to his right. Folders, mostly invoices and receipts. The drawer below it contained a metal lockbox. He retrieved the letter opener and jimmied the tiny latch open. A checkbook, a money clip, maybe a dollar in loose change. Below that, folded in half, was the deed to the house. Grantor was somebody named Theodore Winstead. Grantee was listed as New Century Corporation.

Everything's owned by corporations these days.

He opened the ledger. Dates and numbers, columns of credits and debits, disbursements and deposits. Nothing he understood.

He picked up the newspaper. It was a few days old. It had been folded to a particular article, placed face down on it.

AMERICA'S MERCURY ASTRONAUTS
PUT THROUGH THEIR PACES

Project Mercury astronauts yesterday completed disorientation tests on the Multiple Axis Space Test Inertia Facility at NASA's Lewis Research Center. Also known as the 'gimbal rig,' this spaceflight simulator is made of three cages that revolve separately or in combination to create roll, pitch, and yaw motions at speeds up to 30 revolutions per minute.

"We've entered an exciting phase of the program," said Norman Thurgood, Assistant Director of Research and Development, during a brief question and answer session with reporters. Mr. Thurgood declined to provide details of either the tests or the simulator, citing the need to keep the technology from falling into the wrong hands.

The article went on to discuss the administration's commitment to space exploration and its plans to open new facilities, the details for which officials also declined to comment. It ended noting that the Q&A session was cut short due to the assistant director's travel schedule, which included stops in Florida, Texas, and California.

Texas. As far as leads went, not exactly a smoking gun. Expanding the paper over the desk, he shook it a few times. No keys clanked onto the wood, no slips of paper feathered down to reveal some clue. A piece was cut out from a page of advertisements. Probably a coupon clipped.

He tossed the paper aside and leaned back in the chair. He stared at the phone, started to reach for it. That's when the Dwarf and the Mexican walked in.

Maddox must have let the surprise show, because the Dwarf's rictus stretched even wider than usual.

"Hello, Donald," Maddox said.

The Dwarf eased to a stop a few steps into the room and looked around, rolling his shoulders. "It's Joe, isn't it?"

Maddox said nothing. The little punk knew his name.

"Fancy meeting you here," said the Dwarf. The other guy passed behind him, took a place a few steps farther into the room. He hooked one hand over the other wrist and stood quietly, like a good soldier. Bigger than the Dwarf, average sized, but solid. Black hair, slicked straight back. Thin mustache framing his upper lip. He looked familiar, but Maddox couldn't quite place him.

"I see you've already made yourself at home," the Dwarf added in his nasally voice.

Donald Schwartz wasn't really a dwarf. Or even a midget. He was just a short, wannabe tough-guy from Philly. Five foot three in his shoes. Every cop in town knew him. Word was he'd been a low-level bookie back home who took it upon himself to plug some stoolie that had dropped dime on the local Syndicate, his bid to get in good with the Genoveses. Saw himself becoming the next Lansky or Cohen, climbing to the top on wits and verve. But the Family didn't tolerate unsanctioned hits that well, considered it an affront to their authority, so they let the cops run him out of town. Being slow on the uptake and long on hubris, he assumed he'd earned his bones, asked where they'd like him to go, thought being a point man was a good opportunity to entrench himself in the business. They told him, 'Houston.' Maddox imagined a table of fat Italians laughing it up that night over some pasta fazool. He wondered how long it took the little shrimp to realize the joke. Probably the first time he was hospitalized by a few of the hardened denizens of the Fifth Ward, after he showed up to tell them he was going to be running things and to stay out of his way. Or maybe after a run-in with the greasers over in Schrimpf Alley, when he spoke slowly to them, assuming they didn't understand English. Or the HCSD, the first time they caught him skulking around, looking to start a local racket for a mob that knew better than to set foot within a thousand miles of this place. It was corrupt in ways they just didn't understand and knew they didn't understand. Probably never would.

"Who's your friend, Donald?" Maddox asked.

The Dwarf shrugged, rolling his shoulders again. Couldn't seem to stand still. Being a small guy and a two-bit hood, he did what a lot of small hoods did. He acted like Jimmy Cagney. Sort of like a guy on the Ed Sullivan Show, doing an impression. Right down to the bent elbows and hands pulled in near his sides. Maddox had to hand it to him, though. The Dwarf figured out that hard-nosed oil men and real estate moguls and lawyers with WASPy names needed somebody to do their laundry now and then, somebody not afraid of a little dirt. So he made a living.

"Name's Fabian Sanchez. Maybe you heard of him."

Maddox nodded. He'd heard of him.

To Sanchez he said, "You ever making a comeback?"

Now it was the kid's turn to shrug. And blush a little, too. Sad story, that one. Golden Gloves, turned pro. Promising middleweight. Houston sports pages loved him. Called him the Mexican Mauler. Took a dive to pay off some gambling debts. Had the misfortune of having a photographer catch the punch that missed him by six inches in perfect focus. After that, the papers just called him the Mexican, what had been a term of affection shortened to one emphasizing foreignness.

Now he apparently did whatever it was that boxers do when they lose their license.

"Doesn't talk much, does he?"

The Dwarf smirked but didn't respond. Maddox let it go.

"How can I help you gentlemen?"

"Ha! He called us *gentlemen*! Ya' hear that, Fabo? This guy's a hoot!" The Dwarf pulled out a cigarette and flipped it into his mouth. He lit it with a match, then shook the match out and flicked it onto the carpet. "What do you call that, Fabo? Guy who cracks jokes for living?"

"*Comediante.*"

"Yeah, a regular comedian, that's him." He blew out a long stream of smoke. "Came to see Peele. You know where he is?"

"No."

"What're you doing at his desk?"

Maddox picked up the newspaper, gave it a flap. "Crossword. You know a five-letter word for midget?"

The Dwarf thought about it for a second, then flexed a few muscles in his face. "You think your funny, huh? Well, wise guys usually get what's coming to them."

"I can only hope. What do you want with Peele?"

"That's our business, not yours."

"I'll tell him you're looking for him, Donald." Maddox made a point of calling him that. Everybody knew he hated it. He wanted to be called 'Don,' as in, 'The Don.' But everybody called him Donald, as in, 'Donald Dwarf.'

The more he tried to act like he didn't care, the more obvious it was he did.

"Maybe you oughta just come with us. Somebody might have a few questions he'd like to ask."

"Somebody like who?"

"You sure are—what's the word, Fabo?"

"*Inquisitivo.*"

The Dwarf snapped his fingers. "That's it. *Inquisitive.* As in, if I wanted you to know, I'da told you already."

"Fair enough. But I think I'll pass."

The Dwarf patted his coat near the waist, revealing a bulge "What if I said you didn't have a choice?"

"I'd ask you if your employer really wanted you to get him involved in a homicide investigation. Because I'm not going anywhere with you, and if you try to take me, at least one of us is going to have to be carried out."

The Dwarf twisted his mouth, gave a grudging shrug. He glanced over at Sanchez, made a few mental calculations. Maddox watched his face, realized he'd won this round. The guy may have been annoying, but he wasn't really stupid.

"I'll make you a deal," Maddox said. "You tell me why you want Peele, I'll tell you where he's going to be an hour and a half from now. Best I can do."

"Maybe we already know where he's going to be."

"Then you don't need me to tell you, and we can go our separate ways."

More machinations behind that brow. "There's somebody wants to speak to him."

"I guessed that much. You'll have to do better."

"Let's just say he has something in his possession that he promised to someone else. A deal's a deal. Now, spill it."

"You working for the Devil now? Come to collect his soul?"

"What's that supposed to mean?"

"I mean, either tell me who's looking for him, or what it is Peele has. Then I'll share."

"You sure are pushy. Maybe I oughta just let Fabo here do a number on you and get this over with."

"He can go all Gene Krupka on my face, and Gene Kelly on my ribcage, and I still won't talk. Just tell me what it is. Or who."

"Let's just say it's some valuable object, okay? I don't know what the heck it's called."

"Object?"

"Yeah, like a whatdyacallit... help me out here, Fabo."

"*Artefacto.*"

"Right. An artifact. Or something. Let's just say, party of the first part paid for it, now party of the first part wants it. That's more than you need to know. So where's Peele supposed to show?"

"Buffalo Bayou, beneath Waugh Bridge."

"And how do you know he's gonna be there?"

"That's where he told me to meet him, before he told me to come alone."

"He told you that?"

"Yeah. He called me. You'd never know he'd half caved-in the back of my skull a half-hour earlier."

"Why's he want to meet you?"

"I don't know. He hung up before I had a chance to ask."

"Did he now? So why are you here?"

"Trying to figure out what he's up to. I figure I'd have to be an idiot to show. He's probably just looking for a place to off me without witnesses. Job doesn't pay that well."

"You'd better not be trying to pull a fast one on me."

"You? No man in his right mind would dare."

"That moutha yours is gonna get you in big... Fabo?"

"*Apuro.*"

"Yeah, that's right. Big *apuro* someday."

"So they tell me."

The Dwarf looked him over once more, then slapped the back of his hand against Sanchez and jerked his head toward the doorway. "Just stay out of our way, you got it?"

They were almost out of sight when Maddox said, "Hey, Donald..."

The Dwarf looked back, hand on the door.

"Aren't you even curious who my client is?"

The perpetual smile widened a bit as the Dwarf pointed a finger at him, pistol-like, and mimicked taking a shot. Then he shut the front door behind him.

Maddox checked his watch. The phone rang a moment later.

The Rice Hotel stood on the edge of downtown like a stern schoolmaster. Seventeen stories of brown brick and white stone blocks, the Rice occupied the space formerly the site of the Republic's capitol and, honoring that legacy, catered to the monied and powerful. It boasted the city's first air-conditioned public room, dining in its renowned Flag Room that was fine enough to rival any restaurant one could name, and more wealth and influence in its Old Capital Club than routinely gathered in any one place outside of Washington, D.C.

But Candy Lawrence, in a tight red skirt and a tighter white blouse, didn't know any of that when she stepped into the lobby and sashayed up to the front desk. All she knew was a room there cost big bucks. What she saw did nothing to change her mind.

The furniture was elegant, if a little stuffy. Brass fixtures shimmered under gaslight, making the wood grains seem restless. Her heels clicked on the polished floor, and one caught on the edge of a large Persian rug as she made her way across the cavernous space. She bit her lip to keep from cursing. That's what she got for staring up at the chandeliers.

A small man, barely older than her her twenty-four years, with dark hair and a dark suit manned the check-in counter. A much larger man with a shiny bald head and a gray buzz on the sides was stooped over writing something in a large book not far away. The smaller one manning the check-in dropped his gaze as low as the counter would allow, then raised it just as slowly. Usually men met her eyes with a smile after doing that. Not this one.

"Can I help you, Miss?"

"I'm, uh, supposed to meet someone."

"Is that so." The clerk scratched his head and glanced to the side, lips pursed. " I'm afraid our lobby is for guests of the hotel. You will have to arrange your 'meeting' for somewhere else."

"But the man I'm meeting is a guest. And I was just planning, you know, to go up to his room."

"I see. Now look here, Miss, we are not that type of establishment. I'm going to have to ask you to—."

"I'll take care of this, Leonard."

"But—?"

"Leonard..."

The bald man placed a hand on Leonard's shoulder, nudging him gently but firmly out of the way. The younger man did not resist, but his expression was a mix of surprise and indignation. He trudged off to a corner, the hangdog look of someone preparing to stew and sulk.

"Now, young miss. Whom are you here to see?"

She had to think for a moment. "Norman Thurgood."

The man nodded, more in thought than agreement, and slid the guest ledger closer. He ran a finger down one page, then the next.

"Thurgood... I'm sorry, I'm not seeming to find him."

"Are you sure? He told me this was the place." In a lower voice, she whispered: "*He's from NASA.*"

The man looked up. "Oh, yes, of course."

He flipped the book back a page and ran his finger down again. "Here we are. I apologize. Sometimes guests are noted, uh, differently than normal. Privacy reasons, you understand."

She understood—a hotel for the super wealthy was no different than the motels on the east side of town she was used to. Just snootier.

The man reached for a telephone. "I'll let him know you're here."

"If you'll just tell me his room number, that's all I need."

"I'm sorry, but I have to get his approval first."

She leaned forward, glancing to the side. "Here's the thing..." She checked to make sure he got a good look down her blouse. He did. "He told me the room, and I forgot. I don't want to get in trouble, know what I mean? He might be a little embarrassed that I, you know, talked to anyone."

The man paused, his eyes dropping to her cleavage. Not for the first time.

She added, "I'd be very grateful. Maybe later I could make it up to you?"

He lowered the phone as if his hand were sinking through water. Then he let out a breath and casually spun the registry around, pointing to a name. Next to it was a number.

"Well, as long as you remember... you didn't hear it from me. And my name is Patrick."

Candy knocked on the door of room 714 once. She waited thirty seconds, then knocked again. Sounds of someone stirring, the rustling of sheets, the creaking of a boxspring. Footfalls.

"Who is it? Do you have any idea what time it is?"

"It's me."

"You have the wrong room. Go away before I call the front desk."

"C'mon, Norman. Open up. I think I may be pregnant."

A thump, a click. The sound of the door knob turning. It opened a few inches.

"Just who the hell are—"

Maddox rammed his shoulder against the door, knocking the man back. He rushed inside, grabbing a confused Norman Thurgood and clamping a hand over the man's mouth. Glancing back, he gestured with his chin, indicating the door. Candy stuck her head out, checked the hallway, then closed it.

Thurgood struggled. He was strong for a bureaucrat, not much to look at in his boxers, but his medium frame and slightly expanded midsection hid some taut muscle. Maddox let go and unloaded two fists to the stomach. High, just beneath the breast bone. A good shot to the solar plexus tended to knock the wind right out of a person, and he'd just landed two. It was a prime target for a nightstick, as all cops were trained. A fist was almost as good.

Grunting, Thurgood sank onto the bed, arms crossed over his midsection. He bent forward and started to sag to the floor. Maddox caught him and pushed him back up.

"Listen, I don't want to hurt you."

The man sucked in a breath audibly but didn't speak. Maddox drew his pistol and cocked the hammer.

"I'm going to ask you a few questions. As long as you answer them, we'll leave, and you'll never hear from us again. If you don't, well, how is it going to look when the concierge tells cops the last thing he remembered was sending a hooker up to your room? Your family will be devastated." He raised the Tokarev. "Doubly devastated."

Thurgood coughed a few times, then managed a deep whisper. "What is this about?"

"Your friend. Peele."

Thurgood's head snapped up. *Bingo.*

"I don't know what you're talking about."

"Really? Is that why your eyes about popped out of their sockets when you heard the name?"

"I'm not telling you anything."

"That so?" Maddox backed up a few steps, pistol still trained on his new acquaintance. He glanced down at the desk near the wall. He picked up a wallet and tossed it to Candy.

"Do me favor, Kitten. Look through that wallet and find the driver's license for Mr. Tightlips here. Then get the operator on the line to help you find the number for wherever he lives. I'm sure Mrs. Tightlips will want to hear what you have to say, all about the sordid affair, the way he smacked you around when you told him you were pregnant. " He gestured toward Thurgood with the gun. "Mention the outie belly button and that birthmark on his inner thigh, just for good measure."

"You wouldn't."

Candy sobbed, drawing the man's attention as she picked through his billfold. "*Oh, Mrs Thurgood... I'm so, so sorry. He didn't tell me he was married. Honest! Not until after I told him about the baby. I'm just scared, I don't know what to do. I just couldn't let him keep lying to you. And when he gave me the name of a doctor, threatened that if I didn't...*"

She looked up, cutting off the tears. She held up a yellow card. "Got it."

"She won't believe you."

"I'm sure you're right. I'm sure you'll be able to explain it all. The arrest for beating this woman, who the night manager will say knew your name and went straight to your room and who made such a ruckus screaming in the hall, clothes torn from trying to get away from your perverted clutches, telling everyone in earshot how you were going to kill her."

"What the hell do you want?"

"Information."

"What kind of information?"

"Tell me about Peele. You were supposed to meet him, weren't you?"

"You have no idea what you're dealing with."

"Maybe not, but I will when we're through here. And the quicker you tell me, the quicker we're out of what's left of your hair."

"You're not going to understand."

"There's a lot of that going around. Now talk."

"Who are you with? The Soviets?"

"No. I'm just a fellow American, looking for some answers."

"Since you know my name, I assume you know who I work for."

"Yeah, not exactly a secret."

"Well, what you're asking me about certainly is. Not enough people even know about it for it to be classified. There's just no way I can tell you."

"How secret do you think it's going to be when this lady of the evening is screaming to the press about how before you attacked her you were blabbing about secret missions and hundreds of thousands of Americans being killed?"

Thurgood said nothing.

"Yeah, I know about that, and you'd better start expanding that knowledge, real quick. Why are you here?"

"Officially, I'm here as part of a series of site assessments. NASA is planning to construct a major new facility. A base of operations for space missions."

"And unofficially?"

"It would be very hard to explain."

Maddox raised the pistol.

"For decades now, the federal government has had an... arrangement with an organization. A private company."

"Let me guess. New Century Corporation."

"If you already know all this, why are you interrogating me?""

"I know a little. Just keep talking."

"Well, a 'little' is all anyone knows, as far as I can tell. You may know more than me. From what I was told, this company possesses some remarkable form of technology."

"What kind of technology."

"I don't really know. I swear. But whatever it is, it was capable of spooking the living daylights out of a few highly-placed officials, several administrations ago. My understanding is that each new President is in-briefed in general terms, then strongly advised to decline further information. Only one President has demanded full access, but that was because of the War. The political damage that would be sustained if word got out is incalculable. And political damage isn't even the main concern."

"What is?"

"Some people seem to think whatever it is this firm possesses, it's capable of tearing apart the social fabric. Undermining civilization as we know it."

"So, what are we talking about?"

"I'm afraid I'm not privy to such information. All I know is, whenever these people report a threat, we're supposed to do exactly what they say."

"Sounds like blackmail."

"No, nothing like that."

"You're starting to go all vague on me, Norman."

"This is going to sound ridiculous."

Maddox said nothing.

"They predict the future. It's like an equation. A plus B equals C, and if C, then X. If X, then Y. That kind of thing."

"And they use that information to extort money?"

"No, like I said, it's not like that. Not completely. I mean, yes, I'm sure they're well compensated. But it's more like they dictate exactly what course of action has to be taken."

"To avoid their prediction?"

"Yes."

"In that case, how would anyone ever know if there was anything to it?"

"Because, sometimes they just give us a prediction. In case people are inclined to become skeptics."

"I'm going to take a stab and say this was one of those times."

Thurgood nodded.

"But this prediction was different," Maddox said. "This one had hundreds of thousands of people dying. Americans."

"Yes."

"And they just send you? Why aren't feds and soldiers and armored vehicles swarming to take down these people? Demand to know what they're up to? How to stop it?"

"You don't understand. There are five, maybe six people in the government who know about this."

"Maybe now's a good time to start spreading the word."

"What word? The last time anyone remembers a prediction, it was that there would be over a quarter of a million dead in Japan. No specifics as to what nationality. Those numbers were in line with invasion estimates. Truman almost had a breakdown and ordered us to bomb them until they surrendered. Guess what? That turned out to be the death toll from the A-bombs he dropped. According to our contact, when they give us a prediction with no formula for correction, it's because they don't have one. Should we simply start a panic?"

"You're just going to let all those people die?"

"You're not following me. No one knows enough to do anything. Whatever we try to do in response could be what causes it. Do you have any idea what it would take to evacuate millions of people? What if most of those deaths wouldn't have happened?"

"And this is all supposed to happen tomorrow?"

"What? No, of course not. You think I'd be sitting here if that were the case? They gave us a date. November ninth."

"So, I'm going to ask you again. Why are you here? Just what does NASA got to do with all this?"

"The date happens to coincide with something we have scheduled. I'm supposed to make sure there's no connection."

"What kind of something? A space launch?"

"Look, it's one thing to answer questions about something no one would believe, it's another to give out highly classified information. We're in a race with the Russians, in case you hadn't noticed."

"Tell me what NASA's got planned."

"It's a mission, okay? Someone got the bright idea to—"

The knock at the door was firm and efficient. Maddox glanced at Candy, then back at Thurgood. The look he gave Thurgood was enough to keep him quiet. The raised barrel of the pistol was an exclamation point.

"Excuse me, Mr. Thurgood. This is Mr. Harding from Guest Services." The voice coming through the door was muffled. "Is everything okay?"

Maddox gave Thurgood a nod, raised a finger, indicating the one chance he had to say the right thing.

"Yes," Thurgood raised his voice, eyes on Maddox. "Everything's fine. Thank you."

"We've had some, uh, calls about noise. Loud voices and such. I came personally to make sure I would not be, uh, disturbing you. I must ask that you please keep it down. We have other guests on this floor."

Thurgood took in a breath, then suddenly smiled. When he spoke, eyes on Maddox and voice toward the door, the words strode from his mouth with a swagger. "Sorry, I had some unexpected visitors and we lost track of the time. They were just leaving. Would you be so kind as to see them downstairs?"

Maddox watched as Candy spoke on the pay phone, one of her slender hands gripping the handset, the other winding and unwinding the cord around her index finger. She hung up and opened the glass door to the booth, smiling as she made her way to the car.

She leaned in through the driver's door window, resting her elbows in the opening. "All done."

He was getting a full frontal shot of her chest. And the whiff of perfume made him shift in the seat.

"How'd they sound about it?"

Her face turned mock serious. "Thank you, ma'am. We'll send someone right away, ma'am. You did the right thing, ma'am."

"I'd better get going then," he said, checking his watch. He reached into his coat pocket and took out a few bills. He pressed them into her palm. "Here's a little something for a taxi. You did well, doll."

She glanced down at the wad in her hand. "This is a lot more than cab fare."

"Well, you did a lot more than make a phone call."

"You know, Joe," she said, rolling the bills up and stuffing them into her bra. "It's late. After you're done here, you could... come over to my place. Get some rest. I could make you some eggs."

Maddox peered into her eyes, touched a finger against her chin. "Some other time."

She broke eye contact, ran the back of her hand under her nose like something had tickled it. "Right."

She always asked. He always gave the same answer.

Candy was sexy and more than a little pretty. But he just couldn't bring himself to do it. He liked her too much.

"Thanks for your help tonight. You're a life-saver."

"That's a laugh, coming from you. I'll always owe you."

"You don't owe me anything."

"No, I owe you everything."

He remembered how she looked the first time he saw her. She'd been walking the streets, barely legal and already selling herself. An easy collar for soliciting. She'd reached for his belt buckle like she'd done it a thousand times before, and it turned out she had. A pale and skinny kid with track marks so deep she'd started sticking her feet. She'd been turning tricks since the twenty bucks she stole off her drunken father ran out and had gotten picked up at least a couple times a week by HPD. Never booked once. A few of Houston's finest had been happy to let her keep selling her flesh and burn out on dope as long as she kept swallowing in the back of their cruisers.

Maddox was ashamed to admit he may have given into the temptation had she not looked so wretched that night he picked her up, her breath still sharp from vomiting in an alley, her eyes glazed, her hair stringy, her clothes reeking of smoke and body odors. But she did, so he loaded her in the car and instead took her to the only place he could think of, a Catholic orphanage. Told them she was fifteen. She didn't argue; they didn't question him. They dried her out and as far as he knew she'd been clean since. She never talked about it. Though once she did tell him the nuns brought in a priest who had them tie her down with long belts and handcuffs and fed her nothing but chocolate and orange juice for what seemed like a month.

But she wasn't much for religion. Now, she was what she referred to as an 'escort.' He supposed that was a hooker who charged more money and didn't shoot dope. He was a big enough man to have never asked. But he wasn't a big enough man to overlook it. He only called her when he needed something.

She kissed two finger tips and pressed them to his lips. "If you change your mind, you know where to find me."

Maddox nodded, checked his watch again, and drove the two blocks to the Waugh Street Bridge.

Most people visiting Houston for the first time didn't know the city had a bayou, let alone that it was built smack dab in the middle of one. But it did, and it was, and Maddox couldn't understand how a place that big could have what he thought was its most prominent feature overlooked in favor of TV images of ten gallon hats and cattle drives and maybe a smattering of oil wells. The Buffalo Bayou meandered right through the heart of downtown, snaking for many miles each way, a swampy river banked by oaks and willows and cypress and grasses thick with alligators and snakes and who knew what else. In 1921, a guy by the name of Waugh was the city street and water commissioner, and he built a bridge he named in honor of his son, who'd died in what was supposed to be the War to End All Wars. Several decades and a few wars later, not many people remembered Waugh or his son, but the bridge and the road bearing the family name still stood, spanning the waterway between Memorial Drive and Buffalo Drive, bayou on one side, houses and the occasional retail store on the other.

What mattered to Maddox was that it was inside the city limits and had a path to walk beneath it.

He coasted up Buffalo Drive, keeping a cautious distance and checking his watch. Sure enough, there they were, as inconspicuous as he imagined

Candy was walking though the lobby of the Rice.

They were driving a big Buick 8, light blue in color. Maddox noted the shade and shook his head. It was a habit he couldn't shake, even his mind adding 'in color' to an obvious description. The force drilled it into you. As if describing the vehicle as a 'gold Ford' would really confuse someone as to whether the car was made of solid gold. They'd parked the light-blue-in-color car on the other side of Buffalo Drive in front of a corner grocery store set back in a small parking lot, just like he'd hoped they would.

At the base of the slope, near the path that disappeared beneath the bridge, the tiny glow of a cigarette hopped up and down in the shadows. A dark figure stepped out to sneak a glimpse at Maddox's car, obviously tired of waiting. Maddox could tell it was the Dwarf. He pulled his coupe over to where they'd parked and checked his watch once more. Three minutes since Candy had made the call. Perfect. He swung the car around near the grocery store, then reached beneath the seat and retrieved the brick he'd stowed there. He heaved the brick through the front window of the store and pulled up next to the Buick. The pop of the Tokarev stung his ears, but he could still make out the distinct hiss of air, and he watched driver's side tire start to sag. Then he backed up onto Buffalo Drive and managed to wave at the scrambling figure of the Dwarf just before speeding off. He adjusted the rear-view mirror and watched the man finish scrabbling the hill and race out onto the street, waving a gun.

He could hear the sirens bearing down as he rolled up his window.

The sergeant kept his eyes roaming as they talked. He had a huge face, and the cigarette dangling from his lower lip looked dainty in front of it.

"You know, I could lose my job over this."

"Jesus, Frank—you act like this is the first time."

"Keep it down, will ya'?" He took a drag on his cigarette and nodded a greeting to a cop across the street who nodded back and kept walking to his car.

"Nobody gives a crap if you're talking to some schmo on your smoke break. Did you get it?"

The sergeant scratched at his chin, took another drag. "Maybe you didn't hear the part about me losing my job?"

Maddox shoved a hand into his pocket, trying not to roll his eyes. He pulled out a bill. It made a crinkling noise as he stuffed it into the waiting fingers behind the sergeant's clipboard, where it joined the others.

"This is all I got left," he lied.

The sergeant puffed out his cheeks and lowered his head like he was checking his blotter, ever on the job, ever diligent.

"Yeah," he said. "I got it."

He tore a piece of paper off one of the sheets, looked around, then handed it to Maddox.

"Did either of 'em say anything?"

"No. Unless you count that hubcap spouting off about the injustice of it all, and how if we didn't let him go, his lawyer was going to have our badges and all that. The Mexican didn't say a word."

"Were they armed? You guys confiscate anything?"

"Short guy had a knife in his pocket. Nothing illegal. No guns, if that's what you mean.

Maddox nodded, flicked the piece of paper. "Did they call this number?"

"No. But little man Donald was sure suspicious when I asked him for it. Told him it was a new policy, that he had to give the number for our log if he wanted to make a call. He's still waiting for someone to bring him to a phone." He shrugged, grinning. "Administrative oversight."

"Perfect."

"Eh, what do you expect at this time of night, right? I can probably hold him off another hour. Hey, speaking of phone calls, you wouldn't happen to know who dropped a thin one to make that anonymous tip, now, would you?"

"Me? Of course not."

"Didn't think so."

"You didn't happen to look up a name for this address, did you?"

"Are you kidding? You're lucky you got that. That's all the reverse directory gives. If you want a name, you have to talk to one of the gals at Ma Bell, and I'm not about to do that. That's how guys get caught."

"You're a credit to your uniform, Frank."

The sergeant dropped his cigarette and ground it out under his black patent leather shoe. "Fuck you, Joe. And *DDT*."

"What, and look like you?" he replied, spreading his hands as he backed up a few steps and turned to go. But that last jab lingered, because dropping dead was not something he wanted to worry about at the moment, let alone do it twice. He glanced down at the slip of paper in his hand as he crossed the street and stopped in midstride. He hadn't recognized the address right off the bat, but now he did.

— ❦ —

The home of Sebastian Norwood stood aloft an artificial hill overlooking two cross streets like a secular place of worship. A modern-day Parthenon, with eight marble columns and a wide set of marble steps. The parties at the Norwood Estate were legendary, and the legends they spawned numerous. There was talk of sado-masochism by lottery, of games of spin the bottle for anonymous sex between masked party-goers in the main parlor, of food being served off the bodies of naked women as they pleasured themselves with electronic devices, of special tables where disgusting bodily functions could be viewed up close while sipping champagne or cognac. Of Satanic rituals involving young girls copulating with dogs and horses. There was even talk of a snuff movie having been filmed, shown to guests (to raucous applause), then destroyed in a fire kindled by hundred-dollar bills. But it was all just talk. All anyone really knew was that there were large parties thrown by the eponymous owner, that the wealthy and powerful were invited, if they were lucky, and that what happened at the Norwood Estate, stayed at the Norwood Estate.

The public filled in the details.

Maddox chugged his coupe through the front gate and followed the drive to where it circled in front of the main house. A bow-wielding cherub spit a stream of water into a fountain in the middle, ablaze in colored lights, while two enormous lanterns brightened the entry. There were lights visible through various windows. Despite the hour, the place seemed awake. He parked behind a plain sedan, a nondescript Ford that looked even more out of place on the drive than his car.

He checked his Tokarev. One round down. He'd looked for the brass when he'd returned to the bridge, right after leaving the station, but he couldn't find it. But that was one more reason to be thankful his reloading equipment was still there. He couldn't afford the specialized ammunition otherwise, even if it weren't so hard to find.

The oversized double doors seemed suitable for a castle expecting a siege. Maddox lifted one of the gargantuan iron knockers and let it drop. Once. Twice. He waited.

The door opened a few moments later to reveal a wiry man in a smoking jacket and an ascot. His hair was white and wavy, his mustache thin and trimmed. The man's face widened in recognition of some sort, eyebrows up, jaw dropping, and he raised a martini glass as if he were about to make a toast.

"Ah! You must be the detective! Come in! Come in!"

The man stepped aside in a sweeping gesture, beckoning Maddox to enter. Maddox took off his hat and stepped inside.

"I'm sorry, but I'm a bit confused... were you expecting me?"

"Yes! Well, not exactly 'expecting' you at my front door, but your name was definitely brought to my attention! Joe, isn't it? I'm so glad you decided to pay us a visit. You're just as I pictured you!"

Maddox scratched the back of his neck, uncertain how to respond. Then it dawned on him—the Dwarf and the Mexican. They must have reported back after that run-in at Peele's place. Gave him a description, told Norwood how he was private dick, looking for the same guy.

"In that case, I guess you know why I'm here."

Norwood gave him a collegial palm on the back and led him into the house. "No idea!"

Their footfalls echoing through the cavernous foyer, Maddox got an eyeful of opulence. A staircase with an engraved balustrade depicting figures from Greek mythology spilled out to a first step wider than his living room. The dining room to his right could have seated thirty with ease, an impossibly long table of a grainy, exotic wood spanning the length of it. The sheen of a grand piano glistened in a music room to his left, where it shared space with a standing harp that must have been eight feet tall. That was a first. He wasn't sure if it was gold in color or just plain gold.

"Come," Norwood said, as if Maddox wasn't already keeping pace. "There's someone I want you to meet."

They rounded a corner, crossing in front of steps leading down to a room built for entertaining, with two crescent-shaped sofas as brightly white as a glass of fresh milk. The sofas surrounded a circular glass coffee table in the foreground, and to the left a stone fireplace sporting a hearth big enough to stand in with a mantle wide enough to sleep on comprised the far wall. A wooden cabinet phonograph between two three-foot speakers staked out one corner of the room, and the largest television console Maddox had ever seen claimed the other. The screen must have been twenty-five inches.

Norwood finally led him through a set of French doors into a library. It was a full two stories, walls of books packed side by side like vertical bricks. A huge desk fronted a bay window at the rearmost point. Glass cases and stand-alone displays were situated with such randomness Maddox figured great care must have gone into their placement. There was another fireplace breaking up the mosaic of books, though this one was not quite as grand as the first. A grown man might have had to actually stoop inside of it. Above the fireplace, an enormous aerial photo of Harris County dominated the stone, arranged like a map with typeset place names over areas. Houston in the middle, designated by large block letters, smaller names peppered around it. Pearland, Meyerland, Humble, Spring, Cypress, Jersey Village, Katy, Montrose, River Oaks. It's size and aspect carried a vague suggestion of conquest, the kind of thing one might find in a general's tented field office not far from the front.

A man sat in a high-backed leather chair in front of the empty hearth, swirling the ice in a drink. He looked over as they walked in. His face seemed to animate suddenly, as if he were stirred from a deep thought.

"Joe, here's someone I'd like you to meet. Carl? Carl, this is *Joe*."

He said the name like it meant something, something known by both parties to be highly relevant. Carl raised an eyebrow and cocked his head like he was almost impressed. He stood and took a step forward, extending a hand.

"Very pleased to meet you, Joe."

Maddox took his hand. The grip was firm, but not overly so. The man behind it was average height, but held himself tall. Young, maybe mid-twenties, with the sort of youthful, angular frame that made the gray wool of his suit coat hang loosely from his shoulders. He had long straight hair swooping across his forehead and a bit of an overbite. His mouth was large, but just enough to house a substantial set of teeth that seemed determined to have outgrown it. Peering from his sockets were the twinkling eyes of a child. A very bright child.

"You gentlemen will have to forgive me, but I have no idea what the hell is going on."

Norwood laughed and gave Maddox another slap on the back.

"Of course you don't!" To his other guest, he said, "Well, Carl... now what do you have to say?"

Carl's wide-set mouth grew wider. "I'm withholding judgment."

"Ha! I figured as much! But where the devil are my manners? What's your poison, Joe? I was thinking of opening a twelve-year old bottle of Glenlivet."

"As long as we're slumming."

Norwood paused, then bent over and swung away to let himself have a hearty laugh. "I have a feeling I'm going to like this one, Carl!"

Carl nodded, but the smile seemed a bit forced. "About that bottle, Sebastian." He raised an arm, bending his hand to display his watch. "It's getting a bit late—"

"It's never too late for that. Or too early!"

Another slap on Maddox's back. Carl offered only an amiable frown.

Maddox cleared his throat. "Look, Mr. Norwood—"

Norwood shook his head, waving a dismissive hand. "Please, Sebastian... stay and join us. I insist."

"I appreciate all the hospitality, Sebastian," Joe said, worried the conversation was veering off track. "And the fact you all are enjoying whatever sort of joke you have going on, but I have a number of questions, and frankly some answers would go down better than single malt scotch."

"Naturally! You're a detective, after all! Asking questions is what you do! I'm sure you have some for me, or us, or you wouldn't be here. Ask away! We can drink and talk! Assuming Carl doesn't spoil it by trying to sneak away early."

Carl smiled, the shape of his mouth still seeming a bit forced, and gave a small shrug of surrender.

"I must politely decline the offer of a drink," Joe said. "But I would certainly appreciate some of those answers. To start with, what do you want with Upton Peele?"

"What do I want with him? I'm afraid I don't understand the question."

"You know Peele, right?"

"Well, yes. In fact, Carl and I were just discussing something I acquired from him."

"What would that be?"

"Funny you should ask!"

Norwood turned his body like he was opening a door, gesturing with a sweep of his hand. He stepped to the other side of the room and stopped in front of a table. The table was waist-high, but small. Its sole purpose seemed to be for it to act as a pedestal for the device on it.

"It looks like a stock ticker."

"Doesn't it!"

"You got this from Peele?"

"Yes! For a pretty penny, I might add!"

"I take it this didn't come from some broker's estate sale."

"Ha! No! But you're warm!"

"Okay, I give up."

"This mysterious little device is indeed a ticker of sorts. But it doesn't give stock quotes. It makes predictions."

"Predictions? Like what stocks are headed up?"

"One could describe it that way! But, no—this gadget spits out random predictions."

"Give me a 'for instance.'"

"Well, *for instance*, about fifteen minutes before you showed up, it told us to expect you."

Maddox shot a look over to Carl, who shrugged. Same troubled smile stretching across his face.

"This is all a gag, right?"

"No, but it is fantastic, isn't it?"

"If that's the case, where the piece of paper, the ticker tape with my name on it."

"I tossed it in the fire."

"Why would you do that?"

"Because that's how it works."

"You're losing me, Sebastian."

"Apparently, you must destroy the tape immediately, or the prediction won't come true. Peele called it the 'Cassandra Parameter.'"

"Is that supposed to mean something to me?"

Carl spoke up. "It's from Greek mythology. Cassandra was granted the gift of prophecy from Apollo. But it came with the curse that no one would ever believe her predictions."

"Oh, I see."

"You don't believe it! You're just like Carl!"

To Carl, Maddox said: "How about you? Did you see the tape?"

"Unfortunately, no. But, in fairness, Sebastian did mention your name after he burned it."

"Did he, now."

"Once you destroy the tape," Norwood explained, "you're free to tell people your prediction."

"Is that so?"

"Yes."

"And what happens if you don't destroy the tape?"

"The prediction is never galvanized, and the eventuality remains swirling around, merely one of many in the free chaos of possiblities."

To Carl, Maddox said: "Did he let you try it?"

Norwood interjected. "It has to be programmed for a particular user. Calibrated, I think, was the term he used. He was unwilling to share exactly how that works, but Peele programmed it for me."

Maddox wished he could dismiss what he was hearing, but he couldn't.

"And this thing predicted I would come here?"

"In a manner of speaking. It had your name. Joe Maddox. It also said 'private detective.'"

"You're saying that's the first you ever heard my name?"

"Well, yes. If we've ever met, I certainly don't recall. Then again, I do meet a lot of people."

"I think it's more likely you heard it from the Dwarf."

"The what?"

"The Dwarf. Or maybe his sidekick, the Mexican. You know, the guys you hired to find Peele? The ones cooling their heels in the city lock up, waiting for you to come bail 'em out?"

Norwood threw his head back, guffawing. "Do you hear this, Carl? It's like right out of a movie! A dwarf? A Mexican? Skulking in the shadows, getting arrested! Did I not tell you this would be fun?"

"Are you saying you didn't hire them?"

"Hire them? My boy, I have no idea who these people even are! A dwarf? That's classic!"

"But you say Peele did sell you this contraption here?"

"Yes! Marvelous, isn't it?"

Maddox stared at the glass dome, running his eyes over the tiny brass gears and levers and wheels and ribbons inside.

"But you're not looking for him?"

"Not presently, no. But if he has more delights like this available, I surely will be!"

A stock ticker, Maddox thought. That can tell the future. Yesterday, he'd have called Norwood a lunatic. At the moment, he realized he was unable to disbelieve anything. Almost anything.

"You really think this thing can predict the future?"

"It predicted you!"

"Right. How about you, Carl? You believe it?"

"I'm afraid I would need a bit more evidence to come to that conclusion."

"Carl here's a dyed-in-the-wool skeptic. Aren't you, Carl? But what do you expect from a physicist? They only believe in things they can't see!"

"You two old friends?"

"Ha! Did you catch that, Carl! He's too sly to come out and ask what you're doing here! The indirect approach! I like it!"

"Mr. Norwood is a generous benefactor of my university. I and others in my department make it a point of stopping by whenever we're in town. He's quite gracious."

"That's Carl's way of saying I talk his ear off! But, hey, that's why I give them boatloads of money, so I can have the smartest people in the world fill me in on the latest!"

"And what's the latest?"

"Eh, you don't want to hear about that. What you're asking about seems so much more interesting!"

Carl made a face, and Norwood checked his watch. The gold of it flashed as he turned his wrist. Gold, not gold in color, Maddox thought. "If you have more questions, maybe you can keep Carl here from being the death of the party!"

"As it happens, I do. Have you ever heard of something called the Alpha Omega Protocol?"

"Oh my, but this just keeps getting better! Alpha-Omega Protocol! Next you'll be talking about microfilm!"

"I take it that's a no."

"I'm sorry. I keep forgetting you're here trying to do your job. But how delicious this sort of thing is! Delivered right into my home! Are you sure I can't interest you in some of that Glenlivet?"

"No, thanks."

"What could a drink hurt? I'm sure Mr. Peele will still be missing tomorrow!"

"From what I hear, if I don't find him, that might be true of a lot of other people, too. Permanently."

"Carl, I believe our good detective just let us know this is a matter of life and death! Isn't this fascinating?"

Maddox took the cue to address the other man. "How about you, *Carl?* You know Upton Peele?"

"I'm afraid not, detective."

"You ever hear of the Alpha Omega Protocol?"

"I, uh... no. Sorry."

"Does the date, November ninth mean anything to either of you?"

Norwood thought for a moment, then shook his head. Carl shrugged, did the same. Though he seemed to be giving it some thought.

"This has been absolutely fascinating, detective, but the hour is getting late, or early, depending on how you look at it, and since he seems determined to call it an evening as soon as I'll let him, Carl and I do have some business to discuss. Do you have many more questions, Mr. Maddox?"

"Just one. Do you have any other houseguests?"

"Houseguests? No. Servants quarters are in the back. Carl here is staying in town."

"Know any reason someone would want to call your house tonight, late?"

"No. Can't say I do. Unless they wanted to talk to my wife, of course."

"Your wife?"

"Yes, ah, here she is! Mona! Come in, my dear! Join us! The machine has done it again!"

Maddox turned to see a woman in the doorway. There was a presence about her, a quality that demanded she not be ignored. The hair framing her face was so black it seemed to be mirrored, her skin radiated from what Maddox guessed were a lifetime of lotions and mud treatments. She was draped in a diaphanous ivory gown that flowed around her in wraps, the way a mummy would look in veils.

"Joe, this is my lovely wife, Mona. Mona, Mr. Maddox here is a private detective. The machine spit his name out right before he showed up!"

Maddox dipped his head in greeting. "Mrs. Norwood."

"What brings you to our home, Mr. Maddox."

Mona's gonna be pissed.

"I'm guessing, *you* did."

She crossed her arms and leaned against the door frame. "Is that so?"

"The good detective here believes someone in our home hired a dwarf and a Mexican to follow him! Can you believe it!"

"Not to follow me. To find Upton Peele."

"How about it, Mona? Did you hire a dwarf and a Mexican to find Mr. Peele?"

Mona mouth curled at the edges, her long lashes blinking slowly.

"Of course I did," she said.

Norwood started to speak, then paused. "Well, gentlemen... there you have it!"

"May I ask you why, Mrs. Norwood?"

"I purchased something from him. Something for my husband's collection. I'm sorry, darling. It was supposed to be a surprise."

"What kind of something?"

"I'm not sure what it's called. We just referred to it as 'the Artifact.' It's an old piece of stone, a wheel with text inscribed on it and a crystal in the middle. It once belonged to a man named John Dee."

"John Dee! Outstanding! How thoughtful of you!"

"Oh, but now the surprise is ruined!" Mona said, but without conviction.

"Who's John Dee?"

"He's a famous astrologer, an occultist. Quite the historical figure. Any artifact that belonged to him would be a most prized addition to my collection."

A pause followed, no one quite sure what to say next. Carl stepped in to fill the space before anyone else could. "Sebastian, I'm sorry to disappoint, but I really must be taking my leave."

"But Carl, we're having such a fabulous time! And we still have things to discuss."

"Yes, but I have an early meeting, and I'm quite tired as it is. I must beg your pardon."

"Oh, well, wouldn't dream of keeping you up."

"We can talk tomorrow, I promise. I'll see myself out." Smiling, he added, "I'm reasonably confident I can find the way."

The two men shook hands. Carl nodded to Maddox, then gave a chaste kiss to the cheek of Mona. Maddox noticed that the man's gaze lingered a split second longer as he looked back, then he spun on his heels and departed.

"Splendid conversationalist, that young man."

"I'm sure."

"So, Joe, other than allowing you to ruin my wife's surprise and run off my guest, what exactly can I do for you?"

"If you don't mind, I have a few more questions of your wife."

Mona spoke up. "Oh, can't it wait? It really is late. Aren't you coming to bed, darling?"

"It appears she's not interested in your questions, Mr. Maddox."

"I'll make them brief. Does the term, 'Alpha-Omega Protocol' mean anything to you?"

"No. Darling? Bed?"

"Do you know of anything happening tomorrow? Something involving Peele, maybe?"

"No. Now, if you'll excuse me. Sebastian, I'm going upstairs. Please don't be long."

Maddox watched her leave, the light fabric of her gown fluttering along its many edges. When she was out of sight, Norwood placed an arm over Maddox's shoulders, tugged him to his side.

"You should have seen her back in the day. Queen of the Silent Screen. My jaw dropped the first time I saw her."

"You're a very lucky man."

"Luck? Ha! I made her mine the same way I made my many fortunes—through a sheer act of will. Willpower is the single most potent force in the universe, my boy. Don't ever doubt that. There's no hurdle that can't be overcome, no chasm that can't be cleared, if there is sufficient will to do it."

Maddox thought about that, realized he was, for the moment, living proof of that.

"Now, Joe Maddox, Private Eye, if there's nothing else..."

"One more thing." Maddox tilted his head toward the ticker. "How much did you pay for that?"

Norwood walked over to it and smiled, the proud owner. "Two hundred thousand."

"Dollars? I guess predicting something that's going to happen fifteen minutes from now is quite the conversation piece."

"My boy, I think you may have failed to grasp the full impact of what I told you. This machine doesn't just predict the future." Norwood ran a hand over the tall glass dome, staring down at it with pensive eyes. "*It makes it.*"

Maddox left the Norwood estate with more questions to chew on than answers. So, Mona Norwood had hired Mutt and Jefe. Fine. But what was that crap about Peele welching on a surprise for her hubby being the reason? And how much of a coincidence was it that she has the same name as the landlady for the queer joint Cathy had him go to?

Mona's gonna be pissed.

Not a coincidence, he decided.

He turned onto Memorial Drive and pointed his car back toward downtown. An image of the giant map over Norwood's fireplace filled his vision. It was almost mocking him, the idea that the answers were there, in the bird's-eye depiction. Somewhere, Upton Peele was hiding out, maybe parked in a remote location, maybe tucked away in a cheap motel. Somewhere, other people knew things he didn't. And it was always what you didn't know that got you killed.

Was Cathy in even more trouble than she realized? Did Mona have eyes and ears at Rosie's? That made sense. That might be how the Dwarf found him so quickly. Or did Cathy know Mona was looking for him, too? That one seemed less likely. If nothing else, she seemed to definitely want him to find her husband, and quickly. She would have mentioned something like Mona looking for him. Plus, it was Cathy.

He had a lot of other questions, his head swirling with them, when he saw the figure step tentatively into the road ahead, waving his arms. There was a car parked on the shoulder, tilting sideways down the weedy slope of grass to the drainage ditch that ran the length of the road. Maddox's first inclination was to hit the accelerator, prepared to pulverize whoever it was if there was a flash of hardware, ready to veer around him otherwise.

But then he recognized the man wincing in semi-profile from the glare of the headlights and bracing himself as if he expected to be struck.

Maddox slowed the car to a crawl, stopped a few feet away from him. The man let out a breath like he'd been holding it for quite some time, then straightened his suit coat and made his way to the driver's side window.

"I was hoping I could have a word," he said.

Maddox hummed, glanced around, then reached over and unlatched the passenger door. The man looked through the window in the direction of the passenger seat, a mental abacus all but audibly clicking in his head. Calculations complete, he rounded the car and slid in, shutting the door.

"Mine's a rental. Do you think its okay to leave it here? Like that?"

"For a while, sure." Maddox put the car in gear and drove. "Good motivation to get to the point."

"I suppose that's true."

The man was nervous, that much was obvious. He was straightening out the fabric of his slacks with his palms, having a hard time sitting still.

"What did you want to talk about, Carl?"

"I'm not sure where to begin. I'm not even sure if I should be having this conversation."

"Last I checked, I wasn't the one who flagged you down."

"It's just... a few things you said back there at the house. They bothered me."

"For instance?"

"Did you really mean it when you intimated that many lives hung in the balance?"

"Yes. I'm not sure how many, but something is going on, something weird, and I have a feeling there could be bad stuff as a result."

"Some already think of me as a traitor, you know. That should make this easier, but it doesn't."

"I'm not following."

"The Alpha-Omega Protocol. I think I know what that is."

"Tell me."

"It's a guess, mind you. But an educated one."

"Are you trying to build suspense?"

"No, no, it's just... it's hard to explain."

"Okay."

"I'm not here in Houston as a doctoral candidate from the University of Chicago. I mean, I am one, but I'm here as a consultant for NASA."

"Are you here with Thurgood?"

"You know Thurgood?"

"I've met him. But he wouldn't tell me anything."

"That doesn't surprise me. He's a company man. Anyway, we're both here as part of a site assessment team. Normally, I wouldn't have come, but the university did see the opportunity to pay a visit to Mr. Norwood, so they urged me to volunteer."

"What kind of site assessment?"

"No one knows this, but NASA is planning to construct a major new facility. A headquarters. It will serve as mission control for an enormous space effort."

"And Houston's on the list?"

Carl nodded. "Houston, southern California, Cocoa Beach, a few others. Numbers of people doing reports on various aspects. My particular role is to assess the academic environment, make sure there will be ample technical expertise to draw from in the surrounding areas." He gave the air in front of his face a back-handed swat. "It will all come down to politics, I'm sure."

Maddox shrugged. "Doesn't it always?"

"I'm starting to think so."

"So what's the Alpha-Omega Protocol?"

"You have to understand, NASA is a civilian agency, but it's very much under military control. If the Soviets weren't so far ahead of us, that might not be the case. But they are, so national security is seen as the paramount issue, more important than the exploration, more important than the science."

"And?"

"I was once in-briefed on a program about intercontinental ballistic missiles, ICBMs. NASA and the military use the same rockets. Sometimes they carry a satellite, sometimes they carry a bomb. So I was given clearance to attend an Air Force briefing. This was during testing of the Atlas rockets a couple of years ago. The first one blew up twenty-four seconds after take off. The speaker referenced the possibility a missile might malfunction in some way as to affect a major American population center. He described the national response as the initiation of an Omega Protocol."

"And what kind of response are we talking about?"

"Emergency services, evacuations, disaster aid. Damage control. Vague hints at blaming a foreign power, if possible. Talk of sabotage, that sort of thing. He acted like that would only happen if it were true, but I could read between the lines. The details, I'm sure, were for another briefing."

"Then what's an Alpha-Omega Protocol?"

"This is where I have to engage in some conjecture. I've had a bit of a falling out with the agency over a particular project. It's identified by an alpha-numeric designator."

"English, Carl."

"Project A119."

"A-one-one-nine. You think that's the 'Alpha'"?

"I wouldn't have, except for the date you gave. Then it clicked."

Maddox thought about that. November ninth. Eleven-nine. One-one-nine.

"What is Project A119?"

Carl let a long breath escape through tight lips.

"The Pentagon wants to explode a ten to twenty kiloton nuclear device for all the world to see with the naked eye, on the grandest stage imaginable..."

He paused, waiting for Maddox to look him in the eye.

"The surface of the Moon."

"You're kidding."

"I wish I were."

"And you're sure of this?"

Carl nodded. "I was hired to accomplish some mathematical modeling on the kinetics of the resulting dust cloud, assess the visibility of it from Earth."

"And they actually plan to do this?"

"I don't know. I've been eased off the project. It seems a few of what you might call the brass didn't like my objections. And I may have casually referenced it when I applied for a graduate fellowship." He turned up his palms and shrugged. "Oops."

"You tried to blow the whistle."

"No. I tried to make them think twice by letting some ambiguous information float out that was bound to get back to them. They told me they were scrapping it, reassigned me. But I have no reason to believe they aren't moving forward. Insane as it is."

"If they do, do you think that could result in a catastrophe? Like, hundreds of thousands of Americans dead?"

"Who knows? We are in entirely uncharted waters. Our track record of successful missile launches hasn't exactly been stellar. No pun intended. And predicting the effect of an explosion of that size on the surface of a body like the Moon's... it's hard to say what might happen."

"Can you help me stop it?"

"Is this where I'm supposed to ask if *you're* serious? I could face federal charges simply for telling you. I signed an oath of loyalty and secrecy. We're talking about national defense issues the government takes very, very seriously."

Maddox said nothing.

"What's your interest in this? How did you even come to know about any of it?"

"Someone hired me to find Upton Peele. That someone is convinced a lot of people might die if I don't."

"Does this have something to do with that crystal ball device Norwood was so excited about?"

"Maybe."

"Well, I wish you luck. Believe me, if I knew how to stop it without becoming an enemy of the state, I would. But here's the thing—if we don't do it, chances are the Russians will."

"Does that justify it?"

"I don't know. Do you?"

Maddox pulled up next to the rental car they'd left on the side of Memorial. Carl opened the passenger door. The interior light popped on.

"Thanks for the info, Carl."

"I'm sorry I couldn't be more help. For what it's worth, I'll be doing my part from within to discourage them from going forward. Unfortunately, their official position is, there is no Project A119 anymore."

The man held his hand out. Maddox shook it.

"If you're ever in Chicago, come to the university and look me up. I'm in the department of astronomy and astrophysics."

"Assuming I'm not a statistic before then."

"Yes, assuming that neither of us is."

"Okay. Should I just ask for Carl?"

Carl smiled broadly. "That might be enough, but if not, by next summer you should be able to ask for me by a new title—Dr. Sagan."

Maddox headed in the direction of Rosie's, reserving the right to pass it by and head to his apartment. It was late, bordering on early, and he was starting to feel fatigue set in.

No, he thought. *This is Cathy. I owe it to her to let her know what I found out.* Besides, she was the one person who might be able to shed some more light on what was going on. Maybe the information would jar loose some more insight.

He expected the small unpaved lot to be all but empty, but there were a few cars still near the front. Pam was not at the door, so Maddox parked and crossed the gravel toward the entrance, too tired to park around the corner.

The first thing he noticed was the lights were out. The small lamp over the door sign had been on, but inside the place was dark. Maddox waited to let his eyes adjust, but the light from the doorway barely penetrated. He groped the wall for a switch.

Oh. Shit.

The bodies jumped into view like a trick of light. But they were still there after he blinked and rubbed his eyes.

Pam was on the floor, legs sprawled, head and shoulders against the bar. She had slid down to where most of her was flat, like she'd been sitting up and melted until her chin was on her chest. Her eyelids were slits, barely open, and she stared cross-eyed off to the side. A flap of scalp hung from the wet, red exit wound on her crown. Chunks of her were splattered on the wood above her head.

A revolver lay loosely in her limp palm.

Across from her, face down, was a larger, older woman. It took him a second, but Maddox placed her as the bar matron. She was lying in a smear of blood. Another streak of it near her hand.

Two dead women. Three cars.

He drew his Tokarev, almost as an after thought. Stepping gingerly to avoid any blood, he circled the bodies and made his way to the back. Her burst through a door, fanning the muzzle of his pistol back and forth. Then he flipped a light switch. A stock room, with crates and boxes, bottles of booze and a few kegs. A large sink with exposed plumbing. Off to the side, a bathroom. A utility closet next to it. Empty, all.

Cathy.

He rushed back toward the front of the bar and looked out into the lot. Three cars. Two dead women. An old Chevy. A beat-up Fairlane. And a Cadillac.

Cathy.

Maddox stepped back inside, thinking. Peele? Did he come here for Cathy? He imagined a confrontation, the two women coming to Cathy's aid. Peele using his .45.

But that didn't work. This was too organized. Too staged. He reimagined Peele coming in, his Colt .45 stabbing Pam in the back, her snubnose in his other hand. He'd waited outside, watching for Cathy, waited until he wasn't willing to wait anymore. Pointing the gun at the bar matron's head. Ordering her to keep her hands where he could see them, to come around from behind the bar. Cathy pleading for him to stop, that she'd go with him, do anything. Maybe the barkeep tried to grab his gun as she got close, and he shot her. Before she hit the floor, he wedges his Colt in his belt and grabs Pam, shoves her down against the bar, jamming her own revolver in her mouth and pulling the trigger, all in one motion. Sticks the gun in her hand, then draws his own again. Cathy hysterical, screaming.

It would never fool the cops. But that wasn't his goal. Buying time was. And the initial impression would certainly do that. Days, at least.

Maddox stood there, surveying the bodies. Maybe, he thought. Maybe. And if it were the case, that meant Peele had Cathy.

He moved a step closer, staring. He contemplated running his hand down over Pam's eyelids, then thought better of it. Guilt made his gut feel heavy. The woman had likely had a rough life. Teasing in school, constant awareness of not fitting in. Daily looks of disdain from people she'd never even spoken with. Enduring the sort of cracks he had made to her. It all seemed so petty now.

He crossed over the bodies and knelt next to her, trying to follow her line of sight. Nothing. Just floor. He started to stand again when he saw the blood near the other woman's hand. From this angle, he realized there was more of it under her hair, and it wasn't random. It was writing. Letters. Rough, shaky, smeared like finger paint, but legible. C-Y-P-R. A swipe of blood after the last.

... he asked whether he could take me with him to what he called Sanctuary. He mentioned it was in Cyprus...

It didn't make sense. If Peele had snatched Cathy, why would he take her to a place considered a Sanctuary? For her own protection? Would someone so anxious to save her kill two innocent people to do it?

The whole thing was making his head hurt. He was running on adrenaline now, wired and jittery, his brain needing sleep. He rubbed his eyes, found himself absently gazing at the giant map of Southeast Texas on the wall opposite the bar. He'd done the same thing at Norwood's place. It was just a map. Little cutouts of cowgirls from Life Magazine and some cheesecake from dirty mags pasted here and there. All the paste-ons were scantily clad women with a hint of lesbianism to them, if only because of the way they were presented.

Except for one.

A bird. A parrot. Pasted over a spot northwest of Houston. Beneath it, in small block letters cut from the same source were the words, Norwood Bird Sanctuary. The tiny town's name on the map was just above it.

Cypress.

No sooner did he see the word than a telephone rang from behind the bar.

He knew it was for him.

Finding the bird sanctuary wasn't easy.

The first place he went was back to Peele's house. He parked directly in front of it this time. The door was still unlocked, the light in the study still on. He rummaged through the trash next to the desk, pulling out the newspaper cutting. It wasn't a coupon, it was the back of the article. Norwood had acquired a few acres in the rural area of Cypress. He was dedicating it to the care and protection of exotic birds, a cause he attributed to his wife, Mona. The paper didn't give an address, but it was described as an inactive gravel pit, shut down due to the insolvency of the mining company. The article noted the acreage was located directly off Hempstead Highway.

Little over an hour later, he found it.

Hempstead Highway was a lonely plow of road populated with an occasional gas station, intermittent stretches of farmland, and dense woods. The glowing eyes of longhorn peering from behind barbed wire. Maddox's headlights forged through the darkness, cloud cover making sure there weren't even any stars visible. The treeline in and around Cypress was especially thick in most places. Every dirt road was a possibility, just as every one seemed too much of a gamble to try.

But then a break in the clouds passed nearby and bit of moon glow illuminated the sky just enough to silhouette a tower ahead, off to the right. The trees cleared and a wide dirt road curved in that direction. Maddox slowed and followed it.

The car bounced on the rough terrain, rocks pinged off the undercarriage and jangled through the wheel wells.

The terrain opened into a flat circle, surrounded by a range of mounds. Maddox's headlights flashed off some heavy equipment. A steam shovel. A large conveyor belt of some sort leading up to a tall silo shaped like a giant funnel.

Behind all of it, a long trailer sat at the edge of one of the mounds. Wooden stairs led to a platform in front of the door. A light was visible through one of the windows.

Maddox lit a cigarette, took a deep drag, then held his breath. This was it. He replayed the phone call several times in his head. There was little margin for error.

Snuffing out the cigarette, he exhaled a fog of smoke before getting out and heading toward the trailer. Gravel crunched with each step. His footfalls seemed extra loud on the wood of the decking.

He gave three knocks. A few seconds stretched out. Then the door opened, and he was forced to step back as the Dwarf shoved a pistol toward his chest and walked out.

"Was wondering when you were gonna show up."

The Mexican stepped out behind him. Not quite smiling, but there was an unmistakable sense of business-like satisfaction to the set of his jaw.

Maddox raised his hands shoulder high, palms out. The Mexican shut the door.

"I see you got your gun back. Must've had to scramble to hide it when you heard the sirens bearing down. Your lucky nobody pinched it while you were in the tank."

"Turn around."

"I'm not armed."

The Dwarf huffed like he was trying not to laugh, then reached his free hand to pat Maddox around the waist and under the arms. Maddox spun slowly as he did, stopping when he came full circle.

The Dwarf gestured down the steps with the pistol. "Walk."

Maddox stepped down, began walking.

"Where are we headed?"

"Shut up. Keep going straight."

The answer didn't matter, since he already knew. Ahead of them loomed the dark outline of the conveyor belt.

A short metal ladder hung down from its lowest point, almost twenty feet off the ground. The belt disappeared into a loading bay at that spot, a place where trucks could be loaded, or unloaded, Maddox wasn't sure. On the wall a few feet from the ladder, a large lever protruded at an upward angle, next to that a key stuck out of an ignition switch. The Mexican picked up his pace as they drew near and moved ahead of them. He climbed the ladder and hoisted himself onto one of the large trays.

He drew a pistol from beneath his jacket and let it point down in Maddox's direction.

The Dwarf stabbed the gun toward Maddox. "Up."

Maddox tilted his head back and waved at the Mexican. "Just one question. Who was it outside Rosie's? Pretending to be Peele?"

"That was me," said the Mexican, raising his voice. He spoke with only the barest trace of an accent. Maddox had a flash of understanding. A kid growing up on the east side, learning how quick people were to assume his English would be broken or foreign sounding.

"Nice," Maddox said.

"Quit stalling," said the Dwarf."

"You know something, Donald?" Maddox said, still looking up.

He heard the sound of the revolver cocking.

"Someone once said," he continued, "fool me once, shame on me."

Maddox walked over to the ignition, turned the key, and tugged down on the lever. The huge machine shuddered and jolted, then chugged to life. The Mexican dropped into an awkward crouch, hands spread, trying to keep his balance

The repeated clicking of the revolver's hammer dropping was drowned out by the belt drive. The Dwarf looked at his gun as if it were something that had suddenly appeared in his hand. Maddox took two lunging steps and slugged him in the face. He landed a solid kick to the gut before the little man hit the ground. He kicked him once, twice, three more times, for good measure.

"Remember that reloading equipment you knocked over when you tossed my place? While you were in the clink waiting for your phone call, I removed the gunpowder from each round, tapped out the firing cap. Then I put the guns back under the bridge where you'd hid them, jackass."

Sounds of the motorized belt thrumming the air, Maddox walked back to his car and retrieved his Tokarev from beneath his front seat. The Dwarf was on his knees, propped with one hand, when he looked up. Maddox shot him twice in the face.

"Sorry, Donald."

The Mexican was barely visible now, high on the conveyor belt, still ascending, looking shaky on all fours, staring down and tossing glances haphazardly, searching for an idea.

Maddox pushed the lever back past neutral until it was almost parallel to the wall. The engine moaned and the belt lurched before reversing course. Pistol tucked in his belt, Maddox climbed the ladder, stopping near the top.

The Mexican lifted his .45 and pulled the trigger several times.

Maddox pulled his own piece, waited for the Mexican to draw closer, then fired twice. Both shots hit, one on the shoulder, the other the top of the head. The man's body slumped onto the tray. He was still moving, a twitch here, a blink there. But he wasn't a threat.

The engine sputtered for just a second when Maddox turned off the ignition. He checked his Tokarev again, did a quick mental calculation, then headed toward the trailer.

He didn't knock. The door swung in and he entered, his gun in front of him. Mona sat rigid on a small sofa, stiffening as she saw him.

"Oh, shit," she said.

"Spare me the fake surprise."

"So," Mona said. "What happens now? Do you shoot me? Kill an unarmed woman?"

Maddox glanced around the trailer. It was narrow but uncluttered. Kitchen fixtures and cabinets had been removed or never installed. Beyond the couch, there was a small table at the far end with four chairs. A few dark bottles were scattered here and there. Behind him, an open door led to another small room with a table; documents, maybe blueprints, were spread out over it. Just before the room, a closed door to the side, the space it connected framed out from the wall. A bathroom, he guessed.

"A woman like you is never unarmed. Not as long as you got a head on your shoulders."

"Obviously, I have money. We can make a deal. I'm a practical woman."

Maddox backed up toward the other side of the trailer, gun still trained on Mona. He stopped at the doorway and leaned back to take a look. Empty.

He stood in front of the door to the bathroom, eyeing it. "I'd prefer answers to greenbacks."

"That's reasonable." She patted the couch next to her. "Why don't you have a seat, quit waving that gun around."

"I prefer to stand, thank you. But maybe our friend would like to take a load off."

He stepped to the side, pointing his pistol toward the door.

"You can come out now," he said, raising his voice. "Toss the piece out first. If we both start shooting, my money's on me."

A few beats passed, then the door opened, partially blocking his view. A small black revolver clattered to the floor. Cathy stepped out to where he could see her.

"Shit," she said. "Shit, shit, shit."

Maddox shook his head. "Up until the last second, I was really hoping..."

She shrugged. Maddox gestured with his pistol for her to join Mona. She stepped past the revolver and sat on the couch. Maddox kicked the gun into the bathroom and shut the door.

"Now, would it be a terrible inconvenience for someone to explain to me what the hell is going on?"

The two women stared at him, then glanced at each other, but said nothing.

"Okay," he said. "I'll start. You made this whole thing up to send me on a snipe hunt, setting me up to take the fall. Why?"

"You wouldn't understand."

"For a guy who isn't supposed to understand anything, I'm sure racking up points in the win column."

"All you've done is complicate things."

"Oh, is that what I've done? Let's *uncomplicate* them, then. You called me in to be your patsy, fed me some bullshit story about your hubby, pretended you were afraid for your life, all so I would spend the night looking for him. There's only one reason I can think of for that. It's because he's already dead."

Cathy inhaled audibly. Mona stared at her hands in her lap, watching one fingernail scrape against another.

"He's dead, and you wanted the cops to pin it on me. Or on my dead body, as it were. I've been asking questions about him all over town, so the trail would be easy. Open and shut. My body found next to his, is that it? Gun that shot me in his hand? Gun that killed him in mine? Something like that? Or no, scratch that. My body disappears. Cops think I'm on the lam."

"Why ask?" Cathy said. "You seem to think you have it all figured out."

"Not all. Not yet. You were up to something. Both of you. You just needed a fall guy. But then something went wrong, didn't it?"

Mona shifted in her seat, looking bored. Cathy stared at him, mustering hate. He figured she was good at that.

Maddox unbuttoned his shirt with his free hand, reached down and pulled out a medallion. "You realized you didn't have this."

Now the women reacted. Mona jerked to the edge of the couch, barely seated. Cathy's mouth opened.

"You found it," Cathy said.

"Not exactly. But that's not important. What is important is that you didn't. You thought Peele had it. But he didn't. No, he was too cautious for that. He sent it to me instead."

"He what?"

"This charming accessory showed up on my doorstep less than an hour before you called. There was a note attached. It said, 'Please wear this.' It also said, 'Do not remove it under any circumstances.' I had no idea who it was from."

"But...?"

"I probably would have tucked it in a drawer. But then my phone rang."

"I thought Marge simply gave you my message."

"That wasn't who called. This message was much, much more interesting. It was a call from me."

Cathy's eyes saucered. Mona look confused.

"You mean?"

"I was dead, and I was calling myself."

"It can't be..."

"Well, it was. I had quite an interesting conversation with Dead Me. Several, during the course of the evening. The conversations were short, only twenty seconds or so. That was all the juice I guess he could muster. He/I didn't know a lot. Except that Dead Me had to guide living me in the right direction without changing what happened, and without telling me any details about the future. Dead Me called it a—"

"Paradox."

"Yes. A paradox. First call, Dead Me said, 'Wear the artifact and go meet Cathy. Keep your cool and listen to what she has to say.' When I asked who the hell I was talking to, he said, 'I'm you. I'm dead. Do what I say and maybe we can change that. It's in both our interests.' Of course, I thought it was a joke at first, and a lame one at that. Then I got your message and things started getting real weird, real quick."

Cathy blinked, her gaze bouncing from Maddox to Mona. "Has this ever happened before?"

Mona said nothing, her eyes searching the floor.

"Now, I think it's time for you ladies to explain a few things to me. Like, why did you kill Peele?"

"He... he was going to stop it."

"Stop what?"

"The Project."

"The space mission? Alpha 119?"

"Yes."

Maddox started to speak again, but paused, thinking. "Because it was going to result in a disaster."

Cathy said nothing.

"He wanted to stop it because the missile was going to malfunction and explode."

Cathy shook her head. "No, the missile will work."

"But why——" Maddox felt a chill of understanding tingle down his neck. "It was going to work too well. An H-bomb explosion, on the Moon. An explosion meant to be so big, everyone on the planet could see it. The U.S. of A detonating a bomb on the Moon. Only, the generals and admirals and politicos in charge wouldn't be able to leave anything to chance, would they? They'd make sure it was big enough, bright enough. And what? It showers radiation down on us?"

Cathy sneered, her voice almost a hiss. "Worse."

Maddox thought about that. "It actually blows it up?"

"Yes. Well, a portion of it. A sizable section will break free."

"And come crashing down to Earth."

"An avalanche of meteors, one especially large."

"Destroying Houston."

Cathy said nothing.

"Why, Cat? Why would you want that to happen?"

"Do you know what this country, your beloved USA, did to my father?"

Cathy's eyes flashed. "This so-called *free country*? It hounded him to an early grave. All because he favored a different political system. Favored *equality*."

"You mean to tell me you're working for the Russians?"

"Ha! The Soviets? If there's any country more hypocritical than this one, it's the Soviet Union. Who do you think tipped the government off to my father's activities? Because he refused to act as a courier for their little spy games. And because he tried to protect me."

"I don't understand."

"My father wanted me to be a fellow traveler, nothing more. Some of his associates had other designs. They trained me to be an agent provacateur. To infiltrate. To develop a network. To use my... assets. I thought I could make a difference. My father was furious when he found out."

"Agent provacateur. You mean, they encouraged you to have sex with men and women. To manipulate them. I guess you started with me."

"Started with you? Joe, you are so naïve. You were probably the twentieth guy I was with."

Maddox let that sink in, his brain adjusting to the new information. He imagined Cathy at sixteen, deciding he was a suitable candidate. A loser. A guy who wouldn't feel entitled to sex, who would feel a bond, a debt. An emotional marker to be called in later.

"So, you *are* working for them."

"Too hell with them. The day they hung my father out to dry was the day I realized they were no different. A bunch of men giddy with power hiding behind Potemkin Villages and believing their own bullshit."

"And Project Alpha?"

"Will bring the whole damn system down," she said, her eyes narrowing. "All of it. Once nuclear bombs are seen for what they are, the entire justification crumbles. You think Houston's the only city that will get hit? Chunks will land all over the globe. This will bring the world to the brink of war, and the outcry to stop all the insanity will be overwhelming. Without bombs, the Soviets are just a bunch of drunk peasants. And once forced to demilitarize, the Americans will have no choice but to face up to what a horrible, unfair society this is. I want to see all of them pay."

"And how many people have to die for this fantasy of yours, Cathy?"

Cathy snorted and looked away, her upper lip curling in disgust.

"You don't get it do you?" he said. "Nothing ever goes according to plan. Not on that scale. You can't control the world."

"Oh, no? What do you think the New Century Corporation has been doing for the last fifty years?"

"That's enough!"

Mona leaped from the couch, a hand swung toward Cathy, warning her.

"New Century Corporation, huh? You're saying they're the ones behind all this?"

"Leave, Mr. Maddox. Leave, or you're going to have to kill me. Something tells me you've had enough killing for one day."

To Mona, he said: "They're the ones who were funding Peele. The ones who bought that house he and his *wife* here lived in. Then Peele stole their little gadget, sold it to your hubby. I bet he thought that was poetic. He was going to blow the lid, then use that money to disappear. But I'll bet that gadget's just a parlor trick compared to what you have now. Technology, it keeps advancing doesn't it? From ticker tapes to something much more impressive. What are you using now, Mrs. Norwood? Radio waves? What are you using to communicate with the other side? To predict the future? To make it?"

Mona said nothing. But Maddox could tell from the hardening of her expression that she was about to make a move.

"Okay," he said. "We'll play it your way. I'm going. Let the chips fall where they may."

"Leave the medallion. It's not yours."

"It's not yours, either. Belonged to a guy named Dee, as I understand it. No, I think I'll be taking this."

Mona lunged for him, screaming out like an Indian brave, but it was telegraphed. His left hand was already in a fist, and he landed a stiff punch right on the tip of her jaw. She dropped to the floor in a heap, unfolding onto her back, head lolling.

Cathy didn't move. Maddox raised the pistol toward her, eyes tightening.

"You never overheard Upton at all, did you? He overheard *you*." He paused, sensing the pieces flowing into place. Some of them. "You 'infiltrated,' just like you were trained to. He was a fairy, wasn't he? You offered to be his, what do they call it? Beard? Nice arrangement. Money, big fancy house. Husband who didn't care how or where you got your jollies. You worked your way into things. Learned about their gadgets. About how the future can be not only predicted, but *made*. You made all the right contacts. The poor guy was just doing what I'm going to guess was his job, trying to avert a catastrophe. And you used Mona here to muck it all up, kill him. You convinced her... what? That she would get all her husband's money? The two of you would run off to live happily ever after? But I'm still missing something. Why is she so protective of New Century Corp, Cathy? What else is going on?"

Cathy swallowed hard. Her eyes were rattling from the intensity of her gaze. Welling up with fury.

"I'd shoot you, but something tells me that would be doing you a favor. To think, I once sat shivering in some God-forsaken hellhole hoping to survive one more day, just one more, then another, then another, dreaming the whole time about getting back home and making you my girl. Little did I realize, you're not even human."

He backed out of the trailer onto the deck. She disappeared from view as he shut the door and walked deliberately toward his car. He sat behind the wheel for a moment before inserting the key into the ignition. The windows of the trailer flashed and a loud, muffled pop snapped in his ears.

He closed his eyes, then started the car and drove away.

The recorder stopped dead when Blake rammed two fingers down on one of the buttons like he wanted to hurt it. He wiped a finger from one side to the other beneath his eye patch then inspected it before shaking his head and grunting.

"That has got to be the biggest load of horse shit I've ever heard someone shovel in my entire life."

Wheeler and Corn murmured like they were preparing to crack wise, but Blake shot them a warning look, and they settled down.

"I take it you don't want me to finish?"

"You don't get it. We have three bodies, all tied to you. You just confessed to three more, out in Cypress, admitting that you killed two of them. You think you're clever, but your story means you're either a certifiable nut-case or you're trying to set up some insanity defense."

"At least you didn't use the word *lunatic.*"

"I always thought you were too smart for your own good. Now I realize you were just too stupid."

"I'm telling you the truth."

"You don't say. In that case, where's this magical medallion everyone is dying over?"

"I threw it into Buffalo Bayou."

"How convenient. Where?"

"I don't remember. Somewhere along Memorial Drive. There's a lot of bayou. So many stretches look the same."

"And what about Peele? You're saying his body just happened to show up in your closet?"

"That's where I found him. They put him there to pin it all on me. I'm the one who phoned it in, remember?"

"If balls were brains, you would be working with those NASA folks you weaved into your tale, you know that?"

"It's not like it's a big stretch. It would have looked like I killed him then took off in a panic. My body would have disappeared into the gravel pits. Nobody'd have found me for a long time."

"Except you were wearing the magic necklace, so you were able to call yourself from the future, from beyond the grave."

Chuckles from Wheeler and Corn. Blake didn't discourage it.

"Something like that."

"You know, I would think you could have come up with something better, given how long you waited to report any of this. It's not like you didn't have enough time. What were you doing all day, destroying all the evidence from last night? Hiding more bodies?"

"I went and got some sleep, for one. Then I wrote a couple of letters."

Blake shifted in his chair. "Letters."

"Yeah. One to a lawyer in Dallas. The other to the head of NASA."

"You really are crazy."

"Maybe. But the letter I mailed to that lawyer had a pair of hundred dollar bills with it. It requires that I check in next week, or else he starts doing whatever lawyers do when their client disappears after providing details of a conspiracy. I made it a point to say I would be calling the sheriff's department right after I sent it. I even mentioned you by name."

"Did you, now?"

"Yes. And the letter to NASA detailed what I knew about Project A119. Hopefully, the fact the information is out there, the prospect the Russians might already know about it, too, will make them reconsider going forward."

"You are mad as a hatter, son. But it ain't gonna save you. The only thing left to decide is whether I take care of you myself, or let you spin your fantasy to a judge."

"Salvation may not be part of the deal, but you're going to let me go anyway."

Blake let out a laugh, but the flesh around his eye tensed up just the same. "And why would I do that?"

"Because crazy as it sounds, you know I'm telling the truth, even if you don't believe all of it. And you know you can't afford to have a multiple-homicide investigation that drags Mona Norwood into it without feeling the heat. If I disappear, that lawyer will make sure the US attorney and every media outlet around get a copy of the letter. Plus, you already know the better play. There are other people who'll want to keep this quiet. Other important people."

Blake said nothing. His lone eye shifted from one side of Maddox's gaze to the other.

"Just think about it," Maddox said. "Think about how much money it would involve, money flowing into this county. *Your* county. How much influence an official who delivered a deal like that could wield. How many chits he'd collect. How many people would be beholden to him. All the accolades he'd receive."

Blake lifted his Stetson and combed his fingers through the thin strands of hair still left on his scalp. He leaned his head back and stared at the bulb overhead.

Wheeler chimed in. "Let us take care of him, Captain. He's full of shit. Playing you for a chump."

Blake said nothing for a long moment, continuing to stare in the direction of the bulb.

"A site assessment, you said?"

Wheeler started to say something again, but Blake cut him off with a sharp thrust of his palm.

Maddox resisted the urge to smile. "Yes."

"And the guy's name was what? Norman Thurgood? Rice Hotel?"

"Yes. You can check it out, but there's no need. You know I'm telling the truth. It's why you kicked me off the force, isn't it? This lack of discretion I have when it comes to the truth?"

"You arrogant son of a bitch. You expect you'll just walk out of here and go about your life, business as usual?"

"No. I expect I'll walk out of here and leave town. Get as far away as possible, and you'll never hear from me again. You can name me a possible witness, but as long as I'm not around and that lawyer doesn't go public, you can shape the investigation anyway you want to. There would be some very grateful officials in high places. Especially when the only person relating to them how bad it could be, and how much you are doing to help them, will be you."

Wheeler cleared his throat. "Captain—"

"Shut up."

Maddox held Blake's gaze like he'd just gone all in on a poker hand. Which, he realized, he had.

"You leave straight from here, out of Harris County."

"One stop."

"No. You can't go back to your apartment, can't collect your stuff. We escort you out of the jurisdiction and dump you."

"I'm not going back to my apartment. I've already packed. You have to take my word. Nobody follows me. You know I have no reason not to leave. Where I go has nothing to do with your case and won't affect anything you want to do. You won't hear a peep from me or that lawyer. Thirty minutes from the time I leave this building, I'm across the county line and on my way out of the state for good."

Blake sucked in a breath and hit a button on the tape recorder. The wheels started racing rapidly in reverse. He watched them spin for a long moment.

"You'd better be," he said, finally.

***

"I still can't believe it!"

Maddox smiled at the enthusiasm in her voice and adjusted the rearview mirror.

"I'm serious! This is like a dream! I mean, should I ask you to pinch me or something?"

"Can't it wait till we get a little farther down the road? I thought I pinched you good a few times last night."

Candy dropped her jaw a bit and punched his shoulder, but quickly wrapped her arms around his near one and pressed her cheek against it.

"I love you, Joe. Really."

"Me, too, kid."

"Honest?"

"I'm taking you to California with me, aren't I?"

Candy scrunched her nose as she smiled and pressed her cheek against his shoulder again.

"A surf shop," she said. "This is so exciting! I've never even seen the Pacific Ocean. Is it like the Gulf?"

"Yeah. Only more so."

She patted her purse. "Everything I have saved is in an envelope in here. It's almost five hundred dollars. Do you think it'll be enough?"

"I have my stash, and there's a loan waiting for us when we get there. We'll make do," he said.

The answer pleased her enough that she squeezed his arm again. He felt her weight settle against him.

"You promised you'd tell me what happened on the drive," she said, fingering the medallion around her neck.

"And I will, but right now, I just want to put some real estate between us and the guys with badges. Then, we have to make a stop down south before mapping a route to LA."

"Where?"

"A little place near the Rio Grande, just this side of the border. That's where I'm going to bury that unusual piece of jewelry there around your neck."

"Why there?"

"Let's just say I got a phone call," he said. He checked the rearview one more time, adjusting it. No one seemed to be creeping behind him. Nothing seemed to be following.

"Whatever you say, my handsome man of mystery. Oh, this is exciting, though, isn't it?"

Maddox placed his hand on her leg and she scooted closer to him. He scanned the horizon for the moon, found it lurking off to one side, a bright, white sickle.

"It sure is," he said. He stepped down on the gas and accelerated into the future, determined to make it, or at least part of it, his own.

Haunter

She would not be easy to find, but Matthew knew she was in there. Somewhere deep. Somewhere hidden. But definitely there.

And now, for word on a developing situation in Cobb County, Georgia, we're joined by Jane Riley from our Atlanta affiliate, where she has been following events and is live on-scene. Jane?

The plantation-style house loomed large before him as he made his way down the hillside path. Its white clapboard façade, double portico porch, pitched-roof dormer, and fanlight entryway were exactly as he had envisioned them. The structure looked very old, almost part of the natural landscape. Very old, but recently built.

Just as he'd expected. Just as he'd told himself it would be.

Thanks, Ted. Years ago, a quiet, residential community, similar to the one whose homes line the street behind me now, was stunned by the bizarre slayings of two of its residents…

Matthew heard his own reassuring voice, a running narrative instructing him, giving him directions, telling him to remain relaxed, that he was in control, that there was no reason to be afraid. He was safe in these surroundings. They were his creation; familiar, comforting, known to him. He took a moment to study the features of the house, to concentrate on its details. Details meant focus. Focus was the key to success. Focus was always the key to success.

The edifice was precisely as he'd envisioned it. The roof's split-wood shingles cascaded uniformly in valleys that straddled the dormers. The two-story portico rose high beneath the majestic pediment, protruding forward on columns set one atop another, Ionic over Doric, separated by a balcony. Nine-over-nine double-hung sash windows stared outward, unblinking eyes cocked sideways between louvered-shutter lids.

Everything was just as it was supposed to be.

Matthew walked forward and stepped onto the porch. Glass sidelights with lead dividers separated pairs of colonettes, framing an exquisite set of field-paneled double doors beneath the arching fanlight. He hesitated as he reached for the door handle, his disembodied voice telling him to be calm. Breathing deeply, he listened to it. This was why he came, it said. To go inside, to find her. This is where she would be.

The door opened as he touched it, swinging inward, revealing the foyer and beckoning him across the threshold. Vague light from uncertain sources illuminated dark walls and darker floors. Just past the entryway, a huge staircase wound upward to the second floor, carpeted in red with scrolled face-string paneling and ornately carved balusters. To his right was an open dining room, simply but tastefully furnished. To his left, a library. The books in the library were aligned in tight rows from floor to ceiling, packed around a marble-faced fireplace with a mahogany mantle and Doric pilasters.

When police arrived at the Chambers' home in response to a domestic disturbance complaint, they found twenty-six-year-old Melody Chambers sprawled on her living room floor, the apparent victim of a strangulation. The autopsy would reveal her hyoid bone had been crushed, but police didn't need a medical examiner to tell them she had been, in the responding officers' words, throttled. The imprint of her killer's hands was still clearly visible on her tender throat…

Ignore the upstairs, Matthew told himself. He needed to descend deep, to travel far into the recesses of the house, the house he had so painstakingly designed, the house he had built piece-by-piece for this very purpose. That's where she would be—deep deep deep, pressed back into some distant crevice, dug in like a tick. He took a moment to take in his surroundings, to smell the leather of the library, to feel the wood of the floor beneath him. Only after immersing himself in the details of the place, testing the reality of it, did he continue forward. With calm, measured breaths and steady steps, he moved past the staircase, looking for the opening to the basement.

She had been making her presence known to him for some time now. Sleep was her invitation, her opening. She insinuated herself into his dreams like a virus. More of the computer variety than the biological kind, a piece of malware bent on shutting down his operating system. If he was dreaming of making love to his wife, he might feel a tap on his shoulder, then turn to see her standing there, mere inches away, that rictus smile on her face, baring jagged teeth. If the dream was the product of generalized stress, the type where he'd find himself all but naked as he rushed to meet a crucial deadline, she would pop out of nowhere, taunting him, laughing at him, warning him that eventually there would come a dream from which he would never wake up, because it wouldn't be a dream at all.

Sometimes, he didn't even need to be asleep.

It would start with that voice. Cloyingly sweet, a cocktail of seduction and spite, calling his name. Then, once it got his attention, not sweet at all, just shrill and abrasive as it grated against his brain, vocal fingernails on a chalkboard. He might be in a meeting, discussing the latest marketing campaign. Or in an elevator, surrounded by co-workers. "*Matthew,*" would come the scrape. "*Maaaaaath-yew.*" No one else ever seemed to hear it. Everyone seemed to notice that he did.

But the dreams were even worse. He often woke in a start, bolting upright in bed, his t-shirt damp and clinging, her lingering presence so real, so tangible. He could smell her, taste her. Feel her.

The rude awakenings, the panic-attacks in the middle of the night, the exhaustion that defined so many days that followed so many restless nights—those things were bad enough. Lately, however, he had begun to wake up having left his bed.

The sleepwalking seemed almost planned, controlled, and if that were the case, Matthew knew she was more powerful than before, that she would have to be dealt with, and dealt with without delay. The evidence was impossible to ignore. A week earlier he awoke in the kitchen, having grabbed a knife as she leapt toward him, her eyes blazing, her jaws set wide, her wiry body springing like a leopard. But when consciousness hit him, jolting through him like electricity, the knife in his hand was poised at his own throat, its point depressing the flesh near his jugular. This last time, rather than fending off an attack, he found himself standing beside his bed wielding a large hammer, his arm cocked high above his head, ready to bring the head of it down on the skull of his sleeping wife.

She was building up to something. Something bad.

What police found next would shock the sleepy bedroom community… and make headlines for months to come. The controversy would ignite a debate that dominated local talk radio and raised questions no one seemed able to answer.

Beyond the staircase, the house stretched back in a long corridor, gradually narrowing into darkness. Photos lined the walls of the hall as far as sight could take him. Matthew had seen the images all before. Photos of him. Photos of his new wife, Jill. Stills of the two of them at the beach. In the park. At a dinner party. On their wedding day. There were many doors along the hall. One for every handful of photos. But he knew she wouldn't be behind any of them.

She would be in the basement.

Her space would be dark. Out of the way. Hidden. Buried. Deep, deep, deep—he was certain that's where he'd find her. If she was there at all.

She's there, he told himself. She had to be. The alternative was that he was crazy, and he wasn't crazy.

Matthew paused a moment to remind himself of that. It was something he needed to hear again and again, and he indulged the part of him that demanded it. But such reassurance only went so far. The doubts preyed on his mind almost as much as she did. It was no longer enough to tell himself this was her doing, he needed to *prove* it. Prove it and do something about it. He could live with the voices—her hellish vocals interrupting his day, disrupting his conversations, intruding on his most intimate moments. It was maddening, but he could handle it.

Those dreams were another matter. He couldn't let himself sleepwalk while she was manipulating him like that. It was only a matter of time before she succeeded in making him do something horrible, and he couldn't allow that. He had to confront her. This had to end.

Young Steven Chambers, a two-year old known to friends and neighbors as "Boo-Bear," lay on his parents' bed, his lungs filled with water. Drowned, the evidence would show, in his own bath....

Matthew walked around the staircase, opening a door in the wood-panel wall beneath it. Something was wrong. The entry to the basement should have been there, in the wall beneath the stairs. The door was properly positioned, but it opened to reveal only a closet filled with boxes. The layout of the house had been altered. Matthew wasn't certain what to make of it, but he doubted it could mean anything good. The prospect of not being as familiar with the interior recesses as he had thought was more than disturbing.

Another series of breaths, another pep-talk about focus. He was not about to turn back. No way. The entry had to be somewhere down the hall.

Somewhere deeper.

Surveying the pictures astride him on the walls, Matthew headed deeper into the house, entering the blackened corridor. So many pictures, each joined in some way to another until a larger picture seemed to emerge from the pieces. A happy couple, surrounded by bright colors, beaming smiles on their faces. Then the larger picture receded. With each passing door, the photos showed Jill less and less, until she no longer appeared in them at all, conspicuous in her absence. The scenes that followed were somber, solitary portraits, colors washed out. Most depicted alcohol in some form. There were women in some of them. None of them smiling and never the same one twice.

The light became dimmer as he progressed. Concentrate, he told himself. The hall seemed to extend interminably, stretching forward into the distance like tracks into a tunnel. But he continued to walk. Continued to instruct himself. Continued to focus.

The gathering blackness seemed to embrace him as he moved forward. He could feel it enveloping him, felt it taking his hand, caressing him with unspoken promises, urging him to give into it. He struggled to maintain his concentration, forced himself to perceive the images around him despite the dearth of light. The photos were faded now, and the few scenes he could make out were austere. Sitting alone in a one-bedroom apartment. Drinking himself to sleep. Crying. A few more steps and they were completely colorless, limited to shades of gray, making them even harder to discern.

Ten yards further and the photos were all empty sheets tinged the hue of an overcast sky, held deep in the grip of the shadows. Ahead he saw a door.

Sitting next to Steven on the bed was Matthew Chambers, a prominent, young Atlanta architect. Police described him as all but oblivious to their presence as he stared at his son, stroking his wet hair. "I had to do it," was all the officers recalled Matthew Chambers saying when they covered him with their revolvers and instructed him to step away from the child and to place his hands on his head. Police testimony would later describe the scene as containing ritualistic elements, a bizarre arrangement of crystals and herbs and burning incense.

Behind the door, a steep flight of stairs descended into an inky darkness. Once again there were photos and doors along each side, barely visible, but he avoided looking at them. Down, down, down, stopping at small landings, forcing himself to keep his surroundings in focus. After several flights, the stairs terminated at another door. He opened it and stepped inside.

The room swallowed him. He was standing in the center of it. A shadowy, windowless, dungeon of a suite, one he knew very well. Everything was strangely visible, despite the surrounding shadow and no obvious source of light. The recognition that it was the bedroom from his old house, the place where his world was ripped out from beneath him, was immediate. As was the realization he was not alone.

"I knew you'd be here," Matthew said.

She was sitting on the bed, Steven's head resting in her lap, his eyes closed. She was looking down at the boy, petting his forehead.

The sight caused his throat to tighten, making it difficult for him to breathe. Tears welled up, spilled over his lids and down his cheeks. The child was just as Matthew remembered him. Rosy cheeks and blonde hair. That tiny body prone to marathon sessions of horseplay as if it were powered by a compact dynamo. At that moment, all Matthew could think of was how energetic his son had been, how he was always running or jumping or climbing.

Laying there now, the boy looked peaceful. Angelic.

Melody did not.

"Hello, Matthew." Her voice was raspy, straddling some tonal line it had found between menacing and titillating. Her eyes locked onto his like the jaws of a pit bull. "I've been expecting you."

Matthew Chambers, a man neighbors would describe as a loving father and community pillar, was arrested for murder. If that wasn't shocking enough for the residents of the idyllic neighborhood that the Chambers' called home, Matthew Chambers' defense would certainly prove to be. Matt Chambers' lawyer was to plead the affirmative defense of justification.

She was just as she had appeared in his dreams, only more so in every way. Her face was a death-mask, withered, mummified, her skin shriveled and desiccated, her lips peeled in a constant grimace, displaying a rapacious set of teeth. Her body was thin, angular; leathery gray skin wrapped around long bones that were unsettlingly close to the surface. But none of those features could compete with her eyes. They were wide, round, piercing, with pupils that cut into the bright green of her irises like violent stab wounds. She was all but naked, with only a thin stretch of cloth, decayed and earthen, pasted around her torso. A wild mane of jet-black hair framed her face. Every bit of her seemed feral. Predatory.

"He was a beautiful child, wasn't he?" she asked, dropping her head to gaze at the boy again. "You shouldn't have caused his death."

Matthew felt his heart stomping against his ribcage. Surges of adrenaline and pangs of anxiety shot through his chest, each feeding off the other. He bit down and forced himself to focus, reminding himself of why he was there. What he came to do.

"I didn't kill him," Matthew said, clipping his words. His breath hissed through clenched teeth as he tried to retain control. "I didn't drown my son."

"Oh, you may not have physically held him under the water, but you most certainly were responsible for his death." Melody leaned her face close to Steven's, gently pinching a section of the boy's cheek. "For both our deaths."

The story Matthew Chambers told police caused almost as much controversy as the murders themselves. Chambers, the handsome, up-and-coming architect, admitted killing his wife--but swore he had done it because she, not he, had drowned their son. Investigators initially dismissed his story, but the investigation became more complicated when Chambers passed an F.B.I. polygraph, administered at the request of his defense team, and when forensic reconstructions seemed to support his version of events.

"You killed him, you sick bitch. You sent me outside, murdered him, then waited in the living room to tell me about it. How the hell did you expect me to react? I … *you* deserved what you got."

"*Did* I? Did I *deserve* for you to tell me you wanted a divorce? Did I deserve to be traded-in, like a used car? Did I, Matthew? Did I deserve to bear your child, only to have you fuck that sleazy receptionist? Is *that* what I deserved?"

"We were through, Melody. Finished. You knew that. Why, *why* did you make me go through the motions, let yourself get pregnant? And Steven… God, *Steven*. Why did you—"

"Because I wanted you, Matthew. I was never going to leave you. *Never*. Once we had a child, I thought you would see, I thought you would realize we were meant to be together. I loved you, Matthew. I've always loved you."

Without noticing exactly how it happened, Matthew saw that her appearance had changed. At some point she had transformed into the trim, shapely brunette who'd caught his eye at the gym, the one he had married after a torrid fling. Instead of the tattered cloth, she was wearing a white cotton dress that gently squeezed her at the breasts and hips.

"I remember when it was me you wanted to fuck," she said, lifting a leg beneath her son's body and crossing it slowly, revealing the smooth, tan flesh of a calf and thigh. "All night, sometimes. Long lunch hours, mornings in the shower. Every chance we got. Do you remember, Matthew?"

He remembered. He remembered the desperate feeling of needing to take a breath that wouldn't come, of wanting out, of wanting away from the draining, exhaustive weight of their marriage. Two weeks of unending sex culminating in a hop to Vegas and he suddenly found himself with a wife. He wondered what he could have been thinking, how he could have been so moronic. Maybe his sanity deserved to be questioned, after all.

"That didn't last very long, Melody. You became more obsessive every day, smothering me, calling me at the office a dozen times before lunch, questioning every place I went, every move I made. You drove me away. We weren't meant for each other. Whatever spark there was quickly died out."

"Not for me, you son of a bitch! What happened to love, honor and cherish, Matthew? Huh? What about that? All I ever wanted—all I ever demanded--was for us to be together." Her voice softened as she looked down at the boy again, gently touching her forefinger to his nose. "You know, before Steven was born, when we were starting to have trouble, I even sought out a Wicca. I learned what I could about love spells. I found one that was supposed to link our souls, that was supposed to ensure I'd always be a part of you. But still, you pulled away. So, I tried a stronger one, one I got from a witch everyone told me to steer clear of, one that required I sacrifice a part of me. A part of us. I put off doing it for a long time, Matthew, I agonized over it. But you gave me no choice."

She slowly lifted her head and hitched her shoulders, smiling. "I guess it worked, huh?"

Matthew clenched his eyelids, pressing them tight. It wasn't my fault, it wasn't my fault, it wasn't my fault. Oh, God, don't let her do this to you.

Get a grip. Remember why you came here. This was not unexpected. You have an objective. Focus, man, focus.

When he opened his eyes, Melody was the cadaverous creature she had been before, grinning like a hyena.

"I'm not insane," Matthew said.

"No, Matthew. You're not."

Matthew Chambers was charged with second-degree murder. Women's rights advocates were outraged that a man would attempt to justify the murder of his wife by blaming the victim for her child's death. Protesters carried signs and marched in front of the courthouse every day of the trial. The controversy only intensified when a plea bargain was struck before the verdict, a deal that infuriated the many groups following the trial. Matthew Chambers would plead guilty to manslaughter. Under state sentencing guidelines, he would be eligible for parole in three to five years. As part of the deal, he would also receive psychiatric counseling, despite having rejected an insanity defense. Court documents revealed his lawyers often heard him complain that his dead wife was somehow inside his head ...

"Did you really think you could get rid of me so easily? All those sessions with the psychiatrists, all those useless drugs and therapies. After all those things didn't work, couldn't work, you really thought you could just push me away on your own, shove me deeper and deeper into the dark? Really, Matthew, bury me with willpower? You actually thought I would never come back? I was just biding my time, *dearest husband.* Waiting."

"Waiting? For what?"

"Your new life, of course. To steal from you what you stole from me. Your marriage. Your family."

Jill. The thought sent a tremor though his body. Not Jill. Jill, the woman who had befriended him when he was at his lowest. The woman who heard him crying through the paper-thin walls of his tiny apartment, who wouldn't stop checking on him. The woman who drew him out of his isolation, who cried with him when he confessed what had happened, what he had done. The woman who believed him, who believed in him, who restored his confidence, who straightened his tie before interviews and never let him give up. The woman he loved in so many ways, for so many reasons. The entire structure of the house seemed to shake as he trembled with rage.

"You leave her out of this. Don't you dare touch her."

"Oh, I won't lay a hand on her."

"I'm serious, you psychopathic cunt! Stay away from her."

"Really, Matthew. Such language. You must learn to control your temper. I haven't seen you this angry since, well, you know."

"If you so much as—"

"Come now. How do you suppose *I* would do anything to her? You're the one who is going to do it."

"Me."

"Yes, Matthew. You. And once you do it, you'll have atoned, and then we can be together forever. You can't avoid it. I will make you do it, drive you to do it. Just like you drove me. To do this." She gestured down to Steven's body, which no longer appeared angelic, but suddenly rotted and decayed, with patches of flesh the color of sewer water clinging to its bones. Then she gently lifted the boy's skull off her lap, and Matthew saw she was now holding a baby. A tiny baby, hardly bigger than her hand.

"Your unborn son, Matthew. Carried inside that slut you married." She stretched her smile even wider as she placed a hand over the baby's nose and mouth. "It is every woman's choice."

"No!"

Matthew lunged at her, his arms thrust forward. His hands found her throat, thumbs hooking it. She was laughing as he did it, the same screeching laughter he'd heard mocking him with for so many months. Her face was a grotesquely contorted, teeth jutted forward in a snarl. Mummified cheeks, putrescent lips and savage, feline eyes all now just inches away.

This is why you came, he told himself. *This is what you are here to do.*

He squeezed with all his might, digging his thumb tips into her larynx, feeling the snap of bone and the choking, gasping sound that he had heard only once before in his life and had tried so hard, for so many years, to forget. Then the death mask faded away. The skin became creamy smooth, with a pinkish hue. Everything else melted away, too. Including his dreams. All of them, forever.

"Oh. God," Matthew said, releasing his grip. "Oh God no…"

That was close to nine years ago. Nine long years, and history has apparently--tragically--repeated itself. As I move off the street to the sidewalk, you can see the activity at the home behind me. Police have just arrested Matthew Chambers once again, this time, incredibly, for the murder of his second wife. Officials report that police already in the area responded to a neighbor's call concerning this house. Sources close to the investigation have told Eyewitness News that when police entered, they found Matthew Chambers with his hands still around the neck of his dead wife. Details remain sketchy, but the detective in charge has confirmed that Jill Chambers was pronounced dead by paramedics at the scene...Jill Chambers, age 34, confirmed dead, the apparent victim of a strangulation. A police spokesperson refused to comment on the rumor that Matthew Chambers had earbuds in his ears connected to a smartphone in his pocket at the time of his arrest, that playing on his phone was what the responding officer was overheard describing as a self-hypnosis audio. Police have also refused to comment on other rumors that the victim, Jill Chambers, was approximately three-months pregnant. There are indications she may have just returned from a doctor's appointment when the murder took place, but again, none of this has been confirmed.

I can confirm, however, that witnesses observed a visibly agitated Matthew Chambers shouting hysterically for someone to "stop laughing" as he was led by police from his home, and screaming things like, "She's inside!" and, "Someone get her out of my head!"

One thing is for certain: no matter how he pleads, Matthew Chambers is unlikely to escape punishment this time...Back to you, Ted.

The End

Deepest, Darkest

A Jake Hatcher Story

The most disturbing thought that crossed Hatcher's mind as he scanned the team members lining the interior of the fuselage wasn't that this may have been the first time an audit letter from the IRS was a pretext to coerce participation in a covert op, but rather that it likely wasn't. The C-130 landed on a dirt strip in Malawi, seven miles from the Zambian border. The plane slowed to a bumpy roll, almost coming to a stop, and the pilot turned a tight radius using the right engines and left brakes. She goosed the engines and taxied the big bird back toward the other end.

Hatcher unbuckled from the nylon webbing of the jump seat and stood, hooking a hand on a support along the fuselage wall. A pale glow was spilling in from the front of the plane through the cockpit. The pilot eased the big transport into another turn, then began shutting down the engines, moving sets of controls protruding from a center console. Hatcher stepped toward the cockpit and leaned in.

"How long?"

The pilot tugged her headset down from her ears, letting it hang around her neck. "Ten nautical miles out a minute ago. ETA in about five."

Hatcher nodded. The inbound chopper would take them into Zambia just as the sun was breaking the horizon. It was a short hop to the LZ.

"You know him? The pilot, I mean."

She gave him an enigmatic look, like she had to think about the phrasing of her answer. "Not really. He's Army."

Hatcher glanced at the co-pilot, who looked like he was about to graduate junior high. The kid smiled and shook his head.

"He sure seems interested in knowing *her*," he said. "Or knowing her better. He's been coming up with excuses to check in with her all day." He pointed to a display on the console where there were two sets of numbers. He was indicating the second set. Five digits, the last one separated by a decimal point. Vacant frequency, Hatcher guessed.

"That's quite enough, Lieutenant," the captain said.

"How long are you in-country?"

"Twenty-four hours," she said. "We're flying back to Lilongwe, spending the night there. We're supposed to wait for orders. I suppose those will be to pick you up?"

"Let's hope." He looked at the numbers on the radio again, thinking of the COMSEC limitations his team would be operating under. Zero Airwave Presence.

The whine of mechanisms grew slower and lower, whirring sounds, pinging sounds, ticking sounds. Hatcher stepped back into the main body of the transport and looked over his team, strung together some words in his head. He gave a nod to the one named Woodley, who gave one back. Woodley was some sort of contractor, had done this kind of thing before. Why that guy wasn't team leader, Hatcher still couldn't figure. He hated being in command.

"Alright," Hatcher said, projecting his voice. "You all know the mission and the plan. Time to suit up and go Tom Clancy. If you have any questions, they better be good ones, because the time to ask them was during the six hours of briefing, not now. Otherwise, get your weapon and lock and load."

"I got one." It was Garza. Sniper. Ex-Marine. Short and top heavy. Scar deforming the side of his upper lip. "Why aren't we doing this under dark cover?"

It was a good question. One he'd asked himself, when the operational parameters had been explained to him. He was told not to volunteer the answer if it came up, to give some lame rationale about airspace and international treaties and technical distinctions between hostile incursions and minor violations. But he wasn't going to keep anything from the team.

"The people we're working with on the ground, including our contacts, are superstitious. I'm not sure how else to put it. They believe there are threats in the darkness, risks they aren't willing to take. They insisted on daylight. That's why we're being dropped at the crack of dawn."

Hatcher knew the locals were right. There were threats in the darkness. But he doubted what they were afraid of had anything to do with the kinds of things he knew to be true, the kinds of things he knew to be lurking in the dark. Still, the thought bothered him.

The loadmaster was a small NCO. He stood near the rear and began a roll call of assigned numbers. The first guy to grab his M4 from the man chuckled. His name was Ivy, ex-Navy SEAL. He tapped the magazine against his helmet. Ivy was medium height, medium build. Well proportioned. Very dark skin with high cheek bones.

"Superstitious," Ivy said, chin swaying. "Never known a brother who wasn't."

Some laughs from the group. Zorn, an athletic looking guy with sandy brown hair in a neat flat top, sat up stiff, making a show of concern. "Hold it, now, I was told *you* were the only black guy I'd have to put up with. And they promised you weren't allowed to speak. They ain't paying me enough."

A few more laughs. Ivy made a comment about Zorn's mama having plenty of quarters to spread around, last he'd heard, and Hatcher stepped in to shut everyone up. This, he figured, was why they didn't want that kind of thing talked about. An off-color joke, a poorly-phrased comment—the slightest wrong note at a fragile moment could spell trouble. Cooperation could be cut-off instantly, especially when you were dealing with people who had it rough, people who had little else but their pride.

"Not a word of it. Not to our hosts, not to anyone from this point on. You all have the Ugly-American angle covered well enough with your looks." He stared each of them down, one by one, before catching Woodley's eye. "When the bird lands, you and I are out first. Ivy, Zorn, you're next, but on signal. Garza, you follow them. And watch it with the jokes. Save 'em for the flight back. Gameface time."

Hatcher gestured for Woodley to come closer. He was the first in the group Hatcher'd been introduced to in that basement dungeon of offices, during the carrot portion of the pitch, right after the stick. Tall, athletic in a lean way. Smiled way too much, kept patting Hatcher on the back and talking about how glad he was Hatcher was on board. Hatcher had taken an instant dislike to him. The gung-ho attitude coupled with blond hair and blue eyes screamed poster boy for the Hitler Youth. "You understand why we're first, right?"

Woodley chewed on it, but not for long. He registered his comprehension with a pop of the eyebrows. "Got it."

The muted rhythm of helicopter blades thumped against the aluminum skin of the plane. The rear cargo hatch lowered like a drawbridge. The loadmaster called out the remaining numbers, handing each man his rifle and five magazines. Hatcher went last. After the weapons and ammunition were distributed, the loadmaster unlocked a separate container and handed Woodley a silver metallic briefcase. The men exited single file, headed straight toward the chopper. Hatcher waited for everyone else to board, scanning the tree lines, before climbing on.

There was no preflight briefing. There were headsets, but none of the team reached for one, and Hatcher decided not to, either. The right-seat pilot shut the sliding passenger door and climbed back in. The engine grew louder a moment later and the craft shifted, a sliding feeling, then it rose. The nose dipped before it got twenty feet off the ground, and then they were accelerating forward.

The ride was smooth. It was Hatcher's first time in a Lakota. Much nicer than the Hueys and Chinooks he was used to, but he reminded himself that had been over a decade ago. He watched the terrain roll by below, green concentrations of heavy vegetation, beige-yellow plains. They were barely ten minutes into the flight when the pilot gestured back, then pointed. The helicopter descended into a clearing.

Hatcher slid a hand to the small of his back, feigned like he was scratching. He touched the tiny metal cylinder tucked behind his belt, a tool he'd taken to carrying everywhere, ever since his last run-in with the police. Why the feel of it at a time like this gave him comfort, when he was armed to the teeth, he wasn't sure. Maybe because he felt trapped, roped into an operation against his will, and the reason he always carried it was to make traps seem less hopeless. The idea made him feel silly.

Two automobiles emerged from beyond the tree line, approaching. One was an olive-green Land Rover with an open rear and a large metal frame instead of a roof, what looked like a podium extending over the hood surrounded by a railing. Safari observation platform, Hatcher supposed. The other was a bleached-out tan Humvee. Both were beat up, with numerous dents and Bondo blotches and mud-caked rugged tires that were worn long past their replacement date. The Land Rover had a driver, but no one else in it. The Hummer had a driver and a passenger.

Woodley opened the door and glanced at Hatcher. The others were all in various states of lean, ready to go, but Hatcher held up a fist. He picked a headset off a hook, made sure it was plugged in, and spoke into the mouthpiece.

"There's always a chance they may pull weapons. At the first sign of anything that I or the team member with me can't handle, you get these men out of here and abort."

The pilot nodded. Per the mission rules, there would be no radio traffic. Extraction was set by time and coordinates, with a contingency meeting point set two hours later. There was no host government involvement, so risk of a communication capture was to be avoided with extreme priority. While nobody liked those kinds of orders, Hatcher grudgingly understood. The entire mission was a gross violation of national sovereignty. The ramifications could be far reaching and threaten myriad pacts and alliances, formal and informal. There was no escaping politics.

Woodley hopped out, and Hatcher followed him. They double-timed it in a slight crouch until they reached the Hummer.

The driver opened the door and put one foot on the ground, standing, but didn't get all the way out. He was wearing mirrored sunglasses that reflected the glowing sky to the east. A khaki shirt, pockets but no sleeves. To Hatcher's surprise, he didn't appear to be armed.

The man slapped the outside of the open door, *pop pop*, then held out his hand at an expectant angle. His dark skin was wrapped tight around a lean, corded arm, a bump for a bicep, a knob for an elbow. He snapped his fingers, fanned his hand toward his body.

Hatcher shifted his eyes to Woodley and gestured with his chin. Woodley stepped forward with the briefcase. The man grabbed the handle and tossed the case into the Jeep behind him without so much as a pause to glance at it.

Woodley stepped back. The man leaned on the vehicle door, hiding behind his mirrored lenses. He seemed to be waiting for something else.

"You got your money," Hatcher said. "Now, where are we heading? Distance and direction."

The man stared at Hatcher. His upper lip and the side of his mouth curled enough to show teeth, but he said nothing.

"You're either the leader of whatever gang or outfit or tribal clan you belong to, or the guy sent by the leader. That means you speak English."

Woodley started to say something, but Hatcher threw up a palm without looking at him.

"Well?"

"I am thinking," the man said. He took a long minute eying Hatcher, heading tilting up and down. "About what I am being paid to do. It is not easy to betray someone."

The whine of the helicopter hummed in their ears. Hatcher felt Woodley tense, sensed him shifting his weight forward. He stuck out his arm like a roadblock.

He didn't like any of this. Didn't want to be there, didn't like being in charge, and sure as hell didn't like having been blackmailed into the whole thing. But even if he'd signed up willingly, he would have hated this plan. This was supposed to be a hostage rescue, but they were paying for the location. Half rescue, half ransom. That meant dealing with shifting allegiances and incomplete information of unknown reliability. His objections had been overruled. The plan was put in place at too high a level to change it, he'd been told. And that plan was to pay the money, get the location, and extract the young doctor with the powerful parent back home who'd made the possibly fatal mistake of doing her volunteer work in the wrong country at the wrong time.

"Then don't," Hatcher said. "Stick with the deal as planned. The one you made with the people who sent us. What you're doing will free an innocent woman. That's not a betrayal. That's doing the right thing. No need to complicate things." A moment later, he added, "Any more than they already are."

The man ran his long fingers down the side of his face. His knuckles were cracked and chalky from callouses and scabbing.

"That is a good way to think of it. I will take heed of your words." The man seemed to shift his attention to Woodley for a moment, then back to Hatcher. It was hard for Hatcher to tell with those glasses. "The camp is nine kilometers northwest. We will take you and your men to a location a little less than one kilometer from it. From there, I will escort you and one other to the perimeter. Exactly as agreed. Then, my men and I will take our leave."

Hatcher nodded once. He turned to the helicopter and held up an arm, pointed his index finger to the sky and swirled it. His team egressed one at a time, moving swiftly, head low, weapons in a ready position across their chests.

Leaning in toward Woodley, Hatcher said, "Keep your eye on him." He gestured with his eyes back to the driver. "He's hiding something."

Woodley swallowed. The exchange had clearly rattled him, a greasy film of sweat slicked his forehead.

"Why do you say that?" he asked.

Hatcher'd openly wondered at the first briefing why they hadn't just put Woodley in charge, since he seemed to be the only one in the group with current military ties—though his actual status had been vaguely referenced as 'classified'—and knew more about the situation than any of them. One reason had become obvious. He was jittery, uncertain. Maybe the powers that be weren't as oblivious as he'd assumed.

"Well, aside from the fact I can tell...the only people who don't count money from strangers are ones who are doing it for something other than the cash. And I don't know what that something is. Do you?"

Another swallow, followed by a deep breath. Woodley looked over his shoulder at the driver, thoughts swimming behind his eyes. He dropped his gaze to the ground, his body stiffening, as if gathering resolve.

"I don't know why anyone does anything, anymore," he said. "So, I sure as hell don't know what motivates these guys."

The drive through the jungle was only about five miles, but the indirect route carved out of the terrain made it seem closer to twenty. The road was more of a trail, the destination being a location chosen for its remoteness and lack of accessibility. Branches and fronds draped themselves over the path, rubbery, leafy shapes swatting off the windscreen of the lead vehicle, the wilds of an untamed land trying to reclaim its own.

Far from the chopper, the sound of the vehicles was not enough to drown out the fluty call of birds, the piercing ululations of... what? Monkeys? Hatcher couldn't be sure. He just knew that at each tight curve, as the engines slowed to idle, the hue of wildlife was like a background track. Whistles and whoops and trills.

The lead vehicle pulled to a stop where the path took a sharp turn.

The other vehicle stopped behind it.

"This is as far as I can take everyone but two of you. I will show you the camp. But your men will have to stay back. I do not want to get caught in the middle of a firefight."

"I didn't catch your name."

"Mbuyi."

"No offense, Mbuyi, but this sounds an awful lot like a trap."

The man shrugged. "One of me, two of you. I will take you to where I can show you the path to the camp. But no farther. I have one pistol. You have automatic weapons." He shifted his gaze to Woodley, looking him up and down with what seemed to Hatcher like a palpable disdain. He wondered if it was the blond hair. "I am in no position to control what happens after that. I will do exactly as was agreed."

"How far is it?" Hatcher asked.

"Half a kilometer, perhaps."

Woodley looked at Hatcher. "Your call. We can tell the rest of the team to be ready for a rapid response."

Nothing to like about it, but they needed eyes on the camp to decide the specifics. That was always the weakest part of the plan, which was saying a lot. But they hadn't given him much of a say in the matter. They hadn't given him much of a say in anything.

"Do it. But get us back here in thirty."

Woodley signaled to the others to stand ready in place, threw up three fingers then a circled palm, fingertip touching thumbs, indicating thirty minutes. They understood, as this kind of thing had been part of the brief. If they weren't back at thirty-one minutes, the team was to treat every non-team member as a hostile.

Mbuyi tossed a wave over his head to his associates and started driving again. The path was narrower now, used infrequently, barely two ruts through the trees, whose branches clawed at the windshield and scraped the metal above their heads.

After a few minutes and maybe three or four hundred yards, Mbuyi braked and put the vehicle into park. He stepped out and gestured to Woodley, pointing into the back. Woodley looked down, then handed him a machete that was on the floor. Mbuyi dipped his head toward the heavy brush past him.

"This way. One hundred meters or thereabouts. There is a clearing."

The machete hissed and thwacked its way through branches and stems and vines, fans of green, nets of hairy ropes. The route Mbuyi forged had been cut before, and the jungle had all but reclaimed it, leaving Hatcher to wonder if that sort of reclaiming had taken weeks or only days. The going was slow but steady. Within a few minutes, the growth became less dense. An area opened, a small spread of field. It was littered with the skeletal remains of animals. At least, Hatcher hoped they were all animals. Ribs and spines and giant drumsticks. Straight ones, curved ones, broken ones; jagged and smooth and bleached and yellowing. Large and small.

A light breeze puffed their faces. The stench it carried was unbearable.

"This place is called 'the Garden of Bones.' You will find such gardens throughout the nearby valley. And the areas that surround it."

Hatcher glanced at Woodley, tightened his grip on his M4, raising it slightly. Woodley wrinkled his nose and hitched a shoulder, frowning with one side of his mouth.

"Why are we in the Garden of Bones, Mbuyi? Where's the camp?"

"I'm afraid you will find out soon enough."

Movement along the far tree line. Hatcher dropped to one knee and raised his rifle to a ready-fire position.

"Hostiles. Woodley, cover left."

"Unfortunately," Woodley said, "I'm too busy covering you."

Hatcher turned his head. The barrel of Woodley's rifle was pointed straight at him. Its bearer was staring down the sight, weapon securely in firing position.

Six men emerged from the brush. Most had AKs. One had an Uzi. All were pointed with varying degrees of apparent know-how in his direction. No uniforms, just jeans and sweats and t-shirts and a few caps. A woman was with them. Her wrists were pulled behind her, and a dirty pillow case covered her head down to her neck. Her bare arms were pale beneath smears of grime. It didn't take much imagination to know who she was.

Hatcher eased the grip on his rifle, letting it sag in his arms. "I don't even have any live rounds, do I?"

Woodley gave his head a shake. "Dummies. Had to make sure the weight and balance was just right. Knew you'd check."

The approaching men drew closer, their steps slow and cautious. Hatcher set his rifle down and stood.

"So, what's the play? Me for the girl?"

"That's the general idea."

Hatcher looked at Mbuyi, then back to Woodley. "What could possibly make me so valuable?"

"You'll have to ask them," Woodley said. "I'm sorry about this, Hatcher. I really am."

"I bet."

"Believe what you want, but it's true. They had me by the short hairs. Worse than you, a lot worse. I'm just following orders. Nothing personal, man. It's all part of the plan. Remember how you kept saying, trust in the plan?"

Hatcher never remembered saying any such thing, but saw no use in arguing. One of the men eyed Hatcher as he addressed Mbuyi. Whatever he said was in a tongue Hatcher couldn't identify, let alone understand.

"He says he thought you would be bigger."

"I've never had any complaints."

Mbuyi paused, considering the words. Then his mouth spread into a toothy grin. He said something to the other man, who laughed. The man gestured in the direction of the woman, and one of the others grabbed her above the elbow and led her to Woodley. She stumbled along, almost losing her footing as her head darted. Hatcher guessed her mouth had a gag in it and her ears were plugged, since she seemed to have no idea what was going on around her.

Woodley took the woman's arm, a bit more gently than the guy handing her off, and started to lead her back in the direction they'd come. He stopped after a few steps, guiding her past him, and looked back at Hatcher.

"For what it's worth, they would have killed her. Doing it this way not only saved her, but prevented any other potential casualties on the team. Like I said, all part of the plan. And it sort of makes you a hero."

"In that case," Hatcher said as two of the men came close, weapons raised and shoving toward him, and another produced a pair of handcuffs. "What does that make you?"

Woodley raised his brows high, gave a tilt of his head. "Underestimated."

He winked before taking a step back.

One of the men took Hatcher's helmet while another patted him down and removed the tactical knife from its sheath. Woodley took the helmet and yanked the microphone off. He pulled out some of the internal wiring near the earpiece and threw it into the nearby brush, then tossed the helmet back near Hatcher's feet. The woman flinched when he took her by the arm again.

Mbuyi started to follow Woodley and the woman, then stopped to look at Hatcher. Woodley paused at the mouth of the trail, an impatient set to his stance.

"It is not betrayal if you free an innocent woman. I was having second thoughts until you told me that."

Hatcher held the man's gaze. "In that case, just make sure she actually gets out."

The words seemed to catch him off guard. The man pinched his lips tight and dipped his head. "The joy of life is to be continually surprised. That is also its burden."

The muzzle of a rifle poked Hatcher in the rib, hard enough to make him wince. The leader made a gesture, and his captors started moving. One of them shoved him hard enough to make him stumble.

Mbuyi remained where he was, watching. Hatcher looked back over his shoulder as he crossed through the array of bones, the serpentine weave of vertebrates, the curled fingers of ribs. Mbuyi nodded to Hatcher one final time, then turned and walked away. Woodley guided the woman between the trees, Mbuyi a few steps behind. Within seconds, the jungle had swallowed all three of them.

———— ※✿※ ————

The camp was a collection of huts. Some thatch weaves over cobbled scrap wood, some sheets of corrugated tin nailed to trees. In the middle of the camp was a shot-up armored vehicle without any wheels, collapsed on one side, like it had been driven across an IED and then abandoned where it lay.

They sat Hatcher on a stump at the mangled rear end of the vehicle and ran a dense chain between his arms behind his back, over the links between his wrists, and passed the shackle of a heavy duty padlock through both ends where they sandwiched a large metal loop. The loop was connected to the frame of the vehicle, welded solid.

One of the men tugged on the chain, testing it. Two others stood nearby and nodded their approval.

"Do any of you speak English?"

The three men stared at him, glancing occasionally at each other.

"I speak English."

The voice came from behind one of the men, who stepped aside and looked back. The man it belonged to was seated in front of one of the huts, fashioning something out of a piece of wood with a small knife.

"Mind telling me what you guys want with me?"

"We do not want anything with you."

"Then why am I here?"

"Kongamoto."

The men near Hatcher seemed to grow uneasy at the sound of the word. Their eyes darted, nervous glances from one to the other.

"What the hell is a Kongamoto?"

The man in the knit cap who had seemed to be their leader when talking to Mbuyi—Hatcher hadn't caught his name—barked out a few angry words, slashing a hand through the air for emphasis. The man with the knife sat up straight and kept his eyes down, returning his attention to whittling. The other two hurried away in opposite directions, chastened.

Knit Cap stopped in front of Hatcher, ran his eyes in an arc from one end of his body to the other and back. He was wearing an open military-style green blouse with the sleeves cut off over a faded yellow t-shirt with a worn out soft drink logo on it. His rifle was slung over his shoulder ,and he was holding a walkie-talkie in one hand. He raised it to his mouth and spoke words Hatcher couldn't understand. It squawked, a crackly voice responding in ways equally unintelligible. Then he walked away.

Hatcher kept his eyes on the whittling guy. The man seemed to be forcing himself not to look, which was good. Slowly, Hatcher worked his fingers into the waistband of his trousers at the small of his back. He scissored his index and middle finger around a three-inch rod, fishing it out. It was titanium, with a tooth on one end and the other, sheathed end sharpened to an edge you could shave with. *Slow, slow, slow.* Careful not to move his upper arm or shoulder, working entirely with his forearm, fingers and wrist. The small tube slid up and over the lip of his belt and dropped, landing in the curl of his fingers.

He squeezed his fingers closed as he heard the sound of a car or truck, something with a big engine, rumbling closer until it stopped somewhere to his rear. The motor cut off, a door opened and shut. Voices. Footfalls.

Knit Cap strode into view, rifle across his chest, stock cradled in the crook of his arm. Another person joined him. A woman.

She was tall, as tall as her escort. Her skin was dark and smooth, a sheen to it that gave it an onyx glow. Her lips were full and pouty. Her kinky hair was teased out and pulled back on each side with a clip, a frizzy puff in the back. She wore an unbuttoned tan shirt over a stretchy white tank top, with khaki safari pants.

Even if she hadn't been physically attractive to the point of it seeming absurd, Hatcher would have known by the way her presence made him anxious, that tingly, aroused feeling that her scent caused. She was a Carnate. No doubt about it. A physically perfect half-human, half-demon woman with sexual charms that were all but irresistible. They lived for seven generations and never seemed to age. All they lacked were souls.

"Jake Hatcher," the woman said.

"Small world," Hatcher said. "That's my name, too."

"That famous wit. I am Aleena. You know, some of my sisters in America have talked so much about you, I feel like I've known you for years."

She spoke with a lilt, her voice polished and smooth. There was an accent, but he had no idea what kind.

"In that case, how about you let me go. Just this once. For old times' sake."

"Alas, that I cannot do. My most sincere apologies. I went through a lot of trouble to get you here."

"And why would you go and do a thing like that?"

"I'm afraid that is a bit too complicated to explain at the moment. My friends here have been vexed by an entity you are well acquainted with. Or shall we say, is well acquainted with you. They have been desperately seeking a way to, shall we say, get him off their backs and to stop him interfering with their lucrative business interests. They have sought out the aid of every sorcerer within a thousand miles, created a demand for the body parts of people unfortunate enough to have been born albino in a part of the world where such a condition is believed to carry mystical properties."

"And how do I fit in to all this?"

"Oh, don't you worry, Mr Hatcher. You will find out soon enough. Tonight, in fact."

Hatcher shook his head, frowning. "Ooh, tonight… you know, that just doesn't work for me. Maybe we can reschedule?"

"I have heard the stories, been told how charming others have found you, your manly directness, your facetious banter in the face of perils sure to break the composure of those with lesser mettle. Mostly, they seem amused by your belief you can talk your way out of things, when we both know that has never happened."

"There's always a first time."

"Yes. This will be one of those. Just not for that."

She dipped her head to Knit Cap guy, then turned to walk away.

"What happens tonight?" Hatcher said, calling out after her. "So I know what to wear, what to bring. Not going to make me buy two bottles of wine, just to be safe, are you?"

Aleena pivoted on the heel of her boot, turning herself just enough to look back at him. Her lips spread to show a set of perfect white teeth.

"Red, Mr. Hatcher. The color for tonight is most definitely red."

⬥

Hatcher spent the next few hours evaluating his situation. He could unlock his cuffs—courtesy not only of the escape rod resting in the fold of his curled fingers, a tool he never left home these days without—but also the failure of his captors in not turning his hands palms out before cuffing him. But what good would that do? It was broad daylight, miles into jungle terrain, which was the worst of all worlds. His absence would draw immediate attention, which told him these guys were smart for putting him in the middle of the camp instead of stuffing him into some hut. And even if he found an opportunity, some distraction or diversion, he'd need a firearm. Accomplishing that would draw its own attention. If they had any lying around, asking to be grabbed, he hadn't noticed.

So he waited.

At least one question had been answered, he thought, running through events. This was the real point of the whole production all along, not that garbage they'd BS'd him with. Get him to the Federal Building under the guise of an audit, have him met by Secret Service agents who led him to a sub-basement more secure than a Bond villain's lair, then acquaint him with the velvet hammer. A guy named Keegan, someone high up in the Administration, but exactly how high, or exactly who he was, was never made clear. What was made clear was the offer. Hatcher could either cooperate or face all manner of trumped up tax problems, including civil forfeiture of every dime he had. Criminal prosecution was all but promised, and more than a few not-so-subtle hints were dropped that certain matters involving dead cops may be looked into again with a good deal more scrutiny. Or… he could take what's behind door number two. Help rescue a young woman, a doctor doing volunteer work helping to stop the mutilation and occasional slaughter of albinos whose body parts were believed to be powerful objects for magic. A young woman who just happened to warrant all this attention because she was the Vice President's secret and illegitimate daughter, that last bit being more implied than stated, neither confirmed nor denied.

The more he thought about it, the stupider he felt. Why hadn't he just told them to go fuck themselves, like his gut wanted him to? It wasn't a real question, because he knew the answer, and had from the beginning. Because of Amy. The threats weren't just to him. They were more than willing to go after her, just to prove a point. And they'd clearly done enough homework for the threat to be credible.

Less than four days later, here he was.

The camp was languorous. Heat flowed through like a current, like something that could be touched and scooped and bottled. Hatcher felt the perspiration soaking through his clothes, drenching him with a salty, stinging slickness.

Men moved about slowly, finding shade, playing cards, cleaning their weapons. Hatcher could sense some tension, the buzz of anticipation, but the heat seemed to keep everyone subdued. He could tell they wanted to move, wanted to pace and burn off nervous energy, but they were forced to fidget instead, trying to keep cool.

People came and went. Everyone seemed to stop and look at him more than once. Some of the men from the Garden of Bones, some who were at the camp when he got there, others who arrived later. Most would stand directly in front of him with appraising eyes, some made comments to others that he couldn't understand, some tilted their heads one way or the other, quietly assessing him. A handful smiled. Most didn't.

Around two in the afternoon, there was activity. A vehicle arrived, followed shortly by another. Knit Cap walked up, grunted some words to a few others. Two of them rushed over to Hatcher and unlocked the chain. One clamped a hand on his elbow and half pushed, half dragged him toward an old extended cab pickup truck. There was some sort of mechanical device in the back, taking up most of the bed. Hatcher couldn't quite tell what it was for, but it had the familiar shape of a weapon and what looked like a grapping hook on the end, pointed like an arrowhead.

People were climbing into vehicles. One opened a rear door to the truck, and Hatcher was shoved toward it, then prodded in with the barrel of an AK. The whittling guy slid in next to him and another jumped in the passenger seat up front. Knit Cap got behind the wheel.

Hatcher was in the second vehicle in a four-car caravan. They drove through tapestries of tangled wilderness and stretches of simmering plains. They crossed a narrow river over white water rocks. They passed through a small village of tiny buildings with women in colorful garb and children practically naked. A few minutes later, they were in forest again. Jungle. Vegetation so dense it was like a wild wall, a collective beast that would swallow you whole. Leaving only a Garden of Bones.

"What is that contraption?" Hatcher said, gesturing to the rear with a twitch of his head. He figured asking where they were heading would be pointless.

"That is Chigi's invention." The man jutted a chin toward the driver, whose eyes caught Hatcher's in the rearview mirror. "His father drowned when his truck was swept away, crossing a river."

Hatcher turned to look at it. Calling it an invention was a stretch, but it was definitely homemade. He could now tell it was a catapult. Crossbow design, compound, augmented with what looked like axle springs. He tried to imagine ways it could come in handy. Other than during a flash flood or while teetering on a cliff, he couldn't think of any.

"What's Kongamoto?"

Whittling Guy opened his mouth to speak, but then the brush thinned, and Hatcher saw the first vehicle start to brake and finally stop. They were near the steep embankment of a sizable hill, visible beyond a layer of forest.

The guy in the passenger seat got out and opened Hatcher's door. He tugged Hatcher's arm, pulling him out and shoving him through a narrow gap in the growth toward the hill. Whittling Guy followed, pointing his rifle, a contrite smile on his face.

The side of the hill was rocky, almost a cliff. Vines weaved down its face, fingers and hairs spreading out from ropey trunks to cling, finding purchase in cracks and protrusions. Hatcher expected to see a cave or tunnel entrance, something that would signal why he was being led this way, but the jagged wall of earth and stone looked solid.

He stopped a few feet from the hillside and turned to face the men behind him. Five rifles, all pointed at him, varying states of readiness. He scanned their faces. It seemed like a long way to drive just to have a firing squad.

Two of the men stepped aside to let Knit Cap walk through.

The man stopped a few feet away. His face was grim despite a grin that displayed a good amount of teeth. His rifle hung from a frayed sling around his neck and over one shoulder, the opposite arm holding it steady across his body. He raised the other hand and pointed toward the escarpment. When he spoke, Hatcher had no idea what he was saying.

Two impatient snaps of his fingers, and Whittling Guy hustled forward, followed by another in the group. Skinny, face slick with sweat. The other guy slung his AK over his shoulder and hurried to the wall, the two of them working together, pushing aside some of the vines, grabbing others. Whittling Guy yanked and ripped until he was able to separate the ones he wanted from some overgrowth. Hatcher saw that the vines he'd pulled free had been tied together to form a rope ladder, rungs fashioned out of cable and wire, scavenged material, secured by a variety of screws and nails and even twine, here and there.

More words Hatcher didn't understand. Apparently sensing this, Knit Cap paused. He pointed a finger at Hatcher, then raised it toward the top of the precipice.

"Up."

They expect me to climb. He looked at the one holding the vines. The guy gestured back and another joined him as he took hold of one of the makeshift rungs above his head, tugging it. Looked to Hatcher like someone about to start pulling himself up. Hatcher took a quiet breath, let it out halfway. There were two ways to play this. One was to keep going along. A climb meant parsing out their numbers, and that meant at the top he'd have an opportunity to improve his odds. The problem was, if they expected him to scale a steep wall, they were going to uncuff him. That meant however they handled it, however many they sent with him, before or after, they'd be more attentive, more cautious. Probably have rifles from the ground trained on him the whole way up. He'd lose most, if not all, of the element of surprise.

That left the other way.

Hatcher nodded, lowered his head. He had already positioned the escape key in his fingertips. He slipped it into the left cuff and gave it twist. The teeth disengaged and he felt the strand practically drop open, careful to keep his hand pressed against his back so the metal didn't make any noise.

Knit Cap reached into a lower front pocket of his Army surplus blouse and retrieved a key. He held it up and Hatcher worried for a moment he was going to keep his distance and toss it toward him, make Hatcher kneel down and fumble to pick it up off the ground to open the cuffs himself, which would have been the smart thing to do, but instead he took a step forward. That was all it took.

Hatcher took a step himself, a much quicker one, slamming full frontal into the man, wedging the AK between them. He threw one arm around the man's neck, clenching him tight, hooking his chin from behind and giving it a hard yank. He swung his hand up to grab the stock of the AK between them at the same time, clamping a hold of it to keep it steady, and braced for the sting.

The rifle erupted in a rapid tattoo of shots, *bap-bap-bap-bap-bap-bap-bap*. The sound jackhammered his ears, more distinct and a bit louder than an AR. The barrel swept in a tight arc as Hatcher spun the man by his jaw, the burst of rounds taking out the four men in front of them before they could return fire, their boss being in the way causing all kinds of confusion. A stream of scalding brass bounced off his chest, a few singeing his neck and face.

The firing stopped. No surprise there. Full auto only lasts a few seconds

Other than the guy he had wrapped up, there were two left, the ones prepping to climb the vines. Hatcher gave another violent torque to the man's neck. The guy was trying to resist, most of his efforts directed at regaining his balance, but the laws of kinesiology were governing him for the moment. Where the head went, the body had to follow.

A complete circle, the man stumbling around Hatcher's radial until Hatcher stuck a leg out and threw himself backwards, dropping the man on top of him as he let go of the rifle and stabbed a hand at the man's sidearm. He jerked it free of its holster, aimed at the one of the remaining two who had gotten his weapon the highest, and squeezed the trigger.

The hammer pulled back on the double action, then punched forward with a click. *Son of a bitch.* Hatcher bit his lip in disgust, but didn't have time to curse his luck. Rather than relinquish his grip on his shield's neck, which would have taken more time anyway, he rotated the pistol sideways and slammed it against the man's head, digging the rear sight into his temple as hard and as deep as he could, and in one continuous motion shoved the handle forward. The man screamed as Hatcher racked a round into the chamber.

One of the gunmen let off three rounds, apparently writing his boss off for dead. Two of them hit the man, jolting his body, the other sizzling past Hatcher's skull. Hatcher fired one shot at center of mass that knocked the shooter back just as another round, this one from Whittling Guy, took a chunk of Knit Cap's head and splattered blood across Hatcher's face. Hatcher fired another shot, this one missing, but far worse than that was the sight of the slide open, stuck halfway back, the end of a protruding shell visible in the ejection port. A jam. Hatcher knew before he'd even glanced at it, knew without even thinking about it. Cheap loads, limp wrist. To clear it, he'd have to slap his palm against the bottom of the magazine and rack the slide again. But that would mean tossing off his shield. And there wasn't enough skull left on the body lying on top of him, now dead weight, for him to try another forced rack. He looked to be out of options. To make matters worse, the first gunman he'd shot wasn't even down, he was pressing his hand against a wound in his abdomen, intent on rejoining the fray, a bit hunched over, but looking directly at Hatcher and managing to point his rifle using his other arm. The second one, Whittling Guy, seeing the malfunction, stepped forward, focused on not wasting any more rounds, the set of his jaw dead serious, moving in for the kill shot.

He'd have to risk it. The chances of him not taking hits seemed about zero, but there really wasn't any choice.

Hatcher rocked to the side, ready to throw the body off him, hopefully have enough momentum to roll over it, pop onto a knee on the other side, tap-rack-fire. The closest rifleman snapped his AK higher, sighting it in, just as Hatcher flung the body over.

The eruption of rifle fire hammered his ears. His back seemed to be exposed for dozens of bursts. He braced himself for the burn, tensing in anticipation, figuring at least the pain would let him know he was alive.

He bounced up, one knee down, just as planned. He was already slapping his hand against the bottom of the pistol, jacking the slide back, thrusting the barrel out.

No one was there. No one standing.

Whittling Guy was on his back, body arched and slowly sagging to ground as his neck went limp. The other rifleman was facedown, several wounds in the top of skull leaking thick streams of blood.

A voice projected from the jungle a few yards away.

"Hold fire!"

Hatcher remained still for a moment, then lowered his weapon. Woodley emerged, gesturing above his head. Others appeared from different points, rifles trained on the bodies, barrels snapping from one to another to another. No one appeared to be taking any chances. Only Woodley seemed confident the threat had been neutralized.

Half of Woodley's face tightened into a smirk. "Didn't really think we were going to leave you in the hands of a bunch of guerrillas, did you?"

Hatcher narrowed his eyes at the man before bouncing glances at the others. They were too engrossed in the task at hand, checking the bodies, alert for undetected hostiles, to make eye contact. He let himself exhale fully for what felt like the first time in minutes. His body suddenly felt heavy, his limbs weighted down. He stared at the ground and gathered enough strength to push himself to his feet.

"Why?" Hatcher said, running his gaze over the bodies.

"I know you've got lots of questions. First, let Ivy take a look at you, make sure you're not carrying any unwanted metal or losing any tomato juice anywhere."

"*Why,*" he repeated, less a question this time than a command.

"You're angry. I get it. I would be, too. But you know how it works. Orders."

"Bullshit. That doesn't answer the question, and it sure as hell doesn't let you off the hook."

"Whoa, now. I'm the guy who just saved your ass, remember? Yes, it was a shitty thing to do. The world's a shitty place."

"I'm only going to ask one more time. Why?"

"I can only tell you what I know, which is what they told me. The PMU that had her, that was their price. They asked for you—demanded you—by name. A swap."

Hatcher straightened up. "They asked for me, by name."

"That's what I was told. My orders were to accomplish the exchange, clear the hostage, then track and retrieve you." Woodley took his eyes off

Hatcher, snapped his fingers. "Ivy, check him out, will you?"

Ivy slung his rifle behind his back and approached Hatcher, removing a pack from his belt.

Hatcher barely glanced at the man, keeping his eyes on Woodley. "You have no fucking idea what you've done."

"Hey, it's not like I was the one who came up with the plan or even had a vote. And, in case you're wondering, the others didn't know. Ivy here didn't know. I briefed them once we were clear."

Hatcher flinched as Ivy reached toward his face with a swab.

"There's a lot of blood." The man's expression was apologetic. His lips were pulled tight in a flat smile that was more of a sympathetic frown. "Just let me clean it off and make sure none of it's yours."

The swab felt cool, even as it stung. The smell of alcohol scraped his nostrils. It perked him up a bit. A slant of sunlight stabbed through a net of leaves and fronds, flashing in his eyes. It was almost dusk.

Almost dusk meant almost dark.

There was too much information to process and not enough information to process it with.

"That looks better. Lemme give you a quick exam, and we can get out of here."

Hatcher locked his eyes on Ivy's, then fixed his attention back on Woodley. One piece clunked into place.

"That's not the plan, though, is it?"

Woodley said nothing.

Ivy paused. "What do you mean?"

"Tell him the truth, Woodley. Tell them all what we're really here for. Because I'd like to hear it myself."

"Hold on, now. I haven't lied. I told them after we rescued you, Phase I of the mission would be complete. That's the truth."

"But you didn't tell them extraction wasn't until Phase III, did you?"

"No," Ivy said. "He didn't."

"He sure as hell didn't," Garza said. "Next thing up was supposed to be evacuation."

"Guys, I'm just following instructions, same as you."

"That's a load of horseshit, and you know it. You may be an ass, but you're not a dumb one. If the mission was to rescue a captive, trading me, you could have staged an assault right after the exchange. You could have attacked the camp. You could have done it a dozen different ways that would make a hell of a lot more sense than this. And you would have told them that, so Keegan or whoever was calling the shots had to give you more."

Woodley tilted his head to the side and rolled his eyes. But his embarrassed smirk gave it away.

Another piece clicked into place. "You put a tracker on me. Where? My boot?"

"Yes." Woodley nodded, letting out a weary sigh. "Good call. In the heel."

"And you couldn't let me in on it because they knew I'd refuse, because the plan was stupid and risky and unnecessary. And because I would know if they asked for me by name, there were factors in play that make this whole operation a very, very bad idea. And you couldn't tell the others because they would also point out there was no need to delay the rescue and would have to be let in on the real mission."

Ivy turned his head back and forth between the two men a few times. "What's the real mission?"

"They needed the people who took me to lead them to something," Hatcher said. "Isn't that right?"

"Well, golly gee fucking willickers, Hatcher…" Woodley tossed a hand up and let it drop, slapping his thigh. "You might as well give the whole briefing, if you know so much."

"No, that's about all I got. I have no idea what they were wanting these guys to lead them to. But I can tell you that whatever it is, we don't want to be anywhere near it."

Garza stepped closer. "It was bad enough we find out about Hatcher after the fact, Woodley. You didn't tell us about any other mission, you son of a bitch."

"Yeah," Zorn said. He was the biggest of the group, with pale skin and a corn-fed look that at the moment was turning a shade of red beneath his crew cut. "Why don't you fill us in before you're grabbing your ankles and yelling BOHICA?'"

"Everybody just calm the fuck down, okay? Jesus. Now that we've liberated our asset, the next phase is supposed to be the easy part. All we have to do is kill some animal. A big dumb thing the locals are afraid of."

Hatcher took a breath. "Animal. What kind of animal?"

"Natives call it Kongamoto. Some sort of giant bird. They're very superstitious about it, scares them to death. They practically worship it, like some demon god or something. If things are still going according to plan—and there is no reason to think they aren't—they've led us to where it nests. All we do now is perforate it with a few hundred rounds, and we can get the hell out of Dodge."

"You've got to be kidding me."

"Scout's honor. Look, as much as it pisses you off to hear it, I really am just following orders. We're supposed to kill the bird and get our asses out."

"Why?"

"What do you mean?"

"I mean, *why?* For fuck's sake, Woodley, the 'why' is always what matters. So, why the hell does the US government, or even just some rogue bureaucrat, want us to kill this thing?"

"What can I say? It's all political. You know, do a favor for this leader, have a chit to call in later... Who knows? I'm just a worker bee, here."

"Political? That's—" A piercing screech ripped through the air before Hatcher could finish. The trees shuddered silently as every other sound seemed to disappear. The echo throbbed several times before fading away.

The ensuing silence was finally broken by Garza. "What in the name of Jesus tap-dancing Christ was that?"

"I'm going to go out on a limb and say it was Kongamoto, whatever the hell that is." Hatcher turned to Woodley. "We need to get these men outta here. Right now, like this damn minute."

"Let's just get a grip, okay? Whatever it is, I doubt it's fucking bulletproof. I mean, show some sack, all of you. We've got enough firepower to cause an extinction event. What the hell do we have to be afraid of?"

"What did they tell you?"

"About this thing? It's supposed to fly. Maybe like a pterodactyl or something similar. Possibly related to a bat. But it should be an easy target. It's big. Should be hard to miss."

"How big?"

"They weren't sure. Size of a small plane, they guessed."

"A plane?" Garza threw his head back and did a half-pirouette. "You're talking about a dinosaur, for Christ sake!"

"They assured me it's just an animal," Woodley said, snapping the words. "All we have to do is put some rounds in it. What the hell, people? Going up against armed militia, you don't bat an eye, but shooting some animal that can't fire back makes you piss your pants?"

Hatcher looked through the trees, eyed the dappled golden glow starting to recede. "Woodley, I'm not going to say it again. We need to get everyone out of here. Now."

"In case you hadn't guessed by now, you aren't actually in command here, Hatcher. I know you're pissed, but everything really is going according to plan. Except that, maybe, you forced our hand a bit earlier than I'd have liked."

"*Now*, Woodley. It's getting dark. I don't have time to argue with you about it."

"Darkness is what we're supposed to be counting on. The thing won't show itself in full daylight. We have state-of-the-art NVDs and FLIR. It should be like shooting ducks at a carnival."

"Listen to me. You don't understand *dick* about what's going on. If they wanted me, and specifically me, this isn't just some animal we're dealing with. This has nothing to do with being gutless. This is about being an idiot. And a soon-to-be dead idiot, at that, if you don't shake the shit out of your head and start listening."

Woodley held Hatcher's gaze for a long moment. There was a cloud of doubt in those eyes. Hatcher could see the man thinking, weighing his options, working through how it would play out. Wondering if maybe he'd misread the situation.

He started to speak, but before a complete word escaped his mouth, another screech erupted.

This one was much closer. It stabbed Hatcher's ears, caused him to flinch. He looked up just in time to see a creature diving straight down, ballistic, traveling at something close to terminal velocity.

Garza raised his head just as the thing smashed into him, the sound of bones snapping and crunching clearly audible even in Hatcher's ringing ears, the man's body compressed into a misshapen sack, numerous splintered pieces held together by skin and cloth.

The thing screeched again, a full-throated scream. It was a shimmering shade of black, almost glossy. It stood over Garza's mangled body, stomping a taloned foot onto his chest and spreading its wings. The first thing that struck Hatcher was its size. Enormous, at least eight-feet tall, a wingspan that had to be more than twice that. It had an elongated head, something almost bat-like, but round and protruding downward, shaped like a mule's. Its wings were leathery, and it had four clawed fingers curving out at the apex of each. It looked straight at Hatcher, eyes ablaze with a crimson glow.

Zorn had been the closest. The creature's dive had caught him by surprise, and he dove to the side, rolling a few times to gain distance, and was now popping off rounds. Ivy was doing the same, having dropped his first-aid kit and swung his weapon off his shoulder.

The thing hissed and raised its wing, using the upper part as a shield, then seemed to collapse into itself, forming a tight ball over Garza's body. Hatcher could almost feel it coming, sense the tension coiling, ready to explode.

"Get down!"

Hatcher dove at Ivy, tackling him just as the creature spun out of its curl, the thing spiraling so fast it was barely more than a blur. Garza's skull rocketed past, smashing Woodley in the shoulder and knocking him to the ground.

The creature dropped back onto its feet, grabbed what remained of Garza's corpse in its talons, and leapt into the air. Hatcher felt two powerful flaps of its wings, the gusts forcing him to blink, and when he looked, it had cleared the trees and soared into open sky.

Hatcher pulled himself off of Ivy. The man sat up, peered up into the gloaming and dusted himself off.

"Ho. Lee. Shit."

Pushing himself to his feet, Hatcher looked back at Woodley. The man was holding his shoulder, rolling his arm forward and back. He shook his head and waved Hatcher off. Garza's head lay wedged against a clump of grass a few feet away, mouth open, eyes dead slits.

"Little help!"

Zorn was cradling his abdomen. Hatcher glanced at Ivy, who nodded and picked up his first aid kit. He was a few steps behind when Hatcher reached the man.

"Wouldn't you know it," Zorn said, coughing. He pulled his arm away from his stomach. "Boned by a teammate."

Ivy sucked in a loud breath through his teeth. Hatcher felt himself wince.

Three bones, what looked like ribs, protruded from Zorn's midsection. Flesh and muscle and connective tissue still hung in clumps from each. They seemed joined at a piece of breast bone.

"Can you remove them?"

"Not without a risk of him bleeding out."

Zorn coughed again. "Right here, guys."

Ivy turned to set down the first aid kit and retrieve dressing material from it. Under his breath he said, "He needs an OR, Hatcher."

Hatcher gave a curt nod. "Want to prove what a tough son of a bitch you are, soldier?"

"Not especially," Zorn said, his voice rough, rasping. "Is there a pussy option?"

"We need to get you out of here. Not to mention us. Think you can move without slicing any vital organs?"

"Maybe. If you got some good junk for me to shoot up. Hurts like a bitch, man."

Hatcher glanced at Ivy. "What about it?"

"I might be able to dose him enough to help without knocking him out."

Hatcher tipped his head back, searching the sky. Then he cut his gaze to Woodley.

"How far's the extraction point?"

"Thirty clicks or so west. But not for another twelve hours."

"Failsafe?"

"No. Complete disavowal, remember? No radio contact, no homing. We show up. Or not. Failing that, same as you were told. The embassy."

"Yeah, in Zambia. How far is that? Fifty miles? A hundred?"

"What do you want me to say? I'm in the same boat you are. Our only known contact was Mbuyi. And he took off to drive the hostage across the border. We just have to make it through the night."

"Yeah, but in order to do that, we have to get as far away from here as possible. So, we need to get to the vehicles and not waste any more time arguing about it."

"Look, Hatcher, I know you're pissed. I don't blame you. Really, I don't. But don't you think our best bet is to do what we came here to do and kill that thing?"

"You mean, what *you* came here to do. I came here to rescue a hostage, remember?"

"Still, it caught us by surprise, that's all. We have RPGs in the floor of the Hummer, for crying out loud. If we just prepared—"

"The answer is no. We have one KIA—our sniper, at that—and another down in need of urgent medical attention. And I have no doubt whatever it was could have taken us all out right then if it had really wanted to."

Woodley gave him a skeptical look, brows cinched. "Then why didn't it?"

Hatcher didn't respond. He looked down at Zorn, who gave him a weak thumbs up as Ivy administered a syringe, slowly depressing the plunger.

"What do we have for transportation? Same as before?"

"Yes. Plus what they brought you in."

The words seemed to echo in Hatcher's head for a moment. Something shifted in his head, revealing a new question.

"You never answered my question. Why?"

Woodley shook his head, frowning. "I told you. The brass figured they'd take you to where it nests or hangs out or whatever."

"No, I mean, why do they want us to kill this thing? Please don't expect me to believe they care about the plight of some third-world poverty hole, because they don't."

"What can I say?" Woodley said, shrugging. "Above my pay grade."

"You're lying. I can see it in the direction your eyes moved before you answered, in the timing of the shrug as you spoke, in the way your lids hooded as the words passed your lips, and in the way you curled those same lips back over your teeth, as if to bite them closed and stop more lies from coming out."

Woodley shook his head, grunting an exasperated puff of air as he tossed his arms up.

"And despite being a fucking idiot, you're not stupid. You would have asked these same questions, demanded answers. And you did. So quit holding back and tell me everything."

The man sucked in a deep breath, held it as he searched the ground, then let it out, his body deflating some.

"Cliché as it sounds, it's classified."

"Is it vital enough to national security that you're willing to endure broken arms and missing teeth? Because I wouldn't bank on me being above all that if I were you."

Ivy stood, took a step closer. "Answer the damn question, Woodley."

Seconds passed as the man's gaze volleyed back and forth, Hatcher to Ivy to Hatcher. His eyes lingered on Hatcher for a long moment, then he lowered them, thinking.

"Helium," he said.

Zorn let out a laugh, a rummy, drug-induced chuckle.

"What does that even mean?" Hatcher said.

"Apparently, the world only has a finite supply. Who fucking knew, right? All kinds of high-tech shit uses tons of the stuff. But it doesn't exist everywhere, and supplies have been starting to run low, low enough some places have banned party balloons and that kind of crap. Then they recently found a huge cache of it in Tanzania, enough to supply everyone for a few more years. But not forever. The shortage got a lot of people spooked."

"Keep going."

"Well, it seems that there's another valley like it, same rock formations and satellite indicators or whatever it is, and they suspect this field is even bigger. Maybe two or three times as big. Enough of the stuff to last twenty years. Only when they've tried to drill core samples…"

Hatcher glanced around the jungle, then tilted his head to search the sky. "Their engineers have disappeared."

"Something like that."

"That's just great."

"Hey, it wasn't my goddamn idea. The way they explained it, this was important stuff. Medical devices, lab equipment, all kinds of crap that requires it to function. The world needs an ample supply. Without one, people all over the globe will be fucked."

"By 'they,' you mean, Keegan. And you believed him. *Still* believe him."

"Why wouldn't I?"

"How about because if this were actually about saving the world, you think he'd send a team of five contractors? Guys he had to blackmail? For Christ's sake, wake the hell up. Did he ever show you credentials? I never saw any. Nothing with his name on it. Nothing with anyone's name on it. Just clandestine meetings in government basements. No paper trail. Jesus, Woodley, this is the same asshole who made up some BS story about the Vice President's daughter to explain all the secrecy, why it all had to be off the books, untraceable, when you have to know by now it was just some poor aid worker in the wrong place at the wrong time. Just some good woman trying to help albinos, or whatever. But who do you think orchestrated that? Hell, who do you think arranged for her to be taken in the first place? This was planned from the beginning, right down to the tiniest detail. It had to look real. Real people, real news stories."

"I don't understand…" Woodley blinked. "You're saying there's no helium?"

"No, I'm sure there is. I'm sure there are a gazillion metric shit-tons of the stuff, or however they measure it, just like he said. And I'm also sure the rights to it are worth a few metric shit-tons of money."

"Money? Wait, you're telling me…"

"Yes. That guy cut a deal. Whoever the hell he is. A big, fat gild-your-toilet deal that will make him millions. Maybe hundreds of millions. No wonder he told me he was retiring, that this was his last gig. Jesus."

"But, he must have thought we could do it, then, right?"

"No. He probably thought all of you would die." *All except me*, Hatcher thought. *Me, he needed to keep alive.* He didn't know how he knew that, just that he did. "Open your eyes, Woodley. Why the hell do you think they asked for *me*…by *name*?"

"He said there was a vendetta of some sort. Didn't get into the details. All I was told was, they'd take you somewhere, and we were supposed to retrieve you and terminate the target."

"There's a vendetta, all right. But not with some guerrilla clan." Hatcher turned to look at Zorn. "Think he can move now?"

Ivy hitched a shoulder. "I guess we're gonna find out."

The two of them helped Zorn to his feet. His eyes were glazed, lids half closed. He had a dreamy smile on his face, even as he winced a few times.

"Keep your eyes on the sky," Hatcher said, looking at Woodley. "You have those NVDs?"

Woodley nodded, reaching into a pack.

"You see it, let us know. If it sees *us*, open fire on it. Three round bursts. How're you set on ammo?"

He detached the curved magazine from his rifle and replaced it. "Four mags. A couple dozen more in the Hummer."

Zorn had a few magazines of the same caliber, so did Ivy. But it didn't matter. If they needed more cover than that to make it to the vehicles, they never were going to reach them anyway.

"It'll have to do. Let's move." Hatcher picked up Zorn's rifle and replaced the magazine before shouldering it. He looked through the trees. Little diamond-shaped sparkles between the leaves. "The sun will be completely gone in a few minutes."

He let Ivy point the way, each of them with one of Zorn's arms around their necks and over their shoulders. Zorn, for his part, helped more than Hatcher expected, so it wasn't quite dead weight. He alternated between laughing and grunting. Like he could feel the pain, but would have a hard time caring less.

"How is it looking back there, Woodley?"

"Nothing, and lots of it."

The jungle was thick. The path they were following was recently slashed, broken stems of rubbery plants dangled in places on each side, partially sliced, other parts lay flat from being pressed with boots, various leafy shapes of deep green and purplish red padded the ground underfoot. An occasional caw from what Hatcher supposed was a bird, the call of what may have been a monkey. The trill of insects rose and fell in waves.

To Hatcher's left, those jeweled twinkles of light flashed and then disappeared. Hatcher looked up. Darkness was creeping across the twilight like a weeping wound.

Hatcher tapped Ivy and stopped. "Now might be a good time to break out those NVDs."

Ivy nodded. Hatcher took Zorn's weight and pivoted to look at Woodley, who was a few yards behind. Woodley's rifle dropped from its sling as he got the message and fit the goggles over his head. He made some adjustments along the sides, staring first at the ground, then the sky, then leveling his gaze at Hatcher.

Something wasn't right.

"*Listen*," Ivy said, pausing, goggles near his face, ready to be slipped over his head gear. "You hear that?"

Woodley shrugged his rifle higher and leaned his head back, scanning the heavens. "I don't hear anything. Don't' see anything, either."

"That's what he means," Hatcher said. "Everything's gone quiet."

Darkness seemed to fall like a blanket. The surrounding jungle became a jumble of strange shadows, with shapes suddenly both closer and farther than before. Woodley was still visible, but hard to see. It was gray beyond him, a dark background populated by deep shadows. Something even darker moved. Fast.

"Look out!"

Woodley started to turn, but there was no time to act. Hatcher felt a buffet of air against his face as he raised his weapon, could make out the ink-black shape as it swooped through. The slashing sound of movement whipping through the air, a wet, popping crunch. Something loose bounced off Hatcher's M4 a split second before a large curve of hair and skin and bone slapped his abdomen. In the dying light, he could make out a nose and eyeless lid as the piece of skull slid like a broken saucer off his boot. By the time he raised his eyes, he couldn't make out anything else but shades of ebony beneath a slate sky.

Ivy scrambled to take aim. The air swirled and something cut and fanned just feet above them.

"Jesus, Mary, and Joseph," Ivy said. "It's like, it's like… Hatcher! You gotta see this thing! Oh my *God*!"

Hatcher wasn't sure what the man could be seeing that they hadn't already got an eyeful of, but he didn't have time to ponder it. He could make out Woodley's NVDs on the ground in front of him from the glow and picked them up. A dull, greenish light shone in the view side of the lens. He pulled them over his head, groping the sides with his fingers and fiddling with the sliding controls until the area around him seemed in focus. These were high quality. Not the best he'd ever tried, but good enough.

He panned the sky, then swept his head around. Nothing.

"Gone," Ivy said. "It just pointed itself up and shot like a missile! Never seen anything like it. I mean, damn."

Hatcher looked at Woodley's body. He lowered his head to see the piece of Woodley's face on the ground.

"How far to the vehicles from here?"

"Click, click and a half. We were just behind your convoy. This should take us right to them, more or less."

"Not us. I'm going to draw it away," Hatcher said, heading to where Woodley lay.

"What? No. We should stick together. I can't handle him myself."

Zorn laughed, then gagged for a few seconds. "Too much man for you," he mumbled.

"You can if you're not being attacked. Look, I think it's me it wants. I also think it's going to pick everyone else off one at a time until it gets me. Unless I can draw it away, and it thinks I'm alone."

"How do you know that?"

"I don't. Don't ask me to explain. There's no time, and I really don't have much of an explanation to offer. I want you take him back to where you found me. Just stay there. Hunker down for about an hour. And do what you can to keep him alive in the process. If I'm the only one headed for the vehicles, it may think I'm trying to escape and come after me."

"What if it doesn't follow you?"

Hatcher inhaled deeply, surveyed the sky for a moment. "If I'm wrong, we're probably all dead anyway. That thing can pick us off whenever it wants to. But I'm pretty sure I'm the one it's really after."

"And if you're right? What are you supposed to do if it does come after you? If you don't make it to the Hummer?"

"What I was brought here to do, whatever that is. Don't try to understand, just go."

Ivy shook his head, then nodded. He hooked Zorn's arm over his neck and started to move back the way they'd come, sidestepping past Woodley's corpse. Hatcher watched for a moment, then checked Woodley's pocket's for magazines. He rolled the body over and could see Woodley's face in the greenish monochrome, part of it missing, the face of someone unmasked while straining an organ in the catacombs of an opera house.

A quick calculation of rounds told him he had a hundred and twenty. But part of him was certain for any of them to do any good, he'd have to be up close, practically shoving the barrel in the thing's mouth. It had already absorbed a couple of dozen hits, at least. Its leathery hide must be as thick as an elephant's. There wasn't much doubt its wings were strong enough to handle high velocity rounds. It left him wondering if there was anything it *couldn't* handle.

He stared down the makeshift trail until Ivy and Zorn were out of sight.

"All right," he said, his voice loud but not overly so. Anything louder than necessary would come across as baiting. At least, that was what his gut told him. "Here's your chance."

He let out a breath and broke into a run. The NVDs kept the terrain visible, and he was able to move at a double-time pace. He kept his rifle up, stopping every few dozen yards to sweep the sky to his rear with the barrel, controlling his breathing, listening, watching, watching, listening.

Minutes passed. He had to have traveled over a kilometer. Run stop sweep, run stop sweep. Nothing but eerie glowing jungle with a pitch background to all sides. No choice but to keep moving.

A break in the foliage seemed to jump in front of him. Dirt road. Nothing visible in either direction. He headed to the right, more of a sprint now. Nothing. He was about to turn around when something came into view, a bright monochromatic outline around a curve.

The back of a truck. He recognized it as he drew closer. The one he'd arrived in, with the grappling hook launcher in the rear. He should have turned left. He'd practically come full circle.

He stopped and scanned the sky, swept the dense cluster of forest to each side. His thoughts turned to Ivy, Zorn. For all he knew, they were already dead, or in the process of being dismembered. There was no way to be sure.

But he didn't believe it. He had to be the target.

He jumped in the truck, placing the rifle across his lap. Keys were in the ignition. He closed his eyes and breathed a grateful sigh.

What if you're wrong?

No. He shook the thought from his head. He'd been through too much, seen too much, not to know. He was the one it wanted. It wouldn't just let him go.

But what if you're wrong?

The truck started on the third try. He pulled off his NVDs and turned on the headlights. He shifted into reverse, then drive, then reverse, using all of a seven-point turn to get it aimed in the opposite direction. He maneuvered past the other vehicles, then gunned the engine and bounced down the dirt road.

What if you're wrong?

He made it a couple of hundred yards before the headlights reflected off more vehicles. The team's, he realized. A Hummer and a safari truck. They were pulled slightly to the left, probably to hug the tree line. He could tell they had stopped here to follow him on foot, laying back far enough not to be noticed.

Hatcher slowed the truck, squeezed it by the two vehicles. The road was narrower at this spot. Branches drummed and scraped on the passenger side, a shriek of metal on metal erupted on the right as it side swiped the Hummer.

He was just past the second vehicle and starting to accelerate when something slammed into the roof of the truck, caving it halfway in. The truck swerved. He was barely able to correct it before there was a second hit, this one smashing the windshield and causing him to veer off into the bush.

One wheel of the truck jumped a felled trunk and popped it onto its side.

Seconds passed. He braced himself for another impact. Nothing.

Goggles, weapon.

He turned off the headlights, then climbed out through the driver's side window, jumping to the ground. He adjusted his NVDs, tilted and swiveled his head in every direction.

There it was. Circling overhead. It started to form a tighter and tighter gyre, centered on Hatcher, spiraling downward.

Holy shit.

Through the night vision, he could see what Ivy was talking about. The creature didn't look like some giant bat anymore, not exactly. It seemed to have the same form at its core, but its skull was long and hooked, with enormous horns curving into sharp points. Surrounding its body was a burst of snake-like appendages, tentacling outwards and writhing like antennae.

We even have RPGs in the floor of the Hummer.

Hatcher launched himself into a low sprint. He looked up as his fingers hooked the latch on the Hummer's door to see the creature in a dive bomb, wings swept back, rocketing toward him. Before he could get the door open, it flared, slamming its feet into the vehicle, talons digging into the roof. Hatcher felt the latch rip from his hand as the Hummer jumped into the air. With two slaps of its wings the thing lifted the entire carriage off the ground, a feat Hatcher could barely believe he was witnessing. Another flap, then another, until the wheels were fifteen feet over Hatcher's head.

Hatcher snapped the M4 up, let out three bursts, followed by three more. Aiming was difficult, but he tried, picking areas to target rather than spots. The creature let go, and Hatcher flung himself out of the way as the vehicle slammed onto the patch of road, part of it crunching the back of the safari truck, causing the front wheels to pop up and jounce back down.

The thing soared higher, then started to spiral into a dive.

The wings. It didn't like getting hit in the wings.

In the UV glow of NVDs, Hatcher could see a difference between the upper wings, which seemed to be stiff, flattened arms with joints, and the lower parts, which were flexible, like leather sails. He pictured the way it had curled itself into a ball, using its arms as shields. It wasn't just protecting its body, it was protecting the soft parts of its wings.

He looked over to the pickup truck, still laying on its side. *Maybe.*

The thing was swooping toward him again. He fired two more bursts, held his ground until it seemed he could reach out and grab it, then dropped to his back and fired two more. It shot past him and rounded up, banking into a tight turn. Hatcher flipped onto his feet and bolted for the truck, making a show of ditching his rifle.

This better work.

He dove into the bed, felt the creature's talons rake his back, claws ripping through his shirt and gashing his flesh but unable to grasp. Those feet punched against the cab of the truck, talons smashing the rear glass and puncturing the roof as it clamped down.

Bursts of wind on his back. He felt the truck shift, sensed it break loose from its traction on the ground. The rear of the bed started to hang.

He slid over to the grappling catapult, spinning it around and wedging himself between it and the tailgate. The truck swung beneath him, and he felt gravity go negative for an instant, sensed everything below falling away, then the truck swung back and his own weight pressed him down, trying to pin him.

Struggling against the schizophrenic g-forces, he leveled the sight of the catapult at the creature. The thing's wings would not stay in one place, whipping back and forth, presenting a broad side for just a flash, then disappearing. There would be no perfect shot; at best, it was a Hail Mary. He pulled back the heavy spring on the charge bolt and tugged the enormous trigger.

The mechanism snapped and the umbrella of hooks shot like a spear. Cable spun out behind it, the reel whirring. The tip tore through the lower part of the left wing, barely.

Barely was good enough.

The creature let out a high-pitched shriek. The sound cut through the ringing in Hatcher's ears, stabbed at his brain. A second later, the thing dropped the truck. Hatcher tried to brace himself, his body light and swimming. He tucked his head, wrapping it with his arms, and forced all the breath out of his lungs. The truck crashed into the ground.

His next conscious thought was that he was still alive. He could tell by the competing pain, his hip screaming to be heard over the shouting of his ribs, his wrist hollering even louder when he went to move.

He was on the ground. Breathing was a challenge, as every expansion of his ribcage sent shockwaves through his torso. He managed to sit up. The night-vision goggles were askew on his head, and he fought through the pain in his wrist to adjust them back over his eyes. The scene tumbled back into perspective when he saw the truck on exploded tires a few feet away. Through the buzzing in his ears, he became aware of the whirring of the reel, the cable still letting out.

Then there was a clank, the groan of metal, followed by a vibrating *twang*, and the truck started to move. Across the ground in fits and starts at first, surging up and crunching down, until soon it wasn't touching the road anymore, just swinging forward, rising into the night. Dipping, jerking up, dipping, jerking up, penduluming forward, then back.

There wasn't much time to decide. There were only two choices; go back for Ivy and Zorn or go after the creature. That thing was too smart, too strong, not to figure out a way to free itself. And if it managed to do that before they could all get to safety, it wouldn't end well, he was certain of it. There was too much night left.

He scrambled to retrieve the M4. No choice. He had to go after the thing, find a way to kill it. He hurried back to the safari truck, checked the ignition, the visor, the seat, found the keys hanging from the rear-view mirror on a lanyard.

The vehicle started right away, sputtering until he revved it. The transmission clunked into drive and the truck lurched forward and was moving again. Doffing the NVDs and using the headlights, he tried to keep the truck from fishtailing as he sped down the road at a far higher speed than was wise.

Over a mile had passed before the truck came into view. Still following the road, still swinging in spasms. Never getting higher than fifteen or twenty feet. He closed the distance, studying the tree shadows of the jungle surrounding him.

It can't clear the treeline. Or it's scared to try. It wants an open path.

Hatcher gunned the engine. It whined, and he saw the tachometer was practically redlined, but he only needed it to last a few more minutes. Seconds, if he caught a break.

There it was. Up ahead, a curve in the road. He held the accelerator down until the hood of the truck was almost touching the dangling end of the pickup. The front end of the pickup swayed over the hood then down over the road. Hatcher bumped it a few times as he tried to keep pace.

A blink before the turn in the curve Hatcher stomped on the gas, pressing the pedal to the floor as hard as he could. The truck slammed into the pickup. The safari railing smashed through the windshield, stabbing into the upholstery, hooking itself over the dashboard and steering column. Hatcher held the wheel straight, the pain in his wrist howling curses that burned their way up his arm. He felt the front wheels lift even as he held the accelerator down, until he threw himself out the door the moment before the truck impacted a tree.

He separated his shoulder on impact and tumbled almost twenty feet over the rocky dirt road. He thought he could hear the cracking of several ribs, but whether he actually did or not didn't matter, as he knew several were fractured whether he heard them crack or not. He had a hard time finding a part of his body that wasn't on fire in some way.

No time for a survey of injuries. He struggled to his feet, favoring his left arm. A few of the lights from the safari truck were still on, visible a few yards into the jungle. He took a step and noticed a glint on the ground. The M4. He hefted it, gingerly minimizing the use of his left arm, felt its balance, reseated the magazine and racked another round into the chamber, just to be sure.

The walk to the truck was excruciating, each step a mix of sizzles and stabs. When he reached it, he saw it was still entangled with the pickup, both of them enmeshed in the foliage. He managed to reach through a broken window and retrieve the goggles. Only one lens still worked. It was cracked, but he was able to see through it after a few adjustments.

He followed the cable from the pickup, fighting his way through the webbed reach of plants and limbs. A couple of hundred feet later, he saw the creature. It was impaled in several spots. It had taken a long, thick bone through the stomach on its way down, and one wing was completely broken. Several other long shards of skeleton—ribs, from the look of them—had pierced it in various places. Hatcher could picture the fall, an accelerated arc swinging it down like a huge sledge hammer, pounding it through the growth. Down into a Garden of Bones.

Through the functioning NVD lens, Hatcher could see the parts of it up close, parts invisible to the naked eye: tentacled appendages wriggling; a skull overlay that looked like a cadaverous vulture; a serpentine tail.

To his surprise, it moved, not without difficulty, but enough to cause Hatcher to take a step back. The thing looked at him with eyes that burned a strange shade in the monochrome. It opened its beak-like jaws and made a grating, squawking roar, like the death rattle of a thousand souls. Maybe more.

Hatcher leveled the M4 and squeezed the trigger.

No three-round bursts this time. He unloaded the magazine in barely a second, retrieved another, then unloaded that. He seated his final magazine and moved closer. The thing was no longer trying to move, but a series of hisses and snarls were still coming out of it. He positioned himself as close as he could, held his ground as a tentacle rose like it was going to strike and shoved the barrel into the thing's mouth.

The sound it made drowned out the shots. Hatcher's head felt like it was collapsing in on itself. He managed to look through the NVD as he dropped to his knees, saw a glowing phantasm tear itself from the body and rear back, a shape of flame surrounding a creature even larger than the one it had occupied, an enormous crocodilian skull sandwiched between twin spirals of horns. Just as the thing seemed to be reaching for Hatcher, ready to consume him in some horrific embrace, it flashed out of existence, leaving swirls of tiny wisps flickering like embers before they, too, vanished completely.

He lay on the ground for the better part of an hour, drifting in and out of consciousness, not fighting it either way, finally pushing himself to his feet in response to some mental clock going off like an alarm. He winced at the aches and the burns and the stiffness setting in and forced himself to start walking. He followed the dirt road back toward where the encounter had started, walking for around fifteen minutes, every other step forcing him to bite his lip, suck in a shallow breath.

Headlights. One was a high beam, mismatched. He was too exhausted to worry about whose they were. He stood in the middle of the road, let the beams wash over him, barely able to raise an arm to shield his eyes.

The vehicle slowed to a stop, audibly shifted into park. A door opened.

"Hatcher?" Ivy's voice came from behind the lights. Then his figure cut a shadow. Before Hatcher realized he was that close, he felt a firm but gentle hand take hold of his arm. "Jesus, you look like... what the hell happened?"

The feel of support abruptly caused his legs to give. Ivy helped him to the Jeep. He vaguely recognized it as having been part of the caravan parked along the road.

With Ivy's help, he eased himself into the passenger seat. Zorn was in the back, presumably asleep. Hatcher could make out ragged breathing.

"You're still kicking, at least," Ivy said, settling behind the wheel. "Does that mean that thing isn't going to be a problem?"

"Not for us," Hatcher said. He tried to adjust himself to find an elusive position of relative comfort. Wasn't going to happen. "Not tonight."

"I can't wait to hear all about it."

Hatcher wondered how much he could explain, how much he even understood himself. Whether he even dare try to tell Ivy about the Carnates, about demons, about his tainted soul, his battles with the ruling elite of Hell, and the civil war that seemed to be raging below. Or whether any of it would make sense if he did. Whether he was even able to understand himself why he was growing increasingly certain that this whole thing was part of an even more elaborate plan, a plan within a plan, designed to occupy him, to get him as far away from the States as possible. A giant distraction from something he had no conception of, for reasons he couldn't begin to imagine.

"In the meantime," Ivy continued, "I need to get us to the LZ. Extraction is supposed to be at dawn."

"Don't bother. There won't be any."

"You serious?"

Hatcher leaned back in the seat, closed his eyes. "As a heart attack. The only thing likely to be waiting for us at the extraction point is another group of paramilitary types, all promised a bounty for each kill."

"So, what, then? Embassy?"

"Not if we can avoid it." Hatcher opened his eyes, looked around the interior, grimacing with each twist. "There a radio in this thing?"

"Not that I've seen."

"Well, then, that's our mission, for the moment. Just drive. I think there was a radio in one of the trucks. Two clicks or so ahead."

Ivy shifted into drive, eased the Jeep forward. "Who you gonna radio?"

Hatcher felt the breeze flow over his cheeks and scalp. It stung a bit, and he realized what a mess his face must be, but it was the closest thing to a pleasurable sensation he'd had in a while.

"I know a gal," he said, inhaling as deeply as his ribs would allow. "Who maybe knows a guy."

"Then what," Ivy said.

"Then, we go home. And I track down a certain Fed who thinks he's about to retire a wealthy man and put him through an interrogation he'll wake up in cold sweats remembering decades from now. You're welcome to join me, if you like. But you'd probably be wise to stay out of it and hope they leave you alone."

Ivy shook his head. "You kidding? I wouldn't miss it for the world."

"Good man," Hatcher said, feeling himself slip into a light doze. "Good man."

Psycho Metrics

A familiar aroma, faint but sharp, permeated the house, tickling Colleen's nostrils as she bent forward. She'd been keenly aware of it from the moment she'd entered. "Joshua is certain the killer held this," she said, pulling her head away from her brother's face and straightening her back. Like everyone else in the room, she wore a rubber glove on each hand and used both to extend the thick tome out to the detective who had passed it to her. "He suggests you search the shelves."

"We've dusted everything. Nothing but the owner's prints in here, and a very few from his wife. Two from a housekeeper. No one else seems to have touched anything."

Colleen eyed him and blinked, shrugging. "I'm just telling you what he said."

Landry frowned, then gave a curt nod to another detective, who began to pull books one at a time from a shelf behind a round-backed leather chair. The shelves took up most of the far wall of the room, divided by a fireplace in the center. Rows and rows of thick hardcovers, their spines denoting classic works of literature and other texts bearing esoteric titles and touching upon obscure academic subjects.

"*The Philosophy of the Plays of Shakespeare Unfolded*, by Delia Bacon." he said. "Right out on the table, and we didn't even notice it. The guy's taunting us."

"Tell me about the victim," she said.

"I thought you were supposed to be psychic. You should be telling *us* stuff, not the other way around. And it's *victims*. Plural. Two of them. A college professor and his wife."

"As I already told you, I'm not psychic, and neither is my brother, for that matter. At least, that's not the way I look at it. Joshua simply gets impressions from objects, possibly trapped energy absorbed during some sort of trauma, like an essence, slowly seeping out."

"Yeah, so you say. The prof's name is John Nesbitt. Taught English at the city college. Wife was Margaret Ann."

Colleen nodded. "A college professor. Dignified profession. Authoritative. Someone in a position of trust. What do you think the motive was?"

"I think that when it comes to murder, there are generally only four.

Plus another that we're only now starting to talk about." He stuck his thumb out like a hitchhiker, starting a count. "Revenge, considered the oldest known to man. Jealousy, which is sort of like its first cousin. Profit, which is everybody's favorite. And power, something people have probably been killing over since the first caveman decided he wanted to be able to tell all the others what to do. But it's starting to look like this is the other one that's on the list."

"And what would that be?"

"Well… this is the second set of bodies found like this, last one was about three weeks ago. You probably read about it. We kept the details out of the papers, didn't want a media circus. I'm not ready to rule anything out, but as far as I can tell, the motive here is one society's been slow to acknowledge, but it's probably been around the longest of all. From the looks of it, we got a predator on our hands. Someone who kills simply because he enjoys it."

"I see," she said. "Or maybe that's just what the killer wants everyone to think."

Landry shot her a look. "If you got some pearls of wisdom to share, I'm all ears. You might actually earn some of what the department is paying you."

"I was just engaging in conversation, detective. Exploring the possibilities."

"I'd say the whatever the 'possibilities' are, we're dealing with a psycho who'll keep killing until we stop him. Look, telling us to search in here and pointing out that book on the table is a neat parlor trick, but if your brother really gets *impressions*, like you say, why can't they be useful ones? Like giving us a name and address? Now that would make my day."

"I don't know what goes on in his damaged brain," she said. "I can only interpret the gist of what he is trying to say. Then I do my best to—"

Before she could finish, her brother let out a low groan, almost a growl. He moved his jaw open and closed, but the modulation to his voice failed to produce anything intelligible.

"He wants you to keep looking. This is the room."

The detective gazed down at the man in the wheelchair. A small finger of drool leaked out from one corner of his mouth where the bottom lip sagged. Colleen crouched down next to him and dabbed at it with a handkerchief.

"You're here because the Chief insisted I let you and your brother take a look. I happen to think it's a complete waste of taxpayer money." Landry stared down at the book in his hands. "Whoever this guy is, he's been extremely meticulous. The first scene gave us nothing, only what he wanted us to find. I can't imagine this will be any different. He's too careful."

"You keep referring to the killer as a man. How do you know?"

The detective looked at her. "What?"

"How do you know it's a man and not a woman?"

"I…" He paused, narrowing his eyes. "You're right. I don't. But I've been doing this a long time. You didn't see them. A normal, everyday couple. Not even sure you could call them middle-aged. Mutilated in ways that I wouldn't want to describe in mixed company. Whoever it was took a sick delight in presenting them for us to find."

The man in the wheelchair moaned, managing to shake his body enough to rattle the wheels. Colleen stroked his hair and leaned in close. He gasped a few times, trying to catch his breath. His eyes were red and moist.

"Joshua says the answer is in the books. The books and the bacon."

"That's about as helpful as a fortune cookie."

Colleen started to say something, then paused to reconsider. "You said the killer was taunting you. What did you mean?"

Landry twisted his mouth to the side and lifted his hat, scratching the top his head with his free fingers. "At the first scene, a couple of weeks ago, there was a strip of raw bacon set out on the floor in the center of the kitchen. And now… well, you can smell it. A couple of strips were left in a frying pan for hours, simmering until they burnt. That was no coincidence. Neither is the name on this book."

"And what do you think the significance of 'bacon' is?" she asked.

The detective shrugged. "I'd say it's pretty obvious, isn't it? The perp's trying to make a point, calling us 'pigs,' mocking us."

Several minutes passed in relative silence before the detective behind the leather chair spoke up. "Lieutenant? I found something."

Landry looked over as the younger man carefully raised a square piece of paper he pinched at the corner between two gloved fingers.

"It was in this," the man said, holding up a biography titled *The Life and Times of Sir Francis Bacon.* "It has writing on it."

"What does it say?" Landry asked, casting a wary glance over to Colleen, then down at her brother as she placed a hand on the crippled man's shoulder.

"It says…" The man turned the paper back toward him to check it again before answering. He cleared his throat and swallowed. *"MY KNIFE'S STILL NICE AND SHARP."*

Landry looked at Joshua, studying him. The man's eyes met his, but drifted off, unable to hold on.

"I guess you can add another at bat to your brother's hit streak," Landry said.

"There's something else," the other detective said. "At the bottom." He circled around from behind the leather chair and held the slip of paper out for Landry. The Lieutenant set down the book he'd been holding and took it. He stared at the writing for several seconds.

"What else does it say?" Colleen asked, breaking the silence.

"It says, *'My name is Jack and I've come back.'*"

●⟨⟨⟨⟨⟨⟨⟨⟨⟨⟨⟨⟨●

"It probably won't come as a surprise for you to learn that I'm opposed to your involvement in this case."

Colleen Bender sat in an uncomfortable chair across the desk from Lt. Landry and watched him eye her with barely concealed disdain, every word passing between his lips practically dripping with contempt. All niceties and politesse of the sort he had exhibited the other night, of which there had been none too much to begin with, had been dropped. She decided she did not like the man.

"I'm sorry you feel that way," she said. "My brother and I are just trying to help."

The detective raised an eyebrow. "At twenty dollars an hour, I have a hard time believing you're here out of a sense of altruism."

Colleen shifted in her seat, running a hand beneath her leg to straighten her skirt. "My brother needs full-time care. I can't afford to hire anyone, and

I can't work and take care of him at the same time. I also have to feed and house and clothe him. I eventually intend to set up a non-profit organization and hope to fund any future assistance to law enforcement through donations, but until then I have no choice but to charge for his services… our services. My bank account will eventually run dry if I don't."

She immediately regretted saying that. What she charged was what she charged, and she should have left it at that. Showing weakness to someone like him, someone with an obvious eye to raising questions about her, a desire to discredit her, could not lead to anything good. This man's mien was throwing her off, making her defensive. Defensiveness was counterproductive. She silently resolved to be more circumspect.

"I just don't place any faith in psychics. A bunch of hokum, if you ask me. But the Chief is convinced you saved his baby nephew who went missing, so there doesn't seem to be any reasoning with the man. I sure as hell let him know how I feel about it, though."

"I prefer the term, *psychometrist.*"

"Excuse me?"

"Instead of 'psychic.' This isn't about fortune telling or spiritualism. My goal is to establish this as a method of legitimate, studied inquiry, not something people think of as supernatural. My brother has a unique ability to perceive impressions from objects, especially objects that have been held by a victim of intense trauma. Or a perpetrator of it. I've always maintained it was the trauma he himself suffered, the trauma to his brain, that awakened this ability. But the science is poorly understood."

"Poorly understood." The lieutenant chuckled under his breath and crunched one side of his mouth into a frown. "Well, unfortunately, the D.C. boys in their Brooks Brothers suits seem to have bought into this kind of snake oil."

"You're talking about the Justice Department guidance for law enforcement for consulting psychic detectives."

"You know about that?"

"I've read it. But, like I said, I don't like the term. I don't think of my brother as a psychic. I don't believe he would think of himself as one, either."

The lieutenant frowned, nodding warily. "Where is he, anyway?"

"My brother? He sleeps for two hours or so every day starting around noon. I use this time to run errands, buy groceries, take care of things that would otherwise be cumbersome." She glanced at her watch and adjusted the face on her wrist, hoping he would take the hint.

"Fair enough." He lifted a set of folders off his desk and held them out for her. "Chief says I'm supposed to give you access to the case files. I'll set you up in an interview room. It should go without saying you are not to remove anything. Not so much as a paperclip. Understood?"

"Yes."

"If you don't mind me asking," he said, his tone conveying to Colleen that he could hardly care less whether she minded or not, "why do you need this information? If your brother gets messages from beyond the grave, how does this help?"

She maintained eye contact as he stared from beneath an unevenly furrowed brow. "I never said he gets messages from beyond the grave. Quite the contrary. I maintain that he gets his impressions, his suggestions, from the energy absorbed by certain things, especially objects touched by victims of trauma. Reviewing the files could help identify items that might prove useful."

"More useful than what he sensed from touching that note, I hope."

"Not everything absorbs or maintains impressions. Like I said, the science is poorly understood. But from those impressions we were able to establish that the person is full of anger and hatred and resentment. Violence is an outlet, an avenue of vengeance. I explained that in the memo."

"Yes, you did. You even went so far as to predict whoever this sicko is would kill again within a month. And your theory that he has adopted this Jack-the-Ripper persona as a way of picking his victims I found particularly… interesting."

"It was my brother who you should attribute that prediction to, not me."

"Yes, let's talk about him for a minute. Tell me, why is it you're the only one who can understand what your brother is trying to say?"

Colleen didn't respond for several seconds. It was obvious he was couching an allegation in the form of that question.

"I grew up with my brother, upstate. Not unusual for siblings to grow up together, of course. But our home, the family farm, was far from any neighbors. We spent our entire childhood together, pretty much every day, all the way up to when he had the accident as a teenager. When he emerged from the coma, no one realized how permanent his condition would be. Our parents died in a car accident less than a year later, and since I was the only one left to take care of him, my ability to understand him gradually took shape."

"Want to know what I think? I think it's you."

Having a police officer make a statement like that, one aimed directly at her, devoid of any polite gloss, was unnerving, and she found herself feeling unusually vulnerable. She needed the cooperation of the police involved, not simply the approval of the Chief, and this man was definitely posing a threat to that. Perhaps coming to meet the detective like this to familiarize herself with the investigation one-on-one had been a mistake.

"I don't understand what you mean."

"I think you do. This whole thing with your brother, a crippled guy in a wheelchair who can't communicate except through grunts and moans, it gives you cover."

"The sounds he makes are more than grunts and moans, if you know what to listen for."

"And, conveniently, you are the only one who does."

"What are you saying, Lieutenant?"

"I'm saying you're a smart woman, smarter than you want anyone to know. I think you use your brother as a shield, a device, a way to make people take you seriously. I also think it's you, just you. You get the 'impressions' and what not and pretend they're coming from him. And while we're on the subject, I don't think you're psychic at all. I think you're just a woman playing Sherlock Holmes. A smart woman, like I said, but still just throwing out theories and observations to see what sticks, using your 'psychometric' brother to get people like me to listen."

"Psychometrist. *Psychometrics* is the measure of cognitive ability."

"See what I mean? Smart lady. Maybe a little too smart for her own good, if she thinks she can keep *out*smarting the police."

"And by that you mean, keep outsmarting *you*. That's what this is about, isn't it? You're worried you're being shown up by a woman."

"No. I'm worried I'm being manipulated by one."

She took a few deep, measured breaths to calm her nerves, told herself not to give in to paranoia. This man was not out to get her, he was suspicious by nature and, at least in this instance, simply guarding his pride, as men like him are wont to do. She would have to factor that into her dealings, she decided.

"Look, Lieutenant, if what you said were true, if I were just using my brother as a prop and was merely relying on my wits to assist you, how would I have known to have you look through the bookshelves?"

"I haven't figured that out yet. But, like I said, you're a smart lady. Smart people make lucky guesses. It was the only room in the house that didn't have visible traces of blood anywhere, the only one we hadn't combed down to the nits. Maybe you realized that, figured if there was anything we missed, it would be in there."

Colleen took in a deep breath, released it in a sigh. "Believe it or not, Lieutenant Landry, you are not the first person to suggest something like this. When I started to offer demonstrations of my brother's ability, assisting locals from the nearby town in finding things—missing cattle, stolen property, etcetera—many of them were skeptical. Allegations were whispered in my wake wherever I went, hushed, breathy tones hidden behind curved hands. They see a handicapped person, someone suffering from brain trauma, and they conclude it must be some kind of trick. An illusion. One woman even accused me of witchcraft. That experience is one reason I want to pursue the science of this, establish it as a legitimate discipline. I will say, the suggestion that I'm some kind of genius sleuth, or a 'psychic' myself, or, even better, some kind of 'psychic genius sleuth,' is flattering. But I can assure you none of that is true."

The detective shrugged, the side of his lip tugging down into a frown. "Can't say for sure what your game is, only that I don't believe any of the stuff you're peddling. But, what do I know? We got a former actor in the White House who believes in astrology. Maybe the '80s'll be the decade of crystal balls and tarot cards and psychic detectives and guys like me will be put out to pasture." He gestured toward the bullpen, visible through the interior windows of his office. "Jennings out there will get you situated."

She left the office and was quickly greeted by the younger detective who had searched through the bookshelves and found the note almost a week prior. Without his sport coat, she could see he was in good shape, athletic. He wore a black leather holster on his hip, threaded through his belt. The wooden handle of a revolver angled back from beneath a strap with a thumb break.

"Miss Bender," he said, smiling warmly. "I'm going to let you use interview room three. Would you like a coffee?"

"No. But thank you." Colleen's impressions of this officer were in stark contrast to how she felt about Landry. This man was kind and considerate, his general demeanor pleasant. Even though he was likely a few years younger than she was, she could tell he was attracted to her. She made a mental note of that.

The interview room was small, almost perfectly square. The walls were covered in white textured panels with a large rectangular mirror dominating one of them. She assumed it was two-way, used to observe interrogations. She doubted anyone would be watching her, but she couldn't rule it out. Not that it mattered. All she was there to do was to look through the case files for information she might find useful.

The files had binder clips at the top of each side. One side had crime scene photos, lab results, and documents pertaining to the victims; the other police reports and witness statements. Those were separated from internal memos and investigator notes. Colleen noticed her memo was included among those, which pleased her. Having documented observations in the official police file provided a paper trail that could thwart or at least blunt any attempts by Landry or others to cause problems for her.

One memo in particular was of interest: a summary of what the author, Lieutenant Landry, had referred to as "the Whitechapel Murders." He had clearly done his homework, describing the first five murders as "canonical," and referencing six others over the following three years that were never conclusively determined to have been committed by the same perpetrator. He listed the similarities between the wounds, intimating they were scant, while asserting that these killings were arguably more brutal and less discriminating, as the murders being investigated here were not of prostitutes or even exclusively of women. This killer had already racked up a body count of three after two incidents. Landry ended the memo by speculating the unknown subject may be planning on a total of eleven, after which he may stop, or at least completely change his M.O. He appended a list of sources to the memo and added a footnote referencing the many Jack the Ripper documentaries that had been airing in recent years in anticipation of the upcoming centennial anniversary of the Whitechapel Murders. Colleen noted that despite displaying a lack of imagination or insight in his assessments, the man was nothing if not thorough.

She was particularly impressed with his handwritten comment in the margins—underlined, with a parenthetical question mark after it—pointing to *"order of victims (?)"*.

She perused the files for the better part of an hour, finding commonalities between the decedents, some she'd already been well aware of, others she was just learning. Such details, she knew, would be invaluable in identifying the next potential victim. She took a few notes here and there and resisted the urge to jump to the section she really wanted to see. The one that dealt with suspects.

The information she was looking for was included in an internal data memo created by Landry with a subject line labeled "Investigative Scope." In it, Landry had compiled a list of potential suspects. He'd started from a set of twenty-two names in total, relatives and acquaintances of each victim that may have had motive and opportunity, but Landry had expanded that list after forensic analysis indicated all four victims had been killed by the same person. That list included persons with histories that signaled a potential for randomly targeted acts of violence, citing recent DOJ guidance on "serial murders." He then whittled it down to four prime ones by removing those with alibis for the other killings or who, in the detective's opinion, just didn't fit the profile of the killer. His memo indicated he had consulted with the FBI's newly formed Behavioral Science Investigative Support Unit, who assisted in establishing that profile.

Colleen read through the profile, gratified that it lined up precisely with what she'd expected. Male, approximately 25-35 years old, likely

Caucasian, likely unmarried. No outward signs of insanity, only a strong anti-social personality trait that he keeps well-hidden in daily life. Intelligent and well-acquainted with police investigative procedure.

She stared at the part that mentioned the familiarity with police procedure, allowing it to fuel her thoughts and push her down paths she hadn't seriously considered.

After several minutes of pensive contemplation, she moved on to the primary suspects. One jumped out at her. Dylan Wurtz. White male, twenty-nine. Drifter with a criminal record of petty misdemeanors, though he had also been arrested at least a few times for getting into bar fights, and one physical altercation with a street vendor over receiving improper change for a hot dog. Those never resulted in charges, but it did, in the eyes of the police, mark him as violent. He also had a weapons charge for carrying a knife. Attached to the memo was a photo of each suspect, along with his NCIC record. Wurtz appeared relatively clean cut, handsome even. Single, never married. Of particular interest was the fact he had attended a junior college for two semesters, studying Criminal Justice, before dropping out as soon as the draft ended. Two of his arrests took place at public libraries. He definitely fit the bill. Landry's notes indicated one thing cutting against him as a likely culprit was the fact he had no car registered in his name, only a motorcycle, something no one had reported seeing or hearing in the vicinity of either scene. She copied down the name and his last known address.

She left the precinct after about an hour and a half, making a point to say a cordial goodbye to both Lt. Landry and Detective Jennings, taking a few extra moments to socialize with the younger man. She indulged his affable nature and responded with coy ambiguity to his mildly flirtatious overtures, making certain to smile when he spoke and to offer a laugh at his occasional attempts to be entertaining with jokes about paperwork and donut shops and police never being around when you need one.

Two days later, she received a call from Landry.

"There's been another one," he said. After a short pause, he added,

"Chief would like you and your brother to get to down there right away. Apparently, he got it in his head that the fresher the scene, the more effective your brother's 'skills' may be. Wonder where he got that idea?"

"I'll get there as soon as I can."

"Good. I'll meet you there."

The line went all but silent. She thought for a moment before it occurred to her. "Lieutenant?"

"Yes?"

"Would you mind giving me the address?"

She wrote it down and thanked him. She hung up the phone and let her gaze wander over to her brother, already dressed for the morning and in his wheelchair, agitated as he always was after she received a phone call, emitting moans and grunts, drool starting to gather at the corner of his mouth. She stared absently at him for almost a minute, ignoring his bucking and groaning, wondering exactly what the motivation was behind Landry's attempts to undermine her involvement, if it was something more than pride at work. Still deep in her thoughts, she retrieved a paper towel and wiped her brother's mouth and patted his head. After carefully considering several possibilities, she decided the most likely reason was also the most obvious. Landry was simply an asshole.

She arrived at the home around 10:00 AM. Police had blocked off the suburban street in both directions, moving a barricade to allow her through after she identified herself and dropped Lieutenant Landry's name. A uniformed officer in front of the house informed Landry of her presence, and he came out to escort her and her brother into the home. He called over two other officers to lift her brother's wheelchair onto the porch, eying her resentfully the entire time.

Once in the foyer, she followed Landry, expecting to veer right into the open living room where a number of police personnel—uniformed officers, crime scene technicians, photographers—were gathered, but he instead turned left down a hallway.

"Victim's name is Cindy Einhorn. Thirty-eight. Husband found her when he came home late from work. His story checks out."

Colleen nodded. No surprise there.

"How thoroughly have you searched the house?"

"The bedroom—where she was found—has been gone over pretty well. Chief wanted us to hold off doing the other rooms except for a cursory sweep until you got here. I guess you convinced him too many other people touching things ruins the 'psychic aura' or some BS like that."

Ignoring the remark, she continued to follow him away from the living room stirring with police until he stopped near a door on the right. The gritty stench of blood and ordure was overpowering.

"I suppose I have to ask if you want to get a close look at the body. Coroner will be here any minute."

"No, that won't be necessary. It would only upset my brother."

As if in response, Joshua bucked in his seat and let out a low gurgling howl.

She moved past the master bedroom, pushing her brother quickly by it and shielding his eyes as she stole a glance. The visible walls resembled pieces of abstract art, splattered with blood. The bed was drenched in it. In the middle of the mattress lay a woman with her skirt pulled up over her abdomen. Her throat had been cut through, a deep, sawing gash, almost to the spine. Her arms were at her side, palms up. Her abdomen had been sliced and pulled open. Lengths of intestine had been removed, portions positioned next to the body. One man garbed in synthetic coveralls and a face mask knelt next to the bed, using tweezers to remove a fiber from the woman's body, carefully placing it in a clear plastic evidence bag.

Colleen looked in on the scene until she became aware of Landry waiting a few steps ahead, staring back at her. She pushed her brother forward to catch up.

The detective led them another few feet to a doorway on the opposite side of the hallway near the end. He stopped at the wall to let Colleen push her brother past him and into the room.

It was a bedroom that had been converted to a study. Smaller than the master but able to house a pair of reading chairs and a wall of books. The chairs were separated by a narrow table stand that had spaces to hold magazines and newspapers on each side. A single lamp stood on the table near the back.

She pushed her brother close to the bookshelves. After a pause, she wheeled him in front of the chairs, stopping in front of the table. Joshua grunted several times, his chest heaving with labored breaths.

"I don't think the killer spent any time in this room," she said.

"I thought your brother was the psychic," Landry said. "Shouldn't you be listening to him?"

"Psychometrist. There's nothing in here that appears to have been handled by anyone since at least yesterday. He's not telling me anything. The noises he's making are just general agitation. Being in places like this makes him very upset."

Landry frowned, giving his eyebrows a bounce, and led her back down the hallway, past the master bedroom once more, then to the foyer where it met the living room.

"You wanted me to see that back there," she said. "You wanted me to see the body, even as you pretended you didn't. Why?"

Landry stopped just past where the hallway spilled into the entry way. His eyes were tiny slits being squeezed by their lids. "To remind you this isn't a game of sleuth, Miss Marple. We're not playing at this for our own amusement. These people didn't die for your entertainment or to give you a vehicle to demonstrate some carnival mental trick. We're trying to catch a psychopath. A serial murderer."

"I'm well aware of that, Lieutenant."

Sneering, Landry twisted his head and barked over his shoulder to one of the uniformed officers. "Take Miss Bender and her brother here to the kitchen."

Colleen pushed her brother through the pockets of police. There were a few murmurs, some subdued conversation, but the overall demeanor of those standing around was one of a shared disturbance, if not shock.

The kitchen was next to a dining area behind the living room, with no wall separating the two. Colleen wheeled her brother to a stop at the edge of the carpet and surveyed the scene. There was a sink and counter below a window with a dishwasher to the right, an oven with a stovetop and more counterspace along the far wall, and a refrigerator and counter opposite the sink. The center of the kitchen was open. On the ceramic tile, written in large, carmine brushstrokes of block letters, were the words

CATCH ME
WHEN
YOU CAN

Below the writing, nearer the dining room, was a bloody print the size of a steak, the smear punctuated with a few flecks of tissue and gobbets of gore. It was marked with a numbered piece of tape adhered a few inches away.

"We found a basting brush," said a voice behind her. She turned to see Detective Jennings. He pressed his mouth into a grim smile of greeting, then pointed to direct her attention to a spot on the floor also marked with tape and a number. "We've already dusted it for prints. Chief instructed us to have it available if you want your brother to… examine it."

Joshua let out a moan that caught in his throat and turned into the sound of a cat hacking up hair. The wheelchair shook, rocking slightly from side to side as he thrashed his body.

Colleen nodded. She turned back to Jennings, then looked past him at Landry, who was watching her from across the living room.

"We think that smear of blood next to the writing—"

"Was a kidney," Colleen said, loud enough for Landry to hear. It was also loud enough to cause a hush to fall over the already quiet living room, all eyes suddenly pointed her way. She let her gaze drift back to the kitchen floor.

"Wow," Jennings said. "I'm impressed."

"Are you still going to pretend you're not the 'psychic?" Landry said. He had made his way over after her exclamation, just as she expected he would.

"You don't need to be a psychometrist to know your subject," she said. She caught his stare and maintained eye contact. "And I suspect you weren't surprised, either."

"Is there something going on I don't know about?" Jennings said, shifting his gaze from Landry to her then back again. "Because I'm having trouble following."

"Jack the Ripper sent a piece of a kidney to the police," Colleen said. "It was enclosed with a note. He signed off with '*Catch me when you can.*'"

Jennings looked over to the floor of the kitchen and let out a low whistle.

"You've been looking at this all wrong. The connection between the victims are the women."

"I guess it's a good thing we have you around to tell us how to do our jobs. Let's get one thing straight—you're a consultant, not a detective, not even a member of the investigative team, and, if you want to get technical, it's your brother who's supposed to be the consultant. You're really nothing more than an interpreter, and I don't even think you're really doing that. I think you're just playing us."

Jennings coughed into his fist. "Uh, Lieutenant…"

"Quiet, Jennings. This needs to be said." Landry shifted back to Colleen. "You may have bamboozled the Chief, but I'm not so gullible. I may have to let you in here, but I don't have to pretend you're not a fraud. So just do your little gypsy palm reader pantomime with your brother and go. And keep your Junior Crime Stopper badge in your pocket. It's bad enough I have to listen to you tell us about your brother's *alleged* psychic visions. No one wants to hear your theories."

"Lieutenant?"

Landry glared at the younger detective. "I said, stay out of this, Jennings!"

"I'd actually like to hear the Junior Crime Stopper's theories," said a voice from behind Landry. The Lieutenant spun to find himself face to face with another man, one slightly taller and a bit older, dressed in a sharp wool suit.

"*Chief Roberts*. Why, hello, sir. Didn't realize you were coming."

"Obviously. Ms. Bender, why don't you share your thoughts with this gullible old man, if you would be so kind?"

Colleen nodded, her poker-face expression unchanged. "I was only trying to point out something I would guess the Lieutenant has thought of, but that seemed worth mentioning just to be sure. That being that you likely won't find anything material in common between the men that have been killed, and, more to the point, that it's not what the female victims—the women—have in common with each other that matters. It's what they have in common with the victims of 1888."

"And what is that?"

"The women that have been killed so far all share initials with the women murdered in the Whitechapel district by Jack the Ripper almost a hundred years ago."

"Interesting. That could be very a useful part of the puzzle. Did you notice that, Lieutenant? Or is that the kind of thing you leave to *amateurs*?"

Landry took in a breath, glaring at Colleen before letting it out. "Yes, as a matter of fact, Chief, I did." He produced a notebook from his pocket and thumbed it open to a particular page before showing it to the Chief. "It was going to be part of my briefing tomorrow morning. But, honestly, even now I don't think it would be prudent to jump to conclusions. This whole Jack-the-Ripper thing could be a smokescreen. We just don't know."

"Generous of you to decide to share that with us ahead of schedule. It's a shame Ms. Bender jumped the gun and stole your thunder. Perhaps she would have been more discreet had she been privy to your intentions."

Landry's jaw shifted from side to side, like he was tasting his words before deciding whether to spit them out. "I withheld that information from Miss Bender because I didn't think it should be shared with the public. You were quite clear on how tight a lid we were to keep on the details of the investigation. I would say we've done a pretty good job so far of controlling leaks. And, frankly, I'm of the opinion giving her too much information could lead to, uh, unreliable input from her."

The Chief frowned, swinging his chin ruefully. "I thought I'd also made it clear you were to give her access to any information that she might find of use in assisting you." He turned to Colleen. "You'll have to forgive the Lieutenant, Ms. Bender. Sometimes he forgets what decade this is. He's fifteen years younger and fifty years less evolved."

"I don't blame the Lieutenant for being skeptical, sir," Colleen said. She caught Landry's eyes for a brief moment. "I would guess he's just trying to ensure there's some integrity to the process."

"Speaking of process, has your brother been able to perceive anything helpful here?"

"Not yet, sir," Colleen said. Joshua let out a growling moan, his eyes rolling up and his head lolling.

Detective Jennings leaned forward. "We were just about to provide

Miss Bender with the implement that looks like it was used to make the writing on the floor."

Chief Roberts pursed his lips, his brows rising. "Would you mind if I observed?"

"No," Colleen said. "Of course not."

Landry sighed, then quickly painted a smile on his face as the Chief looked at him. Jennings left the area and quickly returned, holding an object in his hand. It had a tapered wooden handle that protruded from a paper bag secured over one end of by loops of rubber bands doubled over to serve as a clamp.

"The handle's been dusted already and photographed, and the techs have looked it over carefully for fibers or markings," Jenning said. "The brush end is being protected to avoid contamination before we send it to the lab, but samples from it have already been swabbed and bagged."

He looked expectantly to the Chief, waiting for him to nod before handing it to Colleen. She gripped it just below where the opening of the bag was clamped around the wood, then took one of her brother's hands and placed the lower part of the handle into his palm. Joshua bucked in his chair and pulled his head away, grimacing as if in pain. He stretched his neck to the side, leaning over the armrest as far as his body would allow.

Colleen wrapped his fingers around the handle and held it in place with her hand in a tight grip while reaching over with her other hand and cupping the back of her brother's head to pull it closer. He pulled against her, causing the muscles in her arm to strain. She had to give his neck a few squeezes to get him to sit straight.

"Perhaps we can try again later?" the Chief said.

"He gets like this sometimes," Colleen said. "He senses the tension, the recency of the violence. He expects the impression is going to be unpleasant. But I often remind him that more people may have to die if he won't cooperate. A few moments of discomfort is a small price to pay."

She drew his head closer and lowered her ear to his mouth. His breaths hissed through clenched teeth in fits. A rough rumble vibrated from his throat.

"He says the killer left another message in the refrigerator," she said, standing after kissing her brother's forehead and stroking the hair of his crown.

The three men looked at each other for a few beats before Landry snapped on a rubber glove and moved along the edge of the carpet until he was close to the refrigerator door. He took one careful step and opened it.

"I don't see anything but food. There's a carton of milk. Some cheese." He let the door swing open and poked through the contents with his gloved hand. "A bit of meatloaf wrapped in foil."

"What's in the Tupperware bowl?" Colleen asked.

Landry stooped lower and inspected a shelf. He reached into his pocket for another glove and pulled it on before retrieving an opaque plastic bowl with a closed lid. "Looks like more leftovers," he said.

He peeled the lid off and looked inside. His brow furrowed for an instant then he jerked his head away, the muscles of his face crunched in a look of disgust.

"I think we found the victim's missing ear and nose," he said. "Along with what I'd guess is a smattering of bacon bits."

Chief Roberts turned away, wiping his face. Landry gestured to Jennings with a tilt of his head and the detective called for someone to come photograph the bowl and collect it as evidence. Despite the sounds of the photographer, the film being wound, the shutter being activated, and the background murmurs of department personnel, the sudden lack of conversation created an awkward vacuum, filled only when a uniformed officer entered the house and approached the Chief, who stepped away briefly.

"The press is here, in force," the Chief said, returning. "The department's public affairs officer is out front. I'm afraid the informal agreement we had with our local reporters to keep things low key has run its course. Major outlets have gotten wind of what's going on. I'm going to have to issue a statement. Lieutenant, try to extend Ms. Bender the professional courtesies she is due. She has more than proved her worth."

Landry nodded, the muscles along his jaw bunched into tiny fists. As soon as the Chief was out of ear shot, he told Jennings to get the inside of the refrigerator dusted for prints and check on when the coroner would arrive. Then he turned to Colleen.

"I'm sure you enjoyed the hell out of that."

"I didn't set out to make you look bad, Lieutenant."

"Right. Is this where you tell me I'm doing a great job of that all by myself?"

"If that were my intention, I would have asked him why he has you following me."

Landry tightened his mouth and bore down on her with his eyes but said nothing.

"Of course, I'm sure you've been doing that at his request, not on your own, so nothing to worry about there. You didn't think I'd notice your car parked on the side of the road every evening? Some nights I've been tempted to walk up and ask you if you wanted something to drink."

"It wouldn't be the first time in my career I had my ass chewed out by him, and I'm sure it won't be the last. It's not like I ever pretended to buy this Amazing Kreskin routine of yours—oh, excuse me, your *brother's*. It's only a matter of time before I figure out how you're doing it. Then your little scam moonlighting as a detective for fun and profit will be over."

"So, that's what you think this is? A scam?"

"I had someone do some checking on you," he said, leaning in and lowering his voice. "Seems you became a bit of a local celebrity in that jerkwater town you're from, solving petty crimes like a clairvoyant Encyclopedia Brown. Best anyone can tell, a few years ago you moved here, to a city, not quite the big time, but a much larger stage, so you could bring your show on the road. Maybe get some attention."

"Is that all you found?" she said, deciding the time was now, that this was her opportunity to take control. Things were coming to a head, and she knew she may not get another.

Landry shrugged, making a face.

"Did your snooping turn up the fact that I was barely out of my teens when my parents died, and I became my brother's fulltime caregiver? Did you find out about my having to drop out of school because I became involved with an older man and found myself a girl in trouble? How he pressured me to 'take care of it' as if I didn't even have a say in the matter, then completely disavowed me? Spread rumors about me to discredit me? Did you learn about how my parents blamed me for everything—the pregnancy, my brother's accident, everything bad that ever happened?"

"Calm down, there, missy, and lower your voice. I'm a cop, remember? I'm just doing my job."

"Since when does doing your job involve rooting around in my personal life?"

"I just figured I should know who it is the Chief is placing so much trust in. That's all."

"Does Chief Roberts know you were investigating me? You do know he's the one who contacted me, don't you, and not the other way around?"

The Lieutenant said nothing

"Oh, so you didn't know that. How do you think he'd react if I tracked him down outside and told him about all this?"

Landry locked eyes with her. She could feel him taking her measure.

"Okay, sure, maybe I've been a little rough on you. But this is serious business we're dealing with here. I don't like crap like this guiding my investigation. And I definitely don't like having to pay deference to it."

"If I were trying to show you up, Lieutenant, I would have told Chief Roberts what I'm about to tell you, instead of letting you take the credit."

"And what's that?"

"The woman in the bedroom isn't the killer's third victim."

Colleen looked down at the writing on the kitchen floor. "If you read the books you referenced in your report more carefully, you'd have realized that the body of the victim with the initials C.E. was actually the fourth woman killed. Victim's three and four were killed on the same day, within hours of each other."

She turned back to face him. "Somewhere not too far away from here is another body. That one with the initials E.S."

The press and onlookers were thronging outside the cordon the police had set up when Colleen left. Jennings had spotted her as she was leaving, and the fact she was looking at him when he did prompted him to disengage from whatever conversation he'd been having with another officer in uniform and come over to her. He fell in next to her as she pushed her brother's wheelchair toward a temporary barricade blocking the sidewalk.

"That was very impressive, what you did in there."

"My brother is the one who deserves the credit."

"I don't mean just that. I'm talking about the way you knew about the initials. You have the entire department scouring surrounding areas for another victim. I even heard Landry tell the Chief you're the one who figured it out. You're a smart lady. And a tremendous asset to the investigation."

"I'm not sure your Lieutenant thinks so."

"Oh, he does. Don't mind him. He's like that with everyone. He's a pretty smart guy himself. He just likes to be in control. He probably sees you as a threat."

They approached the patrolman holding back a few people from the neighborhood, and Jennings had him move the barricade over to allow her to wheel her brother past without going on the grass.

"And what do you see me as?" Colleen asked.

"What do you mean?"

"You said Lt. Landry likely sees me as a threat." She stopped near her car, a station wagon, and turned to face him. "What do you see me as?"

"I see you as someone I'd like to… get to know better."

She gazed into his eyes, thinking.

"I'm sorry," he said. "That was forward of me."

"No, it's not that." She let her thoughts play out for another few beats. "Don't repeat this to anyone, but Landry's been following me."

"He has?"

"Yes. He camps outside my apartment down the street. Usually gives up around midnight."

"Wow. I didn't know."

"I called him out on it earlier. I have a feeling he'll back off now. For a while, at least. But I only thought it fair to warn you."

"I see. Well, I'm not trying to be pushy. I have to pull a four to twelve all week, anyway. Maybe next week, too. But when things settle down, I was thinking maybe we could get a cup of coffee or something. You could tell me your story, how you got here, how you started… doing what you do."

She trundled her brother over a patch of grass, maneuvering him next to a passenger door. "Four to twelve?"

"Four PM to midnight. Even today. I'll get to leave here in an hour or so, shower and eat something, but then I'll have to pull my regular shift.

Things are crazy right now, with all this going on."

Colleen nodded. She gestured to the car door, and Jennings helped her load her brother into the back seat. She thanked him after he folded the wheelchair and lifted it into the back of the station wagon.

"Tell me something," she said, looking up at him as she stopped at the driver's side door. "Do you have a welcome mat out in front of your door?"

He cocked his head, a bemused smile creasing his lips. "At my apartment? Sure. Of a sort."

"Leave a spare key under it," she said, shifting her eyes past him toward the house where she spied Landry on the porch, looking in their direction. "If I'm not there waiting when you get home, it means he's still keeping an eye on me."

The clock read just after 1:30 when Colleen approached Jenning's desk the next day. She was fresh off a meeting with Chief Roberts.

"Oh, hi," he said, standing when he noticed her. He looked around the room, hesitating for a moment before adding, "I heard. I'm sorry."

Colleen hitched her shoulders. "It was bound to happen."

"It's the press. Now that the Chief 'lost containment of the story'—as Landry put it—the department can't afford to have to answer questions about you, about your involvement. And with the FBI stepping in to officially consult now, it's important we not, you know, create the wrong impression."

"I'm sure that's what he convinced the Chief to believe."

Jennings said nothing.

"Don't be upset about it," she said, reaching into her purse. She placed a key discreetly on his desk, sliding it under the blotter. In a slightly lower voice, she said, "I forgot to give this back to you last night. Or I guess you could call it this morning."

Jennings cast a few glances from side to side. "Thanks. I really am sorry. But on the bright side, this makes it easier. I really want to see you again."

Colleen smiled. "I'd like that. But we still need to be careful. If you-know-who were to find out we were… seeing each other, he'd immediately decide you were feeding me information all along and that it was all a big con."

"I won't say anything. He's the last guy I'd want to know. He gives me a hard enough time as it is. And he can't find out if nobody else does. They found the other victim, you know. Early this morning. I got the call not long after—" the detective caught himself, dropped his voice a number of decibels—"not long after you left."

"Yes. The Chief told me."

"Landry gave you all the credit, for what it's worth. Told the Chief you predicted it."

"That doesn't exactly surprise me. He wants people to be suspicious, to discount my brother's involvement and focus on me, having everyone questioning how I come about the information I provide. He's sowing the seeds of distrust."

Jennings frowned. "Maybe," he said.

A few seconds ticked by in silence before Colleen said, in a conspiratorial tone, "I hope you don't mind. I stopped by your place on the way over here and dropped off a few books on Jack the Ripper. I really think you should study them. I didn't want to risk anyone seeing me give them to you here."

"*Of course* I don't mind. That was kind of you."

Colleen nodded. She thought carefully about whether the time was right, decided it was. "Paul… be careful. Don't trust anyone. Promise me."

"Don't worry about me. I'm a pretty careful guy."

"I'm serious. Promise me. And promise me you won't let anyone know what I'm about to tell you."

"Uh, okay," he said. When she maintained eye contact for a few beats without saying anything, he added, "I promise."

"Let's put aside the distinction between me versus my brother for the moment. How accurate have my predictions been so far? My assessments?"

"Very."

"That's why it's important you listen to what I say…" She scanned the room in multiple directions, then leaned forward. "This isn't based on ESP, this isn't a psychic prediction, this is just me telling you something I'm certain of. Mark my words. The killer is going to turn out to be a cop."

She straightened up before Jennings could respond and angled herself toward the exit. "And if you give me a day or two, I'll be ready to show you just which one."

The night air was heavy as Colleen watched the car pull to the curb and park, the humidity being shoved and jostled around beneath the thumbnail moon by a warm breeze but seeming to always settle back in the same spot. She waited as Jennings locked the driver side door and headed toward her. He was wearing jeans with open shirttails over a t-shirt. She could make just make out the imprint of his service weapon when the cloth moved along his hip.

"Thanks for coming," she said.

"How could I resist?" He scanned the quiet street, swiveling his head in each direction. "Is there a reason you couldn't just tell me on the phone what this is about?"

"Yes. Several. Do you know where we are?"

"City Port Drive, east of town. Harbor District."

"I meant, do you know who lives here?"

Jennings thought for a moment. "One of the early persons of interest. Dylan something-or-other. He got on our radar because of a knife arrest, and he worked nights near the first victim. Missed a meeting with his probation officer the morning the bodies were found, told his PO later that day he'd overslept and talked his way out of being violated. Landry all but ruled him out after an interview. Said the guy was all upset and scared, petrified his employer would find out about his record. Didn't want to lose his job."

"But you haven't had him under surveillance, have you?"

"We followed him for a few days, early on. Not me, I was put on the guy with a rape jacket who got a parking ticket in the vicinity of the first scene on the same night. But, from what I was told, this guy didn't do much other than sleep and grab a sandwich at the local deli and work his late shift at a meatpacking warehouse. We didn't stay on him. The department doesn't have the resources to pay that kind of overtime. This isn't Manhattan. City's not that big. And neither is our budget."

"An unsupervised shift."

"What?"

"He works an unsupervised shift as a security guard at the warehouse."

"What are getting at? You think he's the guy?"

"Let's say, hypothetically, I've been doing what your department hasn't."

"You've been following him?"

Colleen didn't answer. She spun on her heels and headed down the sidewalk, casting a glance over her shoulder to indicate he should follow. She stopped in front of a brick building that housed two storefronts. The building was wedged between two vacant lots surrounded by chain link and strewn with debris, wads and fragments of paper in various colors swirling and flapping with the occasional gust of that warm breeze. In between the storefronts was a battered metal door with a mesh security window. A narrow staircase was barely visible through the glass in the shadowy wash of a lonely streetlight.

"He lives above this sign shop. He won't be home for a couple of hours."

"Okay."

"I want you to come with me and look inside."

"Inside his apartment? Are you crazy? I could lose my badge. Hell, I could be charged. Both of us could."

She took a firm lock of his gaze. "Paul, we're not going to steal anything from him."

"I thought you told me just a couple of days ago you were sure the killer was a cop."

"Yes. That's why we need to go inside."

"I'm totally lost here. What are you talking about?"

"Do you want to know who I was referring to or not?"

The detective looked down, kicked the sidewalk a few times with his shoe. "There's no way for you to know it's someone on the force," he said. She noted his words, however, lacked conviction. "You can't be sure of that."

"How many things have I been wrong about so far?"

Jennings said nothing.

"We need to go inside. There's no other way. I have to show you."

He threw his head back, rubbed his eyes with his thumb and forefinger before pinching the bridge of his nose. "I could get a warrant."

"Based on what evidence? You think Landry would approve that?"

"This is ridiculous," he said, scanning the building, then looking at her. "We shouldn't even be here. Let's go back my place, or yours. Anywhere we can, you know, discuss this, put together a case. You can tell me what you know, or think you know."

"You wouldn't believe me if I did. Worse, you would genuinely think I'm insane. I'm not insane, Paul. We're here right now, and you won't have to take my word for it. I can show you. And you still didn't answer me. How many things have I been wrong about so far?"

Jennings let out a long stream of air that whiffled through his lips, the muscles in his face tensing as he frowned. He stared at the door. "How are we supposed to get inside?"

Colleen pulled a pair of rubber surgical gloves from her pocket and snapped them on, then she produced a small, square leather case and unzipped it.

"Oh, boy… I definitely think we should talk about this."

She removed a pair of thin implements from the case and crouched in front of the door. "Okay, but I'll get started while we do. Time is an issue."

"This is a bad idea. I'm a cop, in case you forgot."

The bolt made a chunky sound as it threw. Jennings reached down and put his hand over hers as she started to withdraw the picks.

"Colleen, I don't think I need to remind you this is highly illegal. I can't just go around committing crimes."

"Tell me," she said, standing and facing him. "Did you join the force because you wanted to enforce laws? Or did you do it because you wanted to be an instrument of justice?"

He took in a breath, dragging his palm down his face. The air whiffled through his lips again as he exhaled and swiveled his head to look up and down the street.

"I can't believe I'm letting you talk me into this."

They entered and climbed the stairs. At the landing, a scratched and dented metal door painted a wooden shade of dark brown stood to their left. Colleen repeated the process with her lockpicks on the deadbolt.

"Where did you even learn to do that?"

"I ordered one of those correspondence courses from the back of a magazine. How to be a locksmith. It wasn't very good, but it taught me enough so that I was able to practice."

Jennings shook his head. "I'm not even going to ask why."

She turned the knob and the door opened.

The place was small. A dim yellow glow suffused the space from a nearby lamppost, leaking in through a window overlooking the street. The area to their immediate left served as a kitchenette, open to the bulk of the floor that served as a living room. A ratty cloth couch and a cushioned chair separated by a small table faced a rabbit-eared television on a makeshift stand. A set of shelves stood against the opposite wall, next to the opening to a narrow hall.

"Tell me again what we're doing here?"

Colleen walked over to a table lamp and pulled the beaded chain. The room jumped as if startled awake.

"Do you have gloves?" she asked.

"I have a bunch in the car."

"In that case, here." She pulled out a pair of latex gloves from her pocket. "Put these on."

She made her way over to the table next to the couch and chair. She pulled open a drawer, then gently picked up an object between her latex-clad thumb and forefinger, holding it out for him to see.

"A switchblade," Jennings said. "You think that's the murder weapon? Forensics advised us it was likely something with a curved edge."

She let the knife dangle from her fingers, holding it as if it were covered in filth.

"How did you know?" Jennings asked. He paused, sighing. "You've been in here already, haven't you? You've already searched this place. By yourself."

"Top of that bookcase," she said. She stepped past the couch and pointed. "Reach up there and tell me what you find."

Jennings looked up, scanning the edge of the shelf above his head. He swung his head from side to side as he flexed his fingers, frowning. "I still can't believe I'm doing this. Will you just tell me what this has to do with a cop being the killer?"

"I'll tell you as soon as you retrieve what's up there."

Jennings gave one more rueful shake to his head and reached a gloved hand to grope the top of the shelf, pushing himself up on the balls of his feet and extending as far as he could.

"There's nothing here."

"Try more over to your left."

"I don't... hold on, I felt something." He stretched higher on his toes. "Almost got it..."

He raised his hand. In it was a short, curved blade, wide, with a thick wooden handle.

"What'd'ya know?" he said as his weight settled back on his heels.

His arm was still extended as Colleen slid her left hand beneath his hanging shirt tail from behind him and pulled his revolver from its holster. At the same time, she thumbed the button on the switchblade in her right, the silver steel of it flicking open with a flash. Jennings barely had time to turn his head before she buried the knife to its hilt in his neck and backed away from him.

"I'm so sorry, Paul. I really am. It turns out the killer cop is you."

Jennings dropped the blade he'd taken off the top of the bookcase and staggered back against the shelves. He reached a hand over and yanked the knife out of the side of this throat. A spurt of blood arced out, followed by another, then another. He tried to cover the wound with his hand as he slid down the front of the shelves, landing hard on the floor. He looked up at Colleen, eyes wide with confusion and panic.

"You just aren't as smart as Landry," she said. "I would've preferred it were him, but that just wouldn't work. I wish it didn't have to be this way. I really liked you. Please believe me. This isn't about anything you did. This is about justice."

The detective coughed, blood running down his chin as it continued to debouch through the fingers of his gloved hand in a slowing rhythm. He slumped, his weight tilting, until he came to rest on his side. He blinked several times and coughed up some more blood. Then his eyes fluttered, gradually closing.

Colleen moved over the table lamp and shut it off. She made her way back to Jennings with cat-like steps, careful to stay away from where he had bled, and lowered herself onto the floor next to him.

"Your heart seems to still be pumping a little, so I hope that means you can hear me," she said, switching the gun to her right hand then gently stroking his hair with her left. "As you fall asleep, let me tell you a story, the kind you told me you wanted to hear. He'll be home soon, but we have a few minutes."

She set her gaze on the front door, barely visible in the shadows.

"It's about a girl who grew up poor, a girl who couldn't afford to go to college. This girl, she had dreams. This girl, she wanted to be a writer. But this girl had parents that didn't care for those dreams, that urged her to stop indulging in fantasies, parents that wanted her to focus on helping out around the farm, which was in constant danger of being lost."

The sound of a motorcycle engine, faint at first, whined in the distance, growing louder.

"But this girl, you see, this girl was determined to carve out a future that didn't involve living in borderline poverty or milking cows or plowing a field or marrying some local rube in coveralls. This girl, she stole away to the library in town whenever she could, and one day, on the advice of the librarian, she contacted a young English professor at a community college a few towns over…"

* ·❮❮❮❮· ✳ ·❯❯❯❯· *

The front half of the coffee shop was bathed in a gentle early afternoon light pouring in from the window walls that looked out onto the street, backlighting Landry when he entered. Colleen looked up from her espresso at the sound of the door, watched as he walked her way and took the seat opposite her in the booth.

"Lieutenant," she said, offering a slight nod.

A waitress in a white cloth apron holding a glass carafe approached as he settled onto the banquette and asked what she could bring him.

"Just coffee," he said, sliding over the saucer already on the table and flipping over the mug without taking his eyes off Colleen. "Black."

The woman poured him a cup and moved to another table.

Several seconds ticked by, marked by the ambient sounds of the shop. The murmured din of conversations, the clinking of silverware, the hum of appliances.

"Well," Colleen said, breaking the silence between them. "You must have had a reason when you asked me to meet you here."

"Where's your brother?" Landry said, maintaining the same wary gaze, the same tight expression.

"Same place he is this time every day. Sleeping. I told you about that, about his schedule."

Landry said nothing. Other than a barely noticeable narrowing of his gaze, he didn't move.

"You really should try the espresso," she said, lifting the tiny cup to her lips and letting the rising warmth caress her face. "It's quite good."

"I know," he said.

She shrugged and took a sip.

"I know," he repeated.

Colleen set the cup down and returned his gaze, her eyebrows cresting slightly, allowing only the hint of a smile to play on her lips. "What is it you know, Lieutenant?"

"Lots of things, maybe everything. Everything that matters, at least. I certainly know enough."

"Is this some police interrogation technique? Am I supposed to confess to something? I'm afraid I have no idea what you're talking about."

"You can drop the act, Faye Dunaway. You know exactly what I'm talking about."

She widened her eyes in mock bewilderment. "I do?"

"I imagine your phone is ringing off the hook these days, with the press having gotten wind of your involvement with the investigation."

"I guess reporters can always be expected to have sources in police departments. Hard to keep everything a secret."

"You know," Landry said, leaning back against the wood of the booth. He pinched a spoon near his hand with his fingers, lifting it off a napkin tapping it gently on the cloth. "When I first figured it out, or first thought I'd figured it out, I was angry, filled with a rage, but beneath all that, I was also smug, telling myself how I hadn't let you outsmart *me*, consoling myself that you couldn't pull the wool over *my* eyes."

Colleen tightened her brow, pursed her lips into a bemused pout.

"But then I realized…"

"Realized what, Lieutenant?"

He stared at her. "They're closing the case."

"The Jack-the-Ripper murders? Yes, I read about how Detective Jennings killed the man, the suspect, after he'd been stabbed. Such a shame."

"Yes, I'm sure you did. You know, that's where I thought you'd fucked up. Making it look like that loser Wurtz was the killer. No way it was him."

"Really? That's not how the newspapers portray it. And what does any of that have to do with me?"

"Yeah, I started putting it together at the scene, that it was all wrong. Staged. The more the evidence was analyzed, the worse it got. Jennings dead, wearing gloves, but not the same type he had in his car. No liftable prints on the knife that seems to be the kind of weapon used in the other murders, and nothing but smudges of blood on the switchblade that punctured Jenning's carotid. Smudges everywhere, even where they shouldn't be. Wurtz shot twice in the chest, point blank. A third shot angled up from the floor, missing him, of course, lodged in the door frame. Powder residue on the latex, but not beneath the blood. The concentrations of barium and antimony less than it should have been for three shots. Wurtz still wearing his motorcycle leather. Ever try to unlock doors in thick leather gloves? It was enough to make someone with a suspicious mind think he must've taken them off and put them on again. Like at gunpoint or something. The whole thing, all of it, was very convenient, meant to look like Jennings was doing an illegal search, no warrant, had been trying to crack the case himself, was surprised by the perp, got stabbed in the neck as he shot the guy in the chest, getting off one more shot from the floor as he lay dying. Guy stumbles back and crumples near the entry way. I really thought that was your mistake."

"I don't understand, Lieutenant. Are you accusing me of something?"

"Can the pretense. I'm not wearing a wire."

"What pretense?"

"Fine, keep it up. It doesn't matter. Like I was saying, I thought that was your mistake. Sure, I hadn't completely made the connection to you yet, I just knew whoever staged that whole thing, that was their mistake. Then we got a warrant for Jennings apartment."

Colleen said nothing. She watched Landry as he eyed her intently.

"And what do we find? Along with books on Jack the Ripper and newspaper clippings about the killings, we find a stash of various objects. Pieces of jewelry, mostly. All belonging to the victims. Trophies."

"Wow," Colleen said. "I don't know what to say. None of that has been in the papers."

"Of course not, and that's just the way you planned it. As soon as the department started leaking evidence pointing to Wurtz as the killer and burying all the evidence about Jennings, the FBI folded up their tents and hopped in their cars. They didn't want any of that spin flinging shit their way. That's when I started to put it all together. Wurtz wasn't the killer, I knew that right off the bat. And Jennings sure as hell wasn't, that was ridiculous. He was cleaner than a preacher's sheets. So how did that stuff get in his apartment?"

Colleen blinked. "Are you asking me? I have no idea."

"A woman, that's how. A preacher's sheets may be clean, but I doubt his were. Not before you laundered them, that is. He's a young guy, a bachelor. No sign of forced entry. *Gee*, I thought, *attractive woman, probably around his age, someone knowledgeable about the Ripper... who did that sound like?*"

"Are you here to arrest me, Lieutenant?"

"Oh, believe me, that was what I expected to do, eventually. Started thinking about it before we'd even finished processing his apartment. All I had to do was figure out how to tie you to the scene, name you as a subject, start collecting evidence. I already had a motive pegged. You wanted to be the star, establish your psychic-brother bullshit as legitimate. Only, the way I figured, I messed up your plans by getting you fired, so you had to wrap it up, pin it on someone. But the more I thought about it, the more the wind fell out of my sails. It wasn't long before I realized you wanted it that way. I hadn't spoiled anything. You wanted me to know."

"I'm sure I have no idea what you're talking about."

"Right. We went over Jennings' apartment with a magnifying glass, looking for anything and everything to tie you to it. Hairs, fibers, *something*. Then it occurred to me that wouldn't prove a damn thing. So what if you were in his apartment? You already had that factored in as a possibility. So I went back to Wurtz's place, searched it a number of times, trying to find something, anything, we'd missed. Something to prove you were there, too. I went back through all the stuff we logged in, which was basically everything that wasn't nailed down. Know what I came across?"

Colleen shrugged. "What did you come across, Lieutenant?"

"A book. It had been in a closet. Tucked in a box. A book of famous quotes. No discernable prints. I flipped through it, back and forth. Then, I happened to see a name. Sir Francis Bacon."

"He *is* a rather well-known historical figure," she said.

"Next to the quote was a faint pencil mark, hardly even visible. A checkmark. Just as faintly, some of the words were underlined."

"Interesting," she said.

"The quote was, '*Revenge is a kind of wild justice*'."

"Pithy. What, again, does that have to do with me?"

"That's when I knew. Not that it was you, that I'd already been pretty sure of. No, that's when I knew that I hadn't figured it out because of *my* smarts, it was because of yours. I wasn't going to make contact on any pitch you didn't want me to. You're too good. Too sharp."

"I'm not sure whether I should be flattered or insulted by these accusations."

"Back when you helped find the Chief's baby nephew, everybody was so relieved, they never thought to question you."

"But they did question me."

"I mean, question your involvement, really question it. Baby disappears, you happen to find the child's pacifier on the sidewalk, out for a walk, wheeling your brother. Say he told you the baby was in the woods somewhere nearby. You refuse any press, say you want to keep you and your brother's name out of it, don't want any credit. Suddenly you become best buds with Mrs. Roberts, who thinks your brother's touched by God or something."

"Chief Roberts and his wife were very grateful. I was just happy to help. They even tried to pay me a reward. I declined, of course."

"Of course. But I dug a little deeper on you. Should've done it sooner, instead of letting someone else run a superficial background check. Found out the police suspected something—or someone—may have tampered with the break lines of your parents' car."

"That's news to me. They asked me a lot of questions about them, but never told me that. Are you saying my parents were murdered?"

"I also found out you were with your brother when he fell from that hayloft."

"I would have told you that, if you'd asked."

"I'm sure you would have. In fact, you told me pretty much everything I needed to know to figure out it was you, right from the beginning."

Colleen said nothing. She tilted her head as if his words made absolutely no sense.

"The only thing that puzzled me was the *why*. Attractive woman, smart doesn't even begin to cover it. So why? My first thought was, same reason as any psycho. The thrill of killing. The satisfaction of taunting the police. But that just didn't seem to apply. Not to you. Then I found the quote, and I was like, 'Aha! Revenge!' But even that didn't make a lot of sense. You couldn't want revenge against all those people, and it seemed like an awful lot of trouble to go through to get it against one or two of them when there were much easier ways to do it. It took me a while, but I finally figured it out. You wanted to commit the perfect crime."

"I'm losing track of all these shifting accusations, Lieutenant."

"The ground I'm on is solid *terra firma*, not shifting at all. Different parts of the same whole. You wanted revenge. You practically came out and told me—'*How do you know it's a man and not a woman?*' It all came together when I figured out who you were after. You see, the sequence of the first two bugged me, from right when we started looking at the Jack-the-Ripper stuff. Why were the first two women's initials out of order compared to the original vics'? Then it dawned on me. You didn't want us looking at those second murders separately, hunting for motive, rather than a serial killer. You wanted those bodies to draw attention to your theme, your red herring, while still planting the big clue, right in front of our noses. The English prof, Nesbitt. I found out that over a decade ago he used to teach at some dinky two-year college about fifty miles away from that little berg you come from. Seems he had a rep back then for working the coeds. I couldn't find any record of you attending, but it all made sense anyway. And guess what I found when I pored over some of those course catalogs from back then? Turns out he taught a class focusing on the Dr. Jekyll and Mr. Hyde archetype in fiction, just coincidentally tying it into media fascination with Jack the Ripper and what the description called the socio-political roots of female victims in literature. You dropped all kinds of hints about that, too, hell, practically screamed it at me, if you recall. Scolding me about how an older man got you in trouble, used you, then tossed you aside. You *wanted* me to know."

"And why would I want that?"

"Because you wanted to prove a point. A number of points. That you could get your revenge. That someone like me would *know* you got your revenge, so someone else would know why he died, know that it was *your* doing. That you were able to commit the perfect crime. And you wanted to prove that you not only could get away with it, which I imagine you already knew, but that you could get away with it even with the lead detective knowing it was you. And, if my instincts are on, you wanted to prove that you could profit from it, too. Because, why not cover all the motives?"

"That's quite a theory. How would I do that?"

"Several ways. Selling your story. Setting yourself up as a psychic celebrity. Hiring yourself out as a guest speaker to groups that believe in that crap to discuss your psychometrics—excuse me, *psychometrist*—bullshit. Haven't quite figured that part out. But I will."

"But if even half of what you're saying were true, how could I risk any of that? I mean, all that attention… wouldn't it be only a matter of time before I was arrested? Charged with murder? Labeled a serial killer?"

"Now you're just trying to rub my nose in it. It's unbecoming. You damn well know you could never be convicted, and that means you'll never be charged, or even accused."

"Because I'm innocent, of course."

"Because your lawyer—any lawyer—would get a verdict before you even put up a defense. The evidence is too confusing. Blood spatter guys can't agree on anything. Forensics, trajectories, stringing—nobody can agree. That's without even getting to the fact Jennings was in the guy's apartment wearing latex gloves, a set of lock picks in his pocket. And, well, by having all that evidence showing up in Jennings' pad, you *really* made sure you'd never be touched. I have to ask, did you know the department would pretend all that stuff didn't exist? Pin the blame on Wurtz and bury all the evidence you planted? Or did you just hope to confuse matters so much it didn't matter?"

"Are you telling me the department covered up an officer's potential involvement in a series of murders?"

"I guess that's my answer." He slid out of the booth, pulled a bill from his wallet and dropped it on the table.

"Why did you want to meet with me, Lieutenant? I mean, really?"

"No particular reason. I guess I just wanted to see your face, maybe get some closure on a few unanswered questions. I suppose, if I'm being truly honest, I wanted to see you in person one more time, see what you looked like to me now, knowing what you really are. I also figured that maybe if I played your game out to the finish, let you know I figured out everything you wanted me to, you may be satisfied and no one else would have to die."

"You've made me out to be a monster. Do I really look like a monster to you, Lieutenant?"

"No. That's what's so terrifying. But you certainly are one."

"If you believe that, you could probably justify doing anything, even engaging in some wild justice of your own."

"I'd be lying if I said it hadn't crossed my mind. But, unlike you, I doubt I'd get away with it. And I value my pension too much. Even if I could get away with it, it takes a certain kind of mind to carry that with you for the rest of your days. No, the burden I'm going to have to carry around is to know what you are and to be the only one who does. No one would believe me, even if I were able to go around telling everyone. I'm sure it will come as no surprise that the Chief has threatened to can me if I even mention your name to anyone, given the shitstorm that would open up for him."

He was a few steps away from the table when she called out to him. He stopped and angled his body to look back at her.

"I suppose I could write a book," she said. "If I were looking to profit from all this. What with all the attention this case is getting, and the hundred-year anniversary of Jack the Ripper coming up, I'm sure it would be a huge bestseller."

Landry's spine seemed to straighten up a bit. She thought she noticed a slight loosening of his jaw. He bobbed his head slowly as he considered her words. Then he turned and left.

She watched him though the window as he crossed the street. She was finishing the last sip of her espresso and planning out chapters when the waitress stopped next to her table.

"Can I get you anything else?"

"Yes," she said, smiling. "Thank you." She looked over the woman's shoulder to the menu posted on the wall behind the counter. "You know what sounds delicious right now? A stack of flapjacks and a few juicy strips of bacon."

Payday

Todd lowered his bicycle by the handlebars as he stepped off, dropping it onto the ground next to Arthur's.

"It better not be much farther, ass-wipe."

Arthur had already trundled over the flattened section of chain link and was wading through the brush, heading toward the trees.

"It isn't. It's in here," Arthur said, looking back and gesturing into the dense thicket of Florida pine.

Todd studied the layers of undergrowth, then eyeballed Arthur before dipping his head and stepping on the overgrown rectangle of fencing. "If I came all this way for nothing, I'm kickin' your ass worse than the last time."

"This isn't for nothing. Promise. Might even be worth some money, eventually. I could maybe sell it to some TV show or something."

"You mean *we* could sell it, cheese-dick. And I'm taking more than half after going through all this bullshit."

Arthur pressed his way through the dense fabric of weeds and flora, stepping over tangles of thorny vine and pushing fronds and branches aside. Todd trailed behind.

"You sure you've been through here before?"

"Yeah. I didn't clear a path in this direction 'cause I didn't want anyone else wandering back here. It's better no one else knows about it."

"What the hell were you doin' out here in the first place, anyway? Other than jackin' off like a butt-muncher?"

"I was looking for a good place to build a fort. I like to scout out places with my dog."

"A fort? Jeez, you really are a little dweeb."

They pushed through an interlocked weave of branches and emerged into a small strip of untamed grass and sweet gum saplings. A faded metal sign angled toward them, bolted to a bent length of ventilated steel. Across the top in washed out red lettering were the words, PRIVATE PROPERTY— DO NOT ENTER. Below that, the paint scratched and chipped, was "By Order of the County Sheriff." At the very bottom was a citation of some sort of statute or ordinance Arthur didn't understand.

"I'd better not get in trouble over this," Todd said, grunting.

"I come out here all the time," Arthur said. "I've never seen any cops or anybody. That piece of fence back there looks like it's been bent forever, with all the stuff that's grown through it. I think people have forgotten all about this place."

Todd mumbled something, then said, "So why'd you want to show this thing to *me*? Why not any of those jerk-offs you hangout with at school?"

"They wouldn't know what to do with it. They'd probably just be scared."

"You got that right. You sure do hang around a lot of pussies. So, is this thing ... I mean, did it scare *you*?"

"Kinda, at first. But I knew right away it could be worth something. Once I thought about it, I figured lots of people would pay. My friends ... they wouldn't understand. That's when you and Chuck came to mind."

"*Fuck* Chuck. You came to me with this. If there's money coming, Chuck ain't getting any of my share. That dickhead left me hanging yesterday. Besides, you already owe me. It's up to over fifty bucks by now. Don't think for a second I'll forget."

Arthur nodded, stepping over a log. His jeans made a ripping, scratching sound as they snagged on the barbs of some sticker bushes. "It's right over here," he said. The sun was almost at eye-level, and he had to shade his eyes with his hand as he looked back. It was early October, but central Florida in the late afternoon was still a hot and humid place to be.

"We should be all-square after this," Arthur added. "That's why I came to you."

Todd snorted. "I'll be the judge of that."

Another nod. The arrangement had been Arthur's idea. He'd read about how mobsters would demand what they called protection money from merchants and local businesses in some areas of town, basically just a payoff to be left alone. He'd gone to Todd and Chuck and offered them the deal. Five dollars a week, payable at the end of the school year. All they had to do was be like mobsters and leave him and his friends alone, stop harassing them in the hallways or when they were out walking somewhere. Each of Arthur's friends in the group chipped in fifty cents. Arthur had been pocketing that money, saving it. Then he came across this and realized it could be worth a lot. An awful lot, the more he thought about it.

"I'm surprised a pussy like you would come out in these woods. My dad used to say they were haunted. Ghosts and shit."

Before he left you and your mom in that trailer and ran off with that waitress, Arthur thought, knowing better than to even hint at that. "Nah, there ain't no ghosts. Grown-ups tell their kids that because they want them to stay away, on account of all the chemicals that used to be dumped out here when the factory was open. The one your dad worked at—" he paused, worried he'd slipped up. When there was no reaction, he finished the sentence, "till the government shut it down."

"I didn't say I thought it *was* haunted, numbnuts. I just figured *you* might buy into all that crap."

The ground swelled upward into a miniature hill, and Arthur tried to keep his balance as he walked the incline, still pushing branches and vines aside. "It's right on the other side," he said.

When the boys reached the top of the mound, Arthur stood looking down into a small gully overrun with weeds and wildflowers, round, uneven clumps of growth every few feet bulls-eyed by reedy seed spouts stretching up until they started to bend under their own weight. To the right, the curved edging of a few rusty fifty-five gallon drums were visible slanting from the ground, swarmed by various lengths of thorny brown vines and green blades.

"There it is," Arthur said.

"There *what* is? Where?"

"Right there." Arthur pointed to the mid-point of the gully. "See that tall thing in the middle?"

In the center of the ditch, emerging through a riot of crabgrass, a dark green stalk protruded toward the sky. Two long stems spiraled out and upward, one from each side. At the top of the stalk was a large, concave flower with red and yellow petals.

"All I see is a fucking plant. You dragged me all the way out here for this? You're one dead little shit if this is all there is."

"No. Look." Arthur took a few steps down into the gully. "On the side. See it? Have you ever seen anything like that before?"

Todd stepped past Arthur, peering in the direction of the plant. "I don't see anything, dork."

"Right *there*," Arthur said, stabbing his finger.

Todd took another few steps, and then stopped. Clinging to the plant was something thick and translucent, with two protuberances at its top-most point. Its shape suggested a gigantic slug, but it was the size of a rottweiler.

"What the *fuck* is that?"

"I don't know, but watch." Arthur picked up a stick and tossed it near the slug-thing. For several seconds nothing happened, but then the protuberances began to extend outward, probing the air, coiling and uncoiling.

"Hot shit!" Todd said in an excited whisper.

"Yeah," Arthur said. "If it touches you, it burns. Your skin, I mean."

"No shit?"

"Yeah. Go ahead and give it a try."

"Fuck you. I ain't getting near that."

"I don't blame you. It is kinda scary. I felt the same way. You're smart to not get too close. I mean, I got pretty close, but I probably shouldn't've."

Todd glared at Arthur for a few seconds, his eyes narrowed into slits. "Shit. If *you* did it, I sure as hell ain't scared."

Todd took a few steps further down toward the plant. He stopped to look back every few feet.

"Be careful, Todd. You might trip and fall."

Todd shot a nasty look over his shoulder, then took a few more steps. He had covered most of the distance, only a few yards left to go, before he stopped again, lowering his head. "What the hell…?" he said, bending down. When he stood, he was holding a tennis shoe out in front of him, dangling it by the laces.

"Oh, that? That's Chuck's," Arthur said.

Todd looked up at Arthur, then over to the plant. Before he could react, the stems whipped forward, wrapping themselves around his chest and throat. He let out a gurgling yelp, grabbing at the tendrils as they dragged him through the weeds. Within seconds, Todd was pinned against the stalk. The slug-thing immediately began to ooze down onto him. It spread steadily over his head, covering his face. His mouth was still open, but the screaming had stopped. At least, to Arthur's ears it did.

"Does it burn?" Arthur asked in a raised voice, smiling. "Chuck said it burned."

Arthur watched Todd struggle in vain inside the thing. Symbiosis, the internet called it, or that was what it called the closest thing he could find, though after it took his dog he couldn't find pictures of anything that really came close. But he knew he'd been right about one thing. It sure was valuable. Oh, yes. He already had a list.

People were going to pay. Plenty of people were going to pay.

Zafari!

(Unlimited)

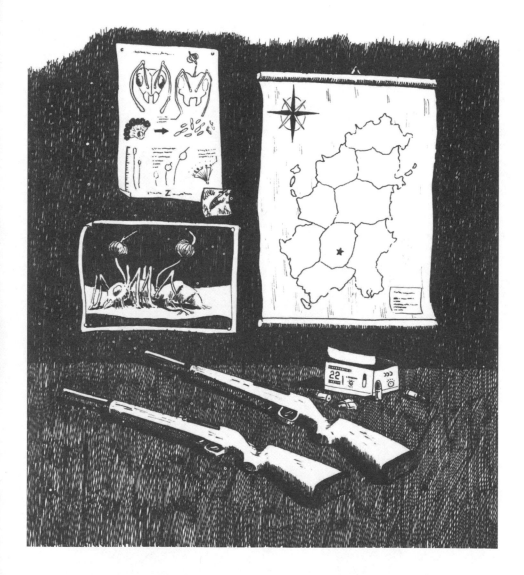

After having cursed the editor chosen to oversee her project for hours with a string of colorful, if blistering, epithets for being so unapologetically sexist ("Misogynistic piece of Neanderthal shit!" … "That brain-dead, troglodytic Boomer fuck!"), as she got off the plane, Ronnie found herself silently thanking a very patriarchal male God that Anthony had conditioned his approval of this assignment on her being accompanied by a man. Even if that man, hirsute and brawny and somehow simultaneously both cautious and cocksure, did seem to embody, more or less, every male quality that made her skin crawl. And worst of all, he reminded her of her father.

The blindfold hadn't been off long, so she blinked and hooded her eyes, turning her face away from the sun and holding up a hand to block it out. The first thing she saw was a tan and black dog staring up at her. A handler in a dark blue military-style tactical outfit stood next to it, holding it by a slack leash. He had a rifle slung across his back, its thin black barrel pointed at an angle from behind his shoulder toward the sky.

"Thank you for flying Zafari Airways," said another man a few feet to her left, his voice rising and falling with an unmistakably Sub-Saharan enunciation. Unlike the dog-handler, who was a stocky, chalky white caucasian, this man was tall and black with wide cheeks and bright, grinning teeth. He wore a discolored shirt over ratty jeans and had a rifle slung across his chest, one hand on the pistol grip, the other on the stock.

"Hey, zip it," said the guard with the dog.

That didn't stop the two other men in similar garb from chuckling at the comment. They were off to the opposite side of the impromptu path they created for her as she deplaned. All the men in sight, regardless of how they were dressed, were sporting black, modern-looking weapons she could only describe as assault rifles. She made a mental note that she would need to brush up on some firearm terminology for her article. She corrected herself: series of articles. She'd already experienced enough to write for days.

The men all stared at her expectantly, as did the dog. Well, she thought, *they're* certainly not zombies.

It seemed clear from their style of dress and general demeanor that the three in somewhat random civilian attire were all native Africans, probably from the same country of origin, but she didn't know accents well enough to place where, or to be sure there was a way to tell even if that weren't the case. She was forced to admit to herself that she had absolutely no idea where she was.

"My compliments to the pilot," Colt—her mandated escort—said. He stepped off the bottom stair behind her and scanned the surroundings. "Not easy to grease a landing like that on a strip of rocky dirt."

The men did not respond, just continued to smile wryly. The dog handler was looking down at the dog, which kept its eyes on both her and Colt, ears erect, shifting its attention back and forth between the two of them.

The guard took a step forward, and the dog responded by moving closer. It sniffed the air, moving its muzzle slightly from side to side, then licked its chops and sat down. Its handler gave it a pat and stepped aside, the dog obediently moving out of the way to take a spot next to him.

"I suppose that's our ride."

Ronnie blinked a few more times and squinted, noticing for the first time a Jeep about fifty yards away. A man was standing in front of it. He was wearing a white polo shirt and khakis under a wide-brimmed white hat, looking the part of a British explorer. Or, more precisely, a caricature of one.

He gestured for them to approach.

Ronnie studied the landscape as they walked. Harsh terrain under her feet. Rolling hills of jungle along the horizon. Tall trees with flat tops in dry, grassy clearings surrounded by green tapestries of vegetation. She thought she could detect a whiff of ocean salt in the air, more than a hint of it in the sultry heat moistening her skin. Were they on an island? She'd wondered for weeks if it would be on an island, sort of a hunch. If so, given how long they'd flow from Mozambique to the first stop—wherever that was—then to here, she figured there would have to be a way to narrow it down later, on a map. Maybe.

"Our bags," she said, turning to the man who'd greeted them with the airline joke.

He gestured to the car. "Just go with Mr. White."

She wasn't sure whether he was referring to the man's name or race. Colt gave her a gentle nudge toward the car and started walking.

"You knew this was coming," he said, leaning in close and lowering his voice. "They want to search them without us watching."

He is right, she thought. She did know it was coming. They had talked about it. They'd also prepared for it. That didn't make it any less disturbing.

"Welcome," the man waiting near the car said as they approached. His voice was a bit high and carried more than a hint of British snootiness to it. He sounded like someone reluctantly reading a cue card. "You may call me Mr. White. I'm going to drive you to your trailer. You'll have thirty minutes to freshen up. Then you'll be escorted to your in-brief. Please hold all your questions. You'll be given all the information you need there."

The man opened a door for them to climb in, then raised an arm and looked toward the far end of the runway. Another Jeep started moving toward them from the rear. This one had a mounted assault weapon of some kind, with two riflemen elevated on swiveling seats behind the driver.

"M60," Colt said. There was a hint of approval in his voice. "And every guy in uniform looks like they have a P90. They're not messing around."

They drove parallel to the landing strip. Another plane was at the very end, a taut chain or cable hanging down from each wing to a point where they were secured to the ground. There were two guards, one with another dog, pacing around, watching the nearby trees.

They rode in slow, bumpy silence for what Ronnie clocked at a little more than five minutes along a dirt road, cutting through a few patches of dense vegetation and stands comprising trees of varying sizes and shapes, before she saw a tall fence of heavy-duty chain link, topped with razor wire. Two fences, she realized, an interior one about ten feet inside the outer one. Beyond the fencing Ronnie could see a single building with a few smaller, temporary structures in the background.

The Jeep with the riflemen tailed a few lengths behind as they followed the road around an edge of the fence until ultimately reaching a pair of gates, one exterior, one interior. A man with an assault rifle stood on a platform atop a metal tower about fifteen feet high, just inside the exterior one. Another man stood inside the outer gate, a dog heeling obediently to his left. He raised a walkie-talkie to his mouth and began to operate some complex type of latch before sliding the gate to the side. Another Jeep approached along the interior perimeter of the fence as Mr. White drove up to the interior gate, and the driver jumped out to repeat the process. Both gates quickly closed behind them as they passed through and covered the remaining hundred feet or so to the building.

The driver that had opened the interior gate pulled up behind them as they stepped out of the vehicle.

"This is Mr. Red. He will escort you to your trailer." Mr. White said, pointing vaguely to the right side of the building. "Your luggage will be arriving shortly."

"We're getting the full Tarantino treatment," Colt said, just loud enough for Ronnie to hear both his words and, in the tone of his whisper, the subtle smile she just knew he'd have on his face.

The man called Mr. Red swung his head for them to follow as he strode toward the corner of the building. He was large, larger than Colt. Like the other guards, he was dressed in dark blue, a full tactical outfit, with black boots. He had a sidearm in a holster and a rifle slung across his back that looked to Ronnie like a stubby little machine gun.

"Another P90," Colt said, as if reading her thoughts. "Pretty sophisticated piece of hardware for standard issue by an NGO of... questionable legality."

Ronnie ignored the comment—*could men like him ever just be serious?*—and took his word for it regarding the weapons. She was still kicking herself for not having done more firearm research while prepping for this assignment. She grudgingly admitted to herself that she was going to have to feign some interest going forward so as not to arouse suspicion from their hosts.

Mr. Red led them around the building and toward a trailer about fifty yards away. There were four trailers in all, two doublewides and two singles. They were heading in the direction of the nearest single.

"Five-star accommodations," Ronnie said. *Oh, great,* she thought. *Now I'm doing it.*

"I've stayed in worse," Colt said. "Looks cozy, though."

Cozy. Ronnie leaned closer, keeping an eye on the man in front of them. "Don't get any ideas," she said in a voice as faint as she could manage while still trying to sound like she wasn't playing around.

"I was about to say the same thing."

There was a small porch in front of the trailer. Mr. Red hopped up the steps and punched in a code to unlock a deadbolt. He stepped aside after opening the door and let them enter before moving into the doorway and stopping there.

"You have thirty minutes," he said. "Bathroom is back there, in front of the bedroom. There's some water in the fridge, along with some snack food if you're hungry. Sandwiches will be provided after the briefing. I'll be outside."

A moment after he shut the door, Ronnie said, "Wow. They're guarding us."

Colt put a straightened finger to his lips, then pointed at his ears before waving his hand to indicate their surroundings. Ronnie supposed it was *possible* the place was bugged, but after seeing it she had her doubts. It was sparsely furnished. A cloth sofa at one end. A tiny dining table with two chairs. A kitchenette. A door past the kitchen to the bedroom their babysitter had mentioned. The space was reasonably clean, at least.

She was going to make a comment about not needing to mansplain the obvious to her, but decided against it.

"I'm going to use the bathroom," she said.

Colt nodded, inspecting the interior methodically like someone searching for a hidden door. "Leave some for me."

The bathroom was tiny and had a small window behind the toilet. Ronnie leaned forward and by cocking her head was able to see Mr. Red on the porch. He was speaking into his walkie-talkie, a cord running from it to his ear. She couldn't make out what he was saying, but she had a strong feeling he was reporting back something about her and Colt.

Where were they? she wondered. *C'mon, Rhonda, think.* They'd flown into Zimbabwe, then took two private flights after. The first one landed without her having any idea where they were, while they were blindfolded for the entirety of the second flight. The only clue she could think of was she thought she'd detected the briny tang of the ocean in the air when she'd deplaned.

Colt was already on her nerves, and she started to wonder why. Sure, he oozed toxic masculinity and condescending arrogance, but that rarely got this far under her skin. She decided it was because of her father, how much he reminded her of the man. Their relationship had been equal parts love and hate. He was a good father, supportive for the most part, but never took her writing seriously. *You keep talking about saving the world,* he'd say to her. *Writers don't do that. Writers write about the people who save the world.* God, how she hated him telling her that, resented him for it until the day he died, a few years ago, his body burned before she was even notified. She stood there thinking about him for a few more minutes before splashing water on her face and patting it dry with a towel that smelled of mold.

When she stepped out of the bathroom, Colt was holding up a piece of paper he'd written on in pencil.

We should make small talk like a couple. I can't imagine they're not listening.

Ronnie rolled her eyes, wagged her chin from side to side. Then she sighed and gave a nod. Like broken clocks, even men like him can be right. Occasionally.

"I expected a little more in the way of creature comforts, given how much the whole thing cost."

Colt smiled. "Hey, you were the one who wanted to spice things up, remember?" he said, his voice obviously if only slightly amplified at the prospect of someone listening. "You could have just agreed to the threesome."

What a pig, Ronnie thought, sneering as he made his way past her to the bathroom.

"You're a pig," she said to his back, trying to stay in character. The mirthful tone in her voice—far different from the one that had uttered the words in her head—came as a surprise to her ears. She grudgingly admitted to herself that while he may have been a pig (*definitely* a pig!) he *was* kind of funny. Sort of. Sometimes.

They passed the time in relative silence, trading only a few bland comments. After thirty minutes down to the second, there was a knock on the trailer door. Ronnie and Colt followed Mr. Red back to the main building. Ronnie was already trying out descriptions in her mind for it, as this struck her as the heart of the operation. The word that kept coming to mind was *vapid.* The structure was painted a pale shade of gray. Beyond the set of front double doors was a wide hallway with three doors on each side and a corridor near the middle to the left. The interior, like the rest of it, was strictly utilitarian and vaguely governmental. Drab, bone-colored walls, metal doors spray-painted an institutional beige.

Mr. Red led them to the second door on the right, and they entered a small conference room. Two long portable tables stretched across the middle of it end to end with folding chairs on the opposite side of them facing the front. There was a dry erase board on the front wall and a large flatscreen TV mounted in the far front corner.

Mr. Red told them to take a seat and that Mr. White and Dr. Blue would be joining them shortly. He left them there and closed the door as he exited.

Ronnie wanted to say something, but was reluctant to break the quiet, which was unsettling, bordering on eerie. She wondered if they were being watched, stealth cameras transmitting angles of the room to monitors one door over. She doubted it, leaned toward this being another manifestation of paranoia, but, again, couldn't rule it out. With more than a little self-reproach, she decided Colt was rubbing off on her.

The length of the silence started to strike her as unnatural. Before she could get a word out to to avoid suspicion, the door opened and a woman entered the room. Mr. White trailed closely behind her, a folder tucked between his arm and his waist.

"I trust your flight and accommodations were all in order," the woman said, not doing much to give the impression that she actually cared.

She was tall and dark and trim, with an aquiline nose and long black hair that shimmered with a rusty tint where it caught the fluorescent lighting. Her accent was British, and Ronnie's first guess was that she was of Indian extraction. She wore a khaki shirt with epaulets and matching trousers with a brown belt and brown flats. Simple and no-nonsense. Ronnie's snap-judgment was that this woman was in charge.

"Yes," Ronnie said. "Fine. Thank you for asking."

The woman nodded. "You may call me Dr. Blue. Before we begin, I'm going to have to ask you to sign and initial the documents Mr. White is about to give you."

Mr. White produced some sheets of paper from the folder and placed a few pages in front of each of them.

"What's this?" Ronnie asked.

"A non-disclosure agreement."

Ronnie looked over the document. It was obviously lawyered, with a number of phrases in legalese the precise meaning of which were hard to understand, but the gist of it was that they promised not to tell anyone about what they learned or did at this location. Conspicuously absent from the document was the name of the party they were making this promise to. The introductory paragraph and the signature blocks all simply had blanks where that information would normally be. She supposed they would fill them in later.

Ronnie signed and initialed where indicated. It wasn't like she cared. She was here under false pretenses anyway.

Mr. White collected the sheets and placed them back in the folder. He glanced at them before nodding to the doctor.

"As I said, you may call me Dr. Blue. I'm sure you've already figured out these names aren't real. And in the same vein, please…let's not pretend. None of this is, strictly speaking, *legal*. You know that and have since you first sought us out. But you may be surprised to learn that none of this is specifically *illegal*, either. I want you to understand that, because it is important that we be on the same page to some extent. If the details of this were to be leaked, if what is currently whispered about and discussed in chat rooms on the dark web were to be confirmed and made public, legal or not, we'd be shut down, probably arrested, with charges manufactured by creative minds determined to bask in the virtuous glory of public opinion while feigning moral outrage. That may not matter much to you, but it matters a great deal to me. To us. What we do here is too important."

Colt spoke up. "How can a zombie hunt be not *specifically illegal*? What happened to all those international accords and UN declarations and multi-lateral whatevers that we've been hearing about for years?"

"It's not that 'zombie hunts' aren't considered a criminal activity by virtually every country on the planet, it's that it's not a criminal activity here. This island is considered an independent principality under a 99-year lease. Don't bother to try to find out where it is on Google. It was part of a classified Cold War program, and the lease was sold off many years ago, after it lost its strategic value. The governmental landlord, as it were, only cares about getting its rent."

"What sort of a *Cold War program*?" Ronnie asked.

The woman who called herself Dr. Blue sighed. "A research facility. We'll leave it at that, if for no other reason than I can't be one-hundred percent sure what sort of research was being conducted here back then. And, no, it had nothing to do with the Zombie Outbreak of five years ago."

"But it *was* a bio-weapons lab, right?" Colt said. "I mean, what other kind of classified offshore research would the government—any government—be doing?"

"That's probably a safe assumption. But enough about the history. You paid for a hunt, and chances are you don't care to know what I'm about to tell you, but I'm going to tell it to you any way. Even if my colleagues strongly counsel against it."

Ronnie leaned her weight forward, elbows on the table.

"As you are undoubtedly aware, over 5 years ago—67 months ago to be exact—reports of persons believed dead becoming reanimated and attacking living people at random began to surface out of Myanmar. The cause was attributed to a previously unidentified virus that was initially passed through swine and which eventually made the leap to human-to-human transmission. That virus became known by the acronym NECRO. Efforts to contain it failed, and within six months zombie outbreaks were happening all over the globe, particularly in the third world, but also in numbers significant enough to cause widespread panic in the US and Europe. Unlike in the movies, however, the outbreak was quickly tamed in the West, where authorities discovered that cremating bodies within two hours of death brought the problem under control. *Burn units*, as I believe you Americans call them, were established in virtually every city. Less than a year later, doctors determined that if the death occurred under medical supervision, reanimation could be prevented through a simple severing of the spinal cord at the base of the skull. This allowed many people to resume having funerals for their loved ones."

"And now, the UN has a task force overseeing compliance with international mandates on the handling of corpses," Colt said. "Reanimated or not."

"Yes. If you're wondering why I'm going over this, what the point is, I'm getting to that. Because of the success of immediate responsive measures, and due to the huge cost of those measures, funding for every other approach began to dry up. Full-time police forces with instant response capability and sophisticated portable burn equipment are, frankly, expensive. Wealthier nations, understanding the threat from poor countries less able to handle the situation to be severe, had to subsidize international efforts to unprecedented levels. Funding for my work here was, consequently, cut off."

"And what work was that?" Ronnie asked.

"A vaccine," she said.

"I thought virtually everyone was infected with the virus, that it just lays dormant until death," Colt said, a heartbeat before Ronnie was about to say the same thing. She wished he would just shut up already.

Dr. Blue nodded, but with a twist to her lips. "That's partly true. There are two types of onset. A flare within the bloodstream triggered by oxygen deprivation to the brain, and a different, lesser-understood type, triggered by the introduction of an active strain of virus directly into the bloodstream, usually through a bite. The evidence suggests the latter involves the presence of a fungus that takes root in the blood and mucus membranes."

Ronnie cocked her head. She'd read about that, but never thought it really mattered. "And what's the practical difference between the two?"

"Through a bite, you become what everyone from the beginning has called a 'zombie' without actually completing the process of dying first."

Ronnie felt her eyes widen. This story was taking on a whole new angle. "That's what you were trying to develop a vaccine to prevent."

Dr. Blue latched her gaze squarely on Ronnie's. "That's what I am *currently* trying to develop a vaccine to prevent."

The room became quiet. Mr. White exhaled audibly, his eyes roaming the floor as he dimpled a cheek. It was clear to Ronnie he did not approve of his colleague's disclosures.

"The point is," Dr. Blue continued, "this *experience* is being offered to you—to people like you—as a means to an end. When our funding was cut off, we were told to clear out and that the facility was being shut down. We were ordered to turn over our research and vacate. We opted to take a different course. That course requires money."

No wonder this little underground hunting retreat was so expensive, Ronnie told herself, and why you can only find out about it by scouring layer after layer of the deepest parts of the dark web. This is how they were keeping the program alive. It was starting to make a different kind of sense than simply a for-profit black-market service. Some of it, anyway.

"They really don't know you're doing this?" Ronnie asked.

"Oh, they know. At the very least they hear the rumors, the internet legends, see the posts that pop up in chat rooms, I'm sure. But they don't know much more than anyone else, no more than the talk of an illicit zombie hunt for people willing to spend lots of money."

Ronnie was about to ask another question, probe deeper, when Colt's voice cut her off. "Well, that's all good to know. But what about the hunt? When does that start?"

"Yes, of course. You didn't come all this way and spend all that money to sit here to listen to me justify our actions. My hope is that I've impressed upon you the importance of discretion after you leave us. As to the hunt, my associate Mr. White is going to explain some rules and give you an idea of what to expect. Afterwards, you'll be taken to a firing range to be familiarized with the weapons you'll be supplied."

"What will we be using?" Colt asked.

Mr. White stepped forward, adjusting has glasses. "Each of you will be given a Ruger 10/22."

"That's it?" Colt straightened up in his chair, the muscles around his eyes and nose clenching. "A plinking rifle?"

"Rest assured, they are more than adequate."

Ronnie bit down on the inside of her lip. Colt's gun-nut macho bullshit could only cause them trouble. He's just supposed to be some guy looking for an adventure with his girlfriend, not some weapons expert asking a bunch of questions. Besides, why was he speaking up at all? He was there to be her security, nothing but hired muscle. She was the friggin' journalist. The nerve of that man! Who the hell did he think he was?

"Mr. White is right," Dr. Blue added. "The caliber is more than sufficient to terminate brain function. You have to remember, these are not normal human brains we are dealing with. They are hijacked, co-opted." Her body went quiet and for a second or two she seemed to stare at nothing in particular, as if reflecting on her own words. "The infection in this stage has jump-started regions that control minimal functionality, walking, grabbing, eating… any transfer of kinetic energy into the brainpan disrupts that delicate balance and causes all revived neural function to cease."

Colt started to say something else, then stopped. Ronnie wondered if he suddenly became aware of the daggers shooting from her eyes.

Mr. White stepped behind Dr. Blue to lower a map on a roller suspended above the dry erase board.

Dr. Blue cast a sudden look at Ronnie, appeared to be considering a thought that had just occurred. "Before Mr. White gives you your instructions for the hunt, it is probably worth noting that the subjects you'll encounter are not alive. Not in any medical or practical sense. These are corpses animated after death by viral repurposing of certain neural pathways. While you will be 'killing' them in laymen's terms, you are not taking what most would consider a life, and certainly not a human one. The people that once inhabited those bodies are gone."

She paused, and Ronnie thought she noticed the woman's eyelids flutter. "Gone and not ever coming back."

The map Mr. White had pulled down was an outline drawing of an island, divided into sectors. The sectors were numbered one through nine. The space numbered 1 was in the southern portion of the island, near the center. The number 9 on the map was contained in an area that looked to be the northwest corner. There was no compass or legend.

It is an island, Ronnie thought. *We're on an island off the coast of Africa.*

"We are here," Mr. White said, extending a collapsible pointer he'd taken from his pocket and giving the map a firm tap at a spot marked by a star near the numeral 1. "Approximately two hours from now, you will be escorted here, to Sector 3." The man gave the map another whack with the pointer.

"With .22s," Colt said.

"Your escorts will have considerably more firepower than that. They will hang back and track your movements from an unintrusive distance, but they will be at the ready to neutralize any threat that gets too close. You can rest assured they are expert shots."

"What's considered *too close*?"

"Inside three meters. Or roughly ten feet."

Colt didn't seem happy with the information, but whatever his misgivings were, he held them back.

Mr. White waited a few beats before continuing. "After you're done here, you will have one hour, give or take, with Mr. Red at the firing range. He will go over the parts of your firearm and let each of you have target practice to ensure minimal competence with the rifle before departing. You will also be given some more time at your trailer to rest or freshen up. Your bags should have arrived by then, if they haven't already, and will be waiting for you there. Now, moving on, it is absolutely imperative that you stay within the area of Sector 3 that is marked by red ribbons. These ribbons are easily spotted and are tied around trees at regular intervals along each side of a fifteen-meter-wide tract that terminates in a zone approximately sixty meters wide and thirty meters deep. To you Americans, that's around fifty feet for the tract and a zone that's two hundred feet wide and a hundred feet deep. You may encounter one or more *zombies* at any point from the beginning of the tract. There will, however, be no more than three, total."

Ronnie noted that he said the word 'zombies' almost ironically, as if the idea of calling them that was crude and ignorant. Of course, that's all the entire world had ever called them, despite initial attempts by governments, mainstream media outlets and international panels to bar use of the term.

"Is there any chance we won't come across any?" Ronnie asked.

"That is unlikely." Mr. White collapsed the telescoping pointer into a short rod. "Once you do encounter any of them, whether one, two, or three, do not panic. As Dr. Blue will explain, these are Stage 2 zombies. As long as you pay attention to your surroundings and do not stand still while missing all your shots, you should be fine."

Ronnie was familiar with the three stages of the zombie condition caused by the NECRO virus's post-mortem phase. The first stage saw the body become ambulatory, but oblivious to its surroundings, like a sleepwalker. It lasted about forty-eight hours. The second stage was when they began to become aware of people and started attacking anyone nearby, persistently, if clumsily, trying to eat them. That lasted anywhere from ten days to two weeks. Stage 3 was the most dangerous stage, where they began to show more physical coordination and apparent awareness that their prey will try to resist, but there weren't many known cases reaching that stage, with only a handful having been documented, mostly from the third world. There had been rumors about a later stage, a Stage 4, stories of them hiding during the day, using darkness and cover to stalk, and attacking in packs, but most people dismissed such accounts as internet legends thrown out there to freak people out.

Sort of the same way they did zombie hunts, Ronnie thought.

"Why all the German shepherds?" Colt asked.

Mr. White and Dr. Blue looked at each other.

"Alsatians," Mr. White said, adjusting his glasses. "They're for security."

"On an island?"

"Once in a while," Dr. Blue interjected, stepping forward, "a zombie will take an unpredictable route and wander off. The dogs are specially trained to track them down."

"If there are no more questions for now," Mr. White said, following an awkward moment of quiet, "we can finish up this briefing and get you on your way."

"Just one," Colt said. "What's the deal with Section 9?"

Mr. White hesitated. Ronnie thought she noticed Dr. Blue cast him a glance, a flash in her eyes, but she couldn't be certain.

"I don't understand the question," he said.

"All those other sections except maybe this one, Section 1, have had a few things written on them in marker and erased. But both this one and Section 9 have had a lot of things written on them and a lot of things erased."

It took a moment, then Ronnie understood what he was getting at. The difference was subtle, subtle enough she wouldn't have noticed, but it was there. The white material was well-used, a vinyl of some sort. Inevitably on these sorts of boards, people sometimes didn't write on it with the kind of marker that easily erased. That meant a less than clean wipe, probably a scrubbing with a cleaner or alcohol. Some parts were slightly shaded a faint gray. Sections 1 and 9 seemed to bear the brunt of it, by far.

"I'm just wondering what you got going on over there." As if sensing Ronnie's alarm over his inappropriate, if not outright suspicious, curiosity, he smiled and added, "is that where the *big game* is? Will we get to hunt there tomorrow?"

Ronnie thought she noticed Dr. Blue's shoulders relax.

"If by 'big game' you mean Stage 3 zombies, no. Not in that Section. Section 9 is where we… house our Stage 1 arrivals until they reach Stage 2. A lot of planning is involved. The logistics and security of it require our team go over every part in meticulous detail."

"Makes sense to me," Colt said. But Ronnie could tell by his tone it made absolutely no sense to him at all. It took all the self-control she could summon not to reach out and strangle him.

"Your Stage 2 hunt will be in Sector 4, tomorrow morning at 10:30. But there will be another safety and procedure briefing with you in this room before that. That should give you plenty of time to return here, eat, freshen up and change, then be flown back to the mainland airstrip for a return flight to Zimbabwe and your personal hotel and flight arrangements. Now, we still have a number of procedures and rules to go over, and we're already a few minutes behind schedule, so if we could please hold off on any further questions not directly related to understanding the information being presented to you…"

Back at the trailer, it took even more of the self-control she'd employed earlier for Ronnie to keep from yelling. Or possibly screaming.

"*What the hell were you thinking back there?*" Her voice was a harsh whisper, harsh enough she was sure he'd be able to hear it above the sound of the water they'd left running in the sink to cover their words.

Colt shrugged. "*They're hiding stuff from us.*"

"*No shit, Sherlock! In case you hadn't noticed, no matter how they try to spin it, this entire operation is a criminal undertaking! The first place you can even make contact was buried so deep on the dark web I thought I was going to end up in China before I got there!*"

There was as much of a smile in Colt's eyes as there was his mouth as he regarded her, which pissed Ronnie off to no end. *Goddamn his masculine stoicism. And damn those handsome eyes, too. Arrogant son of a bitch.*

"*Don't pretend you don't know what I mean,*" he said. "*Do they seriously look like criminals out to make a buck to you? I figured you would have jumped on it at least as soon as I did. They're not just being secretive or careful, they're lying. Why the hell would you need an entire K9 unit for security on an island? Something more is going on here."*

Ronnie stiffened her back and let out a sharp breath, collecting her thoughts for a moment before responding. *"Do you have any idea how much work went into me getting this far? How many hours? How much cajoling and pleading I had to do on top of the dozens—hundreds—of hours of research?"*

"I'm just trying to do my job."

"Your job? I'm the journalist here! You were hired to be my bodyguard! Not to be asking questions that risk drawing unwanted attention to us!"

"I was hired to protect the Post's interests."

Those words cut deep. Frustration was turning to anger, anger that felt an awful lot like hate as it boiled inside her, threatening to overflow.

She started to speak several times, the words halting in her throat. She needed a proper response, something sharp and biting and argument-ending, but nothing whiny or defensive. The proper words were eluding her, adding to her anger.

The thing that made it so frustrating, so enraging, was the fact she was not technically a reporter. Not an employee of the paper, not, in the eyes of many, even a true journalist. She was a blogger. An award-winning, nationally syndicated blogger, but still a blogger. She had no degree in journalism, no pedigree other than the one she'd forged on her own. *Anonymous Reports* had started out as a critique of the news, an outlet for her to share with readers the *real* story, the product of her digging and compiling and analyzing to get overlooked, ignored, or, sometimes, covered-up facts out there. Seven years later, it had grown beyond anything she'd ever expected. When she'd approached the Post about her idea, about them funding an investigative piece regarding whispers of a zombie hunt being offered for a price, they'd been skeptical. But she'd done the footwork, made the case, won them over, and—most importantly—got them to cut the check.

That check came with strings and those strings were so infuriating to her at that moment, she could feel her pulse pounding in her temples.

"All I'm saying is," Colt continued, adopting a conciliatory tone, *"I'm here to keep you safe. Finding out as much as I can about what we may be up against is*

part of that. Besides, it's better for you if they're a little suspicious of me. If you were the one asking all the questions, you'd be in the crosshairs of all their scrutiny. Better to divide their focus."

Ronnie clenched her lips, turning her head away. How dare he be so pushy, so cocky, so... so presumptuous. And how dare he fucking be right.

Worst of all, he was just like her father. Confusing being right on the details with being on the right side of the argument.

She shut off the faucet and didn't say another word to him until Mr. Red knocked on the door, the man once again displaying a punctuality that bordered on preternatural. Even then, her only words were a harsh reproach whispered in Colt's ear.

"Don't you dare go trying to show off at the range after all that."

The range turned out to be a two-by-four and plywood structure in front of an eight-foot tall or so mound of dirt at the rear of the compound with a folding table set up about ten yards away. Stapled to the plywood was a paper target with the plain outline of a person. A man in an outfit matching Mr. Red's was waiting at the table when they walked up. Two identical rifles were laid out on the table.

"This is Mr. Gray," Mr. Red said.

The man nodded once. He was tall and athletic and could have been mistaken for a movie star if it weren't for the conspicuous scar running down the right side of his face, dividing his dark, almost ebony skin with a crooked line of purplish red.

Mr. Gray explained the parts of the rifle and how to operate it. Ronnie listened intently, waiting for Colt to put his two cents in, sure he would be unable to resist flexing his expertise, but he didn't say anything.

After the explanation, Mr. Gray demonstrated how to make sure a round was chambered and how to fire it. He also showed them how to clear a jam. Then Mr. Red gave them each a pair of headphones for hearing protection,and Mr. Gray took three shots at the target, placing all of them in the vicinity of the outlined person's eyes and forehead.

Mr. Gray removed the magazine and gestured for Ronnie to step forward to the table. He handed her the rifle and asked her to insert the magazine as he'd explained. She did it with minimal fumbling. He told her to place the butt against her shoulder and raise the barrel toward the target, careful not to allow the muzzle to point in any direction but straight ahead where it was safe.

"Look down the sight and place it right beneath where you want to hit," he said, "like that spot is resting on it. Then take a gentle breath and let it out without pushing it, and when you're ready, squeeze that trigger finger; don't pull it."

Three shots, one around the throat, one that might have clipped the imaginary person's ear, and one just off the center of the face.

"Good," Mr. Gray said. "If you can group that well from this distance, you would probably notch a kill if you were halfway closer."

Colt took his turn, putting the first two shots where each eye would be, before putting his third near the lower side of the jaw. Ronnie had no doubt he threw that last shot on purpose, guessing he could have put it through either of the eyeholes he'd already made.

If Mr. Gray, suspected the same thing, he didn't show it. He uttered a bland compliment or two, then had them both shoot again. Ronnie's grouping was roughly similar, though in different spots. Colt put all three in the head in a wide pattern that looked random, but it was still obvious to Ronnie he could have lit a match stick with any shot he wanted if someone held it out with their teeth.

"How many magazines will we have?" Colt asked, setting his weapon down.

Mr. Gray removed the rifles from the table and handed them to Mr. Red. "One," he said.

"One?" Colt glanced at Ronnie. "How many rounds?"

"Three each."

"Three? That's it?"

"That should be more than enough," Mr. Red said, interjecting. "Even if you don't see us, we won't be far behind you. And we'll be backing you up with high-velocity cartridges, not to mention laser sighting and red dots. Either of us will be able to wing a mosquito off your shoulder any time we want."

Colt nodded, but Ronnie could tell he wasn't pleased with that information. Not even a little.

The sun was well past the center of the sky when they climbed into the jeep. Ronnie felt fatigue start to set in. By how many hours was her body clock off? Eight? Ten? It was probably well after midnight on the East Coast. But because she wasn't exactly sure where they were, she couldn't be certain how long after.

They drove through the gate, Mr. Red behind the wheel, Mr. Gray in the passenger seat. Both men looked alert, focused, but not the least bit on edge or concerned. *How many times have they done this?* she wondered. About ten minutes later, the rough dirt road ended at another gate. Mr. Red shut off the ignition while Mr. Gray hopped out and punched a code where the gate was latched.

Beyond the gate, tall grass spread out for a hundred yards or more, leaning to the side and twitching in the occasional breeze.

"On foot from here," Mr. Red said, stating the obvious. He retrieved the rifles from a long canvas bag and handed one to each of them. Then he gestured for them to follow.

The road narrowed to a path through the grass as they neared a line of trees. Mr. Red was in the lead, Mr. Gray was some distance back, scanning the landscape to each side as he walked. Ronnie tried to get an idea of the forest past the trees as they approached, but it was hard to discern more than a hodge-podge of various flora. There was an intensity to the verdant tones that struck her as both beautiful and intimidating. She also took notice of how alien many of the shapes were that draped and sprouted and wrapped, shaded by large fronds and thick canopy.

Mr. Red reached into a breast pocket and produced a small rectangular device that looked like a remote control. He tapped it a few times, stared at it until satisfied, then slid it back into his pocket. He looked at Ronnie and Colt as he gestured toward a break in the foliage directly ahead.

"Okay, this is where you advance on your own. We will be covering you from the rear, even if you can't see us. Do not let any of the hostiles get closer to you than necessary, if you can avoid it. We will undertake direct intervention if any get within ten feet."

Ronnie nodded. She started forward, then decided to let Colt take the lead. He didn't hesitate.

They had traveled a few dozen yards before the unsettling beauty of her surroundings struck her. They were traversing terrain that was part canopy jungle, part fantasy forest, and part extraterrestrial landscape. Huge green fronds so bright they almost glowed neon hung off appendages that curled into their path; bursts of yellow, red and blue flowers beckoned from all sides like merchants displaying their wares. The trill of insects, rising and falling, and the exotic sing-song of unseen birds provided a backing track as they moved through a wilderness that gave no appearance of ever prior having been touched by man. Or woman.

Around the hundred-yard point, Colt slowed his already deliberate pace and turned his head to the side to speak over his shoulder.

"You okay back there?"

"Fine." Truth was, she was scared. And not of zombies. "Do you think they intend to shoot us and leave us out here?"

"No. Not these guys who drove us. They're soldiers. Ex-military. They're not murderers."

"I didn't know the two were mutually exclusive."

"I didn't get that vibe." He kept his voice low, barely audible. "They seem to take their job seriously. Besides, there would be no reason for all the production. They could have killed us anytime they wanted to. Who would they be trying to fool? We're on an island. There's no one else here... Anyway, why would they even want to?"

"Because they figured out why we're here?"

"Does this look like an operation that has that kind of reach?"

"What do you make of that story about funding their research?"

"I would guess it's true. Or mostly true. But I'm also pretty damn sure there's a lot they're not telling us."

Ronnie nodded. She thought the exact same thing. Dr. Blue sounded passionate when discussing her reasons for what they were doing here, but there was something guarded about her every word.

Pondering how Dr. Blue was guarded in her remarks reminded Ronnie that she and Colt were literally supposed to be guarded this very moment. Ronnie glanced back over her shoulder, checking from both sides. She could make out the area where they entered the forest in the distance, a bright background to the trees and plants, but not any details of it. She scanned the patches of growth and the gaps between the trees, searching for signs of Mr. Red or Mr. Gray. Nothing.

She rushed a few steps forward to catch up to Colt. "What if they just wanted us to think they were keeping tabs, but instead left us out here on our own?"

"Well, depending on how many boogey-men they let loose, that would be bad," he said. "But it doesn't make much sense from a tactical perspective. They're going through an awful lot of trouble and allowing a number of unnecessary risks." A moment later, he added, "If that is what they're up to, I guess it would explain why they only issued us three rounds of plinking ammunition."

Hearing Colt's words brought home the reality of the situation, bringing with it a wave of anxiety, anxiety that prodded her mind to entertain an array of disturbing possibilities. What if the purpose of this place was far more sinister than her initial assumption that it was an illicit zombie-hunting preserve designed to turn a profit? What if it really was a research facility, but *they* were the subjects? What if the whole thing was designed to see how long people could survive in a so-called zombie apocalypse? To see if a couple fending for themselves would turn on each other? If one would sacrifice the other to survive?

She shook her head with a shiver, tossing the thoughts aside. *Don't let your imagination run wild*, she told herself. *You have enough B-movie plots to worry about as it is.*

They had traveled a bit deeper into the jungle—forest?—beneath a wide cloak of interwoven leaves and branches, when Colt pointed at a tree branch with a red ribbon.

"There's one." He scanned across to the left of them. "And there's the other. At least we didn't screw up the easy part."

The path, or what passed for one, seemed to end around ten yards later. The area was traversable, but there was just no defined trail to take. Ronnie felt a buzz radiate out from the base of her neck. She could only describe it as a feeling they were being watched.

"I see more ribbons up ahead," Colt said, before Ronnie could voice her concern.

A few steps later, Ronnie saw them, too. Then she spotted another pair about the same distance beyond those two. She started to tell Colt when she caught a glimpse of movement off to her left.

She stopped abruptly and snapped her head to the side. She moved her eyes across the terrain, her vision panning from tree to tree, surveying as far into the distance as she could make out. She saw a butterfly flutter around a bush, off to their left a monkey with a long tail jumped from one branch onto another that drooped under its weight. A large beetle bearing the imprint of something prehistoric, with horns and oversized pincers for jaws scaled the trunk of a narrow tree a few feet away. What she had seen, or thought she'd seen, wasn't anything like any of those creatures. She wasn't able to even categorize what it could have been, just movement, a shape, a shadow. A figure in her peripheral vision, gone by the time she was able to train her focus in that direction.

Her mind was playing tricks on her, she decided. Sure, there was a zombie or two (or three?) out here, but they weren't known for their stealth. When the twenty-four-hour news cycle some five years earlier was ZOMBIES! ZOMBIES! ZOMBIES! for almost ten days—before the government stepped in and took over the airwaves with the emergency broadcast system, shutting down what various officials deemed 'disinformation' and 'sensationalism calculated to induce a national panic,' claiming that hostile foreign powers were using the situation to sow unrest—there was no shortage of videos being circulated showing what they looked like, how they moved. So many images of them, all with that stilted, rocking gait, that glassy, vacant stare. She'd never actually seen one live (or dead, as it were)—the outbreak had been quashed quickly and protocols for the handling of dead bodies were implemented with remarkable speed and surprising efficiency—but she had a hard time imagining one being hard to spot.

A few more looks, then she hurried forward to catch up to Colt, bobbing past elephant ears and hopping over branches.

Colt stopped and turned at the sound of her footfalls.

"I thought I saw something move," she said.

"I'm sure you did," he said, nodding. "Lot of creatures in this kind of wilderness. Easy for your eye to catch flashes of things in motion."

Ronnie didn't respond, not appreciating his dismissive reaction, but ultimately supposing he was right. She glanced past him, looking for the next ribbons, seeing one of them up ahead. "The clearing they mentioned shouldn't be too much farther, should it?"

"Assuming they started measuring from the first ribbons, I'd say it's maybe another fifty, seventy-five yards."

She took a breath. She wasn't quite what she'd call tired, but she was already starting to feel the weight of the rifle in her hands. It had felt light back at the range, barely heavier than a toy. Not so light now.

"Lead the way," she said, a hint of sarcasm in her voice.

As much as she hated to admit it, having Colt there made all the difference. The man was confident and, as best she could tell, competent, a reassuring presence for sure. She couldn't imagine being out here like this by herself. What had she been thinking, insisting she go alone? Throwing a fit when her editor wouldn't budge? She *hadn't* been thinking, she realized. Just reacting. She knew nothing about firearms, nothing about hunting, and probably no more than the average person off the street about zombies. It was the story she'd been focused on, getting the story and nothing else, to the point of tunnel vision.

Colt stopped so suddenly, Ronnie almost walked into him. He belatedly held out his arm to the side, angling it back. He was staring ahead to his right.

"What is it?" she said, keeping her voice down.

"I don't know."

"A zombie?"

Colt said nothing. He took a step forward, eyes still in the same direction. Then another.

"Wait here a second. Something's not right."

Not right? She wanted to ask him, *What the hell that was supposed to mean? Did he think there was a zombie out there or not?* She peered in the same direction he was looking to try to see what had caught his eye. It occurred to her maybe zombies weren't the only thing they needed to look out for. Were there predators in these woods? Leopards? Tigers? Something worse?

"Look," she said, as Colt took another step. "Maybe we should—"

Ronnie heard a crack, a snap, a whipping sound, and then a wet thunk, and before any of that registered, she saw Colt's body shudder and pop back a foot or two into the air as if yanked. Her first thought was that he'd run into a tree, because one was now directly in front of him, seemingly appearing out of nowhere. Then she saw the three wooden spikes protruding from his back, covered in blood. She blinked several times, expecting the image to change, to make sense, before she realized he'd been impaled. She let out a sharp shriek, swallowing it as she covered her mouth.

Colt's head jerked, once, twice. She heard a gurgle, followed by a cough. She willed herself to step forward, edging past him, trembling almost uncontrollably.

The flat edge of an imposing log emerging from the ground, about six feet long and vertical, was pressed against the front of him. The impact had lifted him a few inches off the ground and his body was still there, suspended, the soles of his shoes not quite touching the earth below them.

His head rolled in her direction, his eyes trying to reach hers. He opened his mouth, but instead of any words coming out, a large dollop of blood, stringy with saliva, stretched over his lip and extended like a tendril toward the ground.

Ronnie sobbed, almost retching, the muscles of her face tightened and contorted. She reached a hand toward his cheek. "I'm sorry," she said, the words breaking up in her throat. She had no idea what else to say. Her vision blurred. She felt the tears start to spill over her eyelids.

His beard brushed her palm. For a moment she thought he was leaning his head against her hand, like a big puppy wanting to be stroked. Then she saw that his whole body had sagged. She pulled her hand away and his head hung there, eyes narrow slits, staring at nothing.

Her shock and sorrow gave way to a panic. *This was a booby trap*, she told herself, her thoughts screaming, echoing off the walls of her mind. *Someone murdered him.* Her instinct was to run, but her legs felt cemented to the ground.

Without having to think about it, she was certain of two things—one was that that trap wasn't set by some mindless zombie, and two, whoever did set it would have prepared others.

They would be coming after her. And soon.

The mere act of breathing was becoming a challenge, her lungs filling and emptying in rapid succession, her head starting to tingle. She forced herself to hold her breath and count to ten before exhaling. Once, twice, three times. *Calm down. You're still alive.*

The forest around her was unchanged but suddenly far more menacing. She studied her surroundings, careful to keep her eyes away from Colt, certain she would lose it if she looked at him again.

Think, girl. Think. Her thoughts were swirling until she forced herself to look at the situation as if it were a story she needed to write. Writing a story was like solving a problem, after all. What did she want out of it? What did she know? What did she not know? What resources could she use? Who could she consider reliable? What approach would be best, given what she had to work with?

She looked down at her hands. She had a weapon. Three rounds of ammunition. That's something. Or was it?

A feeling of hopelessness swept over her as she reminded herself that Mr. Red or Mr. Gray had loaded both weapons. She fumbled for the button to detach the magazine and thumbed it. One bullet was visible, pressed against the curved edges of the top. It looked real, but how could she be sure? If she pulled the trigger and it fired, maybe that just meant it was a blank. And if it was real, that would just be wasting one of only three. It occurred to her she could take Colt's, have three more, but she remembered how his rifle had been pinned against his body. The thought of him caused her gut to do somersaults and she put it out of her mind.

Her legs gave out and she sunk to the ground. She buried her face, forehead against her knees, and hugged her shins. The rifle slid from her hands. The gravity of her predicament began to settle in. She was on an island, for all intents and purposes alone, stranded, with everyone else occupying it presumably intending to kill her for reasons unknown. There was no way off, no way to communicate with the outside world, and she had no idea exactly where this place was, other than a vague certainty it was off the eastern coast of Africa. She wasn't even a hundred percent certain of that.

Despite herself, she looked up at Colt. From this angle, he seemed to be gazing down at her, a pitying Christ figure. But that only made her more aware of just how alone she was.

Alone.

She jerked upright, groping for the rifle. Mr. Red and Mr. Gray. It had to be their doing. They would be coming for her.

But something niggled at the edges of that thought. Why all the stealth? Why the elaborate trap? And what was the point? Was this some sick sport to them? Did they discover who she was? The purpose of her coming here? If so, why didn't they just shoot her? They were ex-military, with high-powered weapons. Why… she looked at Colt one more time… something like this?

There were too many things to think about, too many things she didn't understand. All she knew for certain was that she couldn't head back the way she'd come. She had to press deeper into the jungle. Once she found some place she could hide, someplace that felt safe, then she could try to figure out what was going on.

C'mon, girl. You need to act. You can't just sit here feeling sorry for yourself.

She stood, averting her eyes from Colt's body, stifling another sob. She moved through the underbrush away from the path she and Colt had been taking between the ribbons, figuring if there were more traps, that's the most likely place they'd be.

A few dozen yards into and over and under and around oversized, leafy limbs of plants and wiry branches of trees and roping slants of vine, she heard something move. A snap of something under a press of weight, the graze of a branch against cloth. She stopped, holding herself still, forcing her body to not move despite the awkward angle she had to contend with having frozen in midstride. Her eyes scanned the area to her right intently. Nothing seemed out of place. Nothing she could see.

She looked down at the ground at her feet, carefully finishing her step, and then raised her head to find a zombie directly in front of her, less than an arm's length away.

Her eyes saucered and a gasp escaped her throat. She stumbled backwards and tripped over a root, landing hard on her ass. The thing continued to look at her, tilting its head, but otherwise didn't move.

It was a man, or had once been. Not much taller than her. Trim, slight of build. Not at all what she had expected from the video footage of the sort she'd seen countless times. This creature wasn't the dead sleepwalker she'd always pictured in her mind. Dead, maybe, as its skin was a pale shade of gray and its hair seemed washed of color, like a faded piece of fabric. But not the same kind of dead. This one looked alert—aware. Focused, like it was assessing her.

And those eyes. Shock white irises with no discernible pupil beyond a pin prick of black in the center.

Her brain seemed to wake up and she scrabbled backward, knocking through leafy branches and sticks, fumbling to get a handle on her rifle to raise it. She brought the barrel up, pointing it at the thing's head. She pushed back with her legs as it took a step, and her head bumped against something behind her, something thin and hard, like a shin. She craned her head and looked straight up, saw another pair of those unnatural white eyes staring down at her. She jerked the barrel up, but the thing shot a hand forward and caught it. It was another man, or what used to be one. It gave the barrel a twist and yanked the rifle out of her hands.

She felt the clawing grip of fingers clench around her ankles. There were several of them descending on her, standing over her, five, six, too many to be sure of the count. She tried to kick, but they were strong. She began to flail as more arms started to restrain her, punching and bucking with everything she could muster. She closed her eyes and screamed, anticipating the feel of teeth ripping into her flesh, tearing at her neck and arms and legs and face. But seconds passed and she felt nothing but the cold grip of those fingers on her, holding her down.

"Are you through?" said a voice. "This will be a lot easier if you calm down. These men are holding on for your safety as much as theirs."

She opened her eyes, her head twisting to various angles, trying to understand what was happening. Three were restraining her, zombies she assumed, dressed in soiled, tattered clothing. They reeked of indescribable odors that made her sick to her stomach and she fought the urge to vomit, even as her pulse was rataplanning in her head and her mind was reeling. Her gaze quickly settled on one to her right. He was standing upright, looking down at her without expression, an air of bemusement to the rake of his head. Those eyes made it almost impossible to think of him as a man, but that was certainly what he once was.

"Let me go!" she said, shouting. The words came out before she could think of something better, more persuasive, to say.

"If I do, will you promise to sit there and listen? Rather than trying to run, or punch, or kick any of us?"

Ronnie swallowed, suddenly aware of the deep breaths she was taking, eager to be free of the smell, of the feel of those hard fingertips digging into her limbs. She nodded, trying not to hyperventilate.

The one standing over her dipped his chin in a gesture to the others. Ronnie felt the pinching grips let go in a cascade, the cool flow of blood releasing into places it had been restricted. She pulled her body away from the one behind her, sitting up, resisting the overpowering urge to try to launch herself off the ground into a sprint.

"What do you want with me?" she said after she managed to gain control over her breathing, casting glances at each of the creatures around her.

"For the moment, I just want you to listen."

"Who are you?" she said after a few seconds of feeling her heart drumming in her ears.

The pale man stared at her with those argent eyes, twin orbs suspended above her like a pair of harvest moons. "You can call me Vic. I used to be Vicente Diego. *Doctor* Vicente Diego. I hope to be him again. Whether I ever can be largely depends on you."

"I…" She took in the sets of white irises gazing down upon her from every direction. "I don't understand."

Vic lowered himself to a crouch, bringing two of those eyes to her level.

"Let's just say most everything you likely know about us, about zombies—everything important, anyway—has been the product of a carefully controlled campaign of disinformation, designed to hide the truth."

His voice carried a hint of an accent, one that struck her as sophisticated, continental. Spain, perhaps. Or Portugal.

"What truth?"

"The truth that the Novel Encephalatic Cerebellum Rhinovirus, the NECRO virus, as you know it, has a lifecycle of approximately two months.

And while it certainly leaves some long term, if not permanent, changes to a person's appearance, the material symptoms ultimately pass. People that die from other causes and are reanimated by the virus unfortunately resume that state, and the virus releases. While those turned from a blood or membrane infection…" Vic raised his arms, offering himself as a visual aid.

Ronnie blinked. "You're saying the virus… runs its course?"

"Yes. I—*we*—are living proof."

She let his words swirl through her thoughts, sifting through them for meaning.

"And you're telling me… they know this?"

"Yes. I'm telling you certain government officials—certainly those overseeing control efforts in the US, UK, China, and a few others—all know, and not only know, but are actively suppressing the information. And let's not deal in obscuring niceties, here… I'm also telling you they are killing infected people and burning their bodies because the cost of dealing with the disease otherwise would simply be too expensive."

The sun was angled low in the sky, flickering through layers of canopy, as Ronnie looked around the informal circle of zombie men. The trek through jungle and plain and rocky hillsides to the makeshift encampment had taken well over an hour. Her muscles were fatigued, and she could feel the crash of an adrenaline drain pull at her limbs as she sat on a flat rock, but her brain was still wired. Her mind was busy trying to decide whether the story she was being told was too fantastic to be true, or too fantastic to be fiction.

"So, where are we?" she asked.

"Sector nine," Vic said. "Northwest portion of the island."

Ronnie shook her head. "No. I mean, where is this place? What is it called?"

"We are on Zafar Island. You won't find it on many maps. It is small. Technically, it's considered part of the Mascarenhas Archipelago, but it's not connected in any practical sense. It's owned by the Republic of Mauritius.

It has been leased to the French government for decades, subleased to the British government more recently. For the past five years, the lease has been held by a private research group, funded under a joint international program. It was highly secretive."

Zafar Island, Ronnie thought. *'Zafar I.', not 'Zombie Safari.'*

"And that funding was pulled," she said, remembering what Dr. Blue had told them.

"Yes. The research group decided to continue its work using… alternative sources of revenue. The officials in Mauritius only care that somebody pays the rent. The French seem happy to be rid of the place. The Brits, they threatened for a few months, but ultimately decided distancing themselves from the whole thing would be safer than pressing the issue and possibly calling attention to things they'd rather stay hidden. After the last election, the American government apparently just decided to pretend this place doesn't exist."

"You were one of them. One of the researchers here. That's how you know all this?"

"Vera and I formed the research partnership, secured the contract. Together, she and I were Zafari, Ltd. We ran this place for over three years. That was, until I was bitten."

"But, if governments know what you say they know, and they are determined to keep it covered up, why wouldn't they…"

"Send in troops and shoot everyone? Because they're scared. They don't know what to do. Not everyone in these government knows, and not everyone who does knows everything. Most of them are bureaucrats, with a few high-level officials calling the shots. The easiest thing for all of them is to do nothing and keep their mouths shut. They don't even know the true extent of what our research has discovered. They figured cutting off the money would end the whole thing and they would not have to deal with the implications. We all signed harsh non-disclosure agreements and agreed to be subject to criminal liability for any breaches or leaks. This involves classified information at levels so high we'd be thrown in cells, cut off from all communication. And we literally have no paperwork officially establishing our research credentials or affiliation. We couldn't prove anything, even if we did go public."

"And this is all about money?"

"Money and panic. If people thought there was even a chance that their loved ones could be cured, the pressure to 'quarantine' infected individuals would be so intense, there would be waves of unrest. Relatives of those who died and were inflicted with post-mortem symptoms, relatives of people who would never recover, they would lie as a matter of routine about the circumstances. People would be hiding those afflicted in basements, in attics. Chaining them, caging them. Most would end up infected themselves. Officials would have to make a choice. Impose a police state and go door-to-door, or bankrupt their economies by funding billions and billions and billions to house, feed, care for, monitor, and give medical attention to everyone infected. And what about the families where the breadwinner was infected? Are they left to starve in the streets? Or will money be printed and handed out like candy until a vaccine is perfected? Entire economies—the world economy—would be completely disrupted either way."

Ronnie turned the bits of information she was hearing over and over in her mind, flipping through them forward and back like they were pages in a book.

"It all sounds like a conspiracy theory," she said.

Vic held her gaze with the impassive intensity he'd shown since she'd first laid eyes on him.

"People seem to think adding the word 'theory' automatically means conspiracies don't exist."

She ran through all the things she'd learned since arriving on the island, all the things she'd learned in preparing for this assignment. The dark web networks she never dreamed existed, internet legends that turned out to be true.

"Why…," she said, her voice cracking slightly, forcing her to clear her throat. "Why did you kill Colt?"

"Your companion? That was *them*. That trap was intended for us. It was triggered remotely. When we overcame the two that were trailing you, stalking us, really, one of them must have triggered it. I am sorry for your loss. That is all the more reason for you to help us."

Could it be true? she wondered. Obviously, some of it had to be. But so much of it didn't make any sense. Or, she conceded, perhaps not the kind of sense she was ready to accept.

Ronnie looked around the circle at the six men seated there, then at the six others milling nearby. Men? Zombie men? She wasn't sure how to think of them.

"Are you the only one who can speak?"

"*I can speak.*"

It was the tall, slim one, the one who she had first seen standing in front of her, looking at her intently. His voice was harsh, like the grinding of a garbage disposal.

Vic interjected. "I've been out here the longest. It takes a while to overcome the atrophy of the muscles connected to the vocal cords."

"I still don't understand. Why are the others here, these researchers, Dr. Blue, hunting you like you say? Trying to capture you, or even kill you? They must know the truth."

"Immortality."

"Immortality?"

"Yes, just not the kind you get from never dying. No, this is the more seductive kind. The kind you get from saving the world. From getting your name elevated to the same status as Salk, Curie, and others talked about reverently in medical schools. Vera wants to be the one. The one who discovers the vaccine. She dreams of spending the rest of her life being feted by world bodies and universities, of having schools and commemorative holidays named after her."

"Vera. Is that Dr. Blue?"

"Vera Dinesh. Brilliant woman. A slave to her own ambition. She's rationalized her obsession. She's willing to keep us in cages, perform test after test after test on us, whether we're willing or not. For as long as it takes. Disposing of us when she's done, or when we try to resist."

"She says she's very close to a vaccine."

"She's been saying that for years. It's always just months or weeks away. But this virus evolves too quickly. And the way it interacts with a highly resilient fungus that seems to accompany it is poorly understood.

She would see us all dead if it meant getting any closer to a breakthrough. Even if that breakthrough were illusory. She would let us rot in a cell until we died in the meantime."

"Surely she can be reasoned with. Or maybe I can call attention to all this, put a stop to it. Nobody here knows this, but I'm a journalist."

"She can't be reasoned with. And calling attention to this would be great, except the powers that be would simply deny all of it, would deny this place even exists. Who's going to come out to confirm any of it? More journalists? How? The best you could do is force them to shut down their fundraising zombie hunts for a while. She'd never allow that to happen. Her goal is to bank years' worth of funding. Which is why she will likely never let you leave this island. She will assume you know about me, about us. And to her that means you know too much. She will talk to you like a friend, like she cares, and then she will have her highly trained mercenaries dispatch you."

"But how can you be so sure?"

"After I was bitten, she put me in a cage, experimented on me with the others. If I hadn't managed to escape, she'd have eventually killed me. You don't know her the way I do."

"You were together, weren't you? The two of you."

"More than just together," Vic said, those white eyes staring off into the depths of the forest. "That was a different person, though, a different me. Whatever we may have had is over and done with."

Ronnie didn't know how to respond. She let her attention drift over the other men, men who were zombies, or used to be, men with eyes like crystals and gazes like a doll's but minds that were obviously functioning, men with hair like matted strands of colorless fishing line and skin like weathered vinyl.

"You said earlier one of you knows how to fly that plane I saw on the runway."

Vic gestured to the tall man opposite her. "Fernando here was a commercial pilot for five years. He can fly anything with wings. But we need to overtake them first, neutralize their ability to stop us. It would never work otherwise."

"And you're sure you need me for this?"

"Yes. Dead certain. None of us can get close enough, not with the dogs, and how we stick out. We'd be shot on sight. You can, though. They'll let you in."

"But why not just try to steal the plane? It only had two guards when I saw it. You took both those men's rifles in the jungle. We could just take off."

Vic stared at the ground, thinking, then he looked over to Fernando and gave the man a nod. Fernando leaned forward, turned his head to the side, and lifted his hair to expose his neck. At the base of his skull was a short, straight line. Ronnie took it to be a surgical scar.

"That cicatrix marks the spot of the implant. It's a tiny incendiary device set to explode upon either being triggered by Vera or if the bearer gets beyond a certain radius that happens to match the width of this island."

"So, they can kill you. All of you. And if what you say is true, they'll have to assume I know too much and as soon as they get their hands on me they'll kill me, too."

"Not right away. Vera will debrief you. She'll act extremely concerned. She'll drag it out a few days. Once she's certain she's wrung every piece of information about us she can, only then will she treat you as a loose end."

Ronnie felt her breath whiffle through her lips. She was having trouble processing all she'd heard. *This is insane,* she told herself. *The whole thing was insane. This island, the story she'd been told, the plan for escape. It was all madness.* She scanned the faces around her, weighing her options. She decided there weren't any.

"What do you want me to do?" she said.

The last rays of light were spearing through the gaps in the tree line as Ronnie came within sight of the main research facility. Vicente had described it as being located in Sector 2. Unsurprisingly, the existence of this place had been left out of the briefing they'd received from Dr. Bluc. She corrected herself: *Vera.* The lab building was a sturdy-looking, utilitarian structure that sat in a fenced-off clearing surrounded by tall tangles of leafy green growth and trees with gnarled trunks that looked like prehistoric spikes hammered into the ground by giants. One vehicle path led to the front gate. There were two guards manning it, two more she could see at the far corners of the compound. Each guard had a dog following at his heel. Another guard was in a tower near the gate. Coils of razor wire topped the fence. Signs on each side of the gate warned of a lethal voltage level coursing through the metal link.

Ronnie took a breath and stepped out onto the rutted dirt road. She increased her pace as she approached the gate, raising her arms and waving them over her head, feigning a slight limp. Her muscles were sore and tired to the point it didn't require a lot of acting.

"Help!" she yelled, breaking into a labored jog. "Help me! Please!"

The guards immediately yanked walkie talkies from their belts and brought them to their mouths. One nodded and reclipped his, then raised his rifle.

C'mon, girl. You gotta sell this.

Ronnie let herself stumble as she drew nearer the gate, flopping forward onto the path with a loud groan. It seemed like a good fall, with a hard landing, and she wondered if she were laying it on too thick.

Both guards looked to the guard in the tower, who gave a thumb's up gesture and nodded. The guard on the walkie talkie engaged a control that opened the gate and the guard pointing the rifle moved through the opening toward her. He crouched next to her, fanning the barrel of his rifle to each side, then reached under her arm and helped her to her feet.

He asked her if she could walk. When Ronnie nodded, he said. "Get through the gate as quickly as you can."

The guard followed behind her, backpedaling, his eyes jumping from the road to the jungle terrain in every direction, swiveling his body and his rifle methodically from side to side.

Once they were past the gate, the other guard quickly shut it then gestured to the one in the tower. Ronnie heard a click and a hum and figured the electrification had been reengaged.

A guard with a dog was waiting just inside the fence line. The dog twitched its nose up and down her leg, its snout lingering longer than she would have hoped, until it finally backed away a few steps and sat.

So far, she thought, *so good.*

The plan was simple, according to Vic. He and his clan brought her to within a few hundred yards of the place. She was to hobble up to the gate, pretend she escaped from a group of zombies, and act frightened and half-hysterical. They would take her into the research facility and place her in one of the conference rooms. While she was waiting for Vera—Dr. Blue—to arrive, and likely Mr. White, too, a man Vic had called Tyson, they would almost certainly leave her alone to keep guarding the perimeter fence, ready to receive Vera and Tyson at the gate. Before they arrived, Ronnie needed to make her way to Vera's office and deactivate both what Vic called the *remote kill switch relay* and then the electricity powering the main security system.

He estimated she would have about ten minutes. The relay had to be done first, precisely the way he described, or the sudden loss of the signal would trigger the devices in their heads. The red light atop the tower would start blinking once the power was cut off and Vic and his men would have approximately three minutes to breach the gate before the back-up generator for the fence kicked in. They would overtake the compound, free her, commandeer a Jeep, take Vera as a hostage to make sure they weren't shot at by any guards unaccounted for, and head to the airstrip.

If that was simple, she wondered what Vic's idea of complex would be.

The first guard escorted her into the building. He hustled her into a small room and asked her to take a seat. He was annoyingly pleasant and polite about it, which caused Ronnie to feel a bit of extra anxiety. Would this man be killed? Did he know what was going on? Or was he just doing his job, guarding a secure research lab? She struck the thought from her mind. He had to know. They all did. Besides, she had more important things to worry about. If she pulled this off, a colossal cover-up would be exposed, countless lives of people infected in the future would likely be saved, and her exclusive write up for the Post would almost certainly win her a Pulitzer.

That last thought brought with it a shudder of shame. Colt was dead, people were being killed with more about to die, and she was thinking of how this would result in a major career boost. She wondered what that said about her, then pushed that thought aside as she had so many others. There would be time to contemplate all such things in the future. Right now, she needed to focus on the matter at hand.

The guard told her to stay in this room, promised her that she'd be safe there, and left, closing the door behind him. She wasn't sure whether he'd locked her in, but decided it didn't matter. She waited a moment to make sure he'd left, then stood, picked up the chair she'd been using and put it on the table. She climbed up onto the surface and reached for the ceiling tile directly above her. It was just within reach. She pushed it up and slid it to the side. Then she slid the chair over to be directly beneath the vacant space and stepped up onto it.

Vic had told her there would be three possible rooms they would put her in and explained how to get to Dr. Dinesh's office from each of them. She had to be careful to use the metal support truss to reach the center of the building and not step on any of the tiles of the suspended ceiling nor the flimsy flashing holding them in place. From the center she would squat and walk in a crouch along the main I-beam support to the south end of the structure. When she got near the far wall, where the building ended, she was to drop in through the third to last tile on her left, two rows over.

The area above the suspended ceiling tiles was dark and hot. Slants of fading light sliced through ventilation slats at haphazard intervals. There were webs hammocked from piping and conduit in every direction. The space smelled of rust and mold and stale air. The muffled sounds of activity were barely audible, voices, squawks, crunchy footfalls on the gravely terrain, but mostly she heard the soft hum of a generator, the rising and falling quaver of a breeze piping through the eaves.

She landed on the floor of the office harder than she'd expected, collapsing to the floor. Her hip hurt and her ankle sent a jolt sizzling through her leg as she tried to stand. The room was small, efficient, purely utilitarian. File cabinets lined one wall, looking a bit anachronistic, with a tall metal locker at the end near the door. A window sat behind a desk with bars bolted across the glass from the inside. The wall opposite the file cabinets was a mish-mash of marked-up maps, newspaper cutouts, magazine clippings, and diagrams of viruses and cells and ants and images of biological matter she couldn't quite place. She tugged her eyes away, knowing she had no time to look any of it over.

The things she was looking for were right where Vic had said they'd be. Below the window on a narrow table was a rectangular black unit. A control panel was positioned along the top of the unit, with a green light and a red light. There was a switch on one end and a red thumb latch on the other. Next to the unit was a console that served as a base for a large round antenna. The two devices were connected by a thick cord. On the side wall a few feet away was the gray metal box that housed the breakers.

Ronnie steeled herself and moved around the desk, the discomfort in her hip and ankle fading to an annoyance. She opened the wide shallow middle drawer and, after minimal rummaging, found the scissors and a paper clip. She turned her attention to the control unit behind her and flipped it over.

The paper clip was a tight fit, but she managed to use it to unscrew the bottom plate of the unit, exposing the electronics within. She took a moment and closed her eyes, slowing her breathing and allowing her nerves to settle.

She repeated the instructions to herself as she scanned the contents. *Follow the two wires leading from the red light to the small circuit board. Pull the board firmly but gently straight up until you feel it separate from the main board beneath it. Keep lifting it until you can see three wires connecting the two boards.*

The small board pulled against her until she felt a delicate pop. She angled it slightly and raised it with care until she saw the wiring. She held the board between her thumb and forefinger and reached for the scissors.

Sounds vibrated through the walls, coming from the hallway. She heard a loud thump, agitated voices.

Green, red, black. She had to cut them in that order, a count of 'Mississippi' in between each. She slipped the scissors over the green wire. *Snip.*

Shouting from the hallway, loud, urgent footfalls reaching her ears.

Snip.

She heard someone at the door, rattling the knob.

Mississippi.

Snip.

Ronnie let out a loud breath, but knew she had no time to collect herself. The knob shook and clicked and rattled for a brief moment before she heard the lock give.

The door flew open. Ronnie lunged toward the breaker box on the wall as Vera burst into the room.

"What the hell are you doing? Stop!"

Ronnie yanked open the box and looked at Vera. A look of horrified understanding spread across the woman's face. Her arm shot forward and she launched herself toward Ronnie.

The first scissor blade fit in the space between the first and second breakers, but the angle of the second one didn't line up with the seam it was supposed to penetrate. Ronnie touched the point of it into the narrow opening and hammered her palm against the handle as hard as she could. Vera slammed into her, knocking her back, but it was too late. The panel of breakers popped and sparked. Arcs of electricity sizzled and jumped around the scissor blades. Then the entire front of the panel erupted in flames. The fire subsided quickly, leaving a small flame shimmering near the center of the scorched panel.

Vera stood looking at the panel, then at the dismantled consoles below the window. She blinked several times and swallowed, staring incredulously. An alarm in the building began to sound.

"What have you done?"

Vera backed away until she bumped into the wall next to the door, her eyes still looking at the consoles beneath the window.

"*What have you done?*" she repeated.

"I put a stop to your operation, Dr. Blue, that's what. Or should I call you *Vera?*"

With what seemed like significant effort, Vera pulled her rapt attention from beneath the window and looked at Ronnie.

"He got to you. Vic got to you. Oh my God." The woman's hands raked though her long black hair. "You have no idea what you've done."

"Got to me? Yes, I suppose if you mean telling me the truth about what you were up to, yeah, he got to me."

"Truth? You don't understand! Dear God…"

"It's all over, Vera. He told me all about it, all about what you were doing, hiding the truth so you could continue your research, experimenting on them, using those men as your lab rats."

"That's what he told you?" She staggered back a few steps, then slowly slumped to the floor, sliding down the wall. She pressed her palms to her face and took a breath. When she looked up at Ronnie, Ronnie didn't like what she saw in her eyes.

"You have no idea what you've done," Vera said. "That wasn't Vic who told you those things."

Ronnie narrowed her gaze, suspicious of this woman, believing she would say anything to save herself, to coopt others to her cause. But Ronnie also couldn't escape the feeling she was about to learn something she wasn't going to like.

"Then who was it, if it wasn't him?"

The woman blinked, staring straight ahead. "It was the fungus."

Dog barks echoed, then multiplied. Gunfire rang out, the report deadened only slightly by the walls. One shot, two, then three in rapid succession.

"They're here," Vera said, looking up. "Aren't they? *They're coming.* You did this so they could overrun this place. That's exactly what he'd want!"

Ronnie ignored those words, having what she considered a much more important question to ask. "What did you mean, a moment ago? Did you say it was the fungus talking?"

"Yes! Don't you understand? It was the fungus! It rewires the brain of the host, taking advantage of the virus's effect on the immune system. It passes the blood-brain barrier and hijacks the system through the cerebral cortex."

"That wasn't a *fungus* I was talking to. It was a person. A man. There were a dozen men out there. I talked to them."

"A dozen? He's got a dozen out there?"

Ronnie didn't respond. A nauseating feeling was worming its way through her gut.

"Listen to me! Those weren't men! And that wasn't Vic! The 'Vic' you were talking to was just his *brain*. It was all the memories, all the intellect, all the mental capacity of a person conversing with you, but *it wasn't Vic.* When they... come back, when they regain their faculties, they're *still zombies.* Don't you get it? *That's* why they shut down the funding, that's why governments spend so much money to burn bodies in the field, without the slightest delay.

That's why they can't let anyone know. Around six to eight weeks after a bloodborne infection, the fungus has brought the speech, memory and problem solving portions of the brain online again, but there is no longer a person in the driver's seat. That brain only has one purpose—to survive and replicate the fungus."

"That's crazy! How...?"

"We don't know! It's almost like it was designed! Like some sort of alien bio-weapon! Or maybe it's a product of evolution that's been hiding in plain sight for millennia, waiting for the perfect virus to team up with. The only thing for certain is that when it takes them, it's like they leave and come back without souls. They're pure sociopaths! That's why I tried to study them! Why I had to continue my research, fund it anyway I could! To find not just a vaccine, but a cure!"

Ronnie's eyes swooned until she found herself staring at the floor. She thought for a long moment. "They showed me the stitches."

"Stitches? Vic showed you stitches?

"At the base of the neck. Where you implanted them." She thought for a moment. "Vic didn't show me his, he showed me the others."

Vera bowed her head, shaking it back and forth as if in disbelief. "There were no others. And there were no stitches. Vic was the only one with the implant. It was administered with an implant gun. The scar is barely perceptible. He insisted on it, after he was bitten, before he... turned. The others... they were zombies we were using for study, trying to track the pathology, testing various fungicides and antibiotics. Nothing worked. A flight crew went missing over a month ago, around the same time those others escaped. Three of them. We found the Jeep, assumed they'd been..."

"Eaten," Ronnie said, after a pause. "That was the crew from the plane I saw, being guarded on the runway."

"I should have known he'd do this. I underestimated him, blinded by my feelings. I just wouldn't let myself think about it. I wanted to find a cure."

"For him," Ronnie said. "You wanted to cure him. That was why you did all this. That's why you continued your research, funded it with zombie hunts."

"Yes! He was my husband! He insisted on the implant, made me swear

I'd use it if he ever escaped. But I couldn't bring myself to do it. And I didn't think I had to, because if he ever tried to leave…"

"*The implant would detonate.*" Ronnie felt her legs buckle. The blood seemed to drain from her head and for a moment she thought she would pass out. This was all her fault. How could she have been so stupid? So gullible? So easily manipulated? She stumbled out from behind the desk, then fell back to lean against it, desperately trying to think.

More shots rang out. Ronnie heard a man scream.

"I don't know what to do…" Ronnie said.

Vera surged forward onto her feet, grabbing Ronnie by the shoulders and shaking her until she made eye contact. "He mustn't get off this island. Do you understand? We can't allow it. He's going to burn this place down, destroy all the research, destroy all evidence of who was here. If he were to get to the mainland… he was one of the most brilliant men, the most brilliant *minds* I've ever met. He would disappear and that fungus… that fungus would use his brain to build an army, to plot a takeover, town by town, city by city, country by country. And, oh my God—he's a signator on the Zafari bank account!"

Vera released her grip, taking a step back. "There's over a million pounds in that account. There will be no limit to what he could do."

She leveled her gaze at Ronnie. "I don't know how else to put this. If we don't stop him, he'll set in motion a plan to make everyone a fungal carrier. *Everyone.* We're talking about the possible end of the human race."

There was a loud crash from the hallway, three shots reverberated inside the building. Vera bolted over and shut the door. She rushed over to the tall cabinet and removed a rifle, the same type Ronnie had seen being used by some of the security on the island. Vera pulled the charging rack and looked in the chamber.

"We have to—"

The door smashed open and two zombies—two of the same ones Ronnie had sat with in the jungle mere hours ago—flashed through it, grabbing Vera and taking her to the ground. One of them clamped its mouth down on the woman's neck and tore off a large chunk of flesh. A gush of blood spurted out, arcing like a fountain. The rifle clattered to the floor, sliding to a stop at Ronnie's feet. There was more commotion in the building, shouts and shots and the sound of things crashing and breaking.

Ronnie felt herself moving, an automaton, her body a step ahead of her thoughts. She picked up the rifle and kicked the zombie nearest her in the face as it turned to look up at her. She leapt past it, over the legs of Vera and out the doorway into the hall. She stopped only briefly, glancing each way, seeing Mr. White fall forward to the floor fifty feet from her, glasses hanging from one ear, eyes wide in horror as a zombie wrapped itself around him from behind and yanked his head back, biting down on his face. She turned the other way and threw herself against the push bar on the door immediately to her left, floundering to a stop a few yards away in the diffuse twilight. The bodies of several guards were scattered on the ground in each direction, their faces bloody, throats ripped out. At least two dogs were down, one twitching. A small building to her left was on fire.

One guard was locked in a struggle with a zombie as another jumped on his back. Ronnie took a step to intervene, raising the rifle, then heard the bump of the door behind her and the slam of it bouncing off the wall. She took off in a sprint toward the front gate, now open.

One was chasing her. She could feel it gaining, heard the footfalls that seemed much more rapid than hers. She could hear the rustle of its threadbare clothing right behind her, felt a hand slap down on her shoulder. She was about to scream, her mind racing, unsure if she could swing the rifle around in time, when she heard a bestial growl surging toward her. She tumbled forward to the ground, losing her grip on the rifle, and rolled to see a huge dog collide with the zombie barely two feet from her, knocking it to the ground. It sunk its teeth into the zombie's arm and shook violently.

Ronnie got to her knees, retrieved the rifle and sprang forward toward the gate. She sprinted through it, only pausing once when she was a hundred yards or more away to look back. The main building was on fire now. She could see figures gathering in front of it. They would be coming for her.

She slipped into the chaotic web of brush and trees to her left, moving as quickly as the terrain would allow. She had to make her way to the runway, had to disable that plane. Shoot out its tires, shoot through the instrument panel, shoot through the engine components. Maybe there were even still guards there, she didn't know. Maybe she could get them to help, maybe she'd have to do it herself and deal with them trying to stop her. She just hoped her instincts were on and the runway was in the direction she was heading.

Whether there would be a story was still up in the air. But she wasn't thinking about a Pulitzer anymore. Her pulse was racing, her body hopped up on adrenaline. Despite all that, she became aware of an almost unnatural calm settling in amid the overwhelming sense of urgency that was powering her legs as she cut and stomped and jumped through and around and over the jumbles of branches and stems and roots and logs. The obstacle course of growth gave way to a clearing and she broke into a run.

There would definitely be a story, she decided. It was merely a matter of surviving to write it. But that was all secondary. This, she knew, was her destiny. She wasn't just going to write about it, she was going to do it. She was taking action. Rhonda Davenport, *Anonymous* no more.

Her father may have been right about some things, but he was unquestionably wrong about the most important one. He never would have predicted this. She wasn't just a writer—not anymore—she was also the story.

She was going to save the world.

STORY NOTES

CAUTION: HERE THERE BE SPOILERS!

(Maybe. Definitely)

The Yearning Jade

I've always been a fan of *noir* and its first cousin, the hard-boiled detective story. Even though the terms are sometimes used interchangeably, the two aren't exactly the same. But as genres go, they do share many similarities and often overlap. "The Yearning Jade" was written for an anthology of stories involving phobias that were supposed to emulate the pulp fiction style of the 1920s and '30s, which immediately got me in the mood to write a piece of horror noir with a private detective searching the mean streets of a concrete jungle. When I was crafting the premise, I decided I needed to come up with a MacGuffin of some sort, something for the detective to hunt for. I remember lying down to sleep one night and the term "yearning jade" popping into my head. I have no idea why; other than the fact I was entertaining ideas about something a lot of people would want to get their hands on. From there, the story and the setting fell into place in my head, helped along by some research into myths and legends I thought would provide interesting context and detail.

Household

It's always fascinating—at least for me—to explore a nexus where the supernatural and the psychological mix, especially when it's unclear in the story if it's one or the other or both at work. I wrote "Household" for an anthology where the theme was stories that had to do with 'home.' I was leaning toward a haunted house premise as I began to plan my writing, but I wanted a fresher and more original take than a classic haunting would provide. So, I asked myself, what hadn't been done before (or done very much)? The idea popped into my head to tell a haunted house story from the perspective of the *house*. A story where the house itself was a character. That got my creative juices flowing, as they say, and I wrote an opening scene for it without having much else in mind, the characters seeming to appear and take shape on their own as I did. I quickly had a plot unfurl itself in my mind. The one question I didn't have an answer for as I wrote it was whether the house's personality was real or just a figment of the main (human) character's disturbed imagination. I had intended to end the story differently than it did, with the house moving on to linking itself to another occupant, but the house, and its human familiar, had other ideas, and I decided that the question of whether it was all just a product of the main character's rupturing psyche was best left for the reader to decide.

Everything Not Forbidden

Sometime back, I came across discussion of something that's come to be known as *Roko's Basilisk*. It was deemed the "most terrifying thought experiment ever conceived" and was deleted and banned from the futurist forum where it had first appeared due to it having caused a tremendous amount of distress among many of its members. The idea behind the experiment was to consider the possibility of an artificial intelligence being created in the future that was so advanced as to be omniscient, almost god-like, and the possibility that if this AI were tasked with perfecting human civilization, it may decide that the first order of business would be to exterminate all those opposed to it having complete control over humanity, including anyone who did not actively work to ensure its creation. This 'Basilisk,' as it was called, would look back in time with a deadly gaze like that of its mythological namesake and punish anyone who knew of it as a concept but who did not lend their efforts to its creation. It would do this by using its absolute knowledge and understanding of the universe to resurrect everyone in the past who fit that description and then condemning them to an eternal existence of unending and unspeakable torture. Oh, and, by the way—having read about the thought experiment meant you were now one of those facing eternal damnation once the Basilisk came into being. Have a nice day.

That thought experiment roamed my mind like a ghost for a long time. I knew I had to write a story inspired by it, but I was having a lot of trouble coming up with an angle, a vehicle for telling it. Then I happened to find an article discussing Roko's Basilisk that mentioned how if a sufficiently advanced intelligence were interrogating you, you couldn't be sure about anything because you would have no way of knowing if you were in a simulation or not. Bingo! I had my angle for the story and while I wouldn't say it practically wrote itself, it did pass through my fingers onto the keyboard with a satisfying thrust of momentum.

One final note regarding this story: the title comes from something called the 'Totalitarian Principle' in quantum mechanics, which states, "Everything not forbidden is compulsory." Many readers may recognize this from T.H. White's *The Once and Future King*, where these words were depicted as appearing on a sign above the entrance to an anthill. The earliest version of this phrase that I can find, however, actually appeared in a story by Robert Heinlein around 1940, in which he described the state as an organism where "[a]nything not compulsory was forbidden." I would guess it derived from a corruption of the legal principle at common law and under U.S. Constitutional theory holding that "anything not forbidden is permitted."

Shifty Devil Blues

As a guitarist and a horror writer, I've naturally been drawn to the story of blues legend Robert Johnson for many years. Whether he actually ventured out to the crossroads one fateful night to cut a deal with the devil or not, he certainly seemed to know how to craft an image of mystery and intrigue around himself that ensured he'd be a subject of fascination almost a century later. It is amazing how little is known about one of the most influential musicians of the 20th century, a man who shaped future generations of rock-and-roll stars with his unique sounds and unusual chordings and haunting vocals. I came across a video about him one day that included an old interview with the stepson of one of Johnson's contemporaries who told him stories about Robert. That got me thinking about what might happen if someone heard one of those stories and decided he could do a better job of dealing with the devil than Robert had.

Moonless Nocturne

I wrote "Moonless Nocturne" as part of a project I proposed to my writing group a few years ago. The idea was for a novel spanning a hundred years and each of us would write a part of it set in a different era. My era was the 50s, and I wanted to capture the mood and feel of a hard-boiled detective story from that time, told through a voice perhaps somewhat more gritty and candid than fiction of that period would have likely produced. The project got derailed after a dispute with the publisher emerged, but I had already completed my portion. What I'd written was a supernatural mystery set at the dawn of the space age and the height of the Cold War. I always liked the way this story turned out, particularly because despite how dark it was, it managed to have a hopeful ending and finish on an up beat. One thing particularly worth noting about it, in my mind, is that the appearance of Carl Sagan as a character at one point was not gratuitous. The project he discloses to the main character involving exploding a hydrogen bomb on the moon was very real, and he really was involved in some aspects of its research and planning. Fortunately, the idea was abandoned, but not before a lot of work had gone into it. Whether it would have turned out the way I imagined it might... who knows? But it certainly provided a fitting backdrop for the story. Not to mention a nice tie-in to the title of this collection.

Haunter

Many years ago, a woman in Houston, which is the metro area where I live, killed her five children, drowning them all in a bathtub one day. It was an absolutely horrific occurrence, which, of course, meant the media was all over it. The news coverage locally was nonstop for quite some time, and the national coverage was not far behind in the amount of airtime dedicated to it. I remember in the days and weeks that followed a number of commentators discussing how heartbreaking the situation was and expressing sympathy for the woman's husband, who lost his entire family one day while at work and now had to face a new, unexpected reality shaped by tragedy.

And then one day I happened upon an editorial by a woman who, rather than expressing any sympathy for the woman's husband, castigated him and placed the blame for what happened squarely at his feet. His wife was overwhelmed, the writer argued, battling depression, yet he got her no help and simply left her at home to care for all those children, children she kept giving birth to because of religious convictions the writer also believed he likely encouraged, if not coerced, her to abide by.

Reading that, I remember experiencing several reactions. Surprise, confusion, uncertainty, pensive contemplation. I thought the woman's take on the situation to be more than a little harsh and obviously the product of an agenda-driven viewpoint, but that didn't mean she was completely wrong. Regardless of the merits of what she was arguing, it definitely got me thinking about that man. Would he be haunted by guilt for the rest of his life? Would he become a different person? Would he eventually remarry? And if he did, would he approach marriage and having children the same way as before? Those thoughts percolated for a while. A few years later, the essence of those questions, the part that remains after the impact and substance of the questions have faded away, found its way into this story.

Deepest, Darkest

My first novel, *Damnable*, featured Jake Hatcher, an ex-special forces interrogator drummed out of the military after his particular skillset was suddenly considered undesirable. It turned out Hatcher also had a talent for attracting demonic attention from the underworld, something he discovered after becoming entangled in an investigation into the death of a brother he never knew he had. Ol' Jake has been battling demons ever since, as detailed in the follow-up novels in the series, *Diabolical* and *The Angel of the Abyss*. I wrote this Jake Hatcher story for an anthology of military sci-fi/horror stories involving black ops where the editor wanted authors to bring established characters to the table wherever possible. Since Hatcher's background as a special forces operator was something I had not had the opportunity to explore in a military setting, I jumped at the chance.

Psycho Metrics

Sometimes ideas for stories come to me without me actively looking for them. Other times, I find them as the result of a search. This was one I found while searching.

I got the idea while I was reading through an old-ish book of real-life supernatural mysteries (twenty years counts as old, doesn't it?). I was flipping from chapter to chapter and came across one dealing with 'psychometry.' If I had ever come across the term before, I didn't recall it. But apparently, it's a thing, or used to be, and it refers to an ability some people have claimed to have that allows them to sense things from touching an object. To be honest, there didn't seem to be much evidence for the phenomenon or much reason to treat it as some big mystery, but I didn't see that as an obstacle. Here was a term I was unfamiliar with involving a supernatural talent, and I knew if *I* was unfamiliar with it, given how extensive my reading into all things paranormal has been since the days of my youth, then there was a good chance this would provide for a story angle, or at least a story device, that was a little different. A little unique. I originally intended for the amateur sleuth I wrote to find the human monster behind the killings, but then get no credit for her efforts and to continue her uphill struggle to establish the legitimacy of this form of extra-sensory perception. But, funny how things work out, this woman had her own ideas for the way the story would unfold and didn't seem in the mood to engage in any debate on the subject. I, of course, as the humble scribe merely documenting her exploits, was forced to oblige.

Payday

"Payday" was a story I wrote many, many years ago that I never sent anywhere (until I did). Not because I didn't like it, but because I had barely written the last word of it when I had a surge of inspiration to start another piece of writing that turned out to be my first novel, and *Payday* dropped off my radar. The idea behind the story was simply a bullied boy who decided to try to 'buy' his way out of the bullying by offering to share something he found—something he believed to be quite valuable—with his tormentor. I can still recall the mischievous feeling I had when I wrote it. I finished it in a couple of days, revised it, polished it—then let it languish on my hard drive while I spent the next eight to ten months writing *Damnable.*

But while I did neglect it, it was through no fault of its own, and I didn't quite ever manage to forget about it. Not completely. And then one day many years later, I was invited to submit a story for the first issue of the reboot of *Weird Tales* magazine. I was quite psyched, given the pedigree of that publication, but I soon learned there was a catch—they were going to press and needed whatever I had by the next day if they were going to consider it (there had been a minor miscalculation regarding the estimate of space for fiction for the issue and the staff apparently decided that while they could easily redo the layout, they preferred to fill that space with more content). So… did I happen to have one ready to go? Yikes. I unsuccessfully lobbied to be given just a couple of days—the weekend—to work on it. But that was a hard no. I was cursing my luck when I remembered I did have one story I never had gotten around to submitting anywhere. I tracked it down and looked it over and was pleasantly surprised that it read better than I'd expected, given how many years earlier I'd written it. I gave it a quick once-over and emailed it. Then I held my breath. Turns out, they loved it. Thought it gave off just the creepy, weird vibe they were looking for. Next thing I knew, my name was on the cover of *Weird Tales* and a bucket-list item for many a horror author had been checked off. The moral of the story is the same one found in the immortal words of Chuck Berry: "'*C'est la vie,*' say the old folks—it goes to show you never can tell."

Zafari! (Unlimited)

The idea for this story was bouncing around the recesses of my mind for several years. I had originally envisioned it as a novel whose plot centered on an illicit 'Zombie Safari,' but I never was able to get started on it, mostly because the contours of what I had in mind didn't quite reach novel-length now matter how much I teased at it. But I was high enough on the premise that I never let the idea go, and this was the first story I sat down and wrote after I signed the contract for this collection.

One note of interest—the premise I present in the story for the zombies being 'controlled' by a fungus, as many readers may be aware, is found in nature. There is a species of ant that ingest a certain type of fungus through cow dung, for example, only to find their brains taken over by it, prompting them to climb to the top of flowers in the field and raise themselves up so that they'll be eaten by grazing cows consuming the plants—thus ensuring the fungus will pass in the bovine feces and the cycle will continue. You combine that concept with the idea of a zombie safari, and you have a story idea I knew I would have to write as soon as the opportunity presented itself. And that's exactly what I did.

PUBLICATION & COPYRIGHT CREDITS

25ANDY.COM

Ouroboros
by Kevin Kauffmann

Chasing Your Tale
by Peter J. Wacks